Shark Girls

Jaimee Wriston Colbert

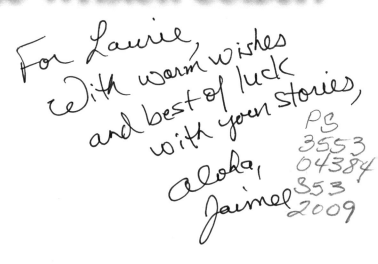

For Laurie,
With warm wishes
and best of luck
with your stories,
aloha,
Jaimee

Livingston Press
The University of West Alabama

Jaimee Wriston Colbert
11-11-09

isbn 13: 978-1-60489-043-3 library binding
isbn 13: 978-1-60489-044-0 trade paper
Library of Congress Control Number 2009931608
Printed on acid-free paper.
Printed in the United States of America by
Publishers Graphics
Hardcover binding by: Heckman Bindery
Typesetting and page layout: Joe Taylor
Proofreading: Joe Taylor, Shelly Huth
Cover design and layout: Jennifer Brown
Cover Photo: Maile Colbert
Acknowledgements:
I want to thank my research assistant, Maile Costa Colbert, who went above and beyond,
swimming with me where the shark attack took place (and for her great cover photo!), and Joy
Passanante, Shawn Shiflett, Leslie Heywood, Arija Weddle, Libby Tucker, Ian Colbert, Maile
Costa Colbert, Nate Colbert and Don Colbert for manuscript consultation; Binghamton
University for research support at various times during the writing of this book, and for the
support of my colleagues; Madison Smartt Bell and Jack Driscoll for their ongoing generos-
ity, and Madison, Jack, and Bobbie Ann Mason for their gracious endorsements. I want to
thank my lovely publicist, Sheryl Johnston, and I particularly want to thank Joe Taylor and
the folks at Livingston Press for believing in this book. My condolences to the family of Billy
Weaver. Although the shark attack in my novel is fictitious, I drew upon various articles and
news accounts referencing his tragic death. I was a child growing up in Kailua, the town next
to his, when it happened. It has haunted me all these years....

Previously Published Acknowledgements:
Excerpts from Shark Girls appeared in the following publications:
Harpur Palate, vol. 5 issue 2. Binghamton: 2006.
F Magazine, F-7, vol. 7. Chicago: 2007.
I Was Indian, vol. 2 (Anthology).
Also, see pages 336-337 for an extension of this copyright page.

Author's note: We have attempted to properly accent the Hawaiian language, but it should
be noted that many sources were published before this became conventional, and when using direct quotes we honored the source's original format

first edition
6 5 4 3 3 2 1

Shark Girls

For My Family,
From Hawai'i to Portugal and the places in between.

Here are reported the passing of the dead into the shark as its commonest incarnation; the transformation of a living person into a shark; and the "exchange of souls between man and shark" (Fox) in which a shark becomes a man's familiar and acts for the man. A shark-man's power passes to his son, who is initiated at birth by the father crooking his arm like a shark's fin and putting the child under his arm. The child and his shark receive the same name. The two are so closely associated that if one dies the other dies. It is said that these are "sharks who have exchanged souls with living men." It is a process of adoption, and what injures one injures the other.

Beckwith; *Hawaiian Mythology*

PROLOGUE

Here is where we begin, what you need to understand. Random things happen, and these are the things that change everything else. When I was a child, just a mile away from our Kailua, Hawai'i neighborhood, a twin-engine plane fell out of the sky before daybreak on top of two houses, a roar and a growl then nothing, a startled moment of absolute silence. The neighbor across the street heard it and called the Kailua police. This was of course many years before planes would be used as missiles against the World Trade Center, back when this sort of thing really was a tragic accident. Back when, perhaps, there was this sort of innocence, naiveté, presumed, assumed, not questioned. It was the nineteen fifties.

The occupants of the first house were killed immediately, sleeping in their beds. The occupants of the second were blessedly somewhere else. On vacation? Who could remember this detail? The people who lived in the house would, of course, for the rest of their lives. Like the Where were you when President Kennedy was shot? question. Where were you when *you* could have been killed? Random chance, one moment sleeping sweet in your home, the next dying under its charred and smoking remains. One of the kids we carpooled from school with knew one of the kids that was killed. This kid, who played jacks, hula hoops, Nancy Ann dolls, jump rope, water balloon fights with Nalani in our carpool, never expected a plane to fall out of the blue onto her roof.

I was the storyteller in our carpool, ghost stories, obake tales as they are referred to in Hawai'i; *get plenty chicken skin*! It is a fact that water flows downhill, yet truth is that in the lush green seat of the Ko'olau Mountains we drove through every afternoon, when the wind rose from the valley wailing against those rigid peaks, you would get the upside-down waterfalls, rush of water blowing up, up—running from the ghosts maybe, the night marchers we all knew inhabited this valley, spirits of the warriors Kamehameha I pushed off the Pali, uniting the islands under his rule. If you try to drive over the Pali at midnight with pork in your car—say a pork sandwich or leftover *lū'au*—your car will rattle and shake so furiously you'd think a hurricane hit. The spirits don't like you to *hele* with pork. Most of us don't know why this is *kapu,* just is.

What about the story of a jeweler named Maung Chit Chine who in 1927 hid under some tree during a rain storm and afterwards his friends could only find his hat and shoes. When they killed the gorged python nearby, they found the rest of Chine's body swallowed feet first and whole inside the snake. In 1993 a fifteen year old mainland boy weighing ninety-five pounds was attacked by the family's python, which killed the boy, though made no attempt to eat him. For sport, perhaps? The way a house cat sated on kibble plays the mouse to death? The way the hunter blasts the bear? What about the way a poacher slaughters the elephant only for his tusks? There are no snakes in Hawai'i. We have mongoose, mean little razor-toothed weasel types who do kill snakes but were imported from Jamaica in 1883 to annihilate the rats in the sugarcane. The problem: mongoose sleep at night. Rats don't.

In 1952 there were Congressional hearings, the House Investigation on the sanctity of showing cleavage on America's new plaything, the television. Here is what else happened in 1952: Ike Eisenhower was elected President of the United States; Queen Elizabeth II ascended to the throne of England; the volcano goddess Pele of the fiery hair and raging temper caused a volcanic eruption in her own home, Halema'uma'u on the big island of Hawai'i; and in Queens Hospital, O'ahu, a child was born. Peevish and selfish as any child, this one would come to be revered as a saint.

In Hawai'i you grow up hearing things, incidents that occurred to one degree or another, that became stories in the telling and the retelling, almost mythic in the transformation of their details from bits of happenings to full blown magical truths. In Japanese folklore one who drowns returns to life as a sea animal. Your uncle, perhaps, who drank too much Saki, in that *honu* turtle's heavily lidded eyes? My grandmother, when she was herself a young woman, told of driving with my grandfather and picking up a beautiful young woman in a long white dress with a little white dog hitchhiking on the side of the Volcano road on the Big Island. Any islander knows this as the goddess Pele in her young woman's disguise. She's silent in the back seat of the car, and when they approach Halema'uma'u' fire pit my grandmother looks back and the woman has disappeared. That night the volcano erupts.

When you grow up on O'ahu, you know always to look over your shoulder, back to the mountains behind, when swimming in the turquoise water or playing on the beautiful white sand of Kualoa beach park. It is said that the night marchers come down from the burial caves at the top of the mountain where there are the remains of more than four hundred chiefs. You can hear their distant drums on a moonless night, see the flickering of torches, and if anyone gets in their path, well, you may never see this unlucky soul again. Their path crosses Kamehameha highway in a place where a lot of car accidents occur. Some say there is a bad curve in the road there, others know differently.

In 1914 the United States government built a dry dock for its Navy over a cave, the home of the female shark god Ka'ahupahau. The Hawaiian natives regarded the building of this with tremendous unease. After years of labor it was finally finished and within hours it fell with a sudden and inexplicable crash. This is real. You can look this up. Engineers speculated there seemed to be earth "tremors" of some sort that prevented the structure from resting on the bottom. But the Hawaiians believed "the smiting tail" of Ka'ahupahau still guarded the blue lagoon at Pearl Harbor.

This also happened: On December 13, 1958, Lanikai beach, island of O'ahu, fifteen year old Billy Weaver was killed by a shark. In my memory Billy is a surfer, and he's surfing when it happens. In fact he was on an air mattress accompanied by five friends, all with their air mattresses, catching waves. The other five didn't notice when Billy didn't catch that last wave. When one of them looked back, he saw Billy slide off his mat, disappear for a moment, then surface, his face ashen. *Help*! he called, but faintly. The ocean churned red. They tried to keep him afloat, bear him back to the beach. But Billy Weaver slipped from their grasp and sank beneath the water. That's when they saw the shark.

In my memory he's a handsome boy and no doubt he was; blond is how I see him, surfer haircut, sun tanned skin, though the news articles showed him as dark haired, that winning smile. He was popular. All of Kailua and Lanikai mourned his loss. I was barely eight at the time; even so there was something of the hero made of me, of any Kailua resident, just by virtue of living beside *his* town, swimming near *that* beach off the bay we shared, one of *ours*. The boys swam frantically back to the shore, and the search boats who went looking for Billy reported seeing a large shark in the area. A diver found his body wedged into a hole in the reef, his right leg bitten clean off to the knee. The *Honolulu Advertiser* reported he was the fifth person known to have been killed by a shark in the Hawaiian islands in 72 years; three of those fatalities were in the past eight years.

I liked to believe I knew Billy Weaver; his loss loomed large in our small town lives. He was from a *prominent island family*, as the papers described it, his father and uncle owners of a family restaurant chain including Tiki Tops in Kāne'ohe, where my own family went on Sundays if we were *good*. They had Peppermint Patty mints at the cash register. We begged our father for one after each meal.

Billy Weaver became mythic, a hero, a legend, the most talked about kid in town. The Territory Of Hawai'i officials and community leaders declared war on the sharks that swam off the island of O'ahu. This I remember: the fear, what was unseen, violent and predatory, our every nightmare lurking in our ocean waters, and how, we were assured, these brave men (for of course they were men in those days) would save us.

Two days after Billy's death, three tiger sharks and two sand sharks were killed off Lanikai. A Billy Weaver Shark Control Fund was started to help finance the destruction of sharks. Fund raisers canvassed our neighborhoods, knocked on our doors, reminded us we lived on Kailua beach, same bay as Lanikai. Once, a dead nurse shark washed up on the beach, riddled with chunks and gouges from being nibbled on by who knows what? Maybe even her own kind; sharks are cannibals, we were told, tiger shark fetuses, brothers and sisters, will eat each other in the womb, survival of the fiercest even before becoming fully formed. The neighborhood children beat it with *kiawe* sticks, coral pieces, whipped it with long smelly strands of kelp, whatever was handy. The dare was to run your hand over it, feel the hateful thrill of its sandpaper-tough and wasted skin. We despised that nurse shark for its perceived power, higher on the food chain than us—once we stepped into the ocean we were potentially its prey. Defiled it in its death, harmless as it might've been.

Merchants posted bounties for any sharks caught, and a local jewelry store offered a quarter for every shark tooth brought in to them from a shark freshly slaughtered. A boat circled O'ahu daily, the *Holokahana I*, chartered through the Board of Commissioners of Agriculture and Forestry, no other purpose than to catch and destroy sharks. At the end of the year long campaign, this was the toll: 697 sharks killed; a total of 641 embryos in the females; nine species, including a sixgill shark, a species never recorded in Hawaiian waters, and the second bramble shark ever caught in Hawaiian waters. These numbers are documented. You can look them up: Ikehara. *Billy Weaver Shark Research and Control Program/Final Report.*

The Hawaiian natives were grieving. Some sharks were gods, *akua*, believed to have guided the original islanders to Hawai'i. Other sharks, *mano kumupa'a*, were *'aumakua*, ancestral gods, guardian spirits, fierce when the occasion called for it, noble and strong. Once when a family member died, his corpse might have been offered by a kahuna, a Hawaiian priest, to a particular shark. The kahuna would point out to the sorrowful family the gradual transformation of the body, the markings of the burial clothes onto the sides, the fin, of the worshipped shark. This particular manō then became this family's own *'aumākua*, believed to drive food into their fishing nets, save them if their boat capsized, protect them from the giant people-eating sharks. *'Aumākua* was thought to ward off sorcery, before Christianity came to the islands in the form of white people, the *haoles*, who labeled this as superstition.

Sharks are not cruising the seas after people to eat, but the ones that do eat people have a name: *niuhi*. To avoid *niuhi* you use your head; you don't go into the ocean at sunrise, sunset, kicking your legs and arms like you are their preferred diet of seals, turtles, or fish; you don't swim at river mouths or in murky water, which appears in the inland seas sometimes after a rain. You use your head. In Hawai'i it is best to try and live peaceably with the old gods. It is a bad omen not to do so.

Part I

"How does the god come to have the shape of a shark?" we asked? "The 'aumakua has no form," he said, "It comes in the shape of a wish into the mother...." The presence of a spirit is indicated by a divine possession in which the person possessed speaks not as he is accustomed but in the character and with the words of the spirit whose medium he is. His utterances are not his own but are the means by which, together with dream and vision, the spirit of the 'aumakua counsels his protégé.

Nakuina; *Nanaue The Shark Man and Other Hawaiian Stories*

CHAPTER ONE

The way I see it you can go two ways with a name like Wilhelmina Beever. You can be a dorky little kid, teased by the masses, enduring persecutions in grease-stinking lunchrooms, girls' bathrooms with their dank secret stalls, their communal watering troughs—as if girl-children, pitted against each other from birth could ever be a community—hair pulled, tugged, knotted, snipped *beaver! beaver!* Or you can be what Willa Beever might have been, the fair-haired queen, one of THOSE GIRLS, the ones whose smiles burn into our queasy little worlds, make our panicky days worth *something* when the smile is aimed at us, golden, scrubbed, white-toothed, birthed under some special star, a kind of brilliance the rest of us can't touch, born *right*. Only Willa could have transcended the tragedy that was her life without even a prayer to become a saint.

Recently I saw a *People's Magazine* article about her, "Victim Soul," they're calling her. It wasn't front cover news, just a quarter page blurb near the back; Willa has a small but insistent following. Apparently these folks don't question she's a savior of sorts. Originally from Kailua, O'ahu, the article said that some people were petitioning their local bishop or cardinal, requesting some tribunal to officiate, the council of the saints or whoever does these "investigated miracles," as they call them, to declare my sister a miracle, or perhaps even canonize her and make her a saint. The article speculated about her having to die first and be dead five years for consideration of the latter; her body must not be *corrupt,* and even then there are steps to be taken. "This person is ineligible for beatification because it is a status reserved for the dead," one holy person was quoted.

Our mother, Jaycee Beever, would have once dismissed this as a Catholic Thing. The article talked about how Willa had been an unusually pretty little girl, popular in school, an average student who enjoyed twirling a baton, who wanted to be a cheerleader when she got older. They showed a photo of eight year old Willa jumping on our parents' bed in the pink tutu Grandma sent her, Willa leaping wide and high, those legs I might have grown up to envy, wee bit of Hawaiian blood that was ours from way back when on our father's side giving them that baby-oiled or *Q.T.'d* mahogany tan, already muscled, perfect split into the golden air. Willa was our golden child. "Life was wide open," our mother is quoted in the article as saying: "Maybe college ahead, a *good* husband, children, the usual, who would've known? I mean," says Jaycee—there's a shot of my mother, not the most flattering, cigarette poking out of her lipsticked mouth, what they must've paid her to put that one in!—"how in God's name can you anticipate such a thing happening? Your whole world comes crashing down around you forever."

Forever is not as long as it used to be. When did forever stop being forever? It's got a finite time to it now, its own itinerary. I sit on alvin-Travis's lānai—that's a word from my childhood, they're called patios here in Maine, or porches or decks—and reflect on this, on how last summer's Johnny Jump-up flowers managed to gravitate out of the flower bed, swimming up every which way now between the bricks, under a bright October sun, steely ocean air, clumps of them and lone little Jump-ups, their array of pansy-like faces jerking spasmodically at each other in the breeze like they're at some kind of cocktail party for wayward flowers, a reunion, the annual gathering of the Rogue Pansies. alvin-Travis will come out before the sun slants down, Salut Vodka in hand, stare for a possessive moment out at the ocean like it really does exist to be part of his own back yard, shift his eyes back to his patio, and say, "Oh no, this can never do. Jump-ups under my patio? We'll have to yank those or they'll bust up the bricks!"

I imagine this, an army of those perky Johnny Jump-ups, all liquored up from their cocktail party, marching across the lānai, little hammers, bats, mallets in viny fingers, whacking at those bricks. Pansy Rebels, out to take over the patio — *No more pussy flower beds for us! We want the hard stuff, feed us brick or bust!* I giggle at this image and alvin-Travis does step outside, frowning in my direction, giving me one of his grey annoyed looks, his *you're such a pain* look. I'm like that these days. My life has ended up nowhere I ever thought it would be, and this does something to a person. I'm living with alvin-Travis, aging 1970's acid rock star, who encourages me to sleep with other men then tell him about it. Because he can't. *It's not a physical thing*, he says. *Just lost that "what-it-takes," that "get up and go." It got up and went*, he says. alvin-Travis is retired now, "off the circuit," he calls it, though sometimes they play special events, state fairs, weddings, or the celebration of a divorce.

I stare at a 5x7 photo of alvin-Travis's family he's tossed down beside me on the chaise lounge; his sister framed it for him in faux gold plating for his birthday. The photo's from five years ago, a significant time, says alvin-Travis, some of them that were in this picture no longer *are*. But I know what he really wants me to notice, the one who is absent, the one taking the picture for the rest. I'm supposed to tell him it's *good*, good composition, clarity, the way he's positioned the shot so the light would filter into the background. It's how we met. I was hired by his agent to photograph his band play an event. I'm a preferred practitioner of a different kind of photography, the chronicling of disasters. Somebody has to do it, is the way I think about it, and do it right — not those sensational anguish shots you get from the local rags' photo-ops. This goes a lot deeper than any mere human factor. It's evidence there is a God and must be shot with this kind of reverence. But then, how many of these do we have in a year that I can get to and make a living off of? Tsunamis, earthquakes that measure above seven on the Richter; *God* has historically shied away from proof, after all, content to let his laurels rest, let his humans practice their own kinds of destruction for a while. In 1950, the year I was born, Mauna Loa on the island of Hawai'i erupted. It was the heaviest destruction in 150 years — seven major rivers of lava ripping down from the west rift zone wiping out houses, a new motel and restaurant, the Magoon Ranch house and pasture land, covering the Ho'okena village, post office, church, service station, burial grounds —

all under a deadly stretch of shiny black lava. I considered this a sign, a prophecy of sorts, forecast of my future.

Even this, what I do, alvin-Travis wants to do better than me. It's nothing personal. It's just that when you've been a star, any kind of a star, even if it's only the big fish in a small pond syndrome, a star in New England but never heard of in New York or new anything beyond the Connecticut border, it's difficult to step back down to being just one of the rest of us.

I say nothing. Study him too, his bullfrog thighs and those skinny calves packed into tight black jeans standing over me—a.T. likes to have the height advantage, when I'm standing we're eye to eye. I'm trying to imagine him relaxed enough to be asleep on his chaise lounge beside me like couples do, but knowing better. alvin-Travis doesn't sleep. At least I've rarely caught him at it. When I do he reacts guiltily, like I've discovered him doing nothing when there's time better spent. Mostly when I wake up beside him he's staring off into the white space of the room. His house, a sprawling contemporary, all bare white walls and angles, the illusion of space he calls it. No illusion, three families, 2.5 kids each and a dog could move comfortably inside. *Sleep's a private thing*, alvin-Travis says. He's still a somewhat pretty man, delicate in that way rock musicians often are, never really having had to *work* for a living, his blond hair mostly white now when he neglects to dye it, his angular shape viny. Like Mick Jagger, ugly as sin some of them, yet they've got that certain something, that power of the publicly known.

alvin-Travis does sit down finally on the chaise beside mine, closes his eyes as if feigning relaxation then immediately slides them open again. Without looking at me, staring at the silver expanse of the Atlantic beyond, he says, "Tell me about your latest." I imagine him slipping out a notebook, a fountain pen, it would be a fountain pen, popping on a pair of bifocals, that concerned look. alvin-Travis, lead guitarist and singer, has confessed to me that what he really wanted to be was a shrink. His band was called the Head Shrinkers. He studied psychology at the University of Maine until he dropped out, and then he bought into those encounter-group therapies of the times, EST, Gestalt, Jungian Workshops. Some of his old clientele who used to attach themselves like lower life-forms to the band, barnacles, algae, pond scum, still come over for dream work, he calls it. They tell him their dream and he tells them what it means. The big picture. alvin-Travis is fond of that phrase, the big picture. *Let me give you the big picture*, he says.

I tell him about the man in the downtown hotel last weekend after the art show in Portland, when I had to stay over because my ride back was leaving too early, I couldn't break down my booth in time, my photographs, mostly of myself at this point, nudes—it's what I do these days in lieu of a major flood or avalanche, what I know—myself, naked. The funny thing though is I'm never wholly there: body parts, my torso, arms and neck, or thighs and butt, the side view; the V between my legs, poignantly shaded, hips and belly over this a cradle of clean white light. To look at these prints one would never guess they are me.

"The song and dance at that hotel, his warming up to me slowly in the slick-carpeted lounge, then quicker, stroking my hair, my neck, and I'm already imagining it," I tell alvin-Travis, "how he'll feel in bed. He's so big, his shoulders massive structures like someone maybe built them out of mortar and brick just kept slapping the stuff on." alvin-Travis leans closer, interest lighting up his tea colored eyes. "I imagined how he'd swallow me whole," I say, "consume me, how underneath his mass I'd disappear, become one with the bed, dissolve into the tangy bleach of hotel sheets." I smile at this; will alvin-Travis appreciate the image?

"And then?" alvin-Travis asks.

"And then, that's it. He leaves. An early morning, he tells me. I go up to my room, shut out the lights, dive into the bed and that's all she wrote."

alvin-Travis looks disappointed. "That's all?"

"That's all she wrote," I repeat. I don't tell him about the way I really felt, the way I always feel after one of these empty encounters, the roar of what I suspect is my own insignificance closing in on me at night, becoming a wail, a moan, a whimper, a *nothing*, when I turn off the light in these strange places. It's the only reason I even considered going to the big man's room, inviting him into mine. If you turn the light out and somebody's there with you, you don't disappear. Not for that night anyway.

I close my eyes into the late afternoon sun, a lemony dance behind them. I have little enough to do these days, my photos sell themselves or not, but it doesn't matter, because I'm living with alvin-Travis, and he will provide, he tells me. Another way of making himself bigger than me. My part is to tell him stories, of the male encounter type especially, but he'll listen to others.

The story I don't tell him much is the one he doesn't want to hear, the one that concerns my sister. It's a story he grows wary even thinking about because it could involve a maybe-god, some sort of holiness or sorcery, the place some stories get to where there are no other answers, no other endings. alvin-Travis is not comfortable with these kinds of stories. He's a reformed Jewish-Catholic-Baptist-Hindu-Janist-Unitarian Universalist, he told me, reformed from buying into any of it. *We're all of us on this earth on our own*, he says, *in it for the long haul by ourselves, and then we die.*

As for me, I like to picture myself back in Hawai'i, in a little *lau hala* hut on a lava field at the base of Kīlauea or Mauna Loa, a place where the earth is as new as earth gets and the forces that create it old as the sky. I'll be there, until I'm not.

This is my story. I have to tell it over and over sometimes, starting at its beginning so I can remember who I am, or who I was, and whether who I was made me who I am. To try and find some sort of understanding, some kind of reason for the way things have turned out. Was there something I could have done differently? What if *it* had never happened? What if Willa grew up into a beautiful young woman, savory and whole, and I, her sister, falling gratefully behind in the shadow of her entirely normal, predictable and more desirable light? Jaycee would grow old, as all mothers must, and my father would just be my father. What if?

****

They called me Scat, Susan Catherine slurred together; I never was a Susany sort of child. I begin in the fifties, in the Territory of Hawai'i. At the end of the fifties, on March 12, 1959, the United States Congress voted statehood for Hawai'i, a day of drifting paper, streamers, confetti and balloons, and people shouting, sirens wailing, bells clanging, horns blowing, and my family, all of us together — Wilhelmina on her two good legs, her enchantress smile — dancing about, happy for who knows what. Hawai'i has always been into a good celebration. We who celebrate this day are mostly *haoles*, local white people, once upon a time from somewhere else. Our mother is from the East Coast; our parents met when Father went east for college. Father's family was originally from California, though since he was born here and his father was born here and his grandmother too, he's not some *malihini*, he's pointed out. It's said we have Hawaiian in us, from our father's father's mother, mother's aunt Wilhelmina Malia, my sister's namesake. Something like that — we're not completely sure how this works — and in my case anyway it's not enough to give me that tough local look that would make the local kids, the *mokes* and the *titas* think twice before they torment. We don't question if this is the right thing, this statehood; it is *the* thing. Says Father, "Now we'll be heard in Washington."

It's the Fifties and jello is for dinner. Not just dessert. Our mother, Jaycee Beever, considers jello the ultimate staple: Throw some chicken scraps and celery on top and you've got yourself a main course; slup it up with peas and nuts and you've got your vegetable, protein too, then serve it with spam and you've hit all the food groups. Make it into a star mold and it's *fancy jello*, or glop it on our plates, mayonnaise, marshmallows, pineapple and it's *filling*. Like we're pillows or something, stuff us with *filling*. Our mother's theory about food: if it's got color and appeals to the eye, no matter the taste, it's a *winner dinner*. I think she got that phrase from some housekeeping magazine she lugged home from Foodland, poring over it, then flinging it down in disgust because our home, she said, could never be *this*. *Just try finding those billowy white chintz curtains in Hawai'i!* The housekeeping magazines always showed billowy white curtains. Sometimes after one of these magazines was devoured she'd make plans: a gold-tone shag carpet for their bedroom, a porcelain white soup tureen on a brand new something or other piece of dining room furniture she just knew we couldn't get *here*. Occasionally she would cry, I remember this — she just wanted our home to be a *nice* home, and Father would promise her things, purchases from the mainland, from one of his trips. We all felt the shame of her tears.

These are the heydays of Tupperware, of chipped beef on toast, sardine sandwiches and avocado colored linoleum, of Wonder bread, Tang, Fizzies, and Ovaltine; pop culture cliché, you might wonder? This *was* our culture, and the cold war brewing a world apart from Kailua, O'ahu, our home town.

Happy Housewife is what Jaycee calls herself, sucking down her gin and tonics, busy as a you-know-what. Our father waters our lawn every evening, hose in hand, won't trust those lawn sprinklers to do a decent job, squirting water across the grass in random arcs, and the grass is *green as green*. That's how Jaycee describes things, as the things themselves: *You're pretty as pretty*, she says to my sister Willa, *bad as bad*, she tells our brother. Other Mothers would say "pretty as a picture" and our brother would be "naughty," never bad, their calm, Madonna-like smiles. It's how I saw them, the other kids' mothers that lived on our street, strolling down to the beach in pin curlers and checkered scarves, pushing baby carriages, saintly presences, their soothing offerings. I longed for one of them to touch me too.

Our mother had just emerged out of her silent years, the years when she birthed us, did little else, lying in her bed day after day under the knotty pine ceiling, counting the patches, the twists, the demented little mole-like shapes. Postpartum depression is what they would call it now; back then it was another thing our family had to hide. Our father hired Kimi to take care of us, little Kimi not much taller than me, who baked us sweet buns, *manapua* and *limu-*wrapped sushi and rice cakes. First thing our mother did when she surfaced was to fire Kimi, saying nobody should take care of us but us, especially not someone who fed us seaweed. "Don't you know what *limu* is, Mr. *Hawaiian*?" she scoffed at our father.

Jaycee became a hula dancer, but not the Hawaiian kind of hula, dancing for the tourists on the Royal Hawaiian lānai under a stripy sunset and Tiki torches, and certainly not the ancient story telling dances of the real Hawaiians. She danced for the Marines on the Air Base in Kāne'ohe, and she danced for the beatnik neighbors up the street—our father called them that. And then our father would show up, red-faced, lug her back home, she's shrieking and cursing and flailing about. He'd take her into their room, and I would hear the tide of their voices behind the shut door, hers shrill, then quieter, a sob, murmurs of comfort then a hush, finally, and I could go back to bed. She was lonely, this much I understand now, and too smart, her calculating nineteen fifties mind presumed to be content with analyzing carpet swatches. Perhaps on some level I knew this even then. Those Other Mothers were suspicious of her, and with good reason it turns out — but we won't get to this until much later in the story.

As a child I longed to be anybody but me. I used to gaze across the street at our neighbors' house in the pink evening light, and think of Kathy Connely who lived in it eating something reasonable for dinner, real meat that's cooked fresh by Kathy's mother and not *stabilized* as my mother called it, by preservatives in the package first (did we even understand these as preservatives then?), a predictable vegetable, carrots maybe, and rice; no jello, not even for dessert. Kathy's mother would make chocolate pudding or haupia, coconut pudding, maybe even a frosted cake.

There's the day our mother takes us to the Kailua Medical Group for our checkup. Willa's weeping because she's scared of shots (I am too, but I don't tell Willa that — *Make A*, as we said in those days, *A* as in *ass*, which we *didn't* say, not yet anyway —), and when we leave, Jaycee's lips are tight as a bobby pin, clenched in that way that announces another family secret about to be unearthed.

"You may have something wrong with you," she tells us the minute we are home, "Scat, and Robbie too. Your father does, you may as well be aware of this, and others in his family could have had it too, but they're dead now so who knows? It's called Marfans Syndrome, a connective tissue disease. They can't do tests for this though, like pricking your finger and sending your blood to the lab. So we'll have to wait and see," she says, those taut, accusing lips.

At our next checkup Dr. Graver tell us it's still a possibility, though it doesn't do much good to confirm it or not, as the medical establishment knows too little about this. He examines my eyes for the telling weakness, *ectopia lentis*, he calls it. Was he trying to impress us with his Latin to make up for not being able to do anything for us? I'm too tall and gangly with a sunken in chest, and if I do have Marfans I might also have a fragile, already aging heart. My maturity in some places is very quick, and in others like *breasts*, well you've got to wonder if these will come in at all.

My mother tells us intelligent people have Marfans, like Abraham Lincoln. But *she* doesn't. And then she gets mad at us for maybe having it, blaming it on our father's genes, our father tall as a door. We may not even make it into middle age, she tells us, her awkward children, Robbie and me, so we have to learn to make the most of every moment. Otherwise, she says, we're a waste of space. *Space is space,* she says. Except for our sister Willa, pretty as pretty, who takes after Jaycee and definitely does not have Marfans. She's more rounded, a symmetrically featured face, as Jaycee calls it, not the *irregular* look of me. And she's small. It's the fifties and pretty girls are small.

I was never considered anybody's friend in those days, my school, my neighborhood, and I wasn't special enough, as Jaycee explained it, to overcome this. "There are consequences," she said, "to being a loner." But I didn't mind it, this loner life, at least not most of the time. I had my sister, "the beavers," our mother called us, beavers before *Leave it to Beaver* a favorite of ours, beavers before *the Beav*! (I'm ashamed to admit it took me until college to learn *beaver* had another, anatomical connotation, even though by then I was engaging mine quite *eagerly,* shall we say.) And I had potato bugs. I played in the dirt with them, built elaborate buildings, tunnels, structures out of twigs and pebbles, made libraries and community centers with playrooms, places nobody had to be alone. Because I'd catch them if they crawled off by themselves, and I'd make them come back into my potato bug school room or my potato bug Foodland. And here it was OK not to be pretty. Potato bugs just aren't particularly pretty.

Then it's the Beatles *I want to hold your hand,* and the teenaged girls no longer parading up and down our street, transistor radios pressed against their ears whining out Elvis, Frankie, Bobby V., bra straps slipping out of white sleeveless shirts tied at their waists, pedal pushers showing off the little round balls of their calf muscles. Now they look like surfer girls, their lemon juiced hair bleached in the sun, ironed straight as straight. I wondered if I would ever have calf muscles. The thing about maybe having Marfans is you don't get much musculature, you're too stretched out.

Willa's only eight and already she's yakking about wanting to be a cheerleader, seems it's her goal now. Willa's got a goal and this is something, Father says. So she practices, *two-four-six-eight, who do we appreciate,* KAILUA! on Father's front lawn every evening, the sky a blaze of scarlet and violet and mynah birds chattering at her to quit it. She's got a crush on Jed Weidemeir, she says, even though it's "highly unlikely" — these are Jaycee's words — that Willa understands what a crush is. He's captain of the Peewee football team and he knows how to surf. "Can't do better than that," Willa says. These are some of the last actual words we hear her speak. *Can't do better than that.* It's the way they talk in the Teen Magazine Jaycee buys for me, since I'm oldest, but Willa's the one who grabs it so she gets to read it first. They were interviewing sweet sixteen year olds about who they most wanted to date. "Dr. Kildare," said one. "He's on TV, he's cute, and he wears *bitchen* shirts. Can't do better than that!"

What I wanted most back then was my own room, small would have been OK, a narrow room filled with simple love and exact emotion. No symbols, no dreams. No Willa Beever in a coma for two weeks, not expected to live at all; Jaycee in the hospital with her, Father's eyes red rimmed and plastered every night on that green as green grass. I see her in my dreams, my little sister, just two years younger than me, lying in that big white hospital bed, still beautiful even after *it* happened, blond hair spread across her pillow like a Japanese fan and the covers caved in, empty as an unfilled balloon where one of her legs should have been. She's lost so much blood, is the thing, transfusion after transfusion just can't seem to pump her life back into her, back to where it was before. Is life measured this way, in blood? You've got to maintain at all times just so much of it to be your normal self, and then you're not?

My dream changes to when she's brought home, wan, sunken, and no artificial leg because she's too weak to manage, just lies in her bed, which used to be in my room. Two twin beds with their pink chenille matching covers, their white rattan table in between, their Nancy Ann doll lights hanging on the wall over each of their heads; one bed is empty now, one light never switched on. Our father waters and waters and waters that lawn until soon maybe we'll have a pond out there, bullfrogs croaking, crickets cricking, palm trees sprouting up and surrounding it like it really does belong, like it's always been there, the way my sister will become: as if she's always been like this, as if all along she's been someone else.

CHAPTER TWO

That was one story I might have told and one way to tell it, the thin way, a skeleton of itself leaving out the meat, the details, the plot. Before *it* happened, the tragedy at the seat of our lives, as Jaycee puts it. I might've told how things were fine. They were what we knew. Hawai'i becomes a state, fluttering of paper in the streets, of horns honking, sirens wailing, an all day holiday — this is what I remember and it's true enough, moments of ecstasy, everything on the brink of feeling almost easy. Jaycee with that glow, the fever in her eyes that seemed almost golden then too, so unquestioningly deserving of all she expected. But listen, even this might have been remembered wrong. Statehood was August 21, Admissions Day officially; that day in March was the vote that made it happen. Which did we celebrate?

Jaycee fixing dinner for her little beavers, a name she called us since our last name's Beever, two ee's no a, two little girls and the son Robbie, who was oldest. Robbie took up space the way a boy did, his things, his loudness, his boy smells, boy friends, disdain for the girls' lives around him. What could we girls hope to grow into in those days? Housewives in starched aprons and Betty Crocker hairdos, luncheon givers, *hostesses*, some of us; fantasy lovers of beatniks, outlaws, the life less normal in our more distant dreams; suckers of Valium, criers of romance and *Peyton Place*, swooners of Elvis and Bobby V. and Fabian, the rest. Whatever was Hawaiian in us had long since succumbed to the conforming pressures of the *haole* fifties. Ricky Nelson singing *I'm a traveling man, made a lot of stops, all over the world...* but he wouldn't stop here, not the Beever house, Jaycee making jello, chopped celery drifting like little green puke boats. Jaycee dancing hula in her cellophane skirt for our boys on the Base, she called them, Kāne'ohe Marines. Hawaiian blood, tuck your little *mo'o* lizard head down and run away fast over the window screens and out the door, like the *'aumakua* gecko. Father once wondered if maybe our ancestral god was the *mo'o*. He was fond of geckos. They cut down the mosquito population that hovered about his ankles, neck and ears when he watered the lawn in those lavender evenings.

And *haole*-hula for the neighbor, Fatboy, shimmery skirt swaying in the light of his windows, Father prodding her out of his house grimly, those lost hands, spiderlike fingers firm on her back. Sometimes if he said anything to her she would clam up for weeks, the cold shoulder he called it. Then the tears, sometimes the tears, and for a little while she's our mother again.

But now I've got to wonder, how *do* I tell it? This story, its fragments, pieces that don't quite connect. Father watering that lawn as if its perfect green growth might make us OK, too.

When Father was gone on one of his trips, Fatboy would come over. "Fatboy *understands* ladies," our mother informed us, and by this we understood she meant her. He has a handsome face, Jaycee told us, though not much hair. He said he lost his hair in the Pali Palms pool where Willa and I were taught to swim, back when they didn't know so much about chlorine. "Put too much in," he said, and he lost his hair, and what little was left turned green so his mother shaved that down like she was mowing it. Fatboy wasn't from Hawai'i, he was from somewhere else, so how could this be true? "Hah!" Fatboy chortled, "I'm pulling youse legs!"

We are playing *spy*, Robbie, Willa and me, which means Robbie gets to be the spy, because only men can be spies, according to our brother, but we can be his deputy spies. Robbie only plays with us when there's no one around who might see him playing with us. It was he who decided we would spy on Fatboy and Jaycee, since he gets to make the rules. We crouch down behind the long, knotty pine bookcase partition that our father built, with its open shelves, separating the living room from the hallway.

"We have our *routine*," Fatboy is saying, and I whisper to Robbie, "what's a routine?" He says it's what you have to do, like taking out the garbage. Fatboy winks at Jaycee like they are somehow complicit in something. Earlier she was in the kitchen fixing their *pūpūs*, Ritz crackers and triangles of American cheese, and now we can hear the clinking of the ice in their drinks, gin and tonics with a squeeze of fresh lime that Willa usually gets to suck on after because she is the littlest.

Fatboy is sprawled on Father's *easy* chair, his big bare legs like hairy tree stumps, rooted to our rug. When we are in the room and he's sitting in Father's chair he asks us how we are. "How are youse kids?" Fatboy speaks with a lisp, a New Jersey accent he calls it but he isn't from there, Jaycee said, wherever that is. Little existed for us beyond O'ahu's aqua shores, those days. But this time he doesn't know we are in the room, hunkered down behind the book shelves, staring at him between the Encyclopedia Britannica, Volumes A through K. Jaycee says she's not ready to sit yet because she needs to spritz their drinks. *Spritz* is her word for topping off their glasses with a *bit* more gin. They've been *spritzing* these all afternoon.

Willa starts to say something, forgetting to whisper and Robbie nails her with his elbow; "shut up!" he mouths. Willa, that scrunched up suckered little face, looks like she's going to cry. She got Jaycee's looks, fine boned as a twig and perfectly symmetrical, though not her fierceness underneath—not yet, anyway. Scat, the plain one, brittle as seaweed, older girl, protector of the Beevers. I wrap my arm around my sister, holding her close. Something about this *routine* makes me uncomfortable. I whisper to Robbie that maybe we could play *Africa* instead, where Robbie is the lion hunter and Willa and I are lions, roaring from the crown flower bushes. But he just shrugs and picks his toes.

There's a sliding door with squared white papery windows, *Japanese door*, Jaycee calls it, separating our living room from the dining room and the kitchen. I can see the shadow of Jaycee moving behind this door, hear the presence of her, our mother. Whoosh! goes the sliding Japanese door, clink of ice and the weighted smell of gardenia perfume. Jaycee swinging back into the room humming.

"Our routine," Fatboy says, taking the gin and tonics out of our mother's hands, setting them on the coffee table. Then he pulls her down on his lap, bumping her around like there's music playing somewhere that only they can hear. Years later this is what will come back to me, reeling through my mind like an unwanted rerun—except that I can't be sure it's a rerun, something I really saw, or whether it's what my own mind created, mystified as I was, my sharp and prideful mother bounced about like a toddler: his hand disappearing under her skirt. She's giggling and the sound of this makes my face flush, eyes burn, can't look at Robbie kneeling beside me; does he know this is dirty? *Is* this dirty? Only dirty girls do these sorts of things, don't they? Easy girls, girls who let a boy onto third base so he'll like her. I can see Fatboy's arm moving, but where is that hand, those fat wormy fingers?

Second base, third base, skipped first base.... But I don't want Fatboy to like my mother! He's spinning her harder now like riding a 45 slick and black on the phonograph. Jaycee's face is the color of an apple. I clamp my tongue between my teeth until the blood burbles out and think about becoming a grown-up and murdering Fatboy. I'll use a gun like they do on *Hawaiian Eye* or *Seventy-Seven Sunset Strip*: *Cookie, lend me your comb*—bang!

Suddenly Robbie is up and running, and I am right behind him. "Wait!" Willa shrieks. My brother throws open the screen door, out into the purpling evening. Always ahead of me, is how I will remember him, never looking back. He is the one who got away.

It's the fifties and it's important to be normal. If you're not considered normal, what could you be? A commie? A beatnik? *Pinko*? The brown-legged children, *poor* children Jaycee clucks, sighs, shakes her pretty head, who live in the broken down Quonset huts in old Honolulu, rusted tin roofs, snarly bushes, doors on broken hinges yawning open and shut, swarming about their cluttered little yards, raucous laughter. How I yearned to be one of them, embraced in a more predictable if not such a *normal* life, following my mother, click click of her high heels, parading the streets of Honolulu on her weekly shopping trip, smell of her perfume wafting into the tarry scent of the streets, not knowing if or when she'll duck into the stone entrance of the Alexander Young Hotel, slip away past the Hob-Nob Room and be gone. What did she do in there? Who did she meet? We didn't know, didn't dare think it, our faces pressed against the dusty cafe windows of the Hob-Nob, watching for her return.

The afternoon its fishy downtown smells, Chinese language crisp around us, Japanese, Filipino, three little mostly-*haole* Beevers huddled on the honking corner of Bishop and Hotel streets, Honolulu harbor's silvery water just beyond. The Aloha Tower where Matson is, its ship the Lurline carrying people to distant places whose names mean little to us other than they are not here: San Francisco, London, Tokyo, lei sellers lining the docks. *Will I ever be the one who gets to go?*

Afterwards she buys us a strawberry shave ice from the shave ice stand on Maunakea if we promise we won't tell Father. We walk, clicking of Jaycee's heels, slurping our strawberry secret to O'ahu Fish Market, faded red awning, the concrete and clay tiled buildings. Chinatown, its dark little fruit and silk and flower shops, smell of the fish, shivery bodies and chopped off heads, people thronging through the streets. They're good at making money, those Chinese, Jaycee whispers darkly. Jaycee, her coifed head above most; "Mahi Mahi!" she snaps. "Be sure you give me your nice ones, yes? Nicest fillets."

"Hey!" Robbie points. "The dragon poles!" Our favorite, on the building across the street, its red and gold arches the tongues of dragons, dancing black shapes on signs that say *something*, but we'll never know. "Gonna eat you up!" he hisses to Willa, shaping a dragon mouth out of his hand. Willa shrieks, buries her head in Jaycee's skirt pretending to be afraid. Didn't know yet what real fear was. Didn't even know all the things we weren't supposed to know. So many secrets, their weight burdensome at times, like schlepping around someone else's skin.

Father's a business man, he tells us. Towering, sad eyed, but angry too sometimes and of course we try to adore him, Beevers should adore their fathers. Jaycee's aqua-green eyes burning like those periwinkle shells we pick up on the beach, the blue hot days, smell of the sea, lowing of the cows from the Castle ranch behind, palm trees dropping unripened coconuts like green bowling balls. And *naupaka* bushes, their fat pale leaves, their broken flowers. There's a legend about *naupaka*, Father told us: The mountain and the beach, two kinds of *naupaka*, their little flowers halved like broken hearts, like lovers who can never come together. *Naupaka kuahiwi*, the mountain, *naupaka kahakai*, the beach.

Jaycee's ironing lessons for her two little girls because *this* is what we can be, she says, caretakers of our husband's homes, ironers of their shirts. And Willa, Wilhelmina after our father's great aunt Wilhelmina, the one who was Hawaiian, who was called Auntie Wilhelmina but we call Willa, Willa—the pretty one, the one most likely to *husband* best.

Life was normal enough, most of the time. It's what we knew. And then it happened. *The tragedy at the seat of our lives.* "Everyone has one," Jaycee was quoted in one of those exposé newspapers, *Star, National Enquirer*, "it's just that mine is so much harder to bear." Father's on the mainland, so Fatboy's around. "A bachelor," says Jaycee. "Not so fat, a childhood nickname that stuck. A man with an appetite is a good thing," she insists. He has a boat, a Lightning sailboat, but this time he's got the motor chugging in the back, sails clamped down. It's a late, yellow-hot afternoon, and we're way out beyond the breakers in Kailua, almost to the midnight deep ocean channel that runs between the islands, the land a blue hump in the distance behind the strip of white beach, craggy Ko'olau mountains like knuckled fists, bright little clumps of cumulus clouds. Robbie, the girls, and Jaycee perched up on the bow in her high-legged, plunging neckline, tight black swimsuit Other Mothers would never wear, with their boxy legs, modestly concealed mother-breasts. Fatboy can't keep his gritty little eyes off her. Jaycee's packed 7-up and bologna sandwiches with mayonnaise, bags of sliced sweet pickles for our *vegetable*.

And maybe it's Robbie who suggests the thing with the tubes; later Fatboy will say it was Robbie, but I remember it as Fatboy himself, perhaps to get us in the water so he's alone with Jaycee. Fatboy's not from Hawai'i, not a local *haole*. If he were local, would he have known better? He's from some place like Montana where he was a trapper, somebody who traps animals, which is somebody I could never accept as a fully human being. "Got a slug bigger than youse hand for a grizzly," he once told Robbie. He could tell you how much money he got from any kind of animal he trapped, his *set*, he called it, what he used to catch and then kill. He could tell you about the furs, what each one of them brings on the market; he said even the men wear certain kinds, like the arctic wolf. He said the red fox is the smartest and the fisher's the meanest and the bobcat never seemed hungry enough when it approached his set, and that's the reason he never caught one of those. Sometimes he did things like clear golf courses of prairie dogs so the golfers wouldn't twist their ankles in the prairie dog holes. He said it's man's work, and that there's nothing he doesn't know about catching and killing an animal.

Off we go, into the wild blue yonder, sings Jaycee, her bob of shiny dark hair fritzing about her upturned face in the salty breeze, sunglasses covering her eyes so those red lipsticked lips leap out, shape themselves into a smile, out pops that tinkly little laugh. Robbie and the girls, three black tubes with ropes attached and tied to the boat, drifting off the back, floating out in three wide and perfect arcs behind the motor, the youngest Beever in the middle, protected in the way (or so we believed!) the smallest among us must be.

Fatboy turns up the heat, he calls it, and we roar, rip, throttle through the blue-dark water laughing and yelling and screaming, the exhilaration, the expectancy, Kailua ocean pulling and tugging and grasping at us, warm and sour as salt. I felt a surge of fear, eyes tearing up but I sucked it back down. Crying is not tolerated from the older of the Beever girls, fright is a private thing and it's never enough, anyway.

So I guess with the noise we're making nobody hears what must have been there to be heard. Must've been just a slight change in those high happy Beever squeals, one now of terror and disbelief, for how could she have known? What could she understand? Pretty little Willa, I remember the way her eyes used to light up, two pale blue flames, little girl teeth, ridges of white like those puka shell necklaces, her uncorrupted smile. She's screaming of course but the motor's a loud and constant roar, and Robbie and I still yelling out our fun, so maybe I'm only imagining it when I feel the yank on my own rope, the water now blurry and too cold, the water a jolt like a bolt of electricity, the water around us suddenly red.

Willa listing, silenced, her head lolling to one side. Robbie's screaming now and I am too, though I'm still not sure why. The boat's motor cut and Fatboy's herding her in, hauling her rope, Jaycee's tugging at mine, Robbie's—*Oh my God! Oh my God!*—she's wailing, drops the ropes and cradling her head, squeezing it between her hands like something she could break in two if only she could, break it, stop all of this now, just *stop*! as Willa comes shooting out of the water, tube attached to the rope, Willa dangling off it but barely. Yank, heave, drag, the water filled with a thunderous sense of some terrible doom, Jaycee howling. Up comes Willa to the deck of the boat, I see her blond wet hair hanging down over her face, the frilly blue palaka checked suit, one leg, foot, another thigh, but where is the rest? And...nothing. Nothing! Empty! Invisible as the hand of God dangling down where the other half should be, *missing*, a flood of red and Jaycee reeling, her high, shrill and anguished scream. Did any of us see the fin, the lurking grey shadow? In our dreams we do, our memories that become part dream, part fear, already shaping this new life.

****

What was life like after a shark dined on your sister's leg? What's it like having a miracle in the family? Years later, those are the kinds of questions you get from the tabloids, *Star, Sun, Globe, National Enquirer*, news shows inviting you to come on so they can get from you the *human* angle. Springer's people call to see if maybe there hadn't been some sort of fight involved, blame laid like hands upon a shoulder, fat fist broad-siding that guilty grin? So people can stare at you and be grateful you are you and not them. Talk of a reality show, *Sharks In Paradise*—How we choose to become survivors of our own catastrophic lives.

Here is what it was like. There's the waiting, mostly, waiting for her to die. "Will she die?" I ask Fatboy, who takes care of us until Father comes home. Robbie won't go to bed when he tells him to, won't do anything Fatboy tells him to do, and Jaycee's camped out at Queens Hospital with Willa. Waiting for her to die? Father's at the hospital too when he's not at work, comes home late in the night but still I hear him out there, watering our yard so that the grass, if nothing else, keeps growing. Fatboy shakes his head when I ask if my sister will die, shrugs.

And then—"Thank God!" says Father—Grandma agrees to cross the ocean on the Lurline, takes her sweet time about it too, he says, moves in. *Just for the time being,* they both say. Grandma's never trusted our father, Jaycee said, because he was born in Hawai'i, which is a little too *native* for her. Even though his family came from California once upon a time, which far as Grandma is concerned, is only one step up on the civilization ladder from Hawai'i.

Grandma's from New England, she tells us, drawing those two words into one stretched-out and exaggerated word, *Newwwwengland,* like it's some holy place. (Who would've imagined then I'd end up there, too.) Newwwwengland. Grandma smokes skinny brown cigarettes, looks like a praying mantis sticking out between her cracked and wrinkled lips. Jaycee's mother. "Always got to be different, that one," Grandma says about Jaycee when we tell her we're supposed to call our mother by her given name. "That's what a name's for," Jaycee said. Grandma's got claws, long arthritic hands that are bent and blue, so Robbie and me have to make the meals. "We have to do it like Jaycee does," I say, and Robbie says he couldn't care less. Dinner jellos with spam, or sometimes bologna bits when Grandma forgets to market, and breakfast jellos when she forgets to buy our cereals, shiny red islands floating in our milk. "Your mother and me, we never much got along," Grandma says.

I wake up in the night a lot, heart bumping and gyrating about in my chest like it wants to pop on out of there do the Chubby Checker twist, *I'm free, I'm free!* my breath barely squeezing in and out like a giant clam shell's gotten around my lungs, clinching shut. *Clamp* shell Willa called them when she was little, when we roamed the Kāne'ohe mud flats at low tide ogling the sea life stuck there, when she was she. I'm sweating and always there's this thin wiry scream behind my throat that never quite comes out. At first I think it's Jaycee's scream, got stuck in me somehow when she let it out That Day; let it rip so long and high and wild, a thing alive, blood, wings, had to go *somewhere* and it flew inside me. That Day, is what it's become, three weeks since it happened and nothing will ever be the same. To say Willa's our mother's favorite because she's the prettiest sounds childish, but we knew this to be true. My sense now is that Jaycee, valued for her looks, probably figured only the fairest of her children had a chance. The Beevers, her little *beavers,* she'd sigh, arm tight around Willa, one hand stretched out as if to touch me, reach me.

"God will love you," insists Grandma, "If you're good."

"Wilhelmina's out of danger, she's out of intensive care, Susan Catherine," Grandma says. Grandma uses our bigger names when she talks to us. She even calls Robbie Robert, which is one more thing he hates about Grandma. Because his name, Robert, is our father's name, and Robbie's gotten into this thing lately where he's *none too fond*, as Jaycee puts it, of our father. Robbie is thirteen, just become a teenager. I'm ten, Willa's eight.

How many *used to's* in our life at this point? Willa's lost her leg, and that's one used-to-be-never-be-the-same. She lost a lot of blood, so much they didn't expect her to live, so much she was in shock a long time, the Lightning ripping back to shore, waiting on the beach for the ambulance, the lifeguards summoned from nearby Kailua beach park racing down the yellow sand with oxygen tanks, a first aid kit, bandaids, iodine, didn't quite have the what it takes for a bit-off leg. Fatboy tore his own shirt, then tied it into a tourniquet to slow the bleeding. Robbie ran to the closest house to call the ambulance, no cell phones those days. Sand a deep crimson under Willa, silent as silent, her eyes rolled back in their sockets, the towel Jaycee put over her turning bright red and that emptiness under it. She's in a coma for two weeks.

Grandma says Jaycee prayed for Willa's life and it worked. "She gets religion all of a sudden and wouldn't you know it, even God believes her. Down the road they can consider prosthesis," Grandma says. I ask what that is and she says it's a fake leg. "They can make them out of titanium," Grandma tells us. Whatever that is. "Only, that Devil!" — Grandma calls the shark 'that Devil!' — "didn't bite in the clean break places, like under the knee or even at the top of poor sister's upper leg." (Grandma won't use *thigh*, says it's a nasty word.) "He bit right in the middle, uneven at that, left more on the left side than the right, a lump of gristle hanging down looks like to me, that poor, poor child. Now your mother won't go bragging about how pretty Wilhelmina is, not anymore, you can bet your booty on that one.

"Sometimes bad things happen when you brag too much," says

Grandma. "It's tempting fate to think you got it so good."

****

Another month goes by and Willa and Jaycee are in some place called Rehabilitation. Robbie and me still can't visit her. "No children allowed in them places," Grandma says. Grandma is not from Hawai'i, she constantly points this out; she's from the East Coast. "Rules is rules," Grandma says, and far as she's concerned Hawai'i needs a sight more of them to be civilized. "You can't trust a place that so recently became a state," she says. "They haven't worked all the kinks out." Grandma tells us Wilhelmina's going to need more than just a leg to get rehabilitated. "She won't speak a word, not a blessed word, your mother's beside herself."

One night Father gets home early enough so that we're still up after our own dinner and I serve him Robbie's and my chunky tuna, baked beans and canned corn dinner casserole (we had no more bread for sandwiches, which he politely told us he might prefer).

"Is it true?" I ask him, my father who himself won't speak much. "Is it true?" I demand. "That Willa's not talking?"

"Scat," he says, "my Kit-Cat-Scat," pulling me onto his lap in his easy chair, lawn already watered, Honolulu *Star-Bulletin* on his knees, staring up into the spaces of our knotty pine ceiling, counting the patches? which is what I do when I'm thinking of things, or even when I'm not. Which is what Jaycee did after she had us, trying to take count of what was left in her life, she said. That was when she made us start calling her by her name. "Not Mommy," she said, "*Mommy's* a job, not a person. Call me Jaycee," she instructed baby Willa, who took to it right off, who had never said Ma Ma anyway.

My father sighs, then running his long fingered hand through my flop of scraggly bangs, pressing his head against mine he whispers: "Maybe Willa just hasn't figured out the right thing to say."

CHAPTER THREE

Would you wonder at this point how things were for Robbie and me, our sister out of her coma and no voice, we're told, a mother on hold, Father mostly gone and a grandmother too arthritic to fix us our meals? We were kids, remember, and when bad things happen in a kid universe life blinks for a moment or two like a light bulb flickering out, darkens, wavering on the brink of absolute blackness then blazes back in again, into its own stifling world with its separate definitions and immediate concerns: who we are in the social order. *Selfishness*, Grandma called it, a word I had previously believed meant sharing my toys with Willa because she'd tattle if I didn't. Another used-to-be-never-be-the-same.

Here is how selfish I can be. It's Lisa Yamamoto's birthday party and I'm the last one invited. I didn't think I'd even *be* invited, except probably Mrs. Yamamoto said, "You have to invite that poor Beever girl, the one whose sister was attacked by the shark." That's who we've become around here, Robbie and me, we're the ones whose sister was attacked by the shark.

So I go to her stupid swimming pool party at the Kāne'ohe Yacht Club, because Grandma makes me, says I can't sit around and be glum all day, a Gloomy Gus. "Be chipper," Grandma says. "It's not the end of *your* life." And I don't have a gift because that's what Jaycee would have done, found me some present to give Lisa, ferreting through her own stuff, a necklace Jaycee doesn't wear or an ugly scarf someone gave her — Jaycee's into *recycling* gifts before this is even a word people use. And I'm sitting on that concrete-rough side of the pool, between the baby pool and the big one, glaring into the turquoise water, sweat drooling down my sunburnt face, as Lisa opens everyone else's gift; *oooh, ahhh, ooh*! Then they're staring at me. "Where's yours, Scat? Where's Scat's present?"

I scramble up and run into the changing room, the *cabana*, Lisa called it, smells like wet floor and cleaning fluids, and I'm remembering how when I was eight, Willa's age, Brenda Dow, one of the bigger girls in my class, part Portuguese, Filipino, and something else making her muscled and dark, probably Samoan; one of the popular girls who can throw a ball like a boy, whom every teacher we've ever had thinks is so smart—I remember how at another one of these swimming parties Brenda made me take off my bathing suit in front of the others and show them the small new bracelet of curly black hairs.

Now I've got a lot down there, spiraling wickedly like barbed wire under my last year's Speedo, got to pull the suit firm and tight between my skinny legs to hide every last piece. And what I decide now is to make them pay to see it, a quarter each and one at a time not the whole blessed bunch of them, then I'll give the money to Lisa so she'll have her present. But it's Brenda Dow who says, peering blandly into my face after cornering me on the shower bench, shoving me down, hissing in the pidgin English Jaycee forbids us to speak, "Your seesta all pau one leg now, eh? How she going walk, just one leg? She come home soon? Have to hop, yeah? Like one Easta rabbit! What she look like no leg, da kine ugly or what! Right or left leg all pau?" The others giggle and snort.

I think about how for a while we were heroes, the first two weeks when nobody knew if Willa would live or die. People, even other kids were actually nice to me and Robbie. They went after the shark, a boat full of Kailua men with guns, and then the state Division of Fish and Game sent out a boat who sent the men home. They were still compiling data on the number of sharks slaughtered after Billy Weaver was killed, the Billy Weaver Shark Research and Control Program, so they knew what they were about. We were supposed to be reassured by this. Killed some nurse shark nosing about the area Willa was attacked in, several sand sharks, even a small black-tipped shark but no tigers, nothing our father called *niuhi*, people-eaters. "I doubt if any of them's that Devil!" says Grandma. "Once a shark tastes flesh and blood he'll come back for dessert, mark my words."

"Used to be one stuck-up little tita, your seesta, now she look like the Monkey Man," Brenda Dow snarls. The Monkey Man sits in his wheelchair in Kailua town where the taxi to Honolulu is, streets gritty, greasy smells from Kress's lunch counter nearby. He's got no legs, lost them in The Big One. The Monkey Man rides around in his wheelchair, Kuulei, Oneawa, Kailua roads, his big muscular arms pumping him about the sidewalks, over the cigarette butt-strewn curbs. He's got a *tapa* print quilt that covers him where his legs aren't and a ratty brown monkey sits on his shoulders, holding out a baseball cap for the people getting on and off the taxi to put some money in. The cap has Hawaiian words printed in black, *no ka mea*. I asked my father what this meant once and he said it's a legal term, means *because of the thing*. "He's a fierce monkey, mean as a drunken sailor," the Monkey Man told us. "Don't go trying to pet him," the Monkey Man warned. "He'll chomp off your fingers and spit them out, easy as gumming a banana."

"It's a *dirty* monkey," Grandma said. *Dirty Monkey Man* she called the man and ordered us not to go near him when she took us into Kailua one Saturday morning, Kress for Grandma's lingerie, Liberty House to shop for Grandma's dresses (Grandma's *dissatisfied* with Liberty House because most of the dresses are mu'umu'us and she wanted *real* dresses like they wear in Newwwwengland), and then to the library because, she said, we have to learn to read *real* books, not comic books like the ones Robbie collects. "Those are summer reading," she insisted. I read real books, always have, but mostly Grandma pays attention to Robbie, the things he does or doesn't do.

The girls are surrounding me now, clambering about the shower benches like crabs, all but Lisa who hangs back a bit. Is she thinking maybe something here is her fault? Or else it's her birthday so who cares, she gets hers? I shrug, feign ten year old nonchalance, stare at Brenda Dow's own fatly muscled legs, little wheels those calf muscles, rolling about under her oily skin.

"At least she won't have nasty legs like yours," I say, not sure if this is any kind of an insult, whether it will even measure up on the tit for tat scale of things; Brenda called Willa a *tita*, after all, which is like calling her a girl *moke* – though if she were either of these she'd be able to beat up Brenda, one legged or not, for comparing her to the dirty Monkey Man.

Brenda punches me in my arm like Robbie does, that place boys know, makes you suck in your breath at the hurt. I push against her, knocking her back against the steel lockers, then make a run for it out of the cabana, away from the big peoples pool and the little kids pool, gleaming turquoise in the late morning sun, down to the pier, Kāne'ohe Bay sucking at its sides, clear green water and the liquidy slime of jelly fish underneath, wormy red and black sea cucumbers, and nutibranchs, which can *look* pretty sometimes but if you touch them they'll feel slick and squishy. I used to imagine falling into this water when Jaycee occasionally brought us to the Yacht Club. (Not very often, only when Mrs. Meehan up the road invited us. "We're not the kind of people that get to be members," Jaycee said, "Your father doesn't make *that* kind of money.") I worried about falling in and touching those jelly fish, the jelly fish grabbing at my toes their slithery, sucking tentacles, or the sea cucumbers, cigar shaped, thick as a sausage. Father told us some sea cucumbers can disgorge their internal organs, like if a predator was after them, leave their organs to munch on instead, regenerate them at a more convenient time. It's called Defensive Vomiting, Father said. *Sharks too, some of them, like tiger sharks, niuhi.*

Now I know there are worse things in the water than jelly fish and upchucking sea cucumbers, make off with your leg and your whole life, whatever you once knew disappears, becomes something else, a life maybe you don't even want. I wonder if the shark that got Willa's leg has *disgorged* it by now, turned his stomach inside out, his intestines, and Willa's leg floating out there somewhere in the deepest part of the ocean like something that belongs.

I hunch down at the end of the wooden pier, cool breeze stiffening my neck, boats blowing in and out of the harbor, hills behind are fist shaped fingers of brown and behind these the Ko'olaus' looming green claws. The Marine Air Base to my right, helicopters whirring in and out, where my mother used to dance, where she won't dance again. I can hear Lisa's party, the girls back in the pool, splashing, laughing, I'm forgotten by now. Eventually Mrs. Yamamoto will come looking when she discovers I'm missing because that's what the Other Mothers do. But for now I let the wind cool me off and I just think. I wanted my own room, it's what I wanted, my own small room apart from my sister, simple love, exact emotion. No symbols and no dreams.

CHAPTER FOUR

You might also wonder about the symbols and dreams. alvin-Travis did. It was the part of my story that intrigued him, in the beginning, when he'd still let me tell it. When he still tried to make love to me and afterwards, in the sweat and the collapse, the privacy of our attempt, we could pretend to ourselves that, yes, we were a regular couple. These things happen to couples, and they keep caring for each other because each other is who they've got.

This is one of the dreams: myself, asleep, then waking up in the night and Willa is standing over me, long blonde hair like moss about her face, like algae, kelp, *limu*, floating strands of something whose home is the sea, standing on something block-like and concrete thick that should be a leg but it's not. And she's calling to me, *Susan Catherine*, who is Scat, using my birth name in my dream even though nobody but Grandma called me that in those days, to get out of my bed. Standing there! And I'm watching myself scream like there's no tomorrow. Then I'm really screaming and I shoot up and race to where my father is sleeping, scramble onto the small strip of couch that is not already filled by him, plastering my skinny shape against his back. I know he'll let me stay here. He knows what's making me scream.

Another dream is more complex, one I can't tell Grandma about because that's where the symbols come in. Everything, it seems, has some hidden message that Grandma ferrets out, symbols she calls these. How many Other Grandmothers make dreams out to be some kind of truth? Was this what drew alvin-Travis to me in the first place,

Mr. would-rather-have-been a shrink, to have such a grandma? And what is it about me that attracts these would be Freuds into my life?

She tells your dreams back to you like the tattooed lady I once saw at the Kailua Carnival who beckoned me over: *Tattooed Lady*! her red and yellow E.K. Fernandez canopy announced, odors of buttered popcorn, teriyaki meat sticks, deep fried sugary malasadas and carnival grease, all mingling with the stink of horse manure steaming up into the sultry Kona wind from the pasture behind. Hawaiian gypsy she called herself: *Kahuna Fortune Teller — Dreams analyzed, Futures foretold*. She said someone in my family would be famous someday and she could tell me about it for a few measly bucks. Father shook his head, scowled, motioned me on. Which was the part that bothered him? I've wondered, the fortune, or that she was part Hawaiian claiming to be *kahuna* at a dollar-a-prediction, travesty of the blood he had himself denied.

"Was there maybe a butterfly in your dream, the one about Wilhelmina standing in your room?" Grandma asks, "Because that's a symbol for freedom. You want your family free from this nasty business got a hold (she pronounced it *holt*, got a *holt*) of us all."

The dream I can't tell her about has Robbie in it and Robbie's friend Paul, the one the neighborhood junior high school girls proclaim to be *bitchen*, *boss* and cute. In this dream Robbie and Paul grab me and force me out back under the old avocado tree where it's dark and secret, where even the grass won't grow, smell of the ancient leaves the smell of a troubled earth, grit and dank. They pull down my pants, stick a pin into the fleshy part of my *ōkole* like I'm a living breathing *voodoo* doll and suddenly I can't walk, can't move, can't even breathe and Paul does something to me with his hand so that I wake up heart thumping and I'm crying, and there's this shaky feeling in the middle of me and between my legs is burning and wet.

I think about the tattooed lady, tattoos in all of those places that somebody would've had to touch, stick the tattoo needle in, press down her skin while the needle carves its meandering and bloodied trail. Nobody touches me anymore. Not Father who's rarely here, and Grandma says she needs her *bubble of space* around her. "We're more of what you call reserved in Newwwwengland," she says, "not the way you all just throw yourselves at each other in these islands."

She's taken to calling Hawai'i *these islands*. Even Fatboy's quit coming over, for now anyway. I saw him going in and out of Mrs. Akana's house up the street. She's *divorced*, a word still whispered, and she's got no children, only a dog. Looks like Fatboy will have to invent a new routine. I doubt Pilikia (that's *trouble* in Hawaiian), Mrs. Akana's German Shepherd, will put up with Fatboy jouncing Mrs. Akana about on his lap. Pilikia barks at anything that moves, even his own shadow.

A couple months later Jaycee comes home for good. Willa has to stay in *Rehab* (this is what it was but damned if I recall what they called it back then, Rehabilitation?) just a few more weeks then she's coming home too, Jaycee tells us. Grandma says there's not much point to it, the cost, the toll it will take, this Rehabilitation. "Wilhelmina just doesn't have the gumption," Grandma says. "She's got to will herself better, make herself *want* a new leg. Got to fix her up with a prosthesis, that's what, a new lease on life."

"Oh good grief!" Jaycee snaps, rubbing her forehead, a white-hot afternoon, perspiration beading there like little pearls. "I can't much see Willa hobbling about on those fake things anyway. She'd have to use crutches, swing herself about. She'd look like, I don't know, some gimp."

"Well," Grandma points out, "she's got no leg, does she? That's the reality of the situation. You expect her to look like a ballerina?"

"She'll look like the Dirty Monkey Man," Robbie offers and Grandma gives him her icy look.

"That's a heck of a thing to say to your mother, just home from Rehabilitation and little sister's not with her. And anyway, Jaycee, they don't stay on the crutches, the ones that have the prosthetic leg, because I've seen them using a cane and walking almost normal too. Mrs. Tibbets down at the Shop and Save back home had to get her one of those legs, from an automobile accident. She used a cane, last I seen. I'll bet over time they don't even need that."

Jaycee shakes her head, sighs. "I don't know. Canes are for old people, not Willa, not that poor little girl. Can't you see? Can't you bloody-well see? Everything's changed! I don't know these new rules, do you? Does anyone? Is it we're supposed to write the damn rules as we go along? Dr. Spock doesn't have a chapter on this, you know, what to do when your beautiful child loses her leg in the mouth of a shark!"

She strides into her bedroom, and I follow her, hoping for...what? Some kind of touch, acknowledgment? *Yes, you are my daughter too!* Pats my head absently, then a little harder—it's a knock knock joke, *knock knock, who's there, I'm here, my mother, I'm here*!—staring at herself in the shell lined mirror Father gave her over her mahogany dresser. Father's dresser is also mahogany but smaller, more plain, the stepchild of Jaycee's. "You think this has taken a toll on me, Scat?" she asks, stretching down her eyelids, frowning. "You think I look older? Well it has taken its toll, I'll tell you. Pretty little Willa, what now? She could've been a model, a movie star, the next Marilyn Monroe. What now, I ask, what now!"

I reach out my hand tentatively against hers, my fingers drumming like rain against the back of her palm. "It's just her leg that's gone," I whisper.

Jaycee frowns. "That tickles, Scat." Yanks back her hand then lets it settle down again on the top of my head. I feel a warmth there, a heat, something like love. I stand very still, will her hand to stay on me, never lifting off.

"*Just* her leg? Well yes, and that's a quarter or so of her body isn't it? That's like telling me your baby sister is three-fourths here!" Jaycee sighs, "Poor Scat, what a foolish thing to say, but you missed me, didn't you." She cups my chin with her other hand, pulls my face up until my dull little brown eyes meet her calculating green ones. "You must be brave, my brave big beaver, set a good example for our littlest beaver, you hear? You'll have to take over for me, Scat, when your sister comes home. Fix the meals, clean up some, you know I can't do it anymore. The nurses there do all the things I'll have to do when Willa comes home, lift her into the bath, bathe her, dress her, even feed her sometimes. Can't say why she won't at least feed herself, Scat. She'll use her hands but not her spoon or fork, like she's a baby."

My mother squeezes my chin hard. "It's like she's being born all over again! An infant for heaven's sake, starting over, only she doesn't have her leg so it can't ever be the same. Not all of her here, it can't be the same." Jaycee releases my chin, sighs. "You know, I wasn't much good with you children when you were infants, it's not my favorite stage. Larval humans, something's still unfinished in the overall design, has to ripen a bit more maybe. I found it all rather pointless."

I swallow hard, nod like I understand, which of course I don't. But I want her to keep talking to me; I need this, my mother's words coming at me like I'm a real person, not just *Scat*, my mother pouring out her heart to me, my mother's other hand still on my head, scalp shuddering under her touch, her fingers slipping lightly through my bangs like these are *something*. Like I am someone.

Jaycee lifts her hand, squeezes my cheek then fiddles with the collection of various sized containers on her dresser, implements of beauty she calls these, creams to soothe her skin, powder to smooth her skin, pancake makeup to color it, more caky colors for her cheeks, eyelids, the tubes of scarlet lipstick for her lips. Stares at her face in the mirror like she's speaking to *her*, this face.

"Willa's doctor said it's probably a sort of prolonged shock," Jaycee says. "She came out of the coma medically speaking, he told your father and me, but she's just not all together with us. He's examined her physically and besides not having her leg anymore there's nothing wrong with her. She lost a lot of blood, it's a miracle she even lived. You remember Billy Weaver? Same thing, only he didn't live. What a good looking boy he was, would've made some lucky girl a fine husband. They pumped a lot more back into her, a whole other being's worth of blood, imagine that! Her heart's fine, brain wasn't deprived of oxygen, well they don't think so anyway, but she *was* in a coma, so what does that mean? What are they not telling us? The lifeguards brought oxygen to her on the beach, remember? Did she *die*, do you think? Stop breathing for a while, little Willa shut down and nobody tells us? There would have been terrible pain, beyond what any of us can imagine, the doctor said—though has this doctor ever had a baby, ever tried to push one of those out a birth canal the size of a shave ice cone? Sorry Scat, you just have no idea what you're in for in this life, being a woman; when God made us bleed every month he was sending a not so subtle message. Willa's doctor seems to think she's locked up inside with the memory of this pain and that her not expressing it is the source of her not talking maybe, all closed up and no language for it. The doctor thinks a psychiatrist should evaluate Willa but your father won't hear of it. What do you think it takes to get that man to put his foot down finally at something? The threat of one of us not appearing normal, you see; looks bad for him, that's what. It's about him, always about him," Jaycee says bitterly, rubbing her eyes.

I nod to agree with her, though I'm not sure what I'm agreeing with. I love my father. Even at this age I sensed his defeat, wanted to crawl into it sometimes, bury myself there so he wouldn't feel so alone. I just wish he were around more, is all. How many meetings and seminars and training sessions does a *businessman* need to go to? "Are we so awful you have to leave us all the time!" Jaycee once shrieked at him, one of her more needy, needling moods. "Not *we*," Father answered quietly. I felt relief, for that moment anyway, thinking it wasn't me somehow disappointing him, Kit-cat Scat the reason for his frequent absences.

"Help me out of this dress, Scat, unbutton me, will you? Then you and your brother run along outside and play. I've got to sleep awhile. I feel like I haven't slept for months, not since That Day."

It wasn't some nurse shark that got Willa's leg. "Highly unlikely behavior," a zoologist from the University of Hawai'i told us, "even in a nurse shark's most agitated state to sever a child's leg." This zoologist worked with Dr. Tester, he assured us, famous shark researcher. *Knows his sharks*, said Father. He determined if it had been a great white Fatboy and Jaycee would have seen it from the boat and most likely we would have too, Robbie and me, gape of a blood-red jaw, teeth like metal shards coming at Willa from behind. (Of course this happened well before Spielberg and *Jaws*, but we needed our images to conceive of this thing.) Like you see in photographs. Like I see in my dreams. "Mostly it's tiger sharks that attack people in Hawai'i," the zoologist said. "It was a fifteen footer that killed Billy Weaver just a couple years before. And the raggedness of the bite, the slant of the serrated teeth marks might be indicative of a tiger too," he said.

The zoologist asked to speak with everyone who witnessed the *event,* and Fatboy was summoned back into our home. In retrospect, he called it, Fatboy wondered if maybe he really *did* see a fin circling where Willa was, the thrash of water the way some sharks do when they're swimming fast toward their prey, the bite, shake of their heads as their teeth tear through the flesh, snake it around, try to yank her under, tube and all.

Grandma whispered to Jaycee, but we all could hear: "Probably Wilhelmina looked like a turtle or a fish of some sort, movement of her legs flying through the water in that tube, being dragged by that boat. What a stupid idea, so deep out there and so late in the afternoon. Why didn't you have the God-given sense to come in?" The zoologist had told us that sunrise and sunset are shark feeding times.

The zoologist said the shark that bit off Willa's leg *could* have been a tiger, which is what most assume, but he personally thought it was more likely an oceanic whitetip. "They don't usually come near to shore, except in Hawai'i when there's a pod of shortfin pilot whales in the vicinity. For some reason they like to swim with these whales," he said, "and these whales frequent Hawaiian waters at certain times of the year." (There's an ancient Hawaiian chant, Father told us...*the great shark Niuhi with fiery eyes that flash in the deep sea. Oh! Alas! When the wiliwili tree blooms, The shark bites....*) "They can be a pretty fierce shark," the zoologist said. "Similar bite to a tiger, jagged teeth designed for tearing chunks out of their prey. They're bold, aggressive, and their diet is broad. Swim straight toward their prey. Plus," he said, "even though it got the taste of the child's blood it wouldn't necessarily stick around the area. If the pod of whales moved on, so would the oceanic whitetip. Which could be the reason for not finding the shark hanging around after the attack." Did we happen to notice any whales about? he asked us. *Requiem sharks*, tigers and oceanic whitetips are from a family of sharks named after the Catholic mass for the dead.

So what this means, I thought to myself, What this means is the shark that got Willa's leg is still out there somewhere. And maybe he's hungry *now* for more Beever blood.

The ocean and me, we develop this weird kind of a relationship, and probably it's that way with the rest of the family too, even Robbie, because we don't go swimming much anymore. And when I do go swimming, I feel like I've got to watch out all the time, look back over my shoulder, only mostly I'd have to look under the water for that long grey shadow, which means sticking my face in it and opening my eyes; no one saw the fin when it attacked Willa. You're supposed to see a fin circling around, aren't you? *Bump and bite attacks,* the zoologist called the attacks that can leave a person with only one leg or a leg so messed up it will take one hundred staples to put it back together. I see this kind of leg in my dreams sometimes and I'm the one who's wearing it. Some species you'll see circling first, the zoologist said, but not the oceanic whitetip. They just zero in on their prey and *Oh! Alas!* the bump is an open jaw.

I stick my face in the water a lot, open my eyes no matter how much the salt burns. And this is hard since none of us goes out beyond the breakers anymore, Father wouldn't let us even if we wanted to. I open my eyes under water and everything is a kind of bleary blue like swimming in a bottle of mouthwash, then suddenly along comes a whitecap and I'm thrown backwards into the surf, which means I've lost my watch for the minutes it takes to pick myself up, feet burrowing into the sagging sand for a grip, mouth open, that silent scream, choking up sea water. Would that be the moment a shark could attack me?

Father says not to worry, that probably no shark big enough to eat any part of me is going to swim in three feet of water. But this is what I think: that even the little ones could come along, baby sharks with their razor sharp baby shark teeth, tear a chunk out of me and maybe I'll just lie down there in that ocean and bleed to death, maybe I don't have as much blood as Willa, enough to keep her alive until they could pump more into her.

****

Willa comes home this afternoon. Robbie and I are waiting behind the louvered windows in the living room, peering out between the wooden slats at the street where the ambulance from Rehabilitation will appear. This time there won't be lights flashing and sirens wailing. "It's just a more comfortable ride," Father assures us. "She doesn't need it."

Jaycee's dusting the furniture, which is something she never does, not since the last time the cows escaped from the Castle ranch near the beach, and one of them got in our yard outside Jaycee and Father's bedroom window so that when she opened the louvers after her nap she was staring right into the big, ornery eyes of a cow. That's how she put it, ornery eyes of a cow. Grandma said Jaycee never liked cows; "Scairt of them," she said, "can't fathom why." That day Jaycee cleaned and cleaned and cleaned like the poor old cow had invited herself into our house and sat down on the sofa, front hooves up on the coffee table, settled in. *What's for dinner, Mom? Chipped you on toast!* Jaycee even scrubbed the slipcovers, then made me iron them. "A girl's got to know how to do these kinds of things," she said. "Who else you think is going to do it, unless you marry a man rich enough to let you hire a laundry woman? That's not your father, I'll tell you."

I pressed the steam smelling iron against the scratchy slipcover, the day white and lazy, and I thought about that cow who got to plod all over our neighborhood, easy as you please, visit everybody's windows before someone had the I-don't-know-what-it-takes, said Father, to call the police.

I'm hoping the Connelys across the street don't see Willa's ambulance, because I don't want Kathy over here prying into what Willa looks like without her leg attached. She'll tell everybody, and then they'll tease *me*, because it would be way too mean to tease Willa. Nobody teases Willa, not to her face. And anyway it's my story. None of *them* ever got to go in an ambulance, although Robbie, who broke his arm falling off the jungle-gym when he was seven, managing to land on top of a centipede and getting bit several times before it died of being squashed (what are the odds of that!) says it's no big *D*.

But we don't get to see Willa's leg, or rather where her leg used to be, not for a long time. She's in Jaycee and Father's room; Father's moved out onto the couch in our TV room. They shoved the big bed against the wall so you can only climb into it on one side, Jaycee's side, and they put one of those hospital beds in there for Willa, the kind that goes up and down. You can arch the back if you're lying flat, or pop your legs up, though Willa's just got the one leg for that particular ride.

We stand outside the closed door sometimes, Robbie and me, just listening. You can't hear much, Jaycee talking at Willa and Willa saying nothing in return. She was never quiet before; matter of fact her talking used to about drive us *lōlō* sometimes. Chatty Cathy, Father called her, after the doll. You pull that doll's chain and she says the things someone thinks toddlers are supposed to say: *I'm hungry, I'm wet, I love you Mommy.* "Willa's got things to say," Jaycee used to tell us, "talkative as talkative." But not anymore. "Quiet as a flea," Grandma says.

Jaycee slips in and out of the room with a powder blue plastic bucket that has white daisies painted on it, like what you might play in the sand with. From that Rehabilitation place, Grandma told us. Grandma's doing the telling of things mostly these days since Willa's come home, because Jaycee is *consumed,* is how Father puts it, and doesn't have much to say to us. Grandma said the pail is Willa's Survival Kit, the stuff Jaycee uses to take care of Willa's *stump:* Phisohex for washing it, Phisoderm for bacteria control, Hydrocortisone to lubricate and kill itches, and some terrible smelly salve, Grandma says, with lanolin and mutton tallow in it, to soothe it. Robbie and I try to imagine what a stump looks like and how you could soothe it. The Monkey Man's are always covered. He lost his legs in a World War. "He was a very brave man," Father said. "It's wrong to call him the Dirty Monkey Man, it's dirty Commies you have to watch out for," Father said.

I think about the Monkey Man's monkey, always got that *no ka mea* baseball cap held out for money from the Honolulu taxi customers. How does it come to this? Will Willa need to do that someday? She's OK with dogs and cats, but I don't know about a monkey.

Robbie says that Willa's stump probably looks like the plumeria tree. "The stump," he snorts, "you know, where Father sawed off the big branch that had the rot in it? It's probably all rotten and nasty!" For a moment I hope Willa heard this from the other side of the door, because normally Robbie saying something stupid like that would make Willa wild and she'd shout a fresh retort right back at him. Or she'd squeal for Jaycee who's taking one of her two or three baths she takes every day now; *marathon baths,* Grandma calls them—"She's afraid to touch your poor sister, what's left of her leg, and yet she can't keep her hands off her, so then she takes a bath." And Willa would tell on Robbie, get him in *Big Trouble, young man*! That's the way things worked around here before, anyway. Nothing. Silence. But I bet she heard all right.

Robbie and I go outside to that plumeria tree, and we climb up into its gnarled branches, the red sticky smell of its flowers all around us. "If you touch that milk be sure to go back in and wash your hands," I caution Robbie, like some Other Mother might have. Plumeria milk is poisonous, and even though Robbie is older than me, I'm the Beever supposed to know best, take care of the rest. We climb up far as we can without getting on a branch too small to support our weight. From here I can look out over the thorny lantana hedge that divides our yards, into Fatboy's lānai. Fatboy's on it, sprawled on a lounger sucking down a Primo beer. He's reading *Hunting* magazine, I can see it from here, a deer on its cover, antlers like stakes poking up and a shiny black nose. It's like those magazines that have the half naked ladies on them, glossy and colorful, like *Playboy,* which once Robbie found a copy of shoved under a YMCA locker after swim practice and he brought it home. We studied the pictures in his closet with the light switched on, door shut and booby trapped so that if someone tried to open it Robbie's stuffed giant panda would fall on their head. I wasn't sure how I was supposed to feel, staring at those ladies. I had wondered how *they* felt, their gleaming smiles, thrusting out their bosoms like a second set of shoulders. And now I wonder how Fatboy is feeling, gazing at this deer that some other hunter shot. He's a Trapper by vocation, he said, and hunting is his passion. We can pretend this has something to do with us, these kinds of pictures, but Fatboy won't ever know that real deer because that deer is already gone.

I stare out over him, pretend I don't notice him, pretend I'm looking into the Keamolemole's yard with its giant avocado tree, so big it won't even bear fruit anymore, up into the pearl and aqua sky over the rest of Kailua. There is trouble in the world; I hear it in school, where we practice hiding from bombs by crawling under our desks and placing our heads between our arms; I hear it from Father talking about the Pinks and the Reds, the *Commies*, places like Cuba and Red China and Russia. But what I know is this: Fatboy doesn't come over for cocktails anymore when Father's on the mainland. Robbie's on a branch above me, his knees hooked over it and swinging like a monkey, Grandma would say. And Willa's in that up-and-down bed, but at the same time it's not really her. It's like a picture of her, her blonde hair, blue eyes, that mouth, but no voice coming out, no words, no laughter, no reflection of a remembered past; as if under it all, this image of Willa, my sister really is gone.

Part II

Such is the form which the shark worship takes in Hawai'i. What is the exact nature of the 'aumakua belief? The ancient Hawaiians worshipped three classes of deities, akua, 'aumakua, and 'unihipili. Akua were thought of as spirits only, not born of humans. 'Aumakua were the offspring of god and human, or those human beings who were marked by an abnormal shape which might be assumed at will, such as that of some animal or object.... Both 'aumakua and 'unihipili belong to the class of akua noho or "gods indwelling," that is, of those spirits who enter into and possess human beings, through whom their messages to their devotees are uttered.

Nakuina; *Nanaue The Shark Man & Other Hawaiian Stories*

(Beckwith — *Hawaiian Shark 'Aumakua*)

CHAPTER FIVE

Enter Gracie. The dream she dreams where she is not herself, surfing the wild aquamarine sea off the coast of Hawai'i; she thinks it must be Hawai'i, where else would it be? Light playing on the waves a clean white, sharp as her mother's white china, bone china she calls it—Gracie used to imagine some poor soul sacrificing a femur for her mother's dinner plates, hip bone for her soup bowls. Turquoise wave, froth of foam sucked up in the tube of this monster she is the air it needs, the breath in its tunnel, split second of calm, of peace, the eye of the storm and then the blue-green crash of the water around her, its flung spray, force of this rolling and flipping her board and she's hanging on, and maybe she's even laughing. Because she knows it's a dream. She knows she'll wake up, who drowns in their own dream? And besides, it isn't even her. At that moment between sleep and wake, or *is* she awake? *sudden dark shadow, its sleek silvery curve.*

In Gracie's dreams she's often someone else, someone she doesn't know, a newly invented life born out of her synapses, out of her but not her. Always the face is perfect. Perhaps she is a man, craggy tan of a surfer, blue eyes, sun lines around those eyes. No other marks on this face. Perhaps in these dreams it really is her, her double, triple, not the face she must show the world but the face under it all, and all she needs is to break free of the one she hefts about, the *unreal* one, into her dream and away.

Unreal! the boys used to say, *So ugly she's unreal!* But only on one side. Want to check out her left side? Here, you see, is the cruel joke, the kicker, her killer left-side profile. When she drives cars full of guys pull up, *guy-flies*, drawn like insects to her long wavy hair, a hank of it blowing out the car window, a flag; welcome to the perfect one-half of Gracie McKneely, the left side of her face. And then they see the rest.

Things often happen to Gracie in triples. Take her face. Here is where it begins. Gracie's father drops her head first on a barbecue when she's thirteen months old like she's just another hamburger, seared to a flavorful crisp on one side. Didn't mean to, he is not a violent man; self-violence certainly, violation of one's own flesh, one's blood, one's soul, and for the rest of his life he will be reminded of this: baby Gracie, slithering out of those helpless hands like some worm, some wet sea thing, like she's not even his, could not possibly be a part of him, his chromosomal material, because how could anyone do *this* to their own child? Her mother shrieking, throwing herself to the ground where little Gracie fell after first hitting those red-hot coals, the grill collapsing under the child's sudden downward projectile; the mother on top as if her weight could press this baby back inside her, make her new again, undamaged, a glint in her eyes, unseen, unmarked, *unknown*; still that possibility of something perfect.

For the rest of his life Thomas McKneely will be unable to forgive himself, staring into the mirror at his own unmarked face, the genetic imprint of his daughter's features, can't escape those features however corrupted in these sure lines. Eventually her father grows a beard which her mother hates and he keeps it there — the thing Gracie is allowed to touch when she reaches up to him, her child arms begging and he turns away, just enough so that it is his beard her fingers come up against, his beard her fingers travel in and out again finding nothing on the other side.

Perhaps it really is Gracie her father hates; she's wondered about this sometimes, can't help but think it. Because every time he looks at her he must be reminded of how he can never forgive himself. Of course he's never said any of this to Gracie, maybe he's never even articulated it to himself. She knows words like this, *articulated*, because she is her father's daughter: her father the professor, lover of books and the languages they speak to him in, of theories and how these offer a way to understand things. Though he never could discover one to live his life by after the *incident*, some theory of survival after you've done the worst. If Gracie hungered for the moon her father would find a way to snare it, prepare it, serve it to her on the fancy *bone* china plate her mother would insist on. Graces, she would say, *How can Gracie live up to her name if we don't show her the way it's done?* But he won't look at his daughter. *Eat,* he'd mumble, ever so gently, liquidy blue eyes fixed on some space above her head. Her father's eyes are the sky, she used to think, staring up at them.

There were the skin grafts, flesh dug from the baby-fat thighs, the formless hips to form a new cheek. She had been airlifted to the Shriners Hospital in Boston, a specially equipped burn center for the surgeries, the physical therapy, and she howled through it all, Gracie's mother told her. "You were never what you'd call a peaceful baby," Maizey McKneely advised Gracie, "even before *it* happened. Always something so unsettled about you, Gracie." This on the eve of Gracie's move to Maine—but we'll get to that in a moment.

Then the Bells palsy seven years later, came on in the dead of night it seemed; maybe she's dreaming someone else's dream and she really does wake up in their face? How much rotten luck can one skin bear? Drooped on one side, the yellowish tinge, like some oversized sunflower neglected to fully open. The side already marred, rippled trenches raw as a new penny now hanging worthless as one too, because although a plastic surgeon some day might attempt to spruce up that scarred skin there's not much to be done for the sag. Her doctor assured Gracie's parents that often times this goes away. "We can't be certain of what causes Bells palsy," she said. "Maybe a fever of some sort." (The time Gracie had the flu and her mother sent her to school because she was hosting a fund-raising luncheon for some Democratic legislator and the child might be in the way?). More likely the trauma Gracie's poor face had already endured, damaged nerves collapsing in on themselves in a sort of exhausted surrender. What makes it go away? "It just does," the doctor told her parents, "in most cases."

Gracie is still waiting. Perhaps it will be the third thing that happens to her, the magical three. Wake up and this time she really is no longer her. Stares at her face in the mirror, firm, smooth, nonchalant and expectant, the face anyone else would take for granted, symmetrically even on both sides, skin the color of her neck, her hands, who cares what color as long as it's the same everywhere? And when she turns to look at both sides, as she always does, holding up the hand mirror to reflect off the larger mirror, gazing at the perfect left, the usual left, and then the right... these are the same. Gracie once read somewhere, in one of her father's sociology texts perhaps, or maybe a *Women's* magazine, that the definition of a pretty face is one that is considered regular, unexceptional in every aspect: average sized features, symmetrical alignment, forehead of medium spread, not too high or too low, eyes nicely ovaled, not protruding, just large enough to announce their color, cheekbones visibly present, medium-full lips, a definite chin. Nothing about scarring, slanting, sloping, none of those *s* words describe a pretty face.

****

The ad in the *Free Press*: *Big Room, no deposit, you clean*. One line, cheapest possible, under Rooms for Rent/Rock Harbor, Maine. And under Help Wanted one line again, same phone number: *Clean Boarding House. Free Room/Board, small compensation*. How Gracie chose Maine was a process of elimination. It had to be a place she could get to in one day on the Greyhound Bus. It had to have the ocean. Living inland, locked in by mountains, endless expanse of field, strip malls, asphalt, highways that connect to other highways riding deeper and deeper into the heart of the country, these terrains of grounded earth, made her nervous. And it had to have as much space with as low of a population density inhabiting that space as possible. A lot of people made her nervous too. You're more likely to have a greater percentage of unkind people, teasing people, bullies, tormentors. A face like Gracie's and you consider these things. These requirements eliminated most of the rest of coastal New England, Cape Cod and all of the Atlantic seaboard states; everything else was too far away for her to afford the bus ticket. And anyway, doesn't everyone want to go to Maine?

Rock Harbor, Maine is the kind of harbor town tourism never discovered. A fishing town whose principle business was it once had a tuna factory and now has a maximum security prison, same concrete slabs of buildings they used to cook and chop and can tuna in, added onto to create a mighty concrete and brick fortress. Those swollen, humid summer days the residents swear they can smell the fish. All this she had learned off the Internet. Head five minutes in any direction you are in the quintessential beauty Maine is famous for—emerald Atlantic, purple mountains, spruce trees clinging to craggy cliffs jutting out over the sea.

Gracie's destination is C Street, middle of the middle of the grittiest part of the town, houses old and chipped, set against the weather like rows of ground-down teeth. Here the streets aren't even named, as if naming them might influence some sort of personality; lettered streets, A B C D E F G. Even the mountains behind seem worn, the poor step-children of the grander mountains, Megunticook, Mt. Battie, the hills in nearby Camden where movies are made, where the summer people from Southern New England, New York and New Jersey have their ocean front houses, where tourists are drawn north in hot-weather hordes, go away thinking they've seen Maine. That too she got off the Internet.

There is another Maine, and the Internet doesn't chat about this one much, a poorer Maine of more meaty, needy people—*salt of the earth,* Gracie's mother calls such people and she doesn't mean it as a compliment; more like a sigh, a resignation, a *There-are-kindnesses-to-be-done-in-this-country-and-that's-why-we-are-Democrats.* Downtrodden lives, like where Gracie grew up in upstate New York, where the economy's been bad for so long a whole new standard has been set to gauge it. A *good* year is one with fewer foreclosures on people's homes, fewer factories closed, businesses shipped off to the Philippines or India, fewer people laid off from IBM and Lockheed Martin and more people shopping at Wal-Mart. Gracie was born in Honolulu, Hawai'i, but that was more or less an *accident,* is how her mother puts it. Her father was at the University of Hawai'i on a research grant, his sabbatical, and her mother spent a miserable year being pregnant in the tropics. "*Hāpai* they called it, sounds like you're carrying a hunk of fruit, about to give birth to a giant papaya!" Maizey scoffed. Twelve years later, awkward Gracie, cowering under the shame of her face and the deeper humiliation of her impending thirteenth birthday—a *teenager* wearing this face!—would be sent back to O'ahu to spend her summer, a poignant and revealing month and a half. But we'll get to this part of the story at the appropriate time; suffice it to say Gracie was born in Hawai'i, then left. Two months old and still those perfect cheeks.

The woman who opens the door, this big hunch of a house on C Street, eyes Gracie up and down, classic double take to the right side of her face, glances away out of politeness, her dark eyes drawn back like being tugged by a magnet. "You can't say you don't attract people's *interest*, Gracie," her mother once remarked. "Why, do you know how many women are virtually ignored?" Maizey the optimist. Perhaps *she* was once ignored. After Gracie's father dropped her the shift of power turned in her mother's favor. Talk about having an ace up your sleeve. *It* hovered, its unspoken presence over every argument they had, the father silenced, the mother getting her way.

Out of habit Gracie tugs a shag of her pale brown hair over her right cheek, covering most of the scarring though it doesn't do much for the droop. Worm-colored hair and it's her best feature, falls to the small of her back full and soft, gliding easily over her face like pulling the blanket down. *Jeanie with the light brown hair*, her father used to sing, stroking her hair, easing it further over her face to avoid touching the damage that crouched under it. Though her name is not Jeanie. The droop, the sag of cheek muscle and jaw, no hairdo can fully disguise this.

The woman nods, looks away again, fixing a stern stare somewhere over Gracie's head into the whiteness of sky. Fall, and the air smells like dried leaves, something cooking, an afternoon well spent. "Feels like rain," she announces. Now Gracie's the one who studies her, grey hair steely and needle-straight tugged into a long ponytail. She's somewhere in the middle of her life, gnarled in a slim, muscled sort of way. Skin the color of translucence itself; Gracie can almost see the blue veins underneath, those wide cheekbones. She's dressed in jeans tight as a teenager would wear them, her shirt a thin, gauzy green.

"Arthritis," the woman says. "Hands and knees my own personal weather forecast, that's how I can tell about the rain. You the one called for the room, comes from somewhere in New York? I warned you, it's a bit of a mess. She splits, boogies, walks out on me whatever name you want to call it, gets abducted by aliens, who knows? One day she just disappears, two months rent overdue and I'm supposed to clean up after her? I do my time, a daughter don't you know, mess incarnate. Lives here, doesn't live here, moves in, out, back in again and each time she's a tornado howling through. She's got that kind of energy, suck the life right out of you if you're not careful. When she leaves you always know this is where she's been. No deposit and I provide the cleaning materials. You interested? Gracie McKneely, that's your name? You don't look much older than my daughter."

Gracie nods, lowering her eyes. At the moment she's not so anxious to hear about daughters, guilt from the way she left her own parents, so *willfully*, her mother's word. "Could I see the room?" Gracie asks, her face still half buried in the comforting scent of her hair, herbal, newly washed. Gracie's hair, her *one good thing. Everyone has at least one good thing, praise the Lord!* shouted a radio preacher on the Greyhound headed for Maine, her seatmate an oblivious Christian, Walkman so loud in her ears Gracie too was bombarded with this news.

The woman nods, motions Gracie inside, shutting the door firmly behind. Gracie sets her suitcase beside the door then follows this woman down a long bare hallway, paint the color of a cloud, that cheap off-white you splash over everything, the paint that hides. She has made a study of things that hide. The woman's pronounced hips sway comfortably as she walks; she has that kind of raw aged prettiness, even the back of her head, her neck, *good lines* that refuse to be hidden in extra flesh. Good lines, Gracie's mother used to say, indicate good breeding. Like people are dogs. Dog-face is what the grade school boys called Gracie. Used to play a game with herself asking God or whomever might grant these things whether she could trade faces with somebody. She'd usually pick someone not too attractive, wouldn't want to be greedy after all, someone just pleasant enough to look at where they wouldn't draw attention to themselves, slip easily through life mostly unnoticed the way most people do—marriage, children, a job, the unremarkable life. In return she would be good, the bargain went, stay away from drugs, try to forgive her parents.

"Before I open this door," the woman starts, turning fully around where they've stopped at the end of the hall, last possible door, somewhat isolated from the rest of the big house, enough so that Gracie's wondering if at another time, a more prosperous time, this house was a prouder, grander house and this was where the servant lived, appropriate enough, if she is to clean the place. "Before we step in," the woman continues, hesitating again as if she knows Gracie hasn't been listening, drifted off somewhere away from her—she's staring into her face which Gracie quickly makes disappear again under her hair—"I want to know, are you saved, Gracie McKneely? Have you accepted the Lord Jesus Christ as your savior?"

Gracie frowns, thinking again of her bus companion, those spandexed thighs leaking over to Gracie's side of the seat, the words in her ears in Gracie's ears too. She shrugs, a professor's kid, the moral orders of C.S. Lewis, T.S. Eliot, E.B. White, even Tolkien more familiar in their home than the Bible.

"You should think about it some, Gracie, because you know He's coming back and you'll want to be ready, won't you? He'll be gathering up His believers. You won't have to hide your face from Him. All faces are beautiful in the eyes of *Jesus*."

Gracie looks away, her cheeks flaming. Of course I would hide! she thinks. If Jesus came tomorrow he'd find Gracie with her hair tugged over her face, eyes cast down upon his sandaled (would they be Birkenstocks, yuppie foot wear?) feet.

"Well, I'm not one to preach," the woman sniffs. "Don't think I'm trying to convert you, just something to think about. What I need to know is whether you've come about the house cleaning job as well. I want someone to help me keep this place up. I got a boy outside, you'll see him around though he won't say much. He does the yard. I need someone inside. Too much for me, the arthritis and whatnot."

"Maybe," Gracie tells her. What else can she do? But she doesn't say this; it's best, she has learned, not to sound too desperate.

"OK," the woman says, flashing Gracie a smile that's more about the mouth than in her eyes. "My name is Berry Waters, by the way, I apologize for not introducing myself earlier." Then she opens the door.

The room is large, Gracie can tell that much, but little else as there seems to be only one high window and a thick beige shade tugged down over it. A peculiarly meaty smell (mold?) and there are things all over the floor, this much she can see, no room to even walk—clothes, papers, books, even plates of food. She understands the smell now, as her eyes adjust, fruit flesh, the natural decay of things organic. She sucks in a breath.

"Ayuh!" Berry Waters nods. "You can see why I didn't tackle it myself, what with the arthritis. Like I was saying before, one day she just up and leaves, we get these strange calls, and the reporters— Lord, you might've thought some kind of saint lived here the way the afflicted were showing up, pressing their faces to my front door like it's the wood's going to heal them. She's gone, just like that."

"The afflicted?" Gracie pushes aside the curtain of her hair, peers into the woman's hard eyes, dead-black circles in this dull light. *Fish eyes.*

"Rumor had it she was some sort of healer, nothing deliberate or studied on her part I'll tell you what, and nothing God-given, that one was no Christian. 'Victim soul' they called her, supposedly she could take other peoples pain into her own body. It's something religious, the concept anyways, Catholic most likely, although I've got my doubts she even believes and—trust me here, Gracie—if you were the Lord this is the last person you'd pick to go healing your flock. No Mother Theresa that one. But I seen it myself once, with my own eyes. This man's standing out in the dooryard, he's got that blood condition, touch him and he bleeds. She goes out, is with him maybe five minutes, they're standing about as close as you and me, and when he leaves she comes in and she's the one that's bleeding. You can still see traces of it on the carpet in my front room, couldn't get it all out of there to save our lives. Didn't know what to make of it then and I still don't. Could be some kind of a trick, know what I mean?"

Gracie nods, but more to stall the moment, to take it all in than from any real comprehension. A *healer*? In this trashed room? "I'm not sure what to think about healers," Gracie says.

"Well," Berry sighs, "stranger things have happened I s'pose. Our Lord works in mysterious ways, I'm just not convinced He works in that one, you know. So I can hardly charge a deposit on this room now can I, mess that it is. No money up front. You move in, clean it, and if you help me to keep the rest of this place up I won't take a cent from you period, meals fixed, eat all you want. I can pay you a bit. I'm not exactly rolling in dollars as I offer most of my own services for free. I mean really, if you're going to designate a victim soul, who you going to pick? Not that I'd want to bleed for somebody. I draw the line at blood."

"What is her name?" Gracie asks, gazing about the room. Its dimness like flaccid grey arms has opened up to her, strange scents not so unpleasant really; rot is a form of life, after all. She's had dreams where her right cheek is rotting, little microscopic bugs settling into the fold of it, nibbling away until one day she wakes up and there it is, her real face under all of that, all this time. This room is beckoning her, *live in me*. "Her name?" Gracie repeats, did she even speak it before?

Berry Waters shrugs. "Don't recollect her giving me any real kind of a name, though I know she had one because of them articles about her. Wasn't used much though, can't say I remember it if I knew it. Always paid the rent in cash. They called her Shark Girl, but this was no girl to boot. Story goes when she was a child she was attacked by a shark and it bit off her leg and another grew back. She does walk with this limp, kind of a dipping off to one side like one of her legs is maybe a smidgen shorter. I've studied it a good bit, shoes she wears, boots mostly. She's partial to them long skirts, heavy socks or tights; can't tell whether it's a prosthesis for sure though I'm thinking it's *got* to be, yet it's not the kind of thing you ask someone now do you?"

Gracie flushes. *This* much she would know about.

"Likely it's just a rumor, you know how things get started. It's not like we have killer sharks steaming about the harbor, looking to snack on little girls legs. Why, that water's so black and cold you don't see much of anything alive in it. Even the lobster boats use the other harbors, Rockland and even Camden, when the summer folks yachts make room for them. Rock Harbor is just this place that gets left, like it's got some kind of drain on it been slowly leaking over the years, businesses fold, children grow up and leave, things just move away from here. But not you, Gracie. You've come all the way here from somewhere else. Why did you come here, Gracie? People who move to Maine, often they're trying to escape something. Yuppies come up to get out of the rat race, after they've made their fortunes in it of course. What was it with you, if you don't mind me asking?"

Gracie is silent for a moment. How would she say it, that it was time to leave and this place, Rock Harbor, Maine, was as far from her home as she could afford? It sounds dumb! "Couldn't she have been from somewhere else too?" Gracie asks instead.

Berry Waters laughs. "Well sure. Some of those *Enquirer*-type articles claim she's not even from this planet. But what difference would it make? She was here, wasn't she?"

****

There are certain mornings, how they linger, the way the light falls into a kitchen that was not her mother's kitchen, and some kind of insect chattering outside, and the pearly cooing of mourning doves and the tang of the sea, aquamarine and salty filling the air like the air is liquid, like you could drown in a breath, go down smiling. It's as if this was her life somehow, this dream of a life, though how could it be? Growing up in upstate New York, in an area that if you go in any direction outside of it there is the land upstate is famous for, low roll of mountains, green ridges, open spaces, but where Gracie's family lived looked like anyplace else: malls, home improvement outlets pimpling the landscape almost as common as the boxy houses they cater to, Wal-Mart, video rental places, fast food stops, chain restaurants specializing in three ways to cook a dead cow, highways intersecting, weaving through the valley and the rivers, two of them, Susquehanna and Chenango, dark threads dissecting the land into twos, cutting and choosing sides; constant rumble of the cars, trucks, endlessly consuming America. The parkways are drive-in strip malls; the entertainment buzz just last year, a Hooters coming to the place where a giant concrete bull once stood, monument to another kind of meat. This was Gracie's home.

She couldn't bear to begin cleaning last night and lay there instead on the double bed, surrounded by someone else's living, remnants of another's life (she did get rid of the plates of old food, half consumed sodas—the former tenant was partial to Diet Pepsi whereas Gracie prefers Coke). In the soft indention of the mattress Gracie imagined *her* form and traced its edges before moving into it, filling it, closing her eyes.

In the morning Gracie's mother calls and Berry Waters raps firmly on her door, leading her straight into the lion's mouth.

She picks up the receiver, breathes into it.

"Gracie? That you? Well honestly dear, I thought you would've at least called us when you got there, can't tell you the trouble I went through to find this number, just try check Information for Rock Harbor Boarding Houses and they give you every bed and breakfast, every Motel 6, I'm telling you, and do you know what the place you are staying at is listed under, what the official name is?"

Gracie shakes her head, though her mother can't see her. But even if she could, would she? Gracie's mother is the kind of talker so consumed with her own words she doesn't speak in sentences — more like phrases and clauses spliced together with conjunctive adverbs, commas, whatever will allow her the quickest gulp of a breath in between, a sort of alcoholism of the voice-box. And she goes on.

"You didn't tell me its name, Gracie, *America's Haunted Housewives*! Now I ask you, what kind of a boarding house is this that calls itself that? Isn't that about the oddest name you ever heard for a place to rent a room in?"

Gracie blinks and stares around the room the phone is in, your basic old house den, walnut stained and paneled walls, bookcases, brick fireplace with its aging, pinkish bricks, worn beige furniture, heavy milk colored drapes still drawn against the morning. A little dark, but the room is livable, not-so-fresh mums on the mahogany end table, its surface mostly covered in a yellowing lace doily, mum leaves browning and crinkling at their edges, petals a toned-down faded gold complementing the neutral-colored everything else.

"Is it women living there? Housewives? Without their own house or a husband, well so how can you call them housewives then?"

Gracie sighs. "I don't know who lives here. I didn't really think about the name, just that it was a boarding house."

"Well, really you can't possibly consider staying on, Gracie, you're a young woman, at a boarding house? I didn't even know they had those anymore, just your motels, your hotels, inns and bed and breakfasts and such, those sorts of places; luckily this was under accommodations in their directory or they probably would never have found the number for me. A boarding house? Gracie, what can you be thinking? For housewives! If you wanted to go to Maine, well, lots of people do, you just vacation there, stay in a motel, or camp maybe and then you come home. I don't understand this notion of yours, to leave home for the sake of leaving home, and so you go up to Maine to a boarding house? Really, what is the point?"

She pictures her mother, standing in her kitchen without a thing out of place, the utensils carefully polished, gleaming from their scrubbed carousel holder, floor a whistling white, white as the cleaning powder she uses to clean it, even the phone receiver pressed against her ear would have already been dusted before she used it. Everyone's life readjusted, recreated to the remaking of Gracie's face. Her father, professor of sociology at the local university who once did one big thing, one noted contribution to his field. Some theory of numbers, groups forever evolving their behavior in the fashion their greater numbers suggest, something obvious sounding like that, though apparently it wasn't to whoever evaluates these things, heralding it as a discovery. Called it Proof of Infinity, a concept taken from math. His theory is outdated now, almost was from the day it was published, but he's still famous for it, for having written it, put his name on it; for having studied something, figured something out. Journal articles, a blurb about him in *Time Magazine*, a book, *Proof of Infinity*, his contribution, twenty-something years ago. And then Gracie's face. And her mother who was a fund raiser *for the good*, she called it, charities that served the needs of children and animals and the Democrats; and then Gracie's face. Her mother cleans their little house now, their three bedroom raised ranch, every day the same routine, preventative cleaning, you never let the dirt, the sloppiness, the detritus of life take hold. And she bosses him around, that look in her eyes, she knows what he's done. It wasn't his fault, she's told him over and over again, an accident, a tragic accident; and yet, he *did* do it, didn't he? This look says it all.

"They offered me a housekeeping position," Gracie tells her mother. There was no such title but suddenly it's sounding like a done deal, a title she should create for herself. Housekeeper for a boarding house on the coast of Maine. How else does she leave home? Twenty-one years old, no job, no degree, no ambition, no plans, no drive, no talents, no future, as her parents would say—still, isn't she too intelligent for such an *unaccomplished* life? Though not to Gracie's face. They wouldn't say this *to* her, but it would be understood nevertheless; the walls of their house would speak it, the ceiling over her as she slept in the little beige bedroom, frowning down: Gracie McKneely, damaged goods. It was time to leave.

"Is it out of spite then, you're doing this? You have a perfectly good home, your own room, a mother to cook for you, we even offered to pay your entire way through college if you'd go through the state system and so you move to Maine to become a housekeeper?"

"It's just until I figure things out. I don't know what I want and I'm too old to be living off of you." (Gracie does know what she wants, though she can't tell her mother this, and it's an impossible wish anyway, a child's fantasy—a way into somebody else's life, someone else's face.) "I have to go now. I'll call, say hi to Dad."

They are cordial at least, the three McKneelys, polite, things mostly hidden that must remain this way to exist with each other, the blame, the guilt, the longing to be somewhere else, someone else, held civilly down below a surface that none of them will pry into, none of them will do anything but skim over the top, like some impenetrable sheen of ice, gleaming a clear dead cold. Gracie's cheek the only visible blade mark on it.

The living room has a grandfather clock that Berry Waters calls a grandmother clock because it belonged to her grandmother, she said, so why should these be grandfather clocks? Her grandmother got only an eighth grade education, Berry said, but she had a healing intuition. She became a midwife and never lost a mother or baby, including her own daughter, Berry's mother, delivered with only the help of a teenaged cousin, after her husband's lobster boat sank. Her husband, who would've been Berry's grandfather, went down with it. Grandmother clock. It chimes five minutes past the hour, five minutes late, its deep and certain throaty bongs.

The house faces Rock Harbor's frigid dark harbor, though they cannot see it, only catch a fishy whiff of it now and then like when the door blows open and Roma parades in. Gracie knows this has to be Roma because Berry Waters said her daughter, whose name is Roma, lives here when she feels like it, leaves again when they fight. "It's become pretty run-of-the-mill," Berry confessed. "Last I saw her the girl had pink hair. Each time that child moves out she dyes her hair a different color, gets another tattoo or a piercing and she thinks that's what will drive me crazy. Hah!" Berry snorted. "She's thin as a stick, shakes off food like some do men, aims to become food-free that one, like food is a kind of drug she's got to wean herself off of."

"I'm back!" Roma announces to no one in particular, flouncing into the living room. Berry is somewhere else and Gracie's caught, dust rag in hand, staring skittishly into dark green eyes, almost black but for a strange yellow tinge, the knobs of her cheekbones under them, her own steady gaze snapping up the distorted right side of Gracie's face. "Uh huh," she says, "so who the hell are you? And what for chrissake happened to your cheek? Got a mouthful of chew stuck in there?" She grins, a ridge of bone-white teeth. "Not to be insulting or anything, but who are you?"

Gracie dips her head down, letting her hair fall over her face. It's the rag she's holding out in front of her now like some kind of an offering, a justification for being here. "I'm dusting," she says lamely.

"No! Big news, that." She smiles again, flash of a cheek dimple. "Let me guess, my mother hired you as cleanup girl number three hundred and thirty-three, huh?"

"Huh?" Gracie echoes, face burning.

"Well, she can't keep them, go figure, like who wants to live in a house full of brain dead, grotesque women? I call them half-lings as in they live half-lives. Broken females, my mother collects them like figurines. Little statues of the saints and Mary and whatall, fetishes you might call them, tries to piece them back together. A regular Queen of Hearts, Berry Waters. You one of the unglued?" She peers at Gracie's face again, scrutinizing her cheek.

Gracie lowers her head further, faking imminent engagement with the scarred wood floor.

"You a Christian? Not that it matters. Berry Waters will try to convert you no matter what you think you are. She's one of those generic brands, hippies for Christ, claims she believes in God and Jesus and that she's been saved, yet if you look around here—I mean it now, just take a look in those shelves you've been swiping that thing at!—she's got Catholic shit and a Buddha and some new agey hemp thing. Icons. My mother likes to keep her bases covered."

Gracie lets her eyes follow Roma's jabbing finger toward the shelves, little plastic statues of saints, she's guessing, one with flowers and animals, another with miniature plastic children gathered about the bottom of his robe where feet should be, Mary, her beatific smile, a chubby Buddha, something (Hindu?) with multiple arms. What should she say here?

Roma is staring at her face again. Steps closer, tugging Gracie's hair aside and Gracie flinches, waiting for the sting of some remark. This close Roma smells like peppermint and her hair, not pink, more of a bright and billowy orange, explodes off her head in sheared angles the way a child might color the sun. Her nose is pierced, a tin colored stud stuck through one side, and both eyebrows have hoops in them the size and color of staples. When she opens her mouth Gracie can see the silver flash of a tongue ring.

"I've got them on my nipples too," Roma announces like she knows what Gracie's thinking, "and my clit. Want to look?"

Gracie shakes her head, little spots flaming like match heads on her cheeks.

"I've seen worse," Roma shrugs, stepping back. "You could get your face tattooed, you know. People will think you did the whole thing on purpose, like maybe you went to a tattoo apprentice and they messed it up. Want to see my latest?" She half unzips a pair of baggy hip-hop pants, juts out the poke of one hipbone. Berry has a point, this girl is very skinny. She has nothing that could even be called a belly, just her belly button dipping into the cave between those sharpened hip bones.

"A canary?" Gracie asks thinly. It's a dull greenish-yellow, more bruise than feathered.

"Yeah, as in born to fly free but, guess what." She steps closer again and tugs a pack of cigarettes out of her shirt pocket, flips one out, holding the pack in Gracie's face. "You know they used canaries in the mines? If it flies out means the air is OK, but if it doesn't.... Smoke?"

Gracie shakes her head. There is something both alarming and strangely appealing about this Roma, and Gracie feels helpless, diminished in front of her, despite being the taller of the two.

"Guess why she named me Roma?" Pops a cigarette between her

lips, quick strike of a match, sucking the stuff in, blowing it out in an arch above both their heads.

Gracie shrugs, takes a step back. She's not used to standing so close to people. Closeness makes her uncomfortable, makes her sweat, bow her head even more. People don't generally want to be close to her. Why would they? Like moths to light, bees to flower, it's beauty draws people in.

"You know Roma means gypsies, right?"

"Your father was a gypsy?"

She snorts. "My *father*?" Exhales another trail of smoke and angling delicately around Gracie, throws that knife-thin body down on the sofa. Gracie notices the whoosh of dust as she bounces and wonders just how long it's been since they had somebody here to clean. Roma gestures impatiently for Gracie to sit down too, and she perches on a stuffed chair, not too close.

Inhales the cigarette, exhales. "I feel like talking," Roma announces. "Tad of the old meth, don't you know—just a taste, that stuff'll kill you. You do any happy herbs or chemicals?"

Gracie shakes her head.

"That'll change, girlie, you're in Maine now and it ain't summer when there's actually something of a life around here." She laughs, sucks off the cigarette, says, "So you want to know about *Daddy*? Disappearo, finito, run away, outasite; a lot of that goes on around here, you'll see, deadbeat is like a profession in these parts, you'd think they'd be offering benefits, a retirement package. *Daddy* was a second rate musician, a wannabearockstar, no gypsy blood there. Rumored to be a blond at that. Whoever heard of a gypsy looks more like some beached California surfer. He got the rock all right, played gui-tar in a rock and roll band, just couldn't quite make it to star. Stars, now that takes something special. You know anything about stars?"

Gracie shakes her head again.

"Let's see, you don't do drugs, no stars and you don't say much. You know anything about *anything*, Miz Cleaning Person?"

Gracie shrugs, feeling helpless in the whirl and meanness of this girl, yet there's something almost likable here too, that thin-person kind of crazy energy, always on the verge of some kind of meltdown; a way of claiming the world as her own, each little piece she stomps on. Gracie admires that, though she can barely imagine it. It's like being in school again when the popular girls, the cheerleaders, preppies, their perfect faces, stoop to talk to you, *slumming* it was called.

"Your new boss Berry Waters was once-upon-a-time a rock and roll groupie." Roma exhales a swirl of grey smoke. "Now if it were me I'd question working for someone like that, a groupie I mean, that's *so* retro. This before she discovered she could be *Jesus'* honey yet even she couldn't grope the stars, you dig? Midlevel bands, those are the ones she got to, ones who do the bars, parties, shit like that." Roma blinks. "It's like fucking mediocrity," she states flatly. "He gave her her name, *Strawberry*, I mean gag me! Her real name is Monica, goes by Berry now. And he gave her me, big whoop, what a fucking surprise."

Gracie makes a tenuous pass with the dust rag over the aging ivory keys of a grand piano, the one piece of furniture she's close enough to reach from where she sits, wondering which one of them plays. Steals a glance at Roma. In Gracie's house, a *professor's home* as her mother insisted on calling it, Gracie was discouraged from using this more *expressive* language. *Coarse*, her mother said, *salt of the earth words. Fuck, fucking, fucked*, she whispers in her head, trying it out. Polite language, her parents house, the kind that deliberately conceals what you'd really like to say, thin veneer of pleasant adjectives, the more delicate, sideswiping verbs (*penetrate, penetrating, penetrated?*), carefully selected nouns. Roma is short and sharp, everything about her child-sized and chiseled china-thin like a worn cup, though she's about Gracie's age, maybe even younger. Gracie had always pictured piano players as long fingered, tall and significant.

"Give up? Gypsies don't do the memory thing. They don't like to talk about the past. If you have no past then how can you die? They don't believe in death. Gypsies believe a person is just *gone*. She named me Roma because she wanted me to *roam*, go places, never die you dig? Like a gypsy, though I doubt the name *Roma* means that, I think it's *Rom*. She wanted me to be at home in the world and so she names me after a nation of outsiders, part myth part real. That's Berry logic for you. I disappointed her though. Because here I am."

At dinner Gracie meets the rest of the household, the other boarders and Anthony, whom Berry introduces as the Yard Boy. She's OK with the women, four of them, oldish, middle aged, near middle age and one maybe just a few years older than herself. They're mostly nondescript, though the middle-ager is pretty enough in that all-things-symmetrical way for another quick and envious look. Names she can't yet start to remember. When she shakes Anthony's hand, a tall, gawky kid looks barely old enough to be out of high school, those squared big fingers with dirt under the nails, she doesn't look at his face keeping her hair drawn over her own. In Gracie's experience it's the boys who make the cruelest remarks. But Anthony doesn't say a word, not even hello, and the pressure of his handshake is so minimal it's almost like he's not there at all.

They sit together in the dining room, a room that once must have been grand in that Victorian sort of way, with its lavender and peach colored wall paper, faded now, the flower print almost rubbed out. The table is a huge wooden one, heavy and dark, the feel of a slab of marble like a giant tombstone or a door to a vault. Berry has positioned woven straw table mats at each place, set with rolled turquoise colored paper napkins and inside these stainless steel implements—one fork, one butter knife, one cutting knife and a spoon, nothing matching. What would Gracie's mother say! A dinner party, she'd call this, anything over the three of them was a party to her and rarer the older Gracie became, requiring her best china, the real silverware and of course everything matched. As if to make up for the two sides of her daughter's face that do not, perhaps, everything in Gracie's mother's house has its perfect double, quadruple, however many of itself it needs to be complete: a set of eight beveled cranberry glass wine goblets, twelve silver napkin rings, place settings; twelve each of the everyday china; two ceramic duck candlesticks for the everyday meals, otherwise the candelabra with its circular sterling spaces for six; four towel sets of the two colors in the bathroom, light tan and deep beige—only Maizey McKneely would be particular about just which shades of a color that mimics dirt or sand, and so forth. Her mother's house, and Gracie's father, the has-been intellectual with his messy books and papers—how can any of *these* have their match?—

self-imprisoned in his walkout basement den.

"Let's hold hands for the blessing," Berry says. "Bless this food, dear Lord, and us to thy service, amen. I do the one meal," Berry announces to Gracie, almost in the same breath. "Dinner, and if you're not here for it at 6:00 sharp there's Old Mickey D's across the way. I'm not a restaurant, but I like the feel of one decent sit-down meal, not enough of them these days what with people all over and so forth, more inclined to slap together a sandwich, plop down in front of the tube. I don't approve of that. I think it's the undoing of this country, civilization as we know it, but there's an issue for another time. I supply food you can partake in for breakfast and lunch, basic cereals and bagels, bread, lunch meat, fruit, don't like these, you buy your own. Though if you need the refrigerator you've got to be prepared to share. An issue with that woman who lived in your room, Gracie. She had some kind of special diet, vegetarian no doubt she was skinny and snooty enough, and she didn't like the others getting into her food so she brought it to her room. In my opinion most vegetarians walk around like they've got a pole stuck up their you-know-what!" — looks significantly at Roma — "That's what you're having to clean up, Gracie, a self-centered vegetarian's mess. How's it going, by the way, the toxic spill cleanup in the site down the hall?" She snickers, and a couple of the others do, too.

"OK," Gracie mumbles, though other than dumping the plates of rotten food, mold covered half filled glasses of something once juicy, crusty forks, spoons, clutching her stomach as if will alone could keep her from getting sick, she's barely touched the room. Something about it makes Gracie not want to move *her* things, change them, replace them with her own. Something about it still claims *her* as resident and Gracie as her guest. Besides, Gracie didn't bring much. Travel on Greyhound is not conducive to humping along the rest of your life too, and Berry kept her busy enough with the general household chores, working out some kind of routine that will move her through the days, get her done in enough time to slip down to the harbor, walk the beach, figure out just what it is she's doing here. Rock Harbor, Maine, of all the places just a bus ride away.

Roma says, "That is so gross you making her clean Shark Girl's room, Mother, you've squatted to a new low!" She flounces out of her seat as if this is *her* issue, slubbing up her mostly untouched plate of food and hefting it to the kitchen. Gracie notices her deliberate slam into Anthony's chair for just a second, kneeing him hard in the ribs. "Oh, excuse me! Clumsy, clumsy, clumsy."

Anthony doesn't look up, looks instead a little to the side, the other side from where Roma knocked into him. He appears a bit dazed and Gracie wonders if maybe he's slow. Maybe that's why he seems to have nothing to say.

The younger boarder sitting directly across is studying Gracie's face. Her hair is the color of winter grass and just as lifeless, lank about her neck. Not pretty, not at all, but nobody would stare at this girl either, she'd go mostly unnoticed about the business of her life. When she sees Gracie look back at her she casts her eyes down, sallow pea colored skin flushing pink. Gracie also looks down, embarrassed for her. Peers furtively, somehow expectantly over at Anthony, but he looks at no one, digging wearily into the plate of stew Berry has served. It occurs to Gracie that maybe he doesn't speak at all, a mute. He's good looking in a hangdog sort of way, only *his* face hangs evenly, dark and sleepy, almost drunken, that sensual manner of some Irish actor acting the stereotype. She too is part Irish, Gracie Kathleen McKneely. *Such a pretty name!* her mother reminds her; no doubt Gracie's parents expected someone else. Someone who starts out pretty and ends up that way too. Someone who goes to college, has a career, marries, moves next door maybe and raises her pretty little family in upstate New York, with a husband her parents would adore. *Someday you'll meet a nice man,* Maizey tells Gracie, often enough such that Gracie figures her mother is trying to convince herself. What her parents don't know of her world fills Gracie with an awful loneliness sometimes. And anyway, Gracie thinks, *drunk* only relaxes her face even more, its one sided hang, its drag, the ultimate pull to the earth. And there's the non-Irish half to consider, Gracie's mother's lusterless mix of things Germanic, Caucasian, your basic Wasp. She'd look like nothing special with or without a symmetrical face.

The attractive boarder is to Gracie's left. She leans in a bit and Gracie feels the warmth of her breath for a second heating up her own arm. "Do you know about the woman whose room you've taken?" she asks, earnest, melodious voice. She appears in her mid-forties, her face having settled into an attractive weave of lines around her eyes, her mouth, a pattern of pleasantness and America's most coveted cheekbones, high and chiseled. She's part Caucasian and something else, something darker, more olivey, Spanish or Indian or maybe African-American. She looks like she could have been a fashion model, and smart enough not to. It's what Gracie's got going for her too, oddly enough, this vague superiority over people who do such things as model for a living, especially scant clothing like underwear no matter how much money they make doing it. What's meaningful about having money if all the talent it takes getting it is about long legs and collar bones? The thing is, and Gracie's been thinking about this, especially since last night when Berry so bluntly asked her why she came here: Gracie wants to be exceptional in some way other than the way she looks, has always wanted this and she just can't settle into not being special enough. Why go to college, for instance, if all it gets you is a degree in something that moves you toward a job any other Tom, Dick or Jane with this particular degree could do too?

Gracie shakes her head, staring down into her stew, floating bits of this and that, unevenly chopped, colors aren't coordinated and packaged white bread to dip in; her mother would not approve of this meal.

"Shark Girl!" the mousy one across from Gracie pipes up. "She's like a mystic or something."

"No," the boarder on Gracie's right shakes her head. She's the oldest of the four, old lady helmet hairstyle, fleshy arms and a face that was probably nice enough in her youth when the skin was more firm, pink, and maybe even considered baby fat. Now it bunches around her mouth, her jaw; other than that it's unremarkable. And yes, Gracie would still rather have this face, she thinks. A trade? This face and she'll clean for eternity.

"She wasn't no mystic, that one," the woman shakes her head, hair holding forth as if encased in plastic, jowls flapping. "They call her a victim soul. That's not magic, it's Catholic."

"Oh, sure, some monster shark bites her leg off and it grows back again? I'd say that's pretty something that's not your usual, not where I come from anyways," says the other woman, maybe late thirties but an older attitude. Gracie gauges middle-age by her own mother who is forty-eight, the what-does-almost-fifty-look-like differential. Her father the social scientist might approve.

"My name's Janie," the boarder says. "Where I come from women are named Mary or Nancy or Sue or Jane, not Shark Girl."

"She had a real name but no one around here seemed to know it," the pretty one beside Gracie explains, that mild voice. "She was such an enigma."

"There you go, Jessie, them fancy words," Berry snorts. "She was a mess, that's what, not a saint, not a mystic, not an *enigma*, your basic slob. I'm sure Gracie can vouch for that, living in her room. Victim soul! I don't suppose one of those can be expected to pay the rent and leave a room tidy for someone else, like a normal person? Let her try do what *I* do!"

Roma reappears suddenly, slithering over to Gracie, snakelike movement of the exceptionally thin. Bends down near her ear though clearly it's for the rest to hear, too. "My mother's a *Spiritualist*, did she tell you? A Christian who believes she can communicate with the dead! It's a New England tradition, a family legacy, her own mother held séances with table tipping and automatic writing. Know what that is? When you write things you wouldn't normally write—possessed by a spirit and they're communicating through you. Though of course my mother doesn't actually *believe* in the dead, being a gypsy wannabe. That's like stealing God's thunder a bit, wouldn't you think? She'd have to raise them like Lazarus, so then they wouldn't be dead. She'd probably be a hell of a lot better with the dead than the living, I'll give her that. Come on!" Roma tugs at Gracie's sleeve, "You don't want the rest of that. Berry Stew should be listed in the historical registry, you can pick out remnants of our past meals for the last six months. It's like an archaeological dig, fishing around in that. Let's go out, I'll introduce you to the night life around here."

"Some in the world would be grateful for my stew, for any kind of food whatsoever, those that don't get the *choice* not to eat it!" snaps Berry. "My grandmother was a midwife who brought life into the world and raised up her family without no help from no one, and *your* grandmother, my mother, assisted those who lost their loved ones."

Gracie, gazing at Roma, swallows hard, her panic rising. *Night life?*

She pictures bars, loud music, gyrating people staring at her shouting rude remarks and she's in the back trying to hide. Anthony pushes back his chair and gets up, stumbling, that glazed expression. "Oh my God, you think we invited you?" Roma sneers. "Or, on second thought..." Her crafty look sizing Gracie up and down, a good shape she at least has and Roma's green eyes blink approvingly. "Maybe we do invite dear old Anthony along with us, what do you say dear old Anthony? He could come and salivate. I do like to see boys salivate, don't you? It's so *llama*."

Gracie's face turns the color of a strawberry, she doesn't dare look at Anthony. She's hardly one who knows what it's like to have anyone salivate around her after all, boy or beast. "I'm just going to finish my dinner," she says, sneaking a look over at Berry who sits straight in her chair, face impenetrable as stone.

She returns to her room after dessert, a dish of canned pears. "Not even the light kind, Mother, for chrissake!" Roma scolded, journeying back and forth into the dining room to see if Gracie had finished *yet*. "If you're trying to fatten them up at least give them something worth its calories." Stepping over Shark Girl, as Gracie has come to see her belongings, like the things could be the person, she picks up a pale blue satin push-up bra, Victoria's Secret-Second Skin, the label says, where it dangles from the radiator like some kind of flag. She's Gracie's size here. *Perfect handful!* the whispered crude remark from a pimply teenaged boy who sat beside her in algebra; *But you'd have to put a bag over the face*, he sneered. *The* face. Like it's not even attached to *the* person. She wonders how old Shark Girl is, a thing no one has hinted at. She could be twenty-six or sixty-six, though Gracie doubts the latter, given the push-up bra. Most of the rest of her clothes, at least the ones scattered about the room are the sort of Maine nondescript she's so far seen on almost everyone here except for Roma and Berry: jeans, your basic shapeless long sleeved shirt, cotton or cotton flannel if it's a man, tee shirts and baseball caps. Where's that LL Bean catalog look? They dress this way where she is from too, utilitarian clothes that don't call attention to themselves or the wearer of them. Big on her own list of Things That Hide. But this bra, and on closer inspection the matching thong panties nosing their minuscule crotch out from behind the radiator like some satiny little animal, don't exactly complete the look.

Gracie tugs open the one window, having to first pound against its wooden frame with her fist. Smell of the fall evening drifting in, dried leaves, that fresh yet dying scent, and still the dank odor of Berry's stew, still the remnants of old food from this room even though she'd gotten rid of any solid evidence of this. And something else, a slight yet lingering perfumy smell. Not sweet though, not flowery. More like if they packaged early morning scent of the sea in a perfume maybe, when the sun has just penetrated its blue, hers would be that. Gracie picks up the shirt that's stuffed on the ledge under the window. This one *is* an LL Bean, pine green cotton velour, missing the two top buttons, the ones that would modestly conceal any evidence of cleavage. Inhales the neckline and there's that smell, almost tropical, almost familiar, though how could it be familiar? Where does Gracie go that's tropical, except in her dreams? Born in Hawai'i then shuttled away after only two months, these would not a fragrant memory make, would they?

The summer on O'ahu, her going-on-thirteen summer after the plastic surgeon told her parents there was nothing she could do for Gracie, that until the palsy goes away, any further grafting could irreparably damage the nerves. *Irreparably*, and Gracie closing herself inside the little beige bedroom, her thoughts, dreams, all of these this color, not of the earth or sky, neither here nor there, barely a color at all. The idea of becoming a teenager and wearing this face! How could she bear it? They sent Gracie to *her* on Mālaekahana beach. *A little vacation*, said her father, *a break*. Whose break? one might have wondered; her parents were not with her.

A friend of her father's, a colleague, though not in the same field, during the time of his sabbatical in Hawai'i. A biologist who worked at the Hawai'i Institute of Marine Biology, Coconut Island in Kāne'ohe Bay, said she'd take Gracie there, show her the shark tanks—shark tanks!—Kāne'ohe Bay a breeding ground for hammerheads. She taught Gracie about invasive alien species and how to collect things. How to look for them, chart them, make them her own while still leaving them in their habitat, leaving them alone. Dr. Robyn Bender. She was missing her right hand. By the end of the summer Gracie would feel like she was missing a piece of her own heart.

Gracie slips back down the hall into the first floor bathroom she shares with two of the boarders, the pretty one she's guessing—there's the hair clip she wore at dinner on the top of the medicine cabinet, pinning up that curly dark hair—and the younger one, whom Gracie had noticed come in earlier in a torn and badly stained chenille bathrobe. They have a shared medicine cabinet over the pedestal sink and a long narrow closet with six shelves divided equally between the three of them, Gracie's two on the bottom naturally. She wonders if Shark Girl used these or whether she had a higher allotment and her stuff quickly exited after her own exit, by one of the boarders tired of stooping so low. She knows little about her, yet already Gracie can't imagine Shark Girl bending down for anything. Earlier she had placed her soap, lotion, toothpaste, hairbrush and a few first aid items on the second to the bottom shelf, the extra towel and sheets Berry had loaned her on the bottom. She has no makeup, what's the use?

She leans over to retrieve her brush then hesitates part way down at the third shelf, the pretty one's? Makeup is here, though not a lot of it; green shadow for her eyes, which Gracie had noticed were a yellowy brown, a mauve lipstick, face powder. Gracie opens the powder compact, running her finger lightly over its silky contents, then onto her own cheek. What would it be like to have this, something so simple, a five dollar purchase make any difference at all?

After she's changed her shirt, one shapeless long sleeved button-down traded for another, cleaner one, and brushed her hair, Gracie heads out reluctantly toward the *Servants Quarters*, Roma had stated meanly, *where dear old Anthony resides*. Berry had corrected her. "The carriage house," she said. "This house is old enough to have a carriage house instead of a garage." Eighteenth century, Berry said and Roma corrected *her*. "*Hello*! Mother, it was built in the 1800s? That makes it the 19th century, duh!"

Gracie is not looking forward to this evening but Roma seems like someone who will not be told *no*, and Gracie isn't much good at saying no anyway. As she approaches she hears Roma shrilling something unintelligible to Anthony and the response is silence. Gracie wonders again if he speaks. He seems slow, his movements hesitant, face unacknowledging. The harvest moon lifts out of a pink-tinged cloud, shining its gold down onto the third story as she gazes up, the attic with its garrets, slope of the unevenly shingled roof. Beyond this house the others in the neighborhood are much the same, oversized but worn down, paint chipping in the salty air, hunched against the chill fall night. And past this the other lettered streets, more houses, then the harbor area. Gracie had walked there this afternoon when her chores were finally finished, downtown, functional shops midst empty storefronts, the kind that might have once been part of a thriving harbor town that didn't know it was supposed to change and cater to tourists: no gourmet food stores, maybe bait shops instead; no gift shops with quaint little odds and ends, mementos of Maine, plastic light house globes, pine-smelling sachets, rubber lobsters and printed gift cards; no trendy shops where incense is burned and gauzy clothes with price tags heftier than the underpaid labor that went into them. Instead there are dollar stores, stores to buy the everyday, pans, forks, pillows to sleep on, the things one needs to make a life, cheap. *Frugal*, Berry had told her; *We're a frugal people, we Mainers*.

There is something strange about this house, Gracie thinks, staring up, the peeling paint even evident in the moonlight; no one and nothing seems quite whole. America's Haunted Housewives! She's beginning to think she's come to the right place, that she'll fit right in. Maybe Gracie had left home to come home, after all.

CHAPTER SIX

Mālaekahana, Hawai'i: Things I Saw on the Beach, July 1, 1994, by Gracie McKneely: (Time was 6:20 in the morning. Dr. Bender said to note the time. That's how you know it happened, she said.) Glass Balls — this was the best! Two of them, one on the sand and one floating in the shallow part. I waded out in between waves and didn't even get my shorts wet, except at the hem. Dr. Bender said these are Japanese Fishing Net Weights, from the time they used to blow handmade glass balls and tie them in their nets to weigh them down. They use plastic now, she said, made by machines, but there are enough glass ones floating in the currents still to last a hundred years!

1. Glass Balls: two of them, one is aqua-blue and round (Dr. Bender said "spherical" — note to self, look up that word). It's four inches at its middle. I measured it because Dr. Bender said to measure everything; everything has a size, she said. Second one is the best: it's cylindrical, I think that's what Dr. Bender said, and notched with two glass nots (I mean knots!) on either end. This one is more blue than the other, turquoise almost. Like if you open your eyes under the lip of a wave this is the color.

2. Beach glass, three pieces, a white and two amber. Dr. Bender said the amber is from beer bottles but the white could be from any kind of a bottle. You can still see through the white, which is just under an inch long, but the amber ones are worn solid from tossing about in the sea. (Note: the best piece of beach glass I ever found wasn't here. It was in New Jersey and it was lavender like an Easter egg.)

3. A rain squall blowing in from the ocean. First it was

purple clouds then the rain came slashing down like needles. I went back to Dr. Bender and Louis's house and had hot chocolate and a cheese and mushrooms omelet that Louis made. (Note: I don't like mushrooms but I didn't say that to Louis.) Louis stared at my face, but not in a mean way. When Dr. Bender looks at my face it's like she's not really looking at it, THE CHEEK. She's looking at me.

Janie catches Gracie in the hallway, at least she thinks it's Janie, the faded out youngish middle-ageish woman who seems older than she should, seems older than Jessie, the darker, prettier one—that's who Gracie remembers. It's beauty, isn't it, that most of us remember, at least in the beginning? It's 2:00 in the morning, not a time you want to be running into anyone and Gracie wonders what Janie (if this is her name) is doing down in this hall since her bedroom and shared bath are upstairs. Gracie doesn't ask, just nods and aims past her toward her own room. Roma had kept Gracie out late, and the strain of meeting her friends, letting the cloak of darkness shield her from them in the park they hung out in is catching up. She's tired, cold, a little sad and wants only to sleep.

"You like that room?" Janie asks.

Gracie sighs, turns back around and shrugs. "It's OK, better when I get it cleaned up."

Janie shakes her head, wisps of hair the color of oak illuminated in the yellow hall light, hair the color of her skin. Here is a woman who appears to blend in with her own self. She moves toward Gracie, clamps a clammy hand onto her wrist, walking beside her down the hall. "Shark Girl was one of them messy kinds of persons, you know? I tell you this, because I'm betting you never had a husband or a family. Some folks are just born to make other folks clean up the messes they make."

Gracie peers down at Janie, she's a lot shorter than her, flips her hair back off her face. "I'm too young to have had a family of my own," she says, annoyed. *Does she think I couldn't have a family, that no one would want me?* For a moment she almost misses her own family, hovering Maizey, distantly concerned Thomas, at least she didn't have to go covering up around them. They were used to her.

At the door to her room Gracie switches on the light, turns to say a firm good night but to her dismay Janie sidles into the room past her, over to the bureau, messing her pudgy hand about in a pile of Shark Girl leavings, emerging with a 5'7 silver-framed photo from underneath. "Know who this is?" she asks.

Gracie shakes her head. She won't encourage her by actually speaking.

"It's her sister, Susan Catherine. See, says so on the back. From your sister, Susan Catherine. She's supposed to live around here someplace; I saw a couple of photographs in the Rock Harbor newspaper, her photographs they was, that terrible flood they had out in Ohio couple springs past. She's a devastation photographer, the paper said, snaps pictures of the bad *natural* things that happen — floods, earth quakes, mud slides, you know. It's her medium, the paper said though she'll do other things too like people. But she's known for her disasters. Made a name for herself in them, you might say, taking pictures of others' tragedies. So wouldn't you think she'd come over here for a visit? You think Shark Girl ever invited her, called her own sister up on the phone? No siree, none of us saw a lick of her. Now, don't you think that's a bit odd, family and whatnot?"

Janie slides over toward the bed. That's how Gracie sees her walk, a sliding sort of movement, someone who's used to having to slip about in places she's less welcome, not the firm step of the wanted (Gracie should know, treading timidly through life herself). Plunks herself down, the only uncovered as in not buried under Shark Girl's things, piece of furniture in the room. Gracie does not want her in her room and is about to say as much, disguised of course by how tired she is. She's not rude, has never been rude; only people confident enough to be rude can actually *be* rude is the way Gracie sees it. But Janie leans forward, her oaky eyes strangely bright. "Things happen when she's around," Janie whispers. "Strange things, bad things sometimes."

"What do you mean?" A chill plays up Gracie's spine, though probably it's just the under-heated air. Berry turns the furnace down when she goes to bed, and it's Gracie's task to turn it up in the morning, but *not* until 6:00, Berry emphasized. Or maybe the late night, strange place, and what is she doing here anyway, this weird, rubbed out little woman perched on Shark Girl's bed, this alien room! How can Gracie even begin to think of this room, this bed as her own without the bleached smell of Maizey's sheets? Berry won't use bleach; says it's toxic and not environmentally friendly. Alien, she called it. *Alien...*

Invasive Alien Species, by Gracie McKneely, July 10, 1994, 4:00 P.M.

Dr. Bender said when an alien species is introduced and it spreads like wildfire causing all kinds of problems then it is considered an <u>invasive alien species</u>. For instance, she said the subterranean (note to self—look up that word so Dr. Bender doesn't know I don't know it) termite is one of the worst invasive alien species in Hawai'i, chowing down whole buildings....

"OK, well how about this then," Janie whines, motioning Gracie closer, her hand fluttering about her mouth, confidentially, like they're friends and she's about to reveal a heartfelt secret. She tugs down on Gracie's hand to sit next to her. "Listen," she says, "Brunswick Naval Air Base has their annual show every July, the Blue Angels and whatnot. You can see them for miles, feel the sonic booms they make in your very bones. So last summer Berry decides we're going. Therapy, she called it, gets us out of the house. 'It's a beautiful weekend!' Berry said, 'Let's rejoice in *Jesus'* light.' Shark Girl wrote us a note, hung it on the refrigerator with this insurance company magnet Berry's got there, the number to call if there's a home disaster, fire and whatnot. The note said she's coming too, though not to rejoice in Jesus' light, it said. Still it was unusual for her to go anywhere with us, she's the type that makes out her own agenda, you know. Maybe she's got a thing for fliers, some of us wondered.

"We get there a little late as it's already started, though not the main event, just some little show they put on for the kiddies, don't even know if it was the Air Base folks. There's this decorated plane painted orange, has a happy face on it and it's doing these cheerful little loops in the sky, acrobatic fliers Jessie told us these were called. So we spread our blankets in this field and Berry lays out the picnic she's brought, fried chicken if I remember correctly which Shark Girl would have nothing to do with being it once had an appetite itself. She saunters off—she's got this limp and darned if on her it don't look like this sexy, deliberate kind of walk—buys herself a fresh squeezed lemonade at the stand. Meanwhile the happy face plane's getting closer to us, its loops, swirls, the kiddies clapping, laughing, a happy time they're all having. Shark Girl sashays back with her lemonade and, I got to tell you, it's like the pilot of that plane sees her for the first time, he's close enough, so what do you think? Boom! That plane is history. Goes into a nose dive. I mean she's not exactly beautiful, I got to say, not exactly. But something about her is, I don't know, arresting. That's the word for it, stops folks in their tracks. Boom!"

"You mean he crashed?" Gracie jerks back a little from Janie who's leaning into her again, smell of something peppery on her breath.

"That's what I'm telling you," she says blandly. "In the field opposite us. Luckily corn was growing so no one's sitting there because it exploded into a fiery ball. You could feel the heat a mile away. Everyone was shocked, crying, wailing, 'Oh my God!' For some reason I turn to look at Shark Girl, the cause of it all I'm convinced and, do you know she's just standing there, sipping that lemonade like not a thing out of the ordinary's going on."

"But you can't blame a plane crash on someone just walking in a field, that's crazy!"

Janie rises off the bed, slips over to the open closet, fingering a black silk blouse hanging inside, one of the few pieces of clothing that hadn't been tossed on the floor. Earlier this evening Gracie too had run the back of her hand up and down the smooth grain of the fabric, for a moment even considered putting it on.

"Don't wear this," Janie warns, as if she read Gracie's thoughts. "Never know what kind of luck it might bring. When Berry's mother used to hold séances she'd sometimes ask folks to describe an article of the loved one's clothing, a shirt or a dress and sometimes, Berry told us, the apparition would appear in it from the waist up, hovering over the table. Guess you don't need your legs and feet when you're floating about in the afterlife. Course, no reason to believe Shark Girl's passed on. Still, if I were you I'd cart all this stuff off to Good Will or the dump. Some folks claim Shark Girl's a healer. Personally? I agree with Berry. I think she's the devil."

"The devil?" Gracie asks Roma the next morning, a little timidly, eyes cast down. You don't make casual conversation with this girl, and Gracie has never been much good at small talk anyway. Chatting assumes a comfort level with another person she rarely feels; hard to when you're sure that whatever they are saying, whatever words they are using, really what they're thinking about is her face in front of them. Roma is making coffee, and Gracie was surprised to see her up, since she's not the one who has to rise and shine this place. The kitchen in the early morning light looks like it was painted with lemons, a sort of squeezed out yellow on the walls, the yolk yellow linoleum floor with black and brown grit in between the tile markers and matching counter tiles. Berry asked Gracie to scrub all this today *but good.*

"Janie told me your mother thinks Shark Girl is the devil," Gracie clarifies, finally looking her in the eye.

Roma scowls, shakes her head, pours a cup of the soupy black into a mug that announces Rockland Lobster Fest, big red letters, a grinning blood red lobster on the other side. Smiling, like it *wanted* to get boiled? Eagerly anticipated this annual carnival to honor its slaughter? Gracie got that one off the Internet too.

"Christ! My mother doesn't believe in any devil," Roma sputters, slurping the coffee. "Even her God is like nobody else's, her own *personal* savior. She just doesn't like people to get the better of her, get more attention than her, upstage her, you dig? These women here are all totally insane, you'll see. Wait till you get invited to a meeting of the Haunted Housewives, is that a hoot! Berry's the boss lady, CEO and self-anointed president of the Jesus Club. What do you think all the *ie* names are about? My mother butchers a serious name like Jessica into Jessie and the woman sheds years of her adulthood right along with it. Janie? That one, Jane, Jan*ie*, she's hopeless. Marie, no comment needed there. And Tia's just a skank, out in la la land anyway. Nothing in a name change is going to affect that loony. You're already Gracie, that pleases my mother I'm sure. Ever consider the grownup version, just Grace?"

"My name really is Gracie, that's what they named me."

Roma inhales the rest of her coffee, grabs her backpack, a U.S. Army field bag off a peg on the wall by the door, runs a hand through the orange spikes of her hair, then stares at Gracie earnestly, her steady green eyes. "I'd revise that sucker if I were you. Your folks named you it because they didn't want you to grow up. Parents either want to keep you a kid or they don't want to keep you at all." Roma shrugs. "I got business to do, *Gracie*, but I'll be back at 7:00 this evening to pick you up. There's someone I want you to meet."

Out of habit Gracie yanks her hair down, curtaining it safely around her cheek. "We just went out last night," she offers lamely.

"Yeah, so? Your dance card filled already? Don't be such a drag, it's cool my mother finally hired someone to clean not about to turn into dust herself." With that Roma flounces out the door, a butt and hip wiggle in Gracie's direction, wheeling around to flash her a dazzling grin. Gracie's blood pumps suddenly into her ears. She can hear that distant roaring, like listening to the conch shell on Dr. Bender's lānai overlooking the beach, the roar and slap of the waves on the sand constant as the trade winds pummeling the trees. Everything had a sound that summer, a scent and a taste and for a while Gracie had felt so *heightened*, felt for the first time maybe she *could* be a part of things, this damaged face, this cringing girl, a small measured piece of this world.

Gracie McKneely's Beach List, July 3, 1994, 8:00 AM
Rain squall, sound of it against the ocean is like a billion tossed pebbles, rubbish caught in seaweed strewn (that's Dr. Bender's word) at the tide line: one tampon case without the tampon; two liquor bottles — can't read their labels; one broken cowry shell and two largish pieces of some kind of purple coral — I need to ask Dr. Bender to help me look this up; is it stag coral? one blue rubber flipper beside one red sneaker.... The long one-legged swim! Louis said.

By mid-afternoon Gracie's chores are done and she accidentally walks in on Jessie in the bathroom. She had been intent on a quick teeth brushing, dragging a comb through her hair then walking down to the harbor. The house was silent, and it didn't occur to her anyone else was home. "Oh! Excuse me."

Jessie is kneeling on the floor by the corner of the painted wooden cupboard and the toilet, and at first Gracie thinks she's vomiting, that stomach tucked down position of the drunk, the sick and the bulimic (which Gracie's beginning to wonder about with Roma, though in Roma's case she has yet to see her actually eat so what would she have to throw up?).

Lifts up that pretty face, presses her fingers to her lips. "Shhh," Jessie whispers, motioning her closer. Gracie notices when she looks at her Jessie doesn't shy away from her cheek, the usual averted eyes. She looks at Gracie like nothing's wrong. Makes Gracie wonder if maybe she doesn't see so well.

Jessie points at a tiny hole in the wall under the lip of the cupboard. "He's scared of you," she says, "but what you do is you let him know it's all right, that you're his friend." She makes a gentle clucking sound with her tongue, laying her hand down lightly on Gracie's arm, now kneeling beside her.

In less than a minute a small grey mouse pokes his head out and Gracie sucks in her breath. "Shhh," Jessie whispers again, "don't say a word. They can read your body language. Think welcoming thoughts and he'll come out."

Gracie stares at Jessie like she's a little touched, as her mother would put it. Jessie slides her arm slowly forward and Gracie inches slowly backward, the unevenly tiled bathroom floor cold under her knees, even through her jeans. It's not that she has anything against mice; in fact, her mother used to set those old fashioned spring wired mouse traps in the basement, looked like a torture device for rodents, from which Gracie would secretly liberate the cheese later in the night and Maizey would become so annoyed at the devilish cleverness of these creatures, she'd say, getting the cheese and making off with it. Plates of warfarin went out next and Gracie got rid of those too. The mice became larger than life in her mother's mind, something to conquer and Gracie became just as determined she wouldn't get them. But this was more about her mother and herself and less about the fate of the mice.

The mouse begins its hesitant humpbacked hobble up Jessie's arm, sniffing at her wrist, sniffing the air, black nose twitching. "Isn't he precious?" she whispers. "Yes you are! You are my precious," she chirps to the mouse.

Gracie raises her brows a bit, peering at Jessie's face, her almost beatific smile. Gracie is not a Catholic and she doesn't know her saints, but somewhere she's seen a painting of one, had to have been a saint, that glorious smile, surrounded by animals, and the plastic figurine of this in Berry's shelves. It's the face she remembers, always the face.

"Does Berry know you're making a pet out of a mouse here?"

Jessie smiles, a little sadly, running a finger lightly over the mouse's clenched back. The mouse stands perfectly still, its nose twitching, staring up into Jessie's face. "It's not for us to make pets out of wild animals," she says. "They have their place in this world too."

Gracie retreats to her room thinking maybe she'll tackle its cleaning instead of that walk, but she is so exhausted from the night out and a day of vacuuming, dusting, mopping, schlepping buckets of water over the kitchen and bathroom floors, that instead she drops down onto the bed and falls into a deep sleep, waking up as someone else in the middle of a dream: beautiful Jessica perhaps, surrounded by legions of mice, so many mice crawling over her arms, her legs, her long graceful legs, their little paws tickling, little noses twitching and they're trying to tell her something but she's unable to listen; she keeps staring at her face, drawing away from her body in this dream that is not her body, this face that she must try and make hers, but quickly! So little time in a dream, after all.

"You have to promise not to tell anyone," Roma is saying. "Especially not my mother. Christ, she'd pitch a fit. That I have a life that doesn't include her makes her mental."

Gracie is following Roma on a winding moon lit path through a field heading up a huge hill. She can feel the dried out stalks of grass and weeds brushing her calves where her cuffed capri pants don't quite reach the tops of her socks. "Wear these," Roma said, barging into Gracie's room, rummaging through the folded clothes still in her suitcase. "With you we'll start your makeover from the feet up," she had said, grinning. Gracie forced herself to not feel hurt by that remark. When Roma's around there's little time to think, ruminate over what anyone says, what they might have meant by what they said. Gracie's father was the one who taught her to always listen for the other message, the real one, *metamessages* under the spoken words. A social scientist thing, or a way of surviving her mother? Penobscot Bay in the moonlight shines pearl colored below and the cold wind smells of pine. Gracie clutches her polar fleece jacket tighter against herself, burying her chin into its fuzzy softness.

"I thought you said we were going out?" she asks Roma.

"Well, this ain't exactly in."

"Last night you took me to the park. I don't know, I just sort of figure when people say they're going out they mean to a club, the movies, someplace."

"This is *some*place, this is Maine! Where do you go where you're from?"

She shrugs, though Roma can't see this in the darkness, Gracie's most comfortable backdrop. "I don't go out much," she tells her.

As they approach the top of the hill Gracie hears music, something whiny, heavy, a lot of electric guitar, shrill laughter. Headlights from a couple pickup trucks illuminate a group lounging about surrounded by the long grass. Her heart quickens, breath stiffens. Groups are the worst. There's a certain mentality, her father's theory perhaps, *Proof of Infinity...*, one torments then the rest will too. Tugs her hair down over the right side of her face.

Closer up she sees they are mostly women, some in fringy leather jackets, some in bomber type jackets, many with piercings that gleam in the headlights and razor cut hair, short and spiky, a rainbow of colors. Not mostly, *all* women. One of them unfolds her long legs, rises up, up and up (Gracie is reminded of Venus on the half-shell, if that's what it's called, a print her father has over his desk in his basement hideaway), hugs Roma then releases her and stares at Gracie. She's maybe the tallest woman Gracie has seen, Roma looks like a child beside her. Her head is completely shaved except for a tuft of razored bangs the color of moonlight over her eyebrows, a gold metal hoop tugging through the pale ends of each brow. Her face, all cheekbones and lips, impossibly long body in a tight leather body suit like she's really some animal encased in a woman's skin. This one could model underwear for a year and retire for life. She holds out her hand and Gracie hesitantly takes it, but instead of shaking the tall woman pulls her closer, Gracie's arm a rope and she's hauling her in.

"So you're the latest *housewife*," she says, voice buttery and low, words carefully enunciated, musky scent of her breath. "You don't look like a psycho. Ms. Waters doesn't usually take them so young."

"I clean," Gracie says lamely. The group titters.

The tall woman nods. "Right," she says, "start out doing something and end up doing nothing. It's a kind of ennui peculiar to that household. Now Roma here, she just exits when she starts to feel it. Will you be able to do that?" She peers at Gracie sharply, judging, what? her face? mostly hidden in the night, she's hoping, despite the headlights.

More laughter from the group, but not unfriendly.

"Why are you here?" the woman asks. "Roma tells me you're from away. You don't look like the boating type. You an antiquer? An outlet shopper? Or just the sort wants to knock Maine off their list of places to see before they die. Why did you come here?"

Gracie shrugs. "I don't really know," she says honestly. "I had to get away from my home," she adds.

The woman nods. "So sit down. You smoke?"

Gracie's about to say no then notices they're not talking about cigarettes. One of the women passes a pipe-like object with a carved out hole to Roma. "Medicinal," Roma says, "Liela is a Source."

"Source?" Gracie asks, folding her legs under her on the cold ground, shaking her head as the pipe approaches, its sweetish smell mixing in with a salt breeze blowing up the hill from the bay. There's something about having her kind of a face, makes you not want to lose control for even a moment.

"Medicinal marijuana," Liela explains. "Glaucoma, cancer, people who need it to control pain. Those who want to make everyone else live by their own moral codes don't approve."

"It's legal here?" Gracie asks, but nobody answers. She peers doubtfully at the circle of women, tattooed and pierced, reminds her of warrior women not sick women, some of whom have their arms around each other, sitting in the possessive way of couples.

"Liela's the only one I know doing something for humanity," Roma states proudly, running her hand over the tall woman's hip bone, poking against her chocolate colored leather-encased shape. Looks like a stretched-out M & M peanut.

"What happened to your face?" she asks. The Question, and Gracie's heart bumps inside her chest. Liela reaches over from where she and Roma are crouched in front of Gracie—Gracie notices they are sitting pretty close too—and lifts the hair gently back off Gracie's cheek, cool night air caressing her damage. A tear in Gracie's eye and she wills it not to fall.

"Ouch!" Liela lets out a low, sympathetic whistle. "Somebody burn you? Looks like skin grafts to me. Maybe they didn't take, there's a bit of a droop."

Gracie sighs. "Palsy," she says softly. "It could go away. They say the palsy could just go away any day. It was an accident, when I was a baby. My father dropped me and I hit the lit barbecue with my cheek on the way down." The crowd goes quiet around her.

"Uh huh," Liela nods, "well, that's gnarly. The world I live in there aren't many accidents. What world do you live in? That shark chick whose room you took in Waters' house? Her leg gets bitten off by a shark so now she's a miracle worker. I think there's another story there. But then you'll get to be the judge of that, won't you." Liela rubs her fingers against Roma's cheek, tilts up Roma's chin, her face, its sharp-boned angles in the moonlight and kisses her long and hard.

Gracie stares down at her hands folded on her lap, her own heart racing. She's not as embarrassed as she might've thought she'd be, or maybe *they* thought she'd be. She remembers coming upon Dr. Bender and Louis one muggy, windy July afternoon, and they were kissing, at the clothesline of all places, lazy flap of the white sheets around them like wings of gulls, of terns, something taking off. Dr. Bender's dark hair usually caught up in a French braid was loose about her shoulders. This too a movement, the sheets, her hair a shadow, flying. At first Gracie was surprised that Dr. Bender even kissed. She had thought of her father's friend as the biologist, only that. *The* Biologist, Thomas always said, like there is just one and Robyn Bender is it. Gracie had felt a pang of something, a hollow sort of longing that started in her stomach, aching there in the pit of her then rising until it was a tight cold fist in her chest. Her throat closed up and she ran back out onto the beach, smell of the salt spray, roar of the waves at high tide, constant as breath.

Gracie has no one to kiss, has never kissed or been kissed by anyone except her parents, and not by them all that often—theirs was not a demonstrative sort of family, not physically anyway, or perhaps just not about displays of love. She studies the shapes of her own fingers in the dimly lit darkness, hands small, useless they suddenly strike her. Wonders what it would be like to have Liela's long-fingered hands, to do something for humanity, as Roma put it, something significant, those hands and the purpose they served. It gets back to that wish of Gracie's, more like a need, the biological feel of it sometimes, like needing to breathe, to eat, to love—to be exceptional in some meaningful way. To be wanted. The background of female voices a high sugary whine and the wind smells sweet like dried grass. Guttural wailing of the boom box guitar, someone singing and Gracie inhales all of it, breathes back into it, trying not to dwell on it, this old loneliness.

CHAPTER SEVEN

This dream I am running running running to catch a long silver train going I don't know where but I've got to catch it or I'll be left behind. I don't know where being left behind is, I don't know where I am or who I am, only that it's critical I catch this train. I try to get a glimpse of my face, see if it is whole, symmetrical, even beautiful. But it's only the back of my head, my long hair that is not my own long hair flying out as the train slows just enough for me to grab onto its silver body, hoist myself up to its hot metal roof black as the shell of a beetle, lean forward, legs apart, riding bare back this searing metal like some mechanical cowboy; fear of this, and the exhilaration.

Gracie wakes up right before dawn feeling triumphant, like she actually did something. Same room, somebody else's things, clothes, remains of her life scattered in greater abundance than Gracie's own belongings still mostly in her suitcase, shoved just inside the closet. She climbs out of bed, walks over to the window, staring out at a grey light paling the roof tops, chimneys of the neighborhood houses, salt tang of the sea as she inches open the window just a little, snap of the frigid air. Gulls wheel and cry, and for a moment she again loses the sense of who she is, where she is, this window facing a sea she cannot see, only breathe, its cold green. There's the purring still of a few fall crickets, though most are dying now. Suddenly she feels such an overwhelming loss, though what could she have lost? Her face— but that's the old story. You learn to be who you are for the most part, don't you? Like you have any choice in the matter, no matter how many dreams, bargains, wishes or prayers that it might somehow be different. Inevitably you wake up.

Gracie walks over to the closet, lifts the black silk blouse off its hanger, Shark Girl's blouse, pressing its coolness against her bare arms. Slides off her cotton nightshirt and puts it on, just like that and it settles in around her like it's meant to be here, perfect fit, intended to be worn by Gracie, after all. It's early, no one in the house stirring except maybe Janie who has a morning shift at Dunkin Donuts. Gracie is careful not to run into her as she slips outside, closing the door gently like this really is her home, her parents are inside and they mustn't hear as she sneaks out...to do what? Creep around this yard, the frosted grass in Shark Girl's shirt, Gracie's own yanked on jeans still unbuttoned at the waist?

There's a silvery sheen on the brambly scrub hedge that separates this yard from the next, and on the low bush blueberry plants, red leafed and dried out now, and the dying maple in the center of the yard, flecks of it shining like dimes. She is reminded of her dream, the fleeting silver of things. Dr. Bender had a silver hook she used for her right hand. It could do almost anything a hand did, she told Gracie. Soon this frost will disappear and the life in this yard move more forcefully into its cycle of shutting down, leaves falling, plants drying up, berries where once there were flowers, its active participation in the fall of the year. Again Gracie feels that loss, a whamp of it in her gut and she's about to turn back to the house when Anthony appears, shouldering a rake. They both jump a little at the unexpected sight of the other. Gracie tugs her hair down over her cheek. "You're up early," she says lamely, like something her mother would say, observations of the obvious.

He gazes off into the grey distance over her head. Does he not even want to look at her, she looks that bad? The night he came out with Roma and Gracie he stayed on the perimeter of things, in the Camden park, clusters of teenagers, young twenties flitting about, and he crouched on the grass, staring out at a moonlit harbor. Gracie doesn't remember him saying anything at all, though occasionally Roma would ram by, drag her hand heavily over his head, pull at his hair, yank his head back and whisper something to him.

She notices that he is eying her shirt now, Shark Girl's shirt. Gracie's face flames, which she hopes he can't see behind her hair. He reaches out his hand, fingers the wrist of the shirt lightly around Gracie's own wrist. Something changes in her stomach, a low ache, the flash of a warning then something more like yearning. She swallows hard. He pulls at the sleeve, indicating she should follow him? Suddenly the back door to the big house is flung open and Berry Waters is there, one hand on one generous hip, a staunch human-shaped tea kettle.

"Gracie!" she calls out. "You got some things to do, don't you?" She stares at the shirt. "Bit chilly out for wearing that one, isn't it?"

It's early yet and Gracie is perfectly warm, or at least she was until Berry said this, but she says nothing. Berry is frowning at Anthony who let go of Gracie's sleeve the moment Berry appeared and stands now almost casually, leaning against his rake though clutching it hard, his knuckles white, eyes riveted at the ground. Gracie thinks about the way Anthony moves, deliberately as if dazed. Is he really that slow or just ignoring certain of life's more disagreeable signals? She looks at Berry standing there expectantly, then moves back toward the house, feeling his eyes on her as she walks, her back, her better side, after all. Again that low ache in the pit of her, the yearning, for what Gracie is not sure.

That night she is invited to her first meeting of America's Haunted Housewives. Roma tries to get her not to go; "Liela has plans for us!" she insists. But Berry is just as determined.

"Gracie is part of the household now," she announces, "so this is what we do." Gracie feels this acceptance — part of the household! — feels grateful for not being thought of as only the person who cleans it, and she follows Berry into the den, carefully avoiding Roma's taunting black-green eyes.

"Fine!" Roma growls. "Hope you have a real hoot. Give it up for the Jesus Club! Say hi to dead Arnie for me. He's a cheap date, you dig? Little bit of kibble and he'll partner in your bed for as long as you like. Just ask Jessie."

Gracie looks at Berry who shakes her head.

The others are already assembled, Tia and Janie on the couch,

Marie and Jessie in opposite chairs, and clearly the plush overstuffed velvet chair is for Madam Waters. Tia tosses Gracie a couple big pillows off the couch and she puts these down on the floor between Marie and Berry, where it is Jessie's olivey face she can see best, other side of the varnished oak coffee table. She starts to pull down her hair, then doesn't. They've seen her, they know.

Berry lights the big vanilla scented candle on the table and Tia and Janie light the smaller cinnamon candles on the end tables, their darker wood either side of the couch. "Tonight is Jessie's night," Berry tells them.

"Welcome Jessie!" the rest chant, as if she doesn't live here too. Then everyone grabs hands, closes their eyes and Berry is mumbling some kind of prayer under her breath, Gracie can pick out a word here and there: "Jessie...help us...her loss," and always punctuated with "Dear *Jesus*!" Gracie is beginning to wonder if she should have gone with Roma, or better yet begged out of both invitations and retreated to their room, Shark Girl's and hers. She's not used to being invited to things and hasn't a clue how to respond other than to do the thing she's invited to do. It's not that she's so uncomfortable around praying either, around religion, even if Roma is correct in claiming that her mother's is like no other. *The church of Berry Waters?*

They didn't go to church in Gracie's family, though they had nothing against it, no particular beliefs one way or the other. As a *functionalist* sociologist, her father claimed the purpose of religion was to provide a societal glue, the bonds of commonality, as well as an explanation for things difficult to understand. Whether or not the explanation was correct was immaterial, he said, as long as it was believed. Maizey's beliefs were political once, and now they came in a Clorox bottle. And Thomas? His were in a different kind of bottle. Some time after the accident that traumatized Gracie's face and then the palsy that seemingly promised this to be more or less permanent, her father decided he would drink himself to death. He didn't say this to them, of course, maybe not even to himself, but it was obvious. He would start as soon as he came home from his classes, before dinner, serial glasses of wine, wine with dinner, then retreat to his basement bearing the rest of the bottle and another just in case, drinking until he collapsed into sleep on his couch. His nose grew red, his belly just grew, but he was never unkind to her mother or her. "Just crawls into that bottle and disappears," Gracie's mother pointed out, her heralding of the obvious. "*We* can ignore it," she said, "but one day his liver will not." Still Maizey did not pray. But Gracie has seen her checking and rechecking their life insurance policies; perhaps this is its own kind of prayer.

"Here is what happened to Jessie," Berry is saying.

"I'm in Wal-Mart one day," Jessie begins, voice soft like it's unsure it wants to tell what it is about to; Gracie has to lean forward to hear her. Outside the wind picks up, pushing against the screen where Berry has left the window cracked slightly open, or perhaps this one, stiff as they are, cannot properly close. The vanilla candle flickers.

"I'm in the Wal-Mart," Jessie starts again, a bit louder now, "and, suddenly I just break down!" She sighs, shaking those black curls. "It was as if something made me unfold, my knees buckle and I collapse onto the floor. I'm crying, and of course there's a circle of people around me asking me what's wrong, but I can't tell them, how can I tell them? So I cry even harder and they call for an ambulance and the EMTs come sprinting in, and even then I didn't stop, my whole body trembling, teeth chattering like I'm plugged in. They loaded me into the ambulance and they took me away. Sobbing. To save my life I could not stop." Jessie shrugs, a faraway look in her eyes. She reminds Gracie of something more animal than human, something sacred and scared, that timid face—a doe maybe.

"Ayuh, and here's where I come in," announces Berry. "I go to the Pen Bay psychiatric ward and I bring you back home."

"She was voluntarily there, wasn't a commitment or committed or whatever," Janie explains to Gracie. "You can't lock a person up for crying in the Wal-Mart now, can you?"

"So what do we need to do?" Berry coaches the group, and they all respond together like some sort of chant or mantra: "Heal Jessie, Dear *Jesus*!"

"Jessie has a broken heart," Tia says to Gracie, looking over Gracie's head at the wall behind her. Tia is the only one in the group who will not look at her face; perhaps her mousiness is too close a cousin to Gracie's ugliness and she worries she'll be downgraded, Gracie thinks.

"And how do we heal Jessie?" Berry asks.

"Bring back Arnie?" Janie answers.

"Ayuh, but let's not forget who we're praying to, who it is we're *asking* to bring back Arnie."

"Jesus!" they howl.

"Dear *Jesus*, help Jessie reunite with Arnie, or at least give us the knowledge he is beside our Jessie in spirit so she can move on," Berry says.

Marie leans over in her chair, whispers to Gracie: "Her husband took Arnie somewhere, we've never been able to discover where. She left her husband but she can't get right with things, not knowing what happened to Arnie."

"*What?*" Gracie hisses. She's picturing body parts in a trash bag.

"Join hands again," Berry commands, and everyone leans in toward the table. Berry grabs Gracie's left hand and Marie her right. Gracie fingers are tingling. She needs to pee and considers saying this, letting herself out of the room, but it's as if Berry knows somehow and her grasp tightens around Gracie's hand. "Close your eyes," she orders them and they do.

Hears a humming that sounds like it's coming out of the ceiling but it has to be Berry, Gracie thinks; can this woman throw her voice? "Come to us Arnie," Berry is whispering, "come back to your Jessie. Dear *Jesus*, bring Arnie to our Jessie. Let Jessie have the sense of him again, to know he is at peace. Dear *Jesus*, whose own life was sacrificed so that we may live ours in your good grace."

Gracie feels the candle's sudden flickering like it's inside her own skin, its synthetic vanilla scent wafting in a sticky breeze pulsing through the cracked window. Jessie is crying softly. "I loved him pressed against me when I slept, haven't slept well since," she sniffs.

"Concentrate now Jessie," Berry murmurs. "Let your positive visualizations and our prayers bring Arnie to you once again."

"He was so innocent! Jack said he had a sleazy purr, that Arnie used to like to watch me undress. Isn't that ridiculous!"

Gracie's eyes pop open. *Purr?*

Berry tugs on Gracie's hand, squeezing her fingers tighter. A sudden gust makes the candle dance wildly and Jessie leaps up. "I'm afraid Jack did something terrible but he won't tell me! It makes me so...crazy sometimes."

Everyone's eyes are open now, hands released, generic mumblings of comfort, we know, we know. Berry sighs, a pronounced, almost violent outtake of breath. "Well, the meeting is over, ayuh? And has it been a successful meeting? I don't think so!" she answers herself, that punishing tone. "Let me remind you, Jessie, of what we're trying to do here, to let Arnie himself tell you what happened. But we can't do that if we don't concentrate now, can we? We're asking for our Lord's help in this and that takes prayer and concentration and...ladies?"

"Faith?" Janie asks. Right answer, Gracie's guessing, ten points and an all-expenses paid trip to heaven for the housewives. She clears her throat, scowls, but says nothing. What would she say?

"Just what made the candle flicker, hmmm? I wonder now! Please try better next time not to make a sham of these special meetings, we were on the verge of something significant."

Gracie stares at Berry, jaw muscle working, twitching, hands squeezing her knees now, beefy and red. It's as though she drained the Maine accent right out of her speech and is talking like some multi-degreed *real* therapist, Gracie thinks. She looks over again at Jessie who has sat back down, head hanging, arms crossed around her chest, hugging herself. She's about the same age as Berry who seems so much older, Jessie diminished almost into a child.

Gracie rises off the pillows a bit uncertainly, but suddenly she doesn't want to be in this room another minute and she doesn't have to be, she reminds herself, the cleaning day is over.

"OK!" she tells them, all of them even Tia staring at her now, "I think I'll call it a night." Which is something her father said, right after dinner, retreating to that basement room; *I think I'll call it a night.* Her mother would spend the rest of the evening cleaning up, poking about the house, looking for more things to straighten, scrub, polish, rearrange, smooth over.

When Gracie returns to her room, their room, Shark Girl's and hers, it's still fairly early, well before midnight and sleep is out of the question. She walks over to the window and stares out into the night, opening it just a bit to let the cold salt air seep in. There's a light on in the carriage house, and for just a moment she is tempted to go out there, knock on his door. This is something a normal young woman might do, mightn't she? Just knock on a guy's door and he'd open it, a shy grin maybe—he'd be glad to see her this normal girl, this good face—and he'd let her in. But who is she kidding?

A knock on Gracie's own door and it opens slightly, Tia poking her head in, her grassy colored hair. Gracie moves away from the window quickly, but as if Tia's guessed what Gracie was staring at she says, "He didn't used to be so quiet, you know. Shark Girl's doing is what most of us think."

"Who?" Gracie asks lamely.

"Anthony, the yard boy. You're in her room so I figured you'd want to know a few things about her. Like, I never heard her speak a word, not one word. But somehow people knew what she wanted, you know? Creepy business you ask me. Couple months after she moved in, he quits talking, too."

She's saying these things and peering all around the room, everywhere but Gracie's face. "Tia," Gracie says, "look at me." She's as surprised as Tia is to hear these words come out of her and almost looks away herself, down at the floor, sliding her hair over the right side of her face, saving them both this embarrassment. But Tia does look, her cheeks flushing, and Gracie doesn't look away. "Why do they treat Anthony the way they do?" she asks. "Berry and Roma. They're so mean to him, especially Roma."

Tia rolls her heavily made-up mud colored eyes. Even her eyes are plain, Gracie's thinking, despite the mascara massacre and she'd still sacrifice several fingers to have this face. "Man oh man," Tia hoots, "Someone's got to catch you up on the household stories! Shark Girl now, she knew them all. Course, she didn't seem to much care, never came to the H.H. meetings, kept to herself mostly. But if she wanted something from you she had a way of digging up your dirt. And let me tell you, she knew your dirt! Don't ask me how. She liked Anthony though. I think she tried to heal him, that was her thing, supposedly. I never saw it myself, course. He had this little stutter sometimes only it must've backfired because one night he comes reeling out of her room and instead of losing just the stutter, next day he's quiet as dirt."

"But why do they treat him so badly?" Gracie asks again.

Tia steps further into the room, shutting the door behind her. Walks over to the bed, perches on the edge of it. "You mind?" she says. "This one's private." Motions Gracie closer. "OK," she whispers, her eyes shifting about the room, "like, what he did? He raped Roma!"

Gracie feels a churning in her gut, sudden sourness in her throat. She too plunks down on the bed, holding her head down between her knees.

"You OK or what?"

Gracie nods, still squeezing her head. This wasn't what she was expecting to hear. Not that she knew what she expected, but not *that*.

"Well, so Berry works out this deal where she won't press charges only he has to come work for her for three years like some slave; I'm not sure she pays him a cent. That way he's forced to remember his crime, be here at the scene of it and, you know, repent like."

"He *rape* raped Roma?" Gracie asks.

"What other kind is there?" Tia says blandly. "I don't know the whole story but there was penetration and penetration's rape in my book."

"But Roma seems to like girls better!" Something in her just doesn't want to live with this bit of news.

Tia laughs, a shallow, mean little tee hee. "Guess nobody told Anthony that! Look, like, that wasn't the actual reason I came in here. Berry asked me to find out from you what you thought about the meeting. She probably meant in the morning but I saw your light was on. I'm a night owl too. In fact I almost never sleep. When you sleep you lose your guard."

Gracie lifts her head up and frowns. "What do you mean?"

Tia shrugs. "Well, like, you're unconscious when you sleep, right? So things can happen when you're unconscious cause you're not conscious of them. I mean look at it this way," she starts, scratching her forehead then rubbing it fiercely. "Say there are other worlds around us, we can't see them but that doesn't mean they're not there. We can't see God but that doesn't mean He's not there, right? So God is good, OK, but what if in some of these other worlds, these entities, maybe they're not? If you're unconscious, it stands to reason they can just pluck you away and then you wake up and you're in no world you ever wanted to be in."

Gracie shakes her head. "Christ!" she moans, the way Roma would say it, trying it out on her own tongue. Maybe this isn't the whole story about Anthony! she thinks, Do I believe it from *this* person?

"Tia," she says, "it's late. I actually do sleep and I have to get up in the morning and mop the kitchen floor."

"Oh yeah," Tia grins, "Cinderella. Do you have a fairy godmother to take you away from all this? OK," she says, rising up off the bed. "Just so you know, Jessie isn't the pervert she sounded like. I mean, so her husband thought she was sleeping with her cat. So whose problem is that? The thing about Jessie, Berry's told us, she's an animalist. Animal Communicator, they're called, some of them even get paid by rich people, therapy sessions for their poodles. Jessie prefers animals to people and animals love her like she's one of them. Berry says probably in a previous incarnation she *was* one of them and they recognize her. Just watch her sometime. If there's an animal in the vicinity, it's all over that woman. Saw a crow land on her shoulder, cluck its head near her ear like it's whispering its heartfelt little secrets. Dogs chomping at the bit to bite you, barking, growling, if Jessie's around they lay down at her feet, quiet as a guppy. So her cat loves her, how not?" Tia shakes her head. "Husbands are so spooked, aren't they? I'd mention those other entities, just hint at them, warn him even about them and mine used to beat the you-know-what out of me. Go figure."

Tia walks to the door, turns around and stands there scrutinizing Gracie's face, her cheek, then quickly looks away again when she sees Gracie watching, her own sallow face flaming. "I don't mean nothing by it," Tia says softly. "Just that it reminds me of what he'd do if I was to ever go home again."

CHAPTER EIGHT

How I am Spending My Summer, July 16, 1994,
by Gracie McKneely:
Dr. Bender said I could call her Robyn but I can't, you know, not to her face. Dr. Bender has the most beautiful eyes in the world. They're so blue it's like you can dive into them, like in the ocean. Louis said what Dr. Bender has is grace. That she makes having a silver hook for a hand look like a fashion statement. Before you know it everyone will want one! Louis said. Louis said Dr. Bender tried out the kinds of prosthetic hands that look like hands but she found the hook more functional. That's Robyn, Louis said. Robyn, Robyn, Robyn....

The top find for my summer collection of the things I list but do not keep — human ashes! They were in a bottle bobbing in the shallow part where the sea is more pale, a brown bottle and a white note inside saying Here Lies Mom! That night out on the lānai (that's Hawaiian for patio) under a billion stars Dr. Bender (Robyn!) tells Louis and me a story about a woman in North Brookfield where she's from (that's somewhere in Massachusetts), who opened a bus station locker after her husband died and discovered photos of another woman. So instead of scattering her husband's ashes in the ocean off Cape Cod like he wanted she kept them in a shoe box under the bed for twenty years. It became the town scandal until her preacher finally said, Enough is enough, time to bury your husband, to err is human, to forgive is divine. I'm not God, says the woman, but it sure looks like I found a way to keep Harold in our bed.

The next morning is a good morning because it's the morning

Berry takes the van and the *girls,* she calls them, down to Portland to shop at the mall. There are no malls in Rock Harbor, or anywhere in a fifty mile radius. Some townsfolk, especially the wealthier ones from the surrounding towns waged a losing battle when the Wal-Mart came in, and now there's talk about a Home Depot. "You woulda thought a strip joint was trying to buy into the area!" Berry grumbled. "Mainers like to support Mom and Pop businesses, don't want to think they're the kind of folk they believe the rest of the country are. Fact is, for the most part we're 'bout as poor as a bag of nails. Fine for the rich to get all up in arms about the chain stores that save the rest of us some pennies. We go down to Portland once a month," Berry explained, "last Thursday of the month. Two hour jaunt," she said, "so if someone's got a birthday coming up, clothing needs, special treats, smell goods to slather on and whatnot, I tell them keep a running list."

Gracie is looking forward to having the house to herself. Those who will not be riding with Berry work early shifts, Janie at the Dunkin Donuts and Marie at Moody's Diner. Her head feels cluttered, too much input. The bizarre Haunted Housewives meeting (the Jesus Club as Roma called it!), seeing Jessie get broken down that way, the talk with Tia afterwards, her 'other worlds.' Is everyone borderline certifiable around here? Where she comes from people are mostly predictable, you know what to expect, one's about as boring as the next. The things Tia said about Shark Girl, and especially Anthony. Anthony. A chill plays up her arms, prickling the little hairs, thinking about how Anthony will be here today and everyone else gone. She watches him now out the kitchen window, sweeping the patio, picking up twigs and tree bits from the blow, Berry called it. "Come in off the bay last night," she said. "No rain, just that heavy mess of wind, kind of wind makes you forget how it is when 'taint any." And another thing: Berry seems to turn on and off her Maine accent like she's choosing whether to speak English or Spanish for the occasion. What's that about? Her own daughter speaks *Roma-ish* like this is its own language. *You dig?* She recalls what Roma said about Berry's mother, her séances, the automatic writing, and wonders if maybe there's such a thing as automatic *speaking*!

The phone rings and for a moment Gracie is wishing it's for her. But who would that be? Her mother, who else would call Gracie?

Someone outside this strange little household reminding her that she too can exist in the *other* world if she wants to, she just has to choose to go back. But her mother's house is not a choice anymore, Gracie knows this much at least. She decides not to answer it and listens to Berry's recorded message on the answering machine briefly welcoming whoever is on the other end, a few details about the boarding house, no space available presently but she'll keep a waiting list, then the names they can leave messages for. Berry has added Gracie McKneely to this list and for this Gracie is grateful; a sort of belonging — you are where your name is on the voice mail. The caller hangs up.

Gracie goes back to the breakfast dishes, scrubbing a soft-boiled egg coated saucer, several cereal bowls, cream-cheesed plates carefully by hand. Berry won't have a dishwasher, doesn't trust them, she says. *Eyes and elbow grease! Got to see the dirt to get rid of it*, she proclaims. It's a beautiful late fall morning, crispness of the air, mild breeze, sky intensely blue and cloudless. Hum of a few crickets still; still no killing frost. She watches Anthony remove his shirt in the sunshine. He's broom thin, no rippling muscles in that back just the ridges of his spine cutting down like the teeth of a comb, and something about the long, Gumby-like shape of him makes Gracie feel a little sad. Something so personal in it, him not knowing that she's watching, studying his thinness, the way he looks without his shirt on. He takes a red bandanna out of his back jean pocket, swipes it against his forehead then ties it around his head. This simple gesture. A *rapist*? She imagines the smell of his skin in the sun. A little sweaty maybe, berry brown scent still spicy from his morning shower, a man's kind of soap. Should she be frightened of him? A rapist for God's sake! Roma, those flashing eyes, barbed tongue, seems like she'd be the one to overpower him.

Gracie finishes the dishes, sweeps the floor then turns off the kitchen light and removes herself to the den. Berry's preferred routine is dust first then vacuum, but once in the den she finds herself at the bookshelves, studying their titles instead of wiping them down. It's the first time she's been absolutely alone in this house. Roma never came home last night and the van is gone. Most of the books are classics, what most people won't read these days, but you'd expect them in an older house that once was grand (its owner would like us to believe still is), set pieces in the antique maple bookshelves: *Pride and Prejudice*, *Portrait Of A Lady*, *Moby Dick*, the requisite Shakespeare collection, *Huckleberry Finn*. Gracie knows books, she's a professor's kid after all and her mother, former Democrat activist turned clean freak graduated from Smith with a degree in Political Science, honors yet! There were so many books in their house that to Maizey's annoyance they'd keep finding their way upstairs, out of place from the massive shelves Thomas had built for them in his basement den. Gracie doesn't mind being alone, involved in a book. She can lose herself, become someone else; she can be part of some other world in someone else's face. She can relax.

Gracie reaches for *Under the Milkwood*, Dylan Thomas, one of the more modern books in the shelves thinking she'll slip away to Wales for a half hour or so. The van won't return until later this afternoon, plenty of time to finish her cleaning routine. But as she pulls it down off the top shelf a folded scrap of heavily yellowed newspaper falls from behind it, fluttering to the floor in its dryness like an old leaf. An article about a band called the Head Shrinkers, photo of the lead guitarist young and hollow-cheeked and blond, arrogant grin. Beside him, a little in the background, what absolutely has to be a younger Berry Waters. There's no mistaking that muscled posture, the chiseled don't-mess-with-me face, her long pin-straight hair, darker here, but it's Berry-hair all right. The article, what you can still read of it, is telling everyone to watch for this Sixties Prototype *Acid Rock* band with its *dynamo* lead guitarist and singer: New On The Scene! Up and Coming! She remembers Roma's words, a "rumored" to be a blond father who had disappeared before she was born; didn't she say he was a rock musician?

Gracie hears the front door open then slam shut and immediately pops the newspaper back up on the shelf, Dylan Thomas on top. She's thinking Anthony and her heart is ramming about her chest like something unleashed.

But it's Roma who marches into the den, sneering at Gracie, the dust rag in her hand she had grabbed up again, just in case.

"Will you look at the cleaning girl! The cat's away and the mouse still won't play!" shaking her head, that electric hair. She's wearing low slung black stretch pants and a short purple sweat shirt, looks like she shopped for it in the toddler section, it's that small, squeezing against her pronounced rib cage, little stairwell of bones. Exposed belly tight and tiny as a baby's fist.

Gracie flushes. "I was thinking about reading for a while."

"Oh, an *intellectual* are we?" Roma flounces down onto the velvet overstuffed chair and Gracie remembers again the meeting last night, Berry Waters presiding over all like some self-ordained preacher, perched regally in that chair, a demented queen. Gracie shivers, sliding onto the couch opposite Roma, anticipating her further harangue. She'll take it sitting down.

"So," Roma starts, "what did you think of Liela?"

Gracie shrugs, tugging her hair down over her cheek out of habit. "I don't know, she seemed nice enough."

"*Nice*? Nice enough? God, you make her sound like one of the housewives or something, chicks with personality lobotomies, know what I mean? What's *nice* have to do with anything? Where you from anyway?"

"I told you, upstate New York."

"Oh, *hello*, that's narrowing it down. Upstate New York, now let's see we're talking maybe three-fourths of the entire damn state, a state big enough to suck up half of New England."

Gracie studies Roma, a slow, careful look. There's fresh unease here, a restlessness, petulance, anger. Beware, she's thinking, watch your step. "I was born in Hawai'i but we didn't stay there long," she offers, then immediately sees this was a mistake.

"Oh really? Born there? Well, Christ, that makes you way cool, doesn't it! An exotic infant-hood. Speak Hawaiian? Gagagoogoohulahulahula? So what the hell you doing *here*?"

"I work here," Gracie shrugs again, trying to fake a nonchalance she's not at all feeling.

"The *intellectual* cleaning slave? They don't have this kind of employment in *upstate*? Maybe you got to get a degree for such a desirable job." Roma shakes her head, yanks at a hank of her hair, newly dyed a tomato red this time, spidery spikes of it. "School is bullshit," she snarls. "All that rote spoon-feeding just so you'll pass some test and the school will look good, get more money. Has nothing to do with learning. How can you test learning? I haven't been back since I turned sixteen. Some of us are smart in other ways, ways that count in the scheme of things. School's where cruelty is bred, don't you know, how to survive it or become it. I'll tell you what, you don't have a life do you Miss Gracie Slave from *Upstate*? That's it, isn't it? You'd rather read about fake lives because you don't have one yourself. Why don't you come with me, we'll get that wicked face of yours tattooed. Then you won't have to hide it."

Now, normally a remark like this would make Gracie cringe, make her silent, shrinking into its hurt like a punch in the jaw; she'd have to work very hard not to let it show. This time it does something else.

"What about Anthony?" she says, surprising herself about as much as Roma.

Roma scowls. "What about him? You want we should get him tattooed too? He will, you know, if I ask it. He'll do whatever the hell I want him to do." She scratches her amber scalp viciously.

Gracie feels something catch in her throat, her voice falters but she plunges in anyway. "Tia told me he raped you. That's why he's working here, she said, as a punishment."

Roma rolls her eyes. "That skank is some mouth. She's too much of a loser to keep her own thing going so she gets into everyone else's. Rape? Jesus, what a drama queen. Tia and Berry. It's what *she* believes." Roma yawns, stretches, slides her eyes over Gracie's face, her neck, her chest, like the whole conversation is a bore to her and she needs to find some diversion. "OK, you want the story? We were both pretty toasted, I hardly remember. My mother tells him she won't press charges but he'll have to come work for her as penance, so he'd see me, be reminded of his sin." Roma grins. "Repent and shit! And, of course, she needed a yard boy."

Gracie's mouth dropping open, snaps it shut then it opens again. "But how can you do that to someone if he didn't really do it? I don't believe this!"

"Well I *was* a virgin, for chrissake!" Roma says. "So he did and he didn't, it's complicated. How old you think I am, anyway?"

Gracie shrugs. "Twenty?"

"Hah! Well there you go. I'm seventeen, *now*. Does the word statutory mean anything to you Miss Intellect? And I wasn't his first, he should've known better. Bled like a stuffed pig. Berry couldn't even get all the blood out of the sheets. She's making Anthony use those sheets out in the carriage house, remind him of his crime." Roma giggles then frowns. "It sets an example for other guys because this shit happens all the time. Girl doesn't want sex, guy gets girl high, maybe she blacks out and he nails her. Girl doesn't even want to have anything to do with guy and he nails her drink with a mickey and she's gonzo, his for the taking. You think that's fair? I'm telling you, Gracie, there's a lot going on out there to be steaming pissed about."

"But you don't know that really happened with you and Anthony!"

"My mother seems to think it did," Roma grins. "And it could've, that's the point."

"But Anthony didn't do it, you said so yourself and your mother's punishing him? What kind of justice is this? Punishing him because he *could've* done it?"

"This is Maine," Roma shrugs. "We take matters into our own hands here. Christ, you're getting to be a bit of a drag, sound like a broken record. *Anthony didn't do it!* You got a thing for this loser? Anyway, I didn't say he *didn't* didn't do it, I said maybe he didn't do it. Where else does he have to go? He was a throwaway kid just like all the other throwaway kids around here, nobody wanted him, no income, living from couch to couch, you dig? Couch surfing. Berry Waters rescued him. She should get foster care money or something. He's got a job now, a place to sleep, meals, how many throwaway kids get those things? That's why when I move out of this place I keep showing up again. Just so my mother knows it's MY choice. Anthony's mom, now there's a peach, she changed the locks on him. He called and she pretended she didn't even know who he was. Maybe she didn't, loaded all the time. And Gracie, folks think she's *nice*. Cashier at the QuickMart, always a smile for the customer."

Roma suddenly lunges forward in her chair, across the oak table and plants her lips on Gracie's mouth, all the while blades of her green eyes the color of wet grass hooked into Gracie's. Gracie pulls back, but not before she feels that electricity in the pit of her, that something yearning wants to knock her off her feet, lay her right down on this sofa. Roma sees this and grins. Pops out of the chair and in a second she's beside Gracie on the couch, whispering, "Don't be mad. I know I come off a little harsh but underneath I'm a pussycat really."

Gracie closes her eyes, her whole body quivering, shivering, can't stop it this crazy tremulous dance of her cells, the prickles of arm hair, her shoulders, neck, all lit up and exposed as a Christmas tree. Roma cups Gracie's chin in her hand, pulls her face close to hers, kisses her. Gracie feels a melting inside, something coming loose, feels like she might cry. Who ever touches her these days? Nobody touches Gracie, just her mother sometimes, fussing over her, correcting her, pulling her hair back off her face, letting it fall forward again.

Roma staring into Gracie's brown eyes her cat green ones, and Gracie imagines little grey doves or mice, a chipmunk, creatures of prey reflected in their golden iris. "Why don't you undress," Roma tells her, "and I'll give you a massage. I've got strong hands, my mother's hands, before her arthritis."

Gracie peers around the room furtively. "What if someone comes?"

Roma shakes her head. "You're so concerned with doing the right thing, Gracie. Dig this, no one around this place does the right thing, that's why they're here for chrissake! Just take your shirt off, we'll start with that."

Gracie, unbuttoning her shirt, fingers trembling, says, "It's just that I'm not sure how to do this."

"What, take your shirt off? You unbutton it, darling, just like you're doing."

Gracie sighs. "No, Roma, you know what I mean. I've never done this. Not the undressing. I mean I've never done…what I think we might do."

"You've never been with a girl before?"

She shakes her head. "No," she says faintly, "with anyone." Gracie can't believe she's admitting this, but how to hide it, these skulking fingers?

"You're a virgin!" Roma says delightedly, clapping her hands like Gracie is offering her favorite ice cream. "I had a feeling about that!" She reaches behind Gracie's exposed shoulders, sliding her unbuttoned shirt off her back, unhooking Gracie's bra, letting that drop to her waist. "So far so good," Roma says, gazing approvingly at her breasts. Gracie has good breasts, at least she has these. Any silicone to spare and it goes to her cheek. "Now stand up," Roma commands, her softer, huskier voice. "Take the rest off. You can do it, girlie! Think of it as therapy."

Gracie rises up off the couch, heart racing. There's something oddly compelling about this girl, her vitality, hardness, even rage sometimes, a driving force Gracie herself has rarely tapped into; but something else is there too, something hungry, a longing, loneliness maybe? Gracie knows *this* a little too well. She stands, gazing down at Roma, heart hammering inside her chest, then slowly she takes her hands hanging limp by her sides and covers her breasts, hugging her arms against herself like it's suddenly cold.

Roma frowns. "What's the matter? You scared?"

Gracie shakes her head, though it is a lie.

"I told you it's just a massage, or is that you're hung up about being with a girl?"

Gracie, her whole body shaking now, squeezes her arms tight across her chest. A memory, did it happen or was this too part dream? She's with Dr. Bender on the lava rocks at Lā'ie Point collecting 'opihi, Dr. Bender showing Gracie how the local fishermen pluck the little snails off the rocks, popping them into their mouths, ocean smashing around them, that fierce and tender blue. A wash of spray and suddenly Dr. Bender yelling at her to jump! The tide's rising! Get back onto the beach! And although Gracie is scared, terrified by these sorts of things really, natural disasters, nature when you come right down to it as out of her control as what happened to her face, Dr. Bender leaps first and when she turns back, holding out her arms Gracie does it, closes her eyes and she jumps.

Roma is waiting, that fiery impatient look of hers. "I just thought..." Gracie begins, but then she can't figure out how to finish this sentence so she starts over again. "This is like, I don't know, going to the doctor or something. I feel like I'm about to be examined." Gracie swallows, blinks, amazed at hearing herself say these things, actually attempting to express some sort of truth of *emotion* to Roma where normally, any sort of conflict, potential disagreement—Gracie at the heart of some uncomfortable situation and she'd fall into a dumbstruck silence. *Who am I?*

And this makes Roma mad. She snakes a hand through her hair, flinging back those pokey razored bangs. "Jesus Christ, what's the matter with you! How many people you think are going to invite you to do anything, anyway? They lining up to *get some* from Gracie McKneely? You think just because I like girls means *I* don't get turned on by a cute face too? I was just messing with you, see how far you would go. At the most you could have gotten a decent back rub. I'm in with Liela, if you haven't guessed it. Maybe you should go running out to your yard boy, Miss Cleaning Slave, he's got some experience popping a cherry!" Roma springs off the couch and flounces out of the den, leaving Gracie there cold.

Just jump? This time she couldn't do it.

That night Gracie is churning about her room, hurling herself down on the bed then up again, plowing through the dresser's drawers, yanking out Shark Girl's things figuring it's time to clean them up — but then again, *do I really want to stay here*? Roma's remarks stung. And normally this would be enough to make Gracie wilt, close up shop, throw in the towel and die one of the thousand little deaths she dies each time the horror that is her is pointed out to her — like she's going to forget? Not this time. This time she's mad, mad, mad. This time she wants to *do something*. It's as if she's a mad someone else — a Roma for instance? — looking to hurt her back. Where is Gracie McKneely, the butt-ugly girl who usually just takes it?

That's when she comes across it, a Christmas card buried under a bunch of paper, pencils, random books (she considers the books' titles, most about oceans, reef life, marine animals, then pushes these aside), rooting, jabbing, bits of this and that, coins, old tissue, all kinds of junk tossed into the bottom drawer of the dresser, this card at the bottom, wedged into a crack. *Mele Kalikimaka, Willa*, it says, picture of a nut-brown Santa, school of porpoises hauling a double-hulled canoe and in parenthesis, the scribbled hand writing — *If you still believe; From Susan Catherine and alvin-Travis*. Not *Love*, just from them. A photograph tucked inside, the woman in the silver framed picture on the dresser, lanky, short haired and sharp, with who Gracie is dead sure is the older version of the lead guitarist in the article she uncovered earlier: alvin-Travis of the Head Shrinkers, no mistaking that grin, that name. How many anemic-haired rock stars—Up and Coming!—are named alvin with a small *a*,Travis?

Math has never been her strong subject but two and two is as simple as it gets, or in this case two plus one! Roma stayed in tonight, at least Gracie never heard her go out, her usual production of stomping footsteps and slammed doors, as if she wants even the house to recognize her leaving it. They had avoided each other most of the rest of the day and now Gracie creeps quietly, triumphantly, out of her room, down the dark hall and up the back two flights of uncarpeted stairs to Roma's attic bedroom, clutching the photograph. I'm going to get her back, she thinks.

It's late, the rest of the house quiet, only the groaning of the old wooden stairs under her weight, sighing of the walls from the wind outside. Roma is playing music, some whiny soprano, a voice filled with complaint, the musky stink of scented candles or a kind of heavy-hitting incense drifting from under her door. Gracie knocks.

Inching open the door a crack Roma sees Gracie and scowls. Opens it enough for Gracie to enter through a waft of fragrant smoke, but she just stands there. Roma snaps, "You coming in or what!" Gracie forces her gaze on Roma's face. It's never been easy for her to do this, stare at somebody, her eyes locking into theirs and not immediately looking down, up, off to the side, anywhere but their face, their eyes peering at her face, thinking what she's sure they must be thinking. But she does it; keeps her gaze focused, Roma's own eyes cutting into hers.

Roma grins, evilly Gracie's thinking. Her guttural voice, "Come up for a fuck, Gracie McKneely? Change our mind, did we?"

"I know who your father is!" Gracie blurts.

Roma looks startled, stares at Gracie like she's crazy then throws back her head. "Hah, hah, hah, ain't you a kick!"

"Shark Girl's got a name!" Gracie growls, figuring she'll feed this girl the news morsel by morsel, smack that smile right off her face.

Roma shakes her head. "Christ, who are you, Nancy Drew? Duh! Shark Girl's got a name, like I thought she was born and her mother names her Shark Girl?"

"Nobody around this place seems to know her name," Gracie

says, a little defensively — this wasn't the reaction she anticipated.

"Nobody around this place has any brains, or haven't you noticed? They all like worship that slut, think she's so interesting, so fascinating, so goddamn different than their own sorry lives, so why let her have something as uncool as a name like the rest of us? I mean what the hell, I find that skank totally boring. Nothing about her life has anything to do with mine. Nothing about her can change my life. You think she can heal me, bleed *my* pain away?"

Gracie doesn't know what to say so naturally she says the wrong thing. She tells Roma her father's name is alvin-Travis and he played with a band called the Head Shrinkers and he may be married to or in some kind of relationship with Shark Girl's sister. "You told me he was a rock star wannabe!" she says triumphantly, pushing the Christmas card photo in Roma's face.

Roma shoves Gracie's hand away, staring her up and down, mean green eyes fixing on her cheek. She doesn't even look at the picture. And Gracie doesn't tug her hair over to hide her face. They stand stiffly face to face, two midnight warrior girls. Gracie is beginning to feel things break apart in her chest, tearing, ripping, slashing, a heaviness like rocks in her stomach, the blood in her veins cold. Still she doesn't budge.

"You're something else," Roma says finally, a little too quietly. "You actually believed I didn't know who my father was? His name, for chrissake? You think I'm an idiot or something? You've been here, what, under two weeks and you've got my life figured out?"

"You told me he ran off, deserted you and Berry you said, before you ever knew him, before you were even born."

"Yeahhhh, *hello*! But did I say I didn't know who the fuck he was, this daddy of abandonment? Christ Gracie, don't you get it? How ignorant can you be? I thought upstate New York was the Adirondacks, not fuckin' Appalachia. I can get Appalachia right here! Come on, girl, what difference could it make? There's nothing about that asshole's life that would make any difference in mine. You think knowing who he is could cure the fact that I've had to grow up in a loony bin with a Jesus-loving new-age *spiritualist*, believes she can have tea parties with the dead? Lazarus in spandex? You think *Strawberry*, my mother, could attract him back into our lives somehow, make him want to pay attention to me, make a bloody difference at all? Where's her *automatic writing* on the goddamn wall for that? Get your head on straight, girlie! Berry Waters was a groupie named Monica and she wasn't even particularly good at that. A loser surrounds herself with even bigger losers to make herself look better, know what I mean? Christ, sometimes I wish she'd of just aborted me, it was all the rage back then and Berry Waters was *trendy* if she was nothing else! Of course I know who my father is and I know it's too late for him to have any impact on my sorry life. Not him, not anyone. Certainly not some lame blond slut thinks she's part fish, whatever name you want to call her! Go to your room, Gracie McKneely, Cleaning Girl. The sad excuses for people around here, who needs humanity?"

Roma starts to close the door but Gracie sticks her foot in it, a bold move, already cringing expecting Roma to shut it on her toes. Roma's trembling, rage radiating from every square inch of her but Gracie is every bit as angry and she's not going to back down, not this time. "So why did Shark Girl come here then? Don't you find it strange? Renting a room from the person who had a child by her own sister's husband or whatever he is? Pretty weird coincidence, don't you think?" Her voice going higher and higher.

Roma shakes her head, smiles coldly. "This is Maine, Gracie *Drew Lysol* detective, there are limits on the possibles. Things that are coincidence other places just *are* here, maybe because there's less of us to bear the goddamn weight of them. Everyone knows what everyone else is about, and we all just mostly ignore it. Now, go to back to your room, scrub down this fucked-up house, do something, anything! But get your ugly face the hell out of mine, OK?"

So what Gracie does is she heads outside, heart stabbing against her chest like it wants to slice itself out of there, even her own heart would take one look at her face and flee. The carriage house light is still on and she doesn't know what she's going to say to him but she wants to see Anthony. There's a quarter moon, a thin cheesy light barely illuminating the walk to his door. Still dark enough she can jump back into the bushes, the beach rose, some thorny comfort! The air smells like popcorn, buttery and cool. Gracie sucks in a breath then raps lightly. Please don't say the wrong thing! she whispers on his behalf; if he says something, anything about her face, that's assuming he *can* speak, or even if he looks at her wrong she'll just die on the spot, crumple up and sink into the ground.

Anthony opens the door dressed in a pair of loose fitting jeans, no shirt despite the late fall night, that awkward Gumby body, hairy belly, his skinny hip bones sticking out like jug handles hitched to the top of the too-big pants.

"Hi," she says weakly.

He stares. Please, please, please! she's thinking, afraid to add words to the plea. If he does the wrong thing it's the end, and she may as well go back to her room, curl up in the bed that isn't her bed and disappear. That was the childhood fantasy: that she could curl up in her bed where no one could see her and she'd be safe. But he steps aside so she can come in, closing the door behind her, though peering first out into the darkness—is he looking for *them*? She follows him over to the only piece of furniture, a sofa bed pulled down for the night. Or maybe it's always like this, open and ready. Gracie blushes, a quick shy look at him, perching herself delicately at one end. Anthony sits at the other end, gazing at his hands, big hands, hands that could do...who knows what.

There's a naked light bulb on a fixture over the bed still swinging from his bumping into it when he sat down, a muted dancing yellow like a moth flitting about, the shadows it makes on the bare wall behind. She's afraid to look at him again, but then she does steal a glance, his skin sallow in the thinness of the light. He's staring at her too now, his eyes on her face, both sides of her face and she struggles not to pull more hair down over her cheek, cowering under his scrutiny. His eyes are fox-colored, pale eyelashes making him look all eyeballs, those dull reddened eyes.

"Want to listen to something?" he mumbles.

"You talk," she says lamely. Why did she think maybe he couldn't, given who he would have to talk to around here! His *employer* who thinks he's a rapist and her daughter who knows he isn't.

He laughs softly. "They tell you I don't?"

She starts to ask him more but he shakes his head, putting his finger against his mouth. For a second she imagines tasting him there, the flesh of his lips and her face goes hot. Anthony gets up, ambles over to the large cardboard box he uses as a table for his stereo, a lawn mower box, Gracie can tell by the picture on its side, slides a CD on. She expects something heavy metal or maybe rap or funk, but to her surprise it's classical. "Beethoven," he tells her, "Opus 18 string quartets. OK?"

Gracie swallows her amazement, nods her head, bit of a lie. Her father played classical, though not as often as her mother who put on something much worse, *easy* listening. "The world's a nervous enough place as it is," Maizey claimed. "Music should be a soothing background, not *dominant*." The kind of dentist office anesthetizes-you type music. Anthony's room, Anthony sitting back down on the other end of the sofa bed, nodding his head to the peaks and valleys of sound (her father's way of describing it), shutting his eyes so that now Gracie can really study him. Dark shagginess of his hair around that long face, like an eggplant his face, purplish from where his skin's broken out, high forehead and squared, flushed cheeks, the drawn-out chin. He looks even more the kid close up, she thinks. Barely has a beard, a few jaw straggles here and there and a puff of facial hair like a Hershey kiss right under his mouth. She wants to touch his face, but she doesn't. She's afraid he would then touch hers. Or maybe he wouldn't, and that would be worse.

"Timing's everything," he mutters, eyes still closed and rocking — she's guessing he's talking about the music. "Beats of silence important as the beats of sound."

Tries to respond, even just the affirmative *hmmm*, but her voice strangles in her throat. *Here I sit!* surrounded by this unexpected music, Anthony's stereo maybe the nicest thing he owns (the room seems hardly lived in, bare walls, conspicuous lack of everything but the sofa bed, several articles of clothing on the floor, tee shirts, shorts, a frayed denim jacket tossed onto his one folding metal chair, the stereo and plastic CD racks with their overflowing CDs on top of the box), and Anthony, Anthony! A *boy* — how old, she wonders? A *rapist* possibly? But maybe, could be...a friend? She hasn't had too many of these, wouldn't even know what the signs are. He's not kicking her out anyway, he opened the door for her and he seems comfortable enough, eyes shut, surging of the string Beethoven.

Gracie wonders if she concentrates really hard, becomes the face she knows must lurk under this other she wears, crouching down under the epidermis, dermis, the subcutaneous (sounds like subconscious, who but Gracie and a handful of doctors might consider its promise?), the deeper layer, this secret skin. If she concentrates on it, what could be possible: that under the scar she really is three blank layers of brand new skin, a clean slate. Then maybe, just maybe, she can try to relax.

Part III

Shark gods may be kāne (male) or wahine (female). Those described are invariably red, shining, light, or spotted to correspond with their sacred character, as allied to the gods. They are of human origin.... They are, in fact, regarded as spirits of half-human beings which, rendered strong by prayer and sacrifice, take up their abode in some shark body and act as supernatural counselors to their kin, who accordingly honor them as household divinities.

Nakuina; *Nanaue The Shark Man and Other Hawaiian Shark Stories*

CHAPTER NINE

Three years after the shark attack and Willa still has not spoken an actual word. She grunts at Robbie and me and he says *in your dreams* when she wants something and I jump to get it to shut her up. If I don't move fast enough her grunt becomes a high whiny shriek and then Jaycee, who's either catnapping, she calls it, on the living room sofa or taking a bath, comes wailing in and I'm the one who gets in trouble. I'm being *grounded* now, when I get into trouble, so I can't go to the Canteen, Jaycee says, our junior high school dance. And this is just bitchen with me, because when she makes me go to those dances—"Try to be *normal*, Scat, for your father's sake!"—I hang around the corners of the gym, all decorated with streamers and balloons and softened lights to encourage us to forget for this one night its daylight reality, a dank and windowless structure of grimy sweat and anatomical tortures, and if I'm lucky I slip out into the night when the chaperones aren't looking, out under the royal poinciana with its lustrous orange blossoms, the palm trees and the stars, the forlorn sky. *Forlorn* is a vocabulary word I learned last summer and so is *lustrous*, something my father made Robbie and me do, his attempts at our education in *normalcy*—look up a new word each day and use it in a sentence at dinner time. I remember how I used forlorn: "Evening is a forlorn time," I began. "Evenings make me feel like something is missing." Nobody said anything except for Robbie, who kicked me under the table, hissing that I made two sentences not one so I was cheating. I kicked him back. Father gave up on our vocabulary lessons after a month.

Folded up small as I can get under the royal poinciana, a sea horse, curled spine, hugging my knees to my chin, my big, bare feet splayed on the ground I think about growing up and proving myself to everyone, making anyone who was ever mean to me or ignored me or teased me or just plain didn't give a you-know-what about me, regret it. I'll transform, become beautiful; I do have potential, my mother's friend Luna says. I'll marry a handsome man and I'll *do it* with him, and this will make us two beautiful children, a boy and a girl. My husband will be famous, a movie star, someone who owns houses all over the world, *villas* (another vocab word—the sentence I used was: I wish I lived in a *villa*, far away from here!), and boats, and maybe we'd even have our own airplane. Maybe I'll marry one of the Beatles, George let's say, he looks cute *and* nice. We'll take the children to the kinds of places children like to go, the zoo, a month at Disney Land, and I'll sit around, *laze* around is how Grandma would put it, reading magazines, tanning myself in our villa's giant yard, squeezing lemon juice on my hair to streak it blond. My hair will have grown down to my *ōkole* and straight as straw; no way will I have to iron it or set it on guava juice cans to try and smooth the *errant* (another vocabulary word, I don't remember how I used it) waves out. Everyone will be jealous.

Once at a Canteen they played Roy Orbison's "Pretty Woman" and my ticket number was the one they drew to claim the 45 when the dance was *pau*. I told Jaycee I won it in a contest doing the mashed potato and the twist, because these are the kinds of things she expects to hear. Fact is, no one ever asks me to dance. I'm a head taller than every boy except for Ronald Wright who's a freak—picks his nose, his toes, chows down on the findings—and it's not like I'd want to dance with any of them anyway. Especially not Ronald Wright.

I go to Punahou School junior high and I'll be there for the real high school too in the Academy, as it's called, where Robbie is. It's a private school in Mānoa started by the missionaries, and our father has to work ever so many longer hours, Jaycee informs us (our mother went into her British phase about this time, mimicking the way she thought English people would speak—who could say why?), to pay for it. He stopped taking the taxi in to Honolulu from Kailua and started driving a used Ford (I don't recall the model, something with fins; everything seemed about fins in those days...), bought from one of *the boys* at work so he could take Robbie and me to school on the way. He gave our mother and grandmother the old Plymouth to use. He didn't offer it to Jaycee before, because when he let her use it she'd end up hightailing down Kalaheo to Kāne'ohe, shimmying her *haole*-hula at the Base. I guess he figured she wouldn't do this with Grandma there, besides which she's too *consumed* with Willa to dance anymore.

We leave in the early morning when it's not even fully light, just this hopeless bone colored sky. We're going to school after all, why should the sun even bother? My father switches the staticky radio on to J. Aku Head Pupule (roughly translated that's *fish-head crazy*) who's real name is Hal Lewis, Father said, on The Coconut Wireless. He laughs at Aku's version of things, his wry commentary on the goings on, my father calls it. (J. Aku Head may have been one of the first ever shock jocks, it occurs to me now, though without so much of the *shock*.) We don't talk much. Unless the subject is lawns or communists, our father pretty much has nothing to say these days. And you don't want to get him started on lawns or communists.

I'm finally growing breasts, small ones with large you-know-whats poking out. Jaycee is too consumed with Willa to notice, to take me to Liberty House, get me a training bra like the Others Mothers would. I'd *die* before I asked her to do this so I hunch over my shoulders, which is kind of the way I sit or walk anyway, a way of willing yourself back into the earth I guess, a tall people thing, comes from having to bend over to talk to just about anybody, and I wear a cotton camisole under my shirts. The straps of the camisole, in the right light and under a white or pastel blouse can look like a bra. But once Andy Moon ran his fingers down my spine when he sat behind me in English class, checking for a bra strap and he told all the boys I don't wear one. *Flat!* they accused me. *Ironing board!*

It has been determined that Grandma's move to Hawai'i is permanent, to help Jaycee with Willa, to help Father with us. Father and some of *the boys* from work built her a room by taking half our two car garage and just plunking down a plywood wall in the middle of it, hammering the thing in, making the one part into a bedroom with a real wood floor built over the concrete, louvered glass windows on the other side. The room isn't big, and Grandma had to put most of her stuff from Newwwwengland into storage. She whines about this, about not having her things around her to comfort her. There are plenty of her things around though, all her little figurines, *pretties* she calls them, watering boys and doughy-eyed girls in long dresses with puffy sleeves and painted sashes, her *Hummels*, swans with china flower necklaces, buggy-eyed porcelain dogs, the breakable sorts of things we're forbidden to touch but who would want to anyway? Maybe the littlest Connely girl, Carrie, who is eight, when she has nobody else to play with and she trails around after me. I don't mind. This bra thing, and the girls in school herding about the hallways, shrill gibberish like they're from another planet, giggling and shrieking, pretending to faint into each other's arms and all over Paul McCartney, the Beatle with the chubbiest cheeks makes me *pupule*. I just as soon play with Carrie Connely.

Sometimes I don't want to grow up. I worry about having to learn how to do things like calculate taxes, which my father gets paid to do by other people so it must not be a very easy thing or why would they pay him? And he's not exactly in a good mood when he does this for our family, either. *Democrats* are the reason there are so many taxes, he tells us. Things Democrat are equated with things Catholic in our family, worth a good hard roll of the eyes.

Growing up is overrated I'm beginning to think, other than growing up is the only way I'll ever be able to leave my house, which is a gloomy house. *Gloomy Gusses*, Grandma calls Robbie and me, always making us go outside, never letting us sit inside our sister's room to just talk to her, try and make her talk back. I wonder, has she forgotten how? Anyway, I don't even think Paul McCartney's cute. George is, but not to have a conniption fit over. In just a few years I'll want to *go all the way*, as we are starting to say, with John Lennon. But in the abstract, not actually imagining the doing of it, only that he's in love with me and everybody knows this. And only because it seems pretty obvious he's the smartest Beatle. Maybe I'll marry him instead of George, have a baby with him, Johnny if it's a boy, Johnnie if it's a girl. I wouldn't want to name a kid after myself that's for sure; my name is enough of a burden for *me* to lug around.

So here is what has become of Jaycee: our mother the shadow, floating in and out of my sister's room, for that's what Jaycee's and Father's room has become now, *your sister's* room. Sometimes you only know her existence by the sounds she makes, the tinkling of ice in her gin and tonics, which she drinks pretty much all afternoon and into the evening now, the running of water for her baths, her sighs and softly spoken somethings to Willa. Eel-like, slithering through the house, ungraspable. And Willa more and more demanding of everybody, though how she manages this without talking beats me.

"She's got your mother wrapped around her little finger," Luna tells me one day, waiting for Jaycee. Luna is really Louanna. She's part local *haole* and part *malihini*, Southern something; her mother was from Texas and Luna was born there, which is something she never tells anybody but we know. When you're local you're supposed to be born in Hawai'i. Luna is taking Jaycee out to lunch, shopping, and the beauty parlor. "A girls' day out," she tells me. "Cheer your mother up. You do understand, Scat," she whispers, bending down, motioning me closer, her perfumy neck. "Your mother isn't...well."

"Jaycee has let herself go," Grandma says. "Too skinny, *scrawny*," Grandma insists. "She puffs those Winstons like there's no tomorrow, drinks enough drinks so she won't barely eat nothing at all," Grandma whines. The doctor ordered Grandma to stop smoking the long brown preying mantis cigarettes because she developed a hacking cough that wouldn't quit and he thinks this might have something to do with it, but she's sneaking Winstons out of Jaycee's pack, I've seen her. Jaycee takes her marathon baths and half the time forgets to wash her hair, which is now cut short as short, anyway.

"Bloody hell!" Jaycee snaps. "Is it hair then I'm supposed to be thinking about, my poor little girl lying in her bed with just the one leg?" Accent high on *hair*, low on *then*, her British phase.

"Those Sassoon hairdos would be just the thing for you, Jaycee," Luna assures her as they head toward the front door. "Put some bounce back, frame your pretty face. A good haircut can make a world of difference."

Jaycee turns to me, wiggles her finger, a *you better listen to me* wiggle. "Watch out for poor Willa now, you hear me Scat? Check on her every fifteen minutes, understand?"

Poor Willa. When they're gone I open the door to Jaycee and Willa's room and stare at her, my eyes narrowed into little slits, like watching her out of my own personal pair of louvered windows. Willa Beever in that bed, her own hair long and blond and brushed something like a thousand times a day, by Jaycee of course. It's a kind of redemption (vocab word, don't ask me how I used it, didn't see much *redemption* those days!), an almost inhuman beauty to it, careening to a waist that will not budge like it's the hair on some statue, an idol, shiny as a thing to be praised, prayed to, *relished*, says Jaycee. Willa's hair hasn't been cut since That Day.

She stares back, unblinking. The TV's been moved into their room and it's turned on; no sound though, is Willa planning on going deaf, too? Lucy is wailing at Ricky but we don't know what she's saying. Ricky grabs at his forehead, *aieyiyi*! Robbie's gone up the street to spy on Alice Keamolemole, see if he can catch her undressing, Grandma's doing Grandma shopping at Liberty House and Kress, so it's just my sister and me, finally. Usually some adult is here. The doctor said not to leave Willa alone. "It appears she's not thriving as well as we'd hoped," he said. No one can tell us why. "They still don't have a clue," Father said. *Still,* like something's going to change, like after three years she's going to suddenly up and talk and demand them to attach that fake leg so she can run out and play; like she's just some normal eleven year old girl and not Willa Beever, dictator of our household. I doubt that Cuban Castro guy (that *commie*, says Father) could be *this* bad, ruling the roost, as Grandma would put it, without even a voice.

Last time we were alone I tried the big sister buddy approach, the remember when we did this and that? sort of thing to get her laughing maybe, get her thinking back on how much more fun life used to be when she talked, when she was Chatty Cathy. But then Grandma came in, said to me, "Are you some kind of a fool or something? You'll get her remembering what it was like having both her legs!" As if she's going to forget.

"I know what you're trying to do Willa, you can't *psych me out*," I say evilly. "You won't let them give you that prosthesis leg because it will make you almost normal, so then you'll have to walk and talk and you'll be just like the rest of us, won't you? The household will stop jumping to your every wish. You're not so special anyway, you know, it's not like you're a princess or something. You're just a regular girl whose leg got bit off by a shark. But you lived, so everyone thinks it's a miracle. And you don't want to talk because then they'll know you're no miracle, you're just plain Wilhelmina Beever, without a leg!" Her face is getting red, eye balls big and frantic and rolling about, pupils like blackheads over her puffed-out cheeks. She's trying to peer around me, out the door to see if anyone else is home; if she does that squealing thing, will someone rescue her and get me in trouble?

"Nobody's home," I tell her, "no one to come save the little crippled princess!" The more I talk the meaner I feel. I'm mad at her, I can tell you that, and it comes tumbling out like something unleashed, how she's faking it and all to make Jaycee belong to her, her own personal mother and so what are Robbie and I supposed to do, huh? Who is going to be our mother, Grandma? No way! Grandma's too old and cranky and Jaycee's cranky but she's pretty and anyway she *is* our mother too! Robbie's and mine! Willa's doing it on purpose, is the thing, and suddenly I lunge toward my little sister and I yank back the covers to expose *it* dangling out of her lacy Barbie nightie, that new doll so naturally it's Willa who gets to have this doll and everything associated with it, dream house, dream car, dream boyfriend, dream make-up, the nightie to dream in, dreaming Barbie maybe, two long and perfect plastic legs! It's completely healed now, rounded and firm, a loaf looking thing, pink scar like a giant ridged finger stretching over it where they sewed her up, where they had to punch in all those staples. I know surgical staples are different than what you slam down to stick pieces of paper together, but this is all I can visualize when they talk about Willa's staples, Willa's leg quivering under Mrs. Bartell's, my homeroom teacher's, mean black staple machine. I've heard that when a person loses a limb, the Monkey Man say or some other soldier, for a long time they still feel it, feel their toes wiggling maybe, in the air around it. This little piggy went to market! I think meanly, think about tickling the emptiness around her stump. But I don't, because suddenly I feel a little sick. I swallow hard. Stare at my little sister, where her leg once was.

Willa starts to cry and I can see I've gone too far, I've done the forbidden thing, *stepped over the line*, as Jaycee will say. I've exposed what Jaycee keeps hidden from all eyes but her own. I quickly slide the covers back up, tuck them around Willa's neck, ever so gently. "Geez Louise, have a conniption fit why don't you," I tell her, which is a thing we say when we're joking around. Willa might've laughed three years ago, but right now I don't think it's too funny either. She's making these stifled sobbing noises, shoulders shaking like she should be heaving out great long wails but they're choked up, muted, a voice unused. I step closer to her, put my hand on my sister's head like Jaycee does to me, patting it, the top of her scalp warm and oily feeling. "It's not so bad," I tell her. "It doesn't look that bad, honest. Like a leg without a knee and the bottom part, but there's still some leg there, Willa, the top part's there. And you've got the other one. You're pretty as ever, honest, your face is much cuter than mine. That's the honest truth, Willa, cross my heart and hope to die! Even with one leg you're cuter than me."

She just keeps making those strangled throat noises, and something deeper from her chest, like even her heart is crying.

Then I get this really terrible thought, so terrible I can't even think it through at this point, not for many, many more years, and then when I do it packs such a painful punch I'm not sure I'm ready to consider it even then. What if it's not *Willa* doing this to Willa, making herself into a helpless baby again, can't talk, can't walk, can't dress or bathe herself, can't do anything at all but lie there in her Barbie nightie, cared for by our mother. What if it's Jaycee who is doing it? Making Willa feel like she lost a whole lot more than just her leg. Making Willa feel like she has nothing left in her life, except what she can depend on Jaycee to give her. It's like Jaycee's become Willa's God in some new world that only the two of them share. Jaycee *is* God, the one making the rules. That's when you got to wonder: If there really is a God, how could he have let this happen?

"He must've had his reasons," Luna says, after she's brought Jaycee home and we're sitting in the living room, Jaycee with her feet in those slick pointy-toed patent leather flats, stuck up on the polished wood coffee table where *our* feet aren't allowed — that's what she calls it, the polished wood table. Jaycee sprays enough Pledge on its surface to make it gleam but then forgets to wipe it, and there are these clear little bumps here and there, the wood looking like it sat out in the sun too long, wood skin blisters. I had asked about God, my eyes bitter and locked into Jaycee's, because when she went in and checked on Willa she came storming out—"She's in a state! She's in a state!"—and slapped my face. Luna sat Jaycee down, pushing gently but insistently against her shoulders. "I'll fix you a drink," Luna said, the magic words around here.

Out comes Luna through the sliding Japanese door bearing the tinkling gin and tonic, crushed and rounded ice shards winking through the glass like little fish eyes, the metal bottom of the ice tray dumped into my mother's Pali Palms hi-ball glass. Rub my hand against my throbbing cheek, refusing to cry, and I'm not going to back down either, not this time. There's a stirring of something inside me—Luna tells my mother later it's the woman I'm to become. I feel this hotness and this MAD sort of thing, and a helplessness too. I'm beginning to grow real breasts, after all, and my own mother won't notice. Little cone shaped ones, and now I'm thinking I don't need Jaycee to take me to the Liberty House: I can save up my 50 cents allowance each week no matter how long it takes, I can babysit the McPherson brats on the other side of us, the ones who wah wah wah all the time and I can earn my own stupid bra money. That's what I'm thinking, glaring at my mother, eyes hot and forcing back the tears. "So? God is a *gentle* god, you said," I spit out at her. "How does a gentle god let a shark bite off a little kid's leg? Maybe the Hawaiians are right. Maybe that shark was somebody's *'aumakua* who's got it in for this family because it thinks Father forgot the Hawaiian in him."

"Oh, for heaven's sake, Scat, you've all got about as much Hawaiian in you as I've got poodle! We have no rights to those myths. No *'aumakua's* out there scouting about for this Beever bunch! Your father's Hawaiian blood could fill his big toes. And it was him who taught you those God things, not me. Being a Christian is the *normal* thing, Scat, goddamnit; it's more important to your father to *look* normal than actually believe in it! Personally I've never bought into it, that there's anything going to save us."

"So keeping Willa covered up all the time is normal? Hiding her stump? And what about that fake leg they used to talk about? It's been three years. Maybe if Willa could walk again she'd talk again."

"Prosthesis," Grandma corrects me; she's suddenly in the room too, back from her shopping, hands planted on both of her pudgy hips like a behemoth pail. Grandma loves a good fight, drawn to one like flies to a picnic, her own way of saying things. Luna rises, she always makes a quick exit whenever Grandma comes into the room because this means there's going to be even more trouble. "Well," Luna says, "I must be going, get dinner on. You all be good now, you hear?" She says this to Jaycee, smacking a kiss on her forehead—a dumb expression, *you all be good now, you hear*? As if anyone judges these things in an adult. From her Texas roots, Father says.

Jaycee waits for the door to slide closed behind Luna, then she rises slowly up from her sitting position on the sofa, carefully, like she's really old, worn out, and painstakingly lifts her drink off the polished wood table. She stares at it thoughtfully, her hollow eyed contemplation, then turns to me, scowling, green eyed darts aimed straight at my chest. I hunch my shoulders.

"Get your grandmother to take you shopping for a brassiere, why don't you," my mother hisses. "Instead of she's always shopping for herself. You look like bloody hell, Scat, are you trying to advertise yourself? Look *cheap*? We're raising you to become a lady and a lady doesn't broadcast her bosom! Your father will have none of that, I'll tell you. He'll wash your mouth out with soap until you can't even speak to say the terrible things you said to your sister. And don't give me that look young lady, because I know. You think I don't? Willa doesn't need to have some damn prosthesis if she doesn't want one. I'll do her walking for her."

All I had wanted was my own room. No symbols, no dreams.

CHAPTER TEN

The thing about wearing a bra is boys like to snap the back strap on you. They think it's funny, and Luna says it's their way of letting you know they know you exist. It was Luna who finally took me shopping for one, came over on a Saturday morning. I was in my pajamas watching Flintstones and she said, "Get dressed now, sister-child, you and me are going to take a little trip uptown to Liberty House." Since then, whenever she comes over to visit Jaycee, Luna always spends some extra time with me, asking me about school, friends, calling me sister-child, a Texas thing, polite in that grown up sort of way but I think she means it. She never had kids of her own; Jaycee said she couldn't, something about her plumbing and then she got *divorced*, which is whispered in my neighborhood even in 1965. 1965, a couple years after President Kennedy's assassination, a heated up summer in Alabama, the Civil Rights March, Martin Luther King's *I have a dream*, but in Hawai'i what I am trying to figure out is how to survive junior high school and my own altered dreams, a little sister who's become a mute.

Luna waited outside the dressing room at Liberty House and the sales lady did too, it would've been really embarrassing to have them in with me, and they instructed me behind the curtain what a good fit should be. I struggled awkwardly with the various bras, red faced, twisting their backs around to my front, fumbling with their clasps then tugging them front-side again. I told Luna and the sales lady when I thought I had a good fit and Luna told the lady we would take two size 32A (least I didn't have to start with a *double* A or a training bra—figured I was well enough trained at that point!), one for when the other was in the wash, Luna said. They have a light fiberfill kind of a lining and I look more *developed* in them, like a real teenager.

Afterwards we sidled over to the lunch counter at Kress's and Luna bought me an egg salad sandwich, chopped up egg and mayonnaise piled so high the white bread and the lettuce become one soggy piece with the rest. My favorite since we hardly ever have eggs in the house—breakfast is Sugar Pops for Willa (finger food Jaycee calls it, Willa still refusing to use a spoon or fork), Corn Flakes for Robbie and me, Shredded Wheat for Father, dry toast and weak coffee for Grandma, nothing for Jaycee who makes it her rule not to eat before noon, she says, though occasionally she'll fix pancakes from the Bisquick box for the rest of us, whenever she gets to thinking maybe a nice breakfast will *cheer things up*. Those are the good mornings, when she thinks we need cheering.

Then one day I become a *real* woman, gym class (P.E. we called it in those days), changing back into our regular clothes and when I saw the blood all over my underwear, running down my legs I felt weak, like I'd pass out, crunched over the toilet. It had this smell like no other blood. I didn't think there'd be so much, a rivulet of it racing down toward my knees and my gym shorts were soaked through— luckily they're navy blue so nobody noticed. I began to cry, because surely this was not *normal*, bleeding like a pig? When they hunt wild boar in the Ko'olaus, they stab them with knives and they bleed like there's no tomorrow. Somebody told Miss Benjamin, the P.E. teacher, that someone was crying in the girl's bathroom. I had braced my feet up against the stall so they couldn't tell by my white sandals it was me and sobbed.

Miss Benjamin never liked me much; she's everything I would never be, a former Olympic gymnastics finalist, small and lithe and muscular and coordinated. She liked girls like Brenda Dow, who weren't afraid to Get In There! Not someone whose mother writes notes saying just in case I really do have Marfans, just in case my heart was fragile I should not have to do anything strenuous.

Miss Benjamin figured out pretty quickly who I was, said, "You shouldn't be crying over *this*, Susan Catherine Beever, you've got The Curse, that's all. Every woman gets it. You're a woman now." She's saying this through the closed stall door, my feet still up but she made me tell her what's wrong and in between great gulps of sob and breath I told her I thought I was maybe bleeding to death.

And then something was really wrong because I just couldn't seem to stop crying. I'd hold my breath, squeeze my eyes shut, slap my hand over my mouth like I'm trying to smother the sobs but under my eyelids I could still see all that blood flowing out of me, taking everything from me, things I wasn't even sure I had yet, the future Scat Beever floating down into that toilet, to wherever the Mānoa toilet water goes, the Mānoa stream maybe, Ala Wai canal, Waikīkī beach, out to the middle of the ocean where the sharks are.

Miss Benjamin sent me home with a note to my mother in a sealed envelope she instructed me not to open, but I did anyway in the back of the Plymouth, my grandmother driving. I could see her beetle-eyed scowl in the rearview mirror, having to drive all the way from Kailua, *over the Pali and everything!* she said, to bring me home.

Dear Mrs. Beever: Please instruct your daughter about the facts of life. She went into hysterics today when she got her menstruation for the first time. Mahalo, Bonnie Benjamin. P.S. Susan Catherine needs to pay attention when we play field hockey. She is a goalie so she won't have to run around much, but she must be daydreaming out there as she lets everything go past.

I balled the note up, stuck it inside the pocket of my skirt and told my mother they sent me home because I was sick to my stomach. She put her hand on my forehead; "Bloody hell, you don't feel warm to me, Scat, no fever here."

Bloody! I'm thinking, the blood the blood the blood.

"Must be that stomach flu going around," said Grandma. "It's a stomach bug so why should her head get hot? Best she just stay right here until we're sure she's better, because I'm not going to drive all the way up over that Pali and back again just to bring her home."

Six months ago a box of Modess had mysteriously appeared in my bottom bureau drawer along with a sanitary belt, no instructions, no explanations. For days I wondered whether to mention these to my mother, at dinner, the only time I was guaranteed to see her long enough to have an actual conversation, the only time she wasn't either moving in and out of Willa's room, in and out of the bath tub, in and out of her own bed or off and on the sofa for her catnaps. But what would I say? My father peering about the table silently, mostly at his food; Robbie darkly contemplating the space above all of our heads; my mother's occasional attempts at animation, at a normal Donna Reed dinner hour: *Well, how did everybody's day go!* Grandma saying, *Pass me this, Pass me that* and I say, *Oh, by the way, someone put a box of sanitary napkins in my dresser drawer, anybody here know something about that?* Eventually I stopped thinking about the Modess, what it might say about what my mother saw in me. Was I growing up in her eyes? One of her little beavers becoming a big beaver? Was this a good thing? Would it free my mother from any further need to be a mother to me, her *ticket to ride...*?

Now I go into the bathroom, shut and lock the door, check then recheck the lock, jiggling the door knob making sure, and I put these on, awkward at first, threading the pad's little tails through the silver clips of the belt, attempting to yank them snug against me, hiding whatever is happening down there. And then I go to bed. Just like my mother.

A few weeks later something else happens that proves I must be growing up. I get kissed. I've sort've been kissed before, but more out of a kind of obligation. Leslie Kam's make-out party, and what you're supposed to do at a make-out party is make out. We obligingly followed Leslie and her steady, Noki Sakamoto, down to Kāhala beach like this was just another party game, spin the tail on the donkey, red rover red rover come over come over. Everyone paired off with everyone else, which left me and Toby Chong together because we were both tall. Toby was a little shorter than me, but not by much. I'd been stuck with Toby before, P.E., those excruciating last two weeks of seventh grade when we had to learn ballroom dancing which meant we had to have gym with the boys. As if P.E. wasn't humiliating enough for spazzes like me. Thankfully Ronald Wright wasn't in that class. Toby at least picked his parts in private.

Toby and I lay on the sand along with everyone else, under a splash of moonlight bright as paint, and he shoved his lips dutifully against mine, mashed them around a bit, tender terror of his tongue slipping about my clenched teeth, then he released and that was that. Mostly I tasted his Bazooka bubble gum. I sat up bolt right on the beach so Toby Chong wouldn't imagine he had any obligation to do it again.

This time it was different. I was home alone one Saturday evening, Grandma and Jaycee had been invited to a Ladies Fashion Dinner with Luna at the Pali Palms. "She's trying to get in good with Grandma," Jaycee said. "Can't imagine why." Father was on the mainland doing what he does and Robbie was somewhere else, so I was assigned Willa duty, which is as good as being alone. "No funny business!" Jaycee warned. "Fix her a TV dinner, turn on the TV if she wants it, that's it."

I didn't mind. Recently Father had bought us a second TV —this was unheard of, a second TV!—since our first had taken up permanent residence in Jaycee and Willa's room. I planned to watch all the things my parents wouldn't usually let me watch, The Twilight Zone, Route 66, Hawaiian Eye, whatever I could find they'd object to. "No violence," Father would insist. "There's enough of it in this pinko world." Jaycee would say, "Bloody hell, you'll get one of your dreams, Scat, watching those kinds of things." But I stopped telling them about my dreams when Jaycee stopped coming to me when I called out in the night. In the morning Grandma would just analyze it, and then she'd tell Jaycee I needed help. "If you catch my drift," said Grandma, "of the psy-cho-log-i-cal kind," as if breaking it into syllables meant I couldn't figure the word out. If Grandma's family had money, and if she had been born in a different time, and maybe if she had been born a man instead of Grandma, she would've gone to college, she told us—"Become a psychiatrist, listenin' to folks problems, telling them what to do." And then she'd be living somewhere else, not in one half of our garage. "You can bet on it," Grandma snarled. She'd have been good at the telling them what to do part.

A couple weeks ago they took Willa into Honolulu to see a specialist of some sort, some doctor from San Francisco interested in Willa's case. They thought he'd be looking at Willa's leg, or where her leg used to be, but he said, peering almost belligerently, as my mother would later tell it, over his glasses at her and my father: "That fish bite is history. Physically your daughter is right as rain. You could have her fit for a prosthesis, she's healthy as you and me. It's entirely psychological," he said. "She doesn't want to walk and she doesn't want to talk. She's made a decision not to be well. She's getting something from this behavior. Our job is to figure out what that is, then convince her there are better alternatives. Three years is too long for this to be some sort of lingering internal damage from the shark attack. Regular counseling isn't enough," he cautioned. "She needs to be in an amenable setting. My clinic in San Francisco could work with her, if you're interested. I'd like to give this one a shot."

"No!" shrilled Jaycee that night. "Bloody hell, no!" Father pleaded, "We have to do something! This is unacceptable, letting her lie around in a bed day in and day out, what will people think? That we're not even trying? And what about school? How long will they keep sending a tutor out here, do you think?"

"She'll let us know when she's ready, she'll tell *me*," Jaycee said. "*Amenable setting,* for crying out loud. Anyway I can teach her, we don't need some tutor around here. In fact, I don't want that tutor anymore, a busybody that one is, always wants to know what we're doing for Willa's *condition*. I'm going to call the school first thing tomorrow morning. My daughter doesn't need a tutor, she's got me. I've almost got a college degree, if you'll recall, just a year away from one. What good it would have done me, God only knows. I'd have still been ironing your shirts. But I can teach my own child, thank you very much!"

"A *junior* college," my father sputtered. "One year toward a two year degree!"

"Yes, well," Jaycee cut a long fingered hand through her hair, "so that's half done now then, isn't it?"

"A degree in home economics!"

"Well bloody hell, that's come in handy around here, hasn't it? Taking care of your home, your kids, your goddamn shirts!"

Then things got weighted, the heavy silence that inhabits our house for days after one of their arguments, like it's its own life force, some*one* to be reckoned with, spoken to—only what could we say to this silence? Father watering the lawn more and more till you'd think he was drowning each blade of grass individually, purposefully singled out for this torture by hose. I can see them curling down under his harsh shoot of water, tender fat little blades of *mānienie grass*—enough, enough, we confess! we let the crab grass in! Jaycee a fixture in the room with Willa, even taking her own meals in there lately, and Grandma, sour as a turnip, whining about how none of us would've managed in this house if she hadn't moved from Newwwwengland. Robbie, sixteen, mostly someplace else. The one who got away.

Except tonight, when I guess he was supposed to be at home, because there's a knock on the door at eight o'clock, just when I'm settling in to watch Route 66. *Get your kicks, on Route 66*! I can see through the louvers in the stoop's yellow light Paul's tall blond head, his hair cut in one of those floppy Beatle cuts, only he would call it a surfer cut. He surfed, and all the girls thought he was *cute, bitchen,* soon to be *groovy,* a *stud* and a *babe.*

"Robbie's not home," I said, opening the door just a crack. I was in my pjs already, my pale pink baby dolls, all settled in with a bag of Maui potato chips and a bottle of icy cold root beer, and I didn't particularly want him to see me that way.

"Yeah?" Paul said, poking his face into the crack in the door right above mine. "So you're going to have to let me in to wait for him, cause I'm supposed to pick him up here, we're going to Scott Oleana's party."

I frown. Peer around uselessly for something to put over my pajamas. "Wait a minute," I say.

"Why should I? I can see you're in your jamies, so what? You don't have anything I haven't seen before, you know." He puts pressure on the other side of the door, pushing harder, and I step back and let him in, face coloring. My legs feel like long strandy noodles leaking out of the frilly short bottoms of my baby dolls; feel like some oversized lollipop standing in front of him and now I hate these baby dolls, something Grandma bought me that I felt I had to wear since she usually doesn't buy us kids much of anything.

I go back to my show, sitting cross legged on the sofa with a zabaton pillow covering my knees. Figured he'd sit over in one of the stuffed chairs or even wander into Robbie's room to wait, but he sits on the sofa, opposite end, worming his hand into my bag of chips I had slung onto the coffee table in front. "Can I have some?"

I shrug, "You already are, aren't you?" I try to concentrate on

Route 66, a car chase, sirens blaring. My cheeks get hot again though because I remember I'm not wearing a bra, duh! who would in baby dolls, but Paul's sitting there, staring at me instead of the TV. To my recollection he hasn't looked at me since I was ten and he was thirteen, and one day he and Robbie shoved me into the hall closet and wouldn't let me out until I howled for Jaycee. That's the kind of dumb stuff boys do when they're thirteen. "Take a picture, why don't you, it lasts longer," I tell him, blushing furiously. Why would I say that stupid thing to a sixteen year old? He'll think I'm *so* immature.

Paul laughs. "You're better looking than you used to be, Scat, I never noticed before. You'll be in high school soon, the Academy, yeah? Few months, eh?"

I shrug. "Duh!"

He leans in toward me, close enough I can smell the potato chips on his breath, and something else. Something sharp and chemically sour, the way Jaycee's gin and tonics smell in her mouth when she's had too many of them. "You gonna be a stuck-up snob like the rest of those high school bitches?" he whispers.

I suck in my breath. That's not a word we use much yet, *bitch*, and it took on a sort of new and dangerous air right then, hanging teasingly brittle between us. He grins, still close to my face and I detect that something else on his breath again, that smell I'm very familiar with, a smell that's become as common as the perfume my mother wears to try cover it.

"You've been drinking booze!" I tell him inanely.

He laughs again, delightedly; hah hah *hah*, up on that last *hah* like it's some kind of question. "You're not so innocent are you Robbie's little sister? And not so little either, not anymore. Anyone else home besides your lame baby sister?"

"She's not lame," I say hotly. We Beevers still rise to each other's defense when under attack.

"I don't mean lame as in *lame, stupid*, I mean she's crippled. Too bad, because she's got a *boss* face, like Kim Novak."

"You think Willa looks like Kim Novak?" I ask him. I feel a twinge of something. Willa still gets to look like a movie star whether or not she ever speaks another word! It occurs to me that I'm sitting on this couch having a conversation with one of my brother's friends, a *high school* boy; every girl in the eighth grade would be jealous if she could see me. I swizzle my bangs back off my face, blow them upwards out of the corner of my mouth, something Sandra Dee might do.

"You should grow your hair, Scat. You could wear it in a flip. You'd look bitchen, like Annette Funicello maybe." He stretches out his legs, bare feet—his slippers left outside our door as in any polite Hawaiian household—sticking them up on my mother's polished wood coffee table, sliding them close to where my hand is reaching for the bag of chips. Then he nails my fingers with his hairy ankle, pressing down hard so I can't move my hand off the table. He grins, "Got ya!"

I try to pull away and as I do he slips up closer on the couch, and I realize bending over like this, my hand on the table, he can see down the top of my baby dolls. I thrust my other hand protectively against my shirt.

"What you doing there Robbie's little sister, copping a feel? I told you, you don't have anything I haven't already seen. Don't you believe me? That I've seen girls boobies before?" He lifts up his leg, freeing my hand and I sit upright, glaring at him, my heart pounding a wild and dangerous dance in my chest. "Stupid head!" I tell him. "*Homo*!" I don't know why I said this, other than it's supposed to be the worst kind of an insult and stupid head wasn't cutting it. *Stupid head*? God, even my tongue isn't as quick as the pretty girls, barbed remarks like they were sharpened on their very own tongue blades. And anyway, personally I don't see why *homo* is so bad. A homo supposedly loves another boy and, far as I can tell, it's not like there's any extra-abundance of love in the world. I mean, who cares?

Paul just laughs, harshly. "I doubt it!" he says. "You know how many babes I've had? Guess, just try and guess how many girls are *stoked* to be with me, how many I've gone all the way with! And the rest I've gotten onto third base." He's sitting very close and I smell the alcohol smell on his breath, sort of sweet and rancid all at once. "You ever been kissed, Scat?" His voice low now, full of that heated up breath, an engine idling, ready to rev.

The skin on my neck prickles, thinking about Toby Chong on Kāhala beach.

"I could show you how, teach you, so you'll know what to do when you go to the Academy next year. It's a favor to you, I'm offering it as your brother's friend. There's not a high school babe who wouldn't want to be you right now. They all want me to kiss them."

"You're stuck-up," I say helplessly, his tan face looming closer and closer, weaving about in front of mine like some flesh balloon. "Anyway I've been kissed before," I inform him. "It's no big *D*."

He sticks out his tongue, wagging it in front of my mouth, plum purple and reeking that boozy stink. "Bet you haven't been French kissed though. Ever have a boy's tongue down your throat?" And then he's doing it, sticking his tongue in my mouth and pressing his body in close against mine, so tight I think I'm going to suffocate under him, his mouth completely covering mine, his dog tongue lapping at the back of my throat like some doctor's fuzzy wet Q-tip checking for strep.

"Mmmph!" I go, "*Yech*!" But he's pushing me further down on the couch, his hand playing with the top of my baby doll shirt, moving down—roving hands, the girls at school call these—and my mind is growing this numb sort of cloud over it; I'm scared to death on the one hand, but something in me doesn't want him to stop, thinking about all those jealous girls. *Boss* Paul Brooker and Scat Beever? I imagine him walking down from the Academy at lunch every day just to see me, we're holding hands by the lily pond maybe, staring into each other's eyes. Brooker and Beever. Mrs. Beever Brooker? The entire eighth grade would know about it!

Suddenly there's a long howl from the next room, Willa demanding something, baby sister to the rescue just as Paul's hand slides over the cone bare top of my braless little bosom. "Jesus!" he leaps off me, off the couch, slamming against the polished wood table, chips blowing across the floor like leaves. "What the hell is that?"

"My sister," I say, flaming cheeks, sitting up and swiping my hand against my mouth like I can remove it, the evidence. "She wants something."

"Jesus!" he repeats. "No duh, sounds like someone's croaking. Tell your loser brother I went ahead to the party without him, eh?" And Paul Brooker, scarlet faced, stumbles back out the front door. Doesn't even offer to help pick up the chips.

I go into Willa's room, my hands crossed over myself like I'm hiding something. "Thanks a lot!" I say sarcastically, like maybe I mean it, maybe I don't. She's staring at me, funny sort of, like she's on to something, somehow she knows. But how could she? She doesn't move from her bed unless our mother's here to move her. "You want to watch the rest of Route 66 with me?" I ask. I turn her set to the right channel, because it's not like she's going to answer. "You've got the better TV in here anyway," I tell her. Suddenly I don't want to be alone. I climb onto Willa's bed with her, plump up the extra zabatons, placing one carefully behind her back, one behind my own, so we can lean against them together, my sister and me.

CHAPTER ELEVEN

I am creating alvin-Travis's forty-fifth birthday party. Creation is the word, he won't settle for anything that hasn't been contrived. The theme this year — a.T. is big on themes — Your Inner Toddler. I've hired a magician who will arrive on a pony, a *big* pony, I specified, and he will give all the partygoers rides on the wide lawn that slopes down from the brick patio toward the sea. The partygoers, alvin-Travis's friends, former band members and the various flotsam and jetsam, the barnacles, algae, pond scum, leechers-on of a past and present music scene, will come dressed in chic diaper paraphernalia, glittery thigh-high satin training pants, tiny tight sequined shirts or perhaps a designer bib and no shirt, little tutu-like sun dresses, frills around their ample asses (in some cases their liposuctioned asses, depending on how high up they married into the music world). Married, partnered, "hooked-up," groped, whichever the case might be, alvin-Travis has managed to avoid successful female musicians in the orbit of his friends, or they've avoided him. Thankfully it's an Indian summer stretch of November, summery cool during the days, good hard chill at night. Where they get these show-all outfits I wouldn't want to know.

It's funny how in junior high I fantasized marrying a rock star. Be careful what you wish for, as they say. Anyway I'm not married to alvin-Travis, I'm free to leave any time. We point this out to each other periodically. I suppose I will never marry anyone again, at least not in the way it was supposed to be, marriage, a home, a family, all that careful ironing training of Jaycee's, her sporadic demonstrations of the correct ordering of the *cutlery*, which fork goes where and why, gone to waste. I feel any potential of a home inside me withering away, drying up, shriveled from disuse.

"Why even hold on to your ovaries if you don't intend to use them, why bother to bleed? Such a nuisance!" Jaycee's sarcastic remarks to me when I saw her a while ago in Boston, drove down and met her at Logan Airport where she flew in from London, a stopover before going back to Hawai'i. Who would've figured Jaycee Beever for a grandmother-wannabe? My sister the *victim soul* was not with her. My mother looked stylish in the way of some grand old dame, expensively garbed in the sort of richly tailored suit only other grand old dames care about. She had concocted a business around granting interviews about The Miracle! Shark Girl! charging mightily for them. Where's the hula dancer now?

I told her, "For the hormones. Monthly bleeding preserves my skin." Figured Jaycee of all people could appreciate this. No doubt she does something to her own face and she's not telling. A face lift? Some sort of supersonic cream injected into the track marks on her forehead from the uterus of llamas? Her face looked the same, drawn tight as a wallet.

"You know," my mother said, sucking off a Winston Light— her voice husky from this habit, an appealing thing on Jaycee, of course—"I've birthed three children and none of you has given me grandchildren. Not that I'm complaining, mind you, I'm not the grandmotherly type, but don't you think your own grandma would appreciate even the hint of great grandchildren before she goes, carrying on the line?"

Are we clothing? The *line*? "Grandma wasn't exactly the grandmotherly type either," I reminded her. What was there to say? Robbie's the one who got away; we're not sure where he is these days and we *don't* talk about this. You'd have to admit parental failure like smacking into the proverbial brick wall when your oldest doesn't even let you know what quadrant of the world he's attempting to have a life in. Last anyone heard from Robbie might have been the birthday card he sent me from Alaska a few years back. Working on the pipeline, maybe, if they're still doing that? Fishing? Who knows? Didn't say much beyond the printed 'thinking of you on your special day,' courtesy of one of those charities that sends cheap cards to guilt you into a donation—children with special needs, the blind, cancer research, Alzheimer's. The return address was a post office box. And of course Willa's excused from any child bearing responsibilities, since she performs miracles. So it's me my mother was pinning her hopes on, jets roaring up and down, off and onto the runways behind us; another way I have failed.

Jaycee sighed, "I bet you believe you still have the wild in you, don't you? You probably still think you can escape getting old."

I busy myself with my created duties, having made out a long list of them, folding it into the pocket of my child's painting smock, my own costume concession worn over a pullover cotton shirt and an adult sized pair of black slacks—a list that will outlast most of alvin-Travis's birthday guests down to the final evening stick-it-outs when they start dragging out their instruments, strumming old sixties and seventies tunes, Remember when...? Which is my exit line, when I can slip off to bed. I won't be missed. I wasn't part of their remember whens. I was barely a conscious participant in my own remember whens, but we'll get to that.

Besides the party my gift to a.T. was to repaint his bathroom a stark glossy white instead of the dull pearl it had become, so his one gold album will stand out hanging there. He wants people to think this is no big deal to him, this gold album, so it hangs in the bathroom; though of course it *is* a big deal and the background is *white as white* to show it off, gold on white. The Head Shrinkers greatest hits, their *only* hits, but I don't begrudge him this little vanity. After all, how many of us will lead the sort of lives that will have any kinds of hits whatsoever? What will I be remembered for, a few poignant black and white shots of ruin, mayhem and devastation? Chronicling the crush of nature, redeeming us in what it destroys?

Presently I'm clipping mums, the flowers of late fall. I'll stick them inside the large imitation Ming dynasty hall vase—mums from the potted plants a.T. brought me last year that I dug into the ground when their blooms were dried out and they actually grew back this year. And the wild cinnamon-scented beach roses that hug the perimeters of the lawn, a few of them amazingly still in bloom, before the lawn drops down to though not quite reaching the Atlantic. It looks like it would like to, each year growing a little further, stretching itself, its necklace of beach rose lurching out over the rocky ledge. I think of this sometimes, is it in us all, human or not, a wish to return to the sea? Could *this* be what happened to my sister, the attack, the shock, the silence, and then one day inexplicably she rises out of her bed, a part of some primal urge residing in all of us but for some reason more acute in her, the return to our briny roots?

At first I think his voice is part of the sea, right behind me, a hum or a roar filling my ears, my throat, the acrid taste of bile.

He says it again: "Fancy meeting you here!" *Fancy meeting you here! Used to say it to us at our front door, like he stumbled upon us purely by accident, when Father was away.*

"What a coincidence I live here," I say numbly. Or is it dumbly? *Numb* is how they say it in Maine, numb for dumb or stupid. But he's not from Maine and neither am I. I turn around slowly, don't meet his eyes, let my own eyes ease up the well packed girth of him; not such a girth anymore, I notice, those traveled calves, hard knots of muscle inside the poorly fitted tan slacks, squat thighs, still that ample belly — '*ōpū*, he'd say, patting it like it's something to be proud of. I remember its tautness pressed up against my mother's back, Jaycee bumping off it like a hard rubber ball as he bounced her on his knees. Or the time I came upon them in the hallway, the light from the window over them beaming down on his bald head, Jaycee's hair shining dark as new tar, his belly shoved up against her so tight you couldn't see any light between them. All these years and still I recall the shape of this nightmare.

"Hah!" he laughs delightedly, "*Scat*, isn't it? Isn't that what they called you? All grown up and with a rich rock and roll musician. Your mother thought your little sister would be the one to marry well, least that's what she told the *Enquirer*."

"Willa performs miracles," I say. "Why would she need a husband?" It is not him, not Fatboy, just some paparazzo, I realize now, hounding me for information about my sister. I look up meeting his eyes, brown and moist, heavily recessed like bits of stuck in wet earth over cheeks less rounded than the ones I imagined, more drawn and pulled down toward his leering mouth. "I don't know your name," I tell him, "and you're in our yard."

"I'm John, just John."

"What are you doing here, Just John?" I grab up the long strandy mums I clipped, already dried out near their roots, pressing them against my smock and start back toward the house. I don't want to be alone with him out here. I haven't seen Fatboy in over thirty years, so why do I do this? Keep imagining I'm going to run into him in some casual way; he's behind me at the grocery checkout line, bumping his cart up against the backs of my legs: 'Scuse me...oh my, is it you? Our little Scat? *Do youse remember me? Fancy meeting you here*! Something about someone who knew your mother so intimately, so privately, so *secretly* before you could even know yourself in these ways. For the rest of your life they come back to you; *like a bad penny*, Father would say, *keeps coming back like a bad penny*. One of his expressions. Did he ever suspect, just how bad *this* penny? My knees feel like rubber bands and there's this quivery jumpy feeling like a caught bird, fluttering in my gut.

"I've outgrown my diapers, if you're wondering why I'm not in costume." He grins, catching up to me, striding along beside me, and a smell escapes his mouth. I remember this smell too, the mordant scent of gin.

"Got to go, Fatboy," I whisper. A million things to do.

****

"Don't forget my list!" Jaycee howls as I fly out the kitchen door, pop back in again, snatching her shopping list out from under the refrigerator soccer ball magnet which clatters to the floor. I don't pick it up. Who among us plays soccer? Robbie who is gone? Willa in bed? Myself, athletic as a towel bar? *I've got a million things for you to do*, she calls after me.

Things are different now. I'm sixteen and I've got my driver's license. And I've got this itchy, panting thing inside me that keeps me moving, keeps me looking too, for what I don't know just yet. There's a boy, Jaycee calls them this but he's not you know, let's get that straight. He's twenty-two and he's an anarchist. The *Honolulu*

Advertiser does this roving reporter thing and they interviewed University of Hawai'i students about what they think the ideal form of government should be. 1968, Summer of Love—*Just call me Mellow Yellow*—Vietnam War heating up, soldiers on R and R prowling the streets of Waikīkī, trying unsuccessfully to blend in with their grunt haircuts, sticking out like sores (we are not friendly toward them; years later I will regret this, those lost boys barely older than we were), tie-dyed hippies, bell-bottomed hippies, hippies without underwear, Haight-Ashbury hippies come to Hawai'i for the *natural* life, doped up, dropped out, high as a grin these long haired *cats* and *chicks*, and activists, students rumbling against the Imperialistic Capitalistic Pig-dom, Tripper calls it. She interviewed Tripper, this *Advertiser* reporter, and he said anarchy's the answer, only thing that'll work.

I start hanging out with him at the Freeway Coffeehouse, part of the Church Of The Crossroads, they called it, though whatever it was that made it a church was mostly invisible to most of us. A shacky building built right under Hawai'i's first freeway, H-1; or maybe they built the freeway over it, it's old enough, run down in that Hawaiian way of run-down, rusted corrugated iron roof, ratchety wooden walls, termite wings littered across chewed up window sills, that tropical almost pleasant smell of wood rot, trade winds breezing through.

The Freeway Coffeehouse serves coffee, of course, your regular oversized raunchy gurgling coffee-machine perked coffee—this is *way* pre mocha lattes and espresso. But mostly we crouch under the spider lily bushes outside toking on *j's*, marijuana joints. I sneak out at night, after Jaycee, who's been chugging down record numbers of gin and tonics these days, slides into bed next to Willa to watch TV, falls asleep or passes out, who could tell the difference? My father goes to bed early in the next room, the one vacated by Robbie who went off to college in California. Only he didn't stay there. Checked in, checked out, stuck out his thumb and headed north, his roommates thought, though it could have been east. We got post cards from Denver at one point, no return address. We don't know where Robbie went and we *don't* talk about it; too much at stake to admit to, too much loss to face. The prodigal son leaves home and keeps on leaving. Father says it's the times, these crazy times. He's confident Robbie will come to his senses, at some point.

Willa still won't speak. She makes sounds indicating the programs she wants to watch: a hum like a kazoo, for instance, does it for the theme song to that new show, Hawai'i Five-O. Blue eyes fix on the craggy face of Jack Lord; does she like what she sees? One night there was blood in Willa's bed and Jaycee freaked out thinking something had happened, *Where her leg's supposed to be.* Turned out little sister had started her period, the life-giving flow from the one who gave up on life.

The strange thing about this was as soon as Willa got her periods my mother's stopped. "Too young for The Change," she told Luna, and none of those *dreadful* symptoms anyway, no hot flashes, no general personality disturbances (though who could tell on that one!). Jaycee felt fine; in fact, better than ever. The hormonal migraines she used to get a week before her period stopped. Jaycee's head never hurt again, and Willa, though she never said anything, was seen rubbing our mother's forehead and then her own, her face crumpled in pain. And then her blood. Is this where *it* begins?

But I had other fish to fry, as Jaycee called it, my lack of interest in The Family anymore, she said accusingly. I started getting interested in Tripper, leaning against the banyan tree under the freeway beside the coffeehouse, whoosh of cars and trucks over us like the pull of some strange mechanical tide, back and forth, something sensual in it, motorized, an electric tingling in my gut, down between my legs. He's sucking on Marlboros, alternating with tokes off a joint passed between us, long wiry hair this hip male Medusa, tanned face, those wire-rimmed John Lennon glasses, supposed to give him the look of an intellectual I guess. He wasn't a surfer, which is what most of the girls in my school still went for, and he's not exactly a hippie, too worked up for that flaccidly stoned image. He's an anarchist.

One night I ask him to help me lose my virginity. "It's a burden," I tell him, "something to get out of the way." All the *far out* chicks get laid, I think, but I don't say this to him.

"Hmmm," Tripper hums, slide of his long hand like a fish swimming toward me, looping his arm around my neck, fingers raining down upon my once again braless breasts. "The thing is babe, I don't usually do virgins, they're a lot of hassle, ya know?" he asks me earnestly. I nod, though how would I know?

He shrugs, sighs, "I could make an exception for you, I guess."

I call Jaycee, tell her I'm spending the night with a friend, and it doesn't occur to her this many gin and tonics into the evening I don't really have any friends. We smoke some hash, sprawled across his mattress on the floor, musty scent of his tie-died sheets; for the pain, he tells me. I'm not sure whose pain he's talking about, his, the burden of this deflowering, or mine, the deflowered. In the morning Tripper hangs the bloodied sheet out in his back yard, slinging it over a monkey pod tree branch, the big old Mānoa house he rents with a litter of other students, anarchists, hippies; a flag of sorts, staking his claim. The others serve us breakfast, scrambled eggs with pot sprinkled on top like flakes of pungent pepper. But wasn't I the victor here? I was the one who got him to do it.

****

The day after alvin-Travis's birthday party I have one of those strange, surreal-like nap time dreams, tossing about on alvin-Travis's bed, sheets like clumps of wet cotton bunched under me. a.T. will only use one hundred percent cotton white sheets, the color of a purity he longs for, color of his regrets. In his own dreams he's no longer fucking me, insisting *I* be the one who is impure instead. How does one get to a place where impotence is transformed into purity? Who is the magician here?

In my dream I am fucking a fat man named Fred who sells me my drug needs at the Rite Aid. I take Anacin, lots of it, aspirin with caffeine in it. Caffeine helps my sometimes overwhelming craving for a drink, the heaviness in my head like it's a normal kind of headache only I know better; plumps up those blood vessels a bit, makes me more alert, vigilant, needfully addicted to something else instead. Reformed alcoholics would call me a dry drunk; any hour any moment and it's all over, one day at a time. It's either caffeine or cigarettes and those damn things will kill you. I feel his belly, firm as a big round inner tube under me, thrusting up against me. In the way of those perplexing nap time dreams this one morphs to an actual tube, large black tire like what might've been on a semi and Willa and me floating on it, bobbing up and down against the silvery-soft

Kailua waves at the moment before they break, before they become white caps mashing toward the shore. When Willa had two legs and a blond smile, Jaycee calling us from the beach, her two little beavers, hair done up in a green and white checked bandanna, young and lithe as the palms behind her. Those days I still mostly believed she loved us equally and life felt about as normal as it got.

When I wake from this dream, clawing my way out of this drenched sleep, I am reminded of something else, the best blowjob I ever gave, also a man named Fred, in San Francisco where I went after college, B.A. in philosophy, one of those humanities you took in the early seventies if you showed no particular talent for anything else thinking it might be *interesting*, an *experience*. Hard to know which was greater, the hopelessness of getting a job with this degree or my lack of desire settling into a job, still searching for God knows what, real love perhaps? Whatever it was I've never found.

San Francisco days white and blearied. Here is where I came to drink, fog horn bleating those low, aching groans, below the belt grief, the way this sound slipped down my throat, my gut, my groin, under my skin it became part of my blood, veins and arteries, nourishing every organ, every muscle, inhabiting me like my own scream, that stifled, strangled, shriek of the hopeless. Even now the hurt of this, calling me back to whatever it was I was unable to discover, something I abandoned, never to return to. Something that still lurks, though, and I can't pin this down, grab onto it, make it mine to forget. Fleeting sense of deja-vu, the life you were supposed to have, a hinting little flash of it then gone.

After the record-breaking blowjob Fred shook my hand, earnestly thanking me, like I had maybe given him the gift of a really good hat.

These days I can barely see this person anymore, this me that I was, a passing glimpse of her in a dream sometimes, the younger me. Where did she disappear to? Did she have any kind of a life? Was she at all aware of it, living this life? When exactly did she make that choice, to disappear.

Part IV

Of traditional adventures with shark 'aumakua Hawaiians tell many stories. Kamakau tells of a certain family descended from a shark, a member of which might be punished for breaking a tapu of the shark god by being "laid beside the shark in the sea for from two to four days close to the fin of the shark" and yet be brought up alive.... Kukuipahu of Hawai'i was swallowed by a shark and lived inside its body many days and came ashore at Hana, Maui, with all his hair worn off, whereupon the daughter of the chief was bestowed upon him as a wife. He is said to have been saved because he was faithful in his offerings to the gods.

Beckwith; *Hawaiian Mythology*

CHAPTER TWELVE

The dreams are changing. Once a luminous blue, the ocean now dank and murky and instead of exhilaration there is fear. This time I am in a cage — the I that is me but is not — and I am being lowered off a boat deep, deep, into the ocean, pea green water slurping, slushing, slopping around me until the cage hits a sand and reef bottom, resting uneasily at the side of a giant coral head. I try to see my face, as I always do in my dreams, but it appears covered in something chain-like, like armor, like I am suddenly some sort of warrior land-knight, out of place in this lurking sea. Where is my steed? My sword? My brave soul?

Peer around outside the cage, between its bars the sea. I must be breathing out of some kind of oxygen tank; I'm not a fish, am I? No gills, no swim bladder, nothing that should be naturally occurring here. At what instance do I run out of air? Fish swim around the cage, colorful parrot fish, umbrella like fish, poking their heads into the reef around me. Tropical fish, it must be the tropics, Hawai'i of course, yet where are the blues, the aquas, my luminous sea?

Suddenly a jolt, a bump against the cage and the cage shudders violently. I peer about, heart (whose heart?) bumping hard inside this chain suit, these bars, see fish heads, bits and pieces of organic matter, bloody dead things drifting through the water leaving their rust-colored trails, chum. Then all around me the giant shadows, the lurking presence of sharks! They are eating the chum, clearing it from the water, a frenzy of thrashing tails, fins, jaws, and when it's gone it is me they are interested in, inside the cage, inside the metal suit, this living breathing skin. One giant shark slams against the cage and we lurch forward, the cage and I — the I who is me — my body falling into the bars on one side where another one waits, gaping, wide open mouth, jagged teeth like the broken ridges of a gargantuous comb, metal cutters, these teeth, the ultimate homicidal saw.

It's a drab rain-spitting Saturday and Gracie has the weekend free. She decides to finally clean her room, and after a breakfast of half a vanilla yogurt and a handful of green grapes—Roma's non-eating eating habits are getting to her—she returns to the room bearing garbage bags and several empty boxes Berry let her cart down from the part of the attic that is not Roma's bedroom, a giant storage closet looking area, heaped full of junk. There are the things Gracie can't throw away. *Make a list! Dr. Bender said; number it, chart it, reference it and it's yours....* Shark Girl's clothes, with the exception of the black silk blouse, Gracie will pack in an ancient brown suitcase Berry has given her for this purpose.

"Don't know why you'd bother," Berry snorts. "It's not like she'll be coming back for them. Goodwill could use them, sell them cheap to real people what need them. She has a history of this, I hope you know. Finds some obscure place—not that we think we're obscure here but the rest of the world barely knows we exist, ayuh? Maine, *Vacationland*—and then one day a paparazzo catches up to her, letters start coming in, phone calls, believers camping out in front like they think it's the sidewalk to Heaven, poof! she ups and disappears. I know this because I looked it up," Berry says smugly. "Got it off the Internet and microfiche down to the library. She's not the only one who can research things. What I don't get though is if she leaves her belongings each time she up and goes, so how does she live? Buys them all over again? Not very thrifty. Them's the habits of someone doesn't have to work for a living. Far as I can tell she never had a job, unless you call bleeding for folks a vocation! The mother is with her most of the time they say, but I never seen her. Maybe she's the rich one, who knows? Doesn't sit well with me I'll tell you, that kind of waste. We Mainers are a frugal people, Yankee mentality and whatnot. These outsiders come in, people from away, and I mean no offense to you here, Gracie, but you folks just have different ways."

She's scowling into Gracie's partly opened door, leaning against the frame, her right arm propped up and encased in a tight lime-green sweater, cozied against the cut of her bicep making it look like a fuzzy tennis ball poking up under her sleeve. "Far as I'm concerned," Berry growls, "clothes to Goodwill then you heave-ho the rest. Give the garbage bags to Anthony, he'll haul them all to the dump. Though if you find anything worth something, remember, that one owes me money. Whoever heard of a healer who skips out on her rent?"

Gracie begins with her clothes, folding things more for the ease of fit rather than worrying about wrinkles or fabric care, placing them into the suitcase. She had removed the blue satin bra and thong from the radiator and the other items spread about the floor, jeans, several long-sleeved cotton shirts, nylon nightshirt, mismatched socks, a pair of knit gloves, hair barrettes, clear nail polish, avocado skin cream and a bent copper bracelet, piling them into the corner, and these she also tosses into the suitcase. The closet is a different story. Taking her few dresses off the hangers, a couple sweaters and the long skirts, Gracie carefully folds and arranges these in the top of the suitcase. She's not sure why, but if Shark Girl felt the need for them to hang and not be part of the general chaos of the room, then Gracie feels she too must care for them. The dresses appear barely worn, especially the shorter ones; these still have that crisp almost new department store smell. A chill prickles Gracie's arms as it occurs to her Shark Girl probably didn't wear short things much, if at all. That whatever is going on with her right leg, prosthesis or not, she's hiding it from the rest of the world the way Gracie tries to hide the right side of her face. There isn't a pair of pants in this closet, just the jeans that had been tossed on the floor. *She was a long skirt person.* Gracie is suddenly hit with the human sense of her, the woman not the myth, and she feels sad. Who is this person that must run away like this, leaving the remnants of a life behind? "Willa," Gracie whispers, "Wilhelmina Beever."

Wilhelmina Malia Beever was born at Queens Hospital, Honolulu, on the island of O'ahu, Territory of Hawai'i, June 3, 1952. Birth unremarkable other than the mother, Jaycee Anderson Beever, fell into a deep depression in the months following this birth, as she did to a lesser extent after the births of her older two children, Robert Morris Beever Jr. and Susan Catherine Beever.

We now understand this depression as post-partum depression, treatable in
all except the most severe cases, diagnosed as post-partum psychosis. Mrs.
Beever was prescribed Valium and bed rest for her "nervous condition," and
the father, Robert Morris Beever, an accountant with the O'ahu Financial
Firm, Smith, Keahui, Beever and Chang, hired help to care for the two older
children and infant Wilhelmina, and to prepare meals. This is only remarkable
in that the initial bonding period between mother and infant was delayed in
the case of Mrs. Beever. It was the hired help, Kimi Matsudo, whom baby
Wilhelmina would first identify with as her "mother."

Queens Hospital in Honolulu, Hawai'i? Gracie was born in Queens
Hospital! Her father's sabbatical, thirteen months away from when
all of their futures, father's, mother's, daughter's, would pay for what
happens to her face. The smell of the sea, drifting into the hospital
room where Gracie's mother lay, where Wilhelmina's mother lay,
where Gracie lay, where Wilhelmina lay? Aqua hauntings of infant
dreams even then? Gracie's mother said: "It's a place where not being
Caucasian meant everything. Your father had his research, at least
he had that and his academic friends, but my skin couldn't take that
fierce sun and I couldn't understand them, the way people spoke. You
were born there Gracie, that's all, an accident of birth."

She discovered the grey metal file box in the far back corner of the
closet, tucked under the bottom shelf, an area Gracie hadn't ventured
into before because of all the junk piled on top, leaking out of the
shelves: old purses, belts, unmatched winter gloves, costume jewelry,
neck scarves, random this and that; in general pretty uninteresting
stuff, not the things that reveal much about a person except for her
taste in accessories, which she seemed to have quite a few of, Gracie
noted, and no problem leaving them behind. No crosses, figures
of saints, Jesus, or any other *icons* as Roma would describe them,
spiritual stuff that might point to her as a healer, a bleeder, the things
people said about her. Girl stuff, heaped on top. The box was taped
shut with a ribbon of duct tape (a lock on it but this looked broken,
maybe picked into given the scratches?), and for all of one minute
Gracie had wondered if she should respect this. But, she rationalized,
if it was really critical that no one look inside than the owner would
have purchased a steel padlock, or taken the thing with her!

Once the top popped open she could see the box was divided

into two sections, the first filled with newspaper clippings, magazine articles, fan mail, if you could call it that, desperate, sometimes barely literate hand-scrawled pleas, a scrap book of sorts minus the book—the life and times of Shark Girl. The blurb chronicling her birth had been in the front. The second part, divided from the rest by a manila folder with an orange plastic paper clip fastened at its side, seemed to contain factual information mostly about sharks (was this what Berry meant about her *research*?), quotes from books, copies of articles, even whole reports. The *Billy Weaver Shark Research And Control Program Final Report*. A chill crawls up her spine, memory of her dream, that cage hurtling to the floor of the sea. But who was Billy Weaver? And why were these things included in what otherwise seemed a more personal collection? This part, she decided, for another time.

From the first section Gracie takes out another clipping, a yellowing photo of a slender young woman with a proud expression she assumes is the mother, holding maybe a two-year-old Wilhelmina Beever, the two other children standing a little apart and behind. The woman, her dark hair a polished and fashionably fifties shaped page boy (Gracie's guessing here, old films styles), is wearing a halter top and a full matching skirt, the kind of skirt Gracie's own mother told her was worn with a petticoat; closer inspection reveals these to be the same green and white checked print as the baby's sun suit. The other two children are dressed unremarkably, almost as if their very presence in the photo was an afterthought; it's the toddler and mother that seem to take up all the space. The article's title: "The Early Years," and underneath this in smaller letters, "of a Victim Soul." Gracie stares at the child's face, baby Wilhelmina, round and petulant, already beautiful. Two chubby little legs stuck firmly, possessively against her mother's side.

There are the letters, scraps of various handwritten notes, lined paper, embossed stationery, flowery stationery, note cards with berries on them, herbs, seashells, rocking horses, anonymous this and that, postcards, childish print and scrawl, computerese, printed e-mail, pages and pages of something typed, something documented, all addressed to Shark Girl. Gracie skims through these, requests for a blessing of some sort, desperate entreaties, prayers to be healed of broken bones, bent over backs, broken hearts, cancer, Tourette's, general lacklusterness, despair, even a husband having an affair (she would settle for a curse on him, the letter writer stated, some sort of pox—Gracie thinks of Dr. Bender's story, the woman who kept her philandering husband's ashes in a shoe box under her bed). Offers of marriage, seduction, sisterhood, even one knighthood! Some have previously reported to other healing sources, the Virgin of Guadeloupe a favorite. Others just beg for a miracle, any miracle, some kind of a change in their lives. They entreat, they don't need much, a basic healing of *this*; bleed for them, Shark Girl, bleed....

Gracie's own head suddenly aches, a coldness in her stomach. The trades she has bartered with, prayers over the years to a God she was never even taught to believe in—*I'll give you this, if you would only give me a new face*....

She pulls out a small stack of letters underneath the others, tied together with a little girl's shiny red hair elastic. They are still in their envelopes; in fact, many appear unopened. The return addresses are varied but the ones on the top, seemingly the most recent, are from around here, Rock Harbor, Maine. S.C. Beever. Her sister? *Susan Catherine*. Gracie's pulse accelerates, throbbing in her neck, her heart beating too fast. But why? Like she's suddenly intruding, these particular letters? She's just gone through an entire room's contents of someone else's personal stuff! She's handled her *underwear*, for God's sake.

Gracie removes the contents from the top envelope, one that has been slit open, a neat and perfectly straight tear as if a letter opener or some such implement was used instead of Shark Girl's own fingers. Odd, because the "fan" mail had all been torn open, the more impatiently ripped results.

Dear Willa,

I hope you are well, and I hope this reaches you. I'm reasonably sure of this address, as this time Jaycee was the one who gave it to me, but as always I wait for you to answer me, wait to be invited to see you. I would like to see you, Willa, you know that. Since you choose to not answer my mail, or perhaps somehow you are not getting it?

I just never know if I, if any of us, are welcome in your life. I've tried e-mailing you, but apparently you keep changing your cyber address even faster than wherever you actually reside. It bounces back to me. Appropriate, I suppose; everything about you but you yourself seems to find its way back to me. I lost a lot of years, wasted them, and that's the truth. Those years were me deserting my own life though Willa, not yours, not you. I didn't try to contact you then because I didn't even know who *I* was. I'm living here now, the same town as you, if this address for you is correct. Who knows? Please answer me. I won't show up on your doorstep until.

Your sister,

Susan Catherine

Glancing through the other letters from Susan Catherine, the ones that are opened, suggests the same kind of message. Not a lot of news, nothing about Susan Catherine herself, just a heart breaking desire to see her sister, a plea at times, almost begging. And always the emphasis on wasted years—*those years were me deserting my own life*. An unwillingness to appear uninvited in her sister's life.

Gracie rocks back on her heels from where she's been crouching too long, plunks down on the floor, stretching her sore legs out. This all strikes her as very sad. She never had a sister or brother; seemingly after the accident her parents were reluctant to risk such a venture again. Or maybe they despised each other too much at that point to do what it would take to give Gracie a sibling. But shouldn't having a sister or brother mean there's a person out there you don't need an invitation from to visit? Why would Shark Girl not answer these, not even open more than half of them? The ones she did sliced coldly with a tool, a knife, a letter opener, apart from her own fingers as if she didn't even want to touch the contents. Where does such willful distance come from? A cruelty here that just doesn't fit with what has been saved in the rest of this section of the file box, the pleas for healing, articles proclaiming *Shark Girl* something of a miracle. Why would she deny her own sister the same interest? This just seems to be some sort of mean sibling stuff, that seething resentment peculiar to families.

Gracie realizes she's been hunkered down on the bare floor for almost two hours, and she's aware of how bad she feels besides being stiff and sore, her helplessness, that all too familiar despair. Would she, *could she*? If Shark Girl really is a healer of sorts, as the fan mail indicates, the articles about her—a Victim Soul!—could she...*heal her face?* It seems ridiculous, even presumptuous; after all, Gracie's scarred and sagging cheek is not the pain of bone cancer, the wasting away of AIDS. It's not even leprosy for God's sake, in spite of its ravaged look! She can hear her mother: "Well honestly, Gracie, how self-absorbed can you be? You have a warm bed to sleep in, food on your plate, so much more than so much of the rest of the world, you have your *cake* so now you're insisting on the frosting too?" Gracie thrusts the box into the closet, refusing to indulge these thoughts any further. Though not all the way to the back this time. Accessible. Her life, *our life*, becoming more accessible.

Gracie McKneely's List of Facts About the Animal and Plant Kingdoms of Hawai'i.

July 21, 1994: (Source is Dr. Bender. Dr. Bender said always identify your source.)

Animals:

> *1. Dogs—brought by the Polynesians for food. (My note: gross!!!)*
>
> *2. Rats—may have also come with Polynesians but also Western ships; a plague in the sugarcane.*
>
> *3. Mongoose—imported to kill rats in sugarcane but sleep at night when rats are out doing bad things. (My note: OK, that was dumb!)*

Plants:

> *1. Kukui (candlenut)—can use oil from green nuts for aching muscles and a laxative too. (Yuch! How gross is this? also when you find the black nuts on the beach they stink!)*
>
> *2. Mango—more people in the world eat them than apples.*
>
> *3. Papaya—bisexual (Note: I asked Dr. Bender what this meant, she said self-pollinating. Louis laughed.)*
>
> *4. Passion fruit (Liliko'i)—10 sepals and petals for the ten apostles at Crucifixion; fringed crown for crown of thorns; 5*

stamens for 5 wounds; tendrils for scourges; leaves for hands of persecutors....

(Note: Is it about Jesus' death? I asked Dr. Bender, and Louis spit a seed from the yellow pulpy stuff at me then stuck a part of the fruit that was in Louis's mouth in Dr. Bender's mouth. Gross! But Dr. Bender must have liked it because she laughed. A bunch of seeds from my own liliko'i but I swallowed them whole.)

CHAPTER THIRTEEN

Where is Shark Girl? I hear this question in my dream, but who's asking it? There are two of us, a he, a she (the she is me?). When he takes off his clothes, his body tall as a tree, I am aware of the flatness of his stomach, the bark of his skin, concave of his chest beckoning me to lean and loll and lie against him the way certain trees lure you in, reach out to you to sit under them, climb up them, cradled in their crotch the fit of this. We are on some bed I recognize though the room, its edges dark and liquidy, is unfamiliar. Then I'm on top of him, the I who may or may not be me, plum-soft hair covering this face, sliding down his torso. He places my hand between his thighs, one of his own hands on my naked breasts. Grab onto that surging MALE of him and am amazed at this solidity, how whole and real it is like a big warm pickle. Feel strong and sure, my body against his; yes! This is me, me who is I, normal after all, hadn't I always suspected it? Under those layers of skin, epidermis, dermis, the subcutaneous tissue — even in my dream I can recite them like vocabulary words, a science test, digging into the subconscious, going down down down — the me who all along was under it all.

Attempt to swing my right leg over his thigh, straddling him, BUT IT WON'T MOVE. Like it's concrete or rock, built into this bed. Sour taste of something in my throat, panic? Horror? Am scared to peek out behind the wall of this hair, afraid to see whose face it is I wear. My leg! I whisper. Did I say it? Brushes his hand across my hair, sliding it slowly away from my face. I cringe, am afraid to look but the dream forces me, this beautiful globular baby face, the one in the photograph, two baby fat legs fierce against the mother, still perfect.

On Oʻahu, in upper Kamana Nui Valley, is a ridge named Manō. Legend tells of a shark-man who lived in a cave there. Both shark and man were known as Keanaokamanō (the cave of the shark). The man followed swimmers to the sea and killed them, but he was finally killed himself by the victims' families. Hawaiian stories of men who turn into murdering sharks are suggestive of European legends of werewolves.... Both are based on fearsome predators.

Sharks of Hawaiʻi; Leighton Taylor, p 30 *(As compiled by S.G.)*

As compiled by S.G.? Tearing through the collections of quotes, researched reports, factual articles from the other section of the file box Gracie sees how she has signed everything. No, not signed, initialed, though not her initials, not her real name. And not her words. Everything, biological, cultural, even spiritual has these initials. S.G. As compiled by. She snaps shut the box. Won't even pretend to re-tape the duct tape. Was Shark Girl some kind of scholar? Gracie's father would approve. Shark researcher, cultural anthropologist, marine biologist? No, she thinks, doesn't fit. Can't be a scientist *and* a healer, a miracle worker, a bleeder for God's sake! can we?

Can *we*...?

Dear Dr. Beever, can you make me a new face...? Bangs her fist against the box. Yanks off the tape, access of the owned.

****

"If wishing would make it so!" Marie is saying. "Just thinking the thing, wishing for it and it's yours."

Roma shakes her head, silver this time, she had the tomato color stripped and now her hair pokes straight up and out of her scalp like steel spikes. When she moves her head it's as if the hair refuses to move with her, has decided to by-God inhabit its stuck-in position, the steel stick-to-it-iveness of a railroad track. "That's just so profound, Marie, honestly you are such an original thinker," Roma sneers. "Golly gee, wish I could be you. Don't think I can touch this meal now, have to go ruminate on those heavy thoughts, you dig?" She slides her chair away from the dinner table, all eyes on her. It amazes them how each night she joins them at the table Roma is able to find an entirely new excuse not to eat. "Marie's brain is the stuff of a Disney animation," she proclaims, sauntering out toward the kitchen, full plate of food in her hand. "They should concrete a star for it on Hollywood boulevard."

Marie grins her crooked teeth smile, unable to understand she's been made fun of. Tia laughs, too, but at Marie, and Berry scowls darkly into her own plate of food. "She's making some ritual out of not eating," Berry grumbles, "like not eating's the whole point of it all."

Janie sighs, "How does she stay alive, you've got to wonder? She's tough, I'll guess, one of them skinny tough girls. I'd have her hips though. Take 'em in a New York minute."

Berry forces a pained smile. "What Roma is or isn't, is, after all, not our decision, is it? Whose decision is it, Janie, who gets to choooose here?" Berry draws out choooose, like this is the word we are supposed to concentrate on.

"The Lord?" Janie says meekly.

"What's a New York minute?" Tia asks.

Berry's eyes are drills boring into Tia, who shrugs and stares at her food. "Correct answer, Janie, we've got to pray to our gracious Lord, ask Him to see to it that Roma develops some lick of sense in that thick skull of hers, let Jesus lead her to food again!"

"You can lead a horse to water..." Roma sings from the kitchen, poking her spiky silver head half out the open kitchen door like some misshapen moon, grinning evilly.

"Speaking of horses or animals," Berry begins, ignoring her daughter, her glare focused on the rest of them now, "I'd be curious to know which of you might have some information about a mouse nest in the downstairs bathroom?"

Gracie glances quickly at Jessie who seems to have paled a bit but says nothing. They are all reduced to children under Berry's inquisitions.

"I s'pose you are aware I am not a wealthy woman, no trust fund baby summer person here, ayuh? I do my best, by God. I do not take funds from the State, though the Lord knows I have little enough whereas I probably could, and I don't require no support from any man. My mother and grandmother before me made their own ways too. We Waters women ask no man for nothing. All I request is a bit of money for your board and the good Lord supplies the rest." Berry sighs, and again cuts her black eyes over all of their faces. Gracie can't imagine where this is going and looks questioningly up at Roma, still hanging in the kitchen doorway. Roma shakes her head, crossing her arms over her bony chest. "This oughta be rich," she snorts.

"What I'm getting at," says Berry, shooting Roma a scathing look, "is as proprietress and owner of a boarding house what offers rooms for poor and troubled women down on their luck—sound familiar to any of you?—sleep in, be warm in, feel they have a home in along with nutritious meals for them to eat, there are certain rules and regulations I have to follow, health standards and whatnot. The state imposes them, I got no choice in the matter. There are rules about animals, although I have nothing personally against pets mind you, cats or dogs. And especially there are rules about cleanliness in a place where food is served." Berry slashes a hard glance to her right, staring sternly at Jessie. "They can shut me down if they find mice running around in my house, you hear!"

Jessie sits quietly, barely lifting her eyes, glazed perusal of her plate. Nods contritely. "What did you do with them?"

"Flushed them down the toilet!"

Jessie jumps a little then crunches down like she's been hit, *hunh* intake of her breath. Roma's howling from the doorway, "Man oh man, I knew *this* would be sweet!"

"Well, what did you think I was going to do with them, invite them to dinner? For crying out loud, don't you dare make an issue out of this, Jessie. I told you, the state could shut me down and you would all be out on the street!"

Tia chirps, "Personally I don't much like rodents."

"You *are* a rodent, Tia!" Roma sneers.

Jessie pushes her chair back from the table, folding her napkin beside her half finished plate of food, still these graces. Downcast eyes, trying to hold straight her quivering chin. "I know it's my turn on the dishes," she assures everyone, "I will do them shortly. Please excuse me."

"Oh, honestly!" Berry smacks her fist down on the woven table mat. "I'm sorry, Jessie, I know you love animals and I'm here to tell you the Lord does too, the beasts of His kingdom on earth. But they are not people, they will not ascend to His kingdom in Heaven. There's a pecking order to things, pits the strongest against the weakest. I am who I am because a mouse can't flush *me* down the toilet. We can pray for them, is what we'll do, along with our prayers for my daughter's return to her God-given senses and her appetite!" Berry picks up her fork, squeezing it hard, her knuckles hamburger-red.

"Score three for Madam Waters!" Roma claps her hands in mock appreciation, her finger swizzling a number three in the air. "You can justify murdering baby mice, make Jessie cry and diss me all in less than a minute. Damn you're good, put your *mouth* in concrete next to Marie's brain. Gracie, you about done with that mess on your plate? We have plans, remember?"

Gracie nods and pushes her chair back from the table. She doesn't remember any plans with Roma but if the meal is turning into a prayer session for mice, this, she's decided, is her exit cue. She has nothing against prayer. What she is beginning to realize though, is she has some real "issues" as Berry would put it, with Berry Waters orchestrating them into it. Gracie didn't leave one hyper-meddling mother to become stuck under the muscular arms and sharpened tongue of another.

"Gracie," Berry starts, her cold hand suddenly clamped around Gracie's wrist before she can take half a step back from her chair — she swears sometimes this woman seems to read her every thought — "better make it an early night. I need you to begin your routine an hour early in the morning. We have our meeting tomorrow night, offering prayer and counsel for Marie, and I'd like you to wash the curtains in that room, give them a chance to air dry. I'll pay a little extra for your time."

"Like clean curtains are going to make a difference in the life and times of our very own Marie Osmond! Why don't we bake her a plate of chocolate chip cookies and be done with it?" Roma hoots.

"OK," Gracie assures Berry and she releases her wrist.

She follows Roma back into the kitchen where Roma makes an about face, snatches Gracie's plate of half eaten dinner from her hand, tossing it into the sink without even rinsing the food off. "Jessie's turn on the dishes tonight, she won't mind. She can have a heart to heart with the ants living behind the drain board," Roma giggles, "tell them all about the tragedy of the drowned mice."

"What did you mean about Marie Osmond?" Gracie asks.

"Oh, don't tell me Marie hasn't broken out into a trite little Osmond ditty for you, lamented on how she misses brother Donny? She believes she's Marie Osmond reincarnated!"

"Did Marie Osmond die? I don't remember her dying. Wasn't that Karen Carpenter who died of anorexia? You said that thing about the cookies. And isn't this Marie too old, anyway?"

Roma grins, "*Hello!* Man, Gracie, you sure are one literal-minded little bitch. We're talking about a crazy person here! What's one mud-haired wholesome faced song girl to another, huh? The world is not a sensible place! That's one thing you'll learn living with my mother, Berry creates her own little world. Marie had a psychotic break, fool, that's how she ended up here, after they let her out of Augusta. You know, the state mental hospital? Or doesn't *upstate* have one of those? They let her out because they figured she was harmless, I mean Marie Osmond never hurt anyone unless you call bad music a type of psychic pain! Marie thinks Marie Osmond has been sending her messages, willing her own soul into our Marie. She thinks Marie Osmond is trying to become her, make her the mother of her seven children. This is straight up the Haunted Housewives alley of course, twisted as all hell. Though if my mother succeeds in bringing the real Marie Osmond, dead or alive into this place I'm outahere."

Roma grabs a worn suede jacket off the peg by the back door, tugs open the door, turning to Gracie. "You coming? Or maybe you rather go back to the dining room, offer prayers for deceased rodents and the hunger of my soul!" Roma giggles again, then throws her skinny noodle of an arm around Gracie's shoulders, hugging her. Gracie feels its warmth all the way through.

The house on D Street has music pouring out of the cracked open windows, in some cases broken windows. There are motorcycles on the lawn, patches of scant grass and frozen, crackly mud. Gracie stares at the motorcycles, that familiar surge of fear thinking *males*. But as Roma pushes open the door, gusts of musky, female scent, she remembers Liela and her friends. They're sprawled about the front room, cloth covered, ancient furniture, its fetid smells, a blue bulb stuck into a dangling light fixture, a lava lamp spewing its red and wormy designs. "Is this Liela's house?" she whispers to Roma.

Roma makes a noise in her throat. "Christ, Gracie, you think Liela would live in a dump like this? Liela's a *source*, I told you that!"

As if on cue a caterpillar shaped bong filled with pungent marijuana is headed their way. Roma grabs it, sucks in a big breath and in one smooth movement whips around toward Gracie, tugs open her jaw and blows the smoke down her throat. Gracie chokes, her automatic gag reflex. The group laughs.

Roma inhales again, motioning Gracie to open her mouth. Gracie shakes her head, her eyes smarting and again Roma yanks down on her jaw, blows the stuff in. "Hold it in this time!" she hisses. "You born in a barn? You don't let good bud escape unsmoked into the air! This stuff's cut with something costs more than a month of your cleaning wages."

Gracie holds it like she's told (good girl Gracie always doing what she's told!), and this time after the burning in her throat subsides, her head starts spinning, not unpleasantly and she feels a melting sensation slinking down her spine like someone's buttery fingers tendering each disc. She curls up with these fingers, cross-legged onto a gritty yet soft enough carpet.

"How's she doing you?" Roma calls down.

"My throat's sore," Gracie squeaks, her voice sounding like it's coming from far away.

"Pass her a hit off the coffee brandy," someone suggests. A cool lip of a bottle is pressed against Gracie's own dry lips, creamy stuff, its gentle sweet singe coating her mouth.

"One more time," Roma demands, kneeling beside Gracie. "This is your night, girlie, I've decided. Your turn to be the bride." Several of the women hoot. Roma blows the smoke in and this time her tongue follows it for a second, a quick lick off Gracie's own coffee-brandied tongue like it's candy. "Now close your mouth," she whispers, "and breathe in deeply."

Gracie does this and her head grows lighter, her mind a cloud floating at the top of her skull, can't help her simpering, silly smile, tattooed and pierced faces swimming in and out of her vision, jellyfish with attitude. *Something about a box jellyfish, Dr. Bender told me, comes in on the south shore after a full moon, little boxy creatures floating graceful as angels, making the ocean unswimmable for people, their fiercely burning sting.* "Get the gown!" Echo of a voice lofty and melodious, *get the gown, the gown, the gown.* Hands are around her, salt smell of woman flesh, skin touching hers. Understands she's being undressed and she doesn't care. Then dressed again, this time in some sort of garment that feels smooth and satiny, if huge, settling about her breasts her hips like a folding of wings.

Someone asks, "Who's the groom?"

"I'm on it," Roma says, and disappears.

Gracie floats for a while, in this dress, this room, this richly scented house, marijuana a fragrant cloud over her head—inhale, exhale, this life, her life at the moment feels strangely OK. She ponders the meanings of things, to eat or not to eat—*did* Marie Osmond have anorexia, or wasn't that indeed Karen Carpenter? Her father's Proof of Infinity. Where did it get him? What did it prove? What is infinite in the long haul? Same job at the same university year after year, same classes, same faces with different names, the Bobs and the Marys, Matthews and Jennifers, Seans and Briannas, whatever the hit names of the decade, but in the end aren't they all really the same anyway, these faces, drifting in then out of his life like balloons, bright and eager or not so eager, then gone? Life in the basement of a ranch house, drinking away the guilt of having to witness his most permanent, most lasting, most *infinite* mark, Gracie's face, day after day. What she refuses to think about now, is her face.

It's some time later, after midnight by the silence of the night around them, the disappearance of cars on the road, quiet enough the stars seem to be ticking, illuminated little shocks of breath in the dark. The night is cold and clear, though in the distance a fog bank starting, and in acknowledgment the sudden mournful wail of the fog horn at the tip of the Rockland breakwater, answering groan at the Owls

Head lighthouse. The breakwater before them in the thin light of the stars, sliver of moon, a giant's finger of rock stretching almost a mile into the sea.

"Your aisle, milady," Roma bowing dramatically, shudder of her astonishing thinness. The others, those that chose to come out into the cold night, snort. "Go ahead," Roma urges. "Walk, you dig? right foot, left foot, repeat. We'll be right behind you."

Gracie looks skeptically down at her own body as if surprised to find herself still in the giant white gown. "This is insane, Roma, I can't walk out on some dark bunch of rocks in this, I'll trip and fall! Why are we doing this?" Suddenly she is sober as stone.

"It was Liela's," Roma says, like that answers something. Though this would explain why it's so long on Gracie, long enough to be incredibly dangerous out here.

She peers about the faces lit up by the lights from the Samoset Resort, its wide lawn at the edge of the rocks, checking again for Liela as if she might suddenly appear. Apparently she is running one of her groups tonight, marijuana joints for glaucoma and cancer victims, and Gracie out on this breakwater in freezing temperatures, a wind kicking up, wearing something Liela failed in or that failed her. "What's the point?" she whispers. "Is there really nothing else to do around here?"

Roma shrugs, "This is Maine, Gracie. You chose us. Besides, as in every good journey there's a prize at its end. So come on, bride, walk!" She slaps Gracie's butt, squeezes hard.

"God," Gracie moans, "I don't believe this." Steps timidly out on the first rock. Why do I let her boss me around? she thinks, this mop-thin, steel-haired girl, four years younger than Gracie and she obeys her every command. At least it's dark, conscious again of her cheek, who she is in this world.

The farther Gracie walks out on this spit of rock the harder the wind swirls about, its pelting scents of salt and seaweed, dried and rotting near the water line. She can hear the dark water lapping at either side, sucking back, a silvery play of an occasional ripple, the tiny break of a small wave. Gracie did not grow up with the sea, though she was born near it. Her parents took her to the New Jersey shore two weeks out of every summer, *The shore* they called it. (Except for her summer in

Hawai'i, of course; where did Maizey and Thomas go that year, 1994? Gracie shipped home again in August, two weeks early.) Yet it isn't unfamiliar to her, Gracie thinks, maybe because the sea is so often the backdrop of her dreams, though never this dark, this cold. She thinks about Berry's comment that first day, the unlikeliness of sharks out cruising these cold water harbors, looking to snack on a little girl's leg. But Gracie knows now and surely Berry did as well, that Shark Girl was not from anywhere around here. She too chose this place, for what reasons Gracie and everyone else it would seem, can only guess. The articles Gracie keeps reading and rereading from the file box (can't stop herself at this point, reading every spare minute; had she found something this engaging at school instead of school being the place most urgent to hide from, she might've gone on to college as her parents expected, made *something* of herself!), these clippings seemed to indicate a woman perpetually on the run, searching for out of the way places to hide, perhaps. Someone who possibly has the gift of healing (some of these speculated) and would have to periodically vanish, because if too many of the afflicted caught up to her this fragile calling could be destroyed. Others hinted at the opposite, that perhaps this *gift* was really a hoax, a sham, a plea for attention—even a slap in the face for the Catholic Church, one suggested, miracles and *stigmatic* healings and the girl wasn't even raised a Catholic! And so Shark Girl disappears.

Gracie concentrates on walking in this dress, one foot then the next, a black and frigid night, trying not to step on the satiny material bunched up high as she can lift it in her freezing fingers, toward the destination point, the lighthouse at the end of the breakwater. She figures she's better than half way there and not totally consumed with panic yet, as would normally be her way. That is if she regularly did stuff like this, which she most certainly does not. Gracie McKneely has led a self-protected life, goes with the territory of hiding. (She could give some of those articles authors, Internet bloggers, pontificating on Shark Girl's whereabouts an insight or too about disappearing.)

It occurs to Gracie she no longer hears Roma and the others. Turns around slightly, slap of cold wind in her face, the black gnaw of emptiness. So! This *is* some kind of a hoax, an initiation into something she wants no part of. Now Gracie does have to swallow down a gulp of panic, alone in a dark, strange and slippery world. She pinches her cheek, the good one, to remind herself *I am here, I am me*, and then the other, her fingers drifting over the stretched tight ripple of scar. A branding, an identity.

She's closer to the lighthouse than the place where she started and so Gracie pushes forward, not because of this supposed "prize" at the end, but because if this is some sort of initiation, even though she'd want no part of *this* club, for once she doesn't want to be thought of as chicken, either. Especially not by Roma. Gracie would never hear the end of it. I can do this, she thinks.

Gracie is muttering to herself about how there must be too little to do around here, even less than upstate, it would seem, clutching the long gown up and away from her ankles, feeling tenderly for each shadowy rock with her sneakered foot. Luckily Liela's feet were so unforgivably larger than hers she didn't have to wear the shoes that would go with such a dress. *Strappy* mile-high platforms, probably, heralding Liela's six foot plus frame into seven. Why is it others who are different in some way, standouts from the masses as in they don't get to slide through unnoticed, unremarked upon, *normal*, manage to turn this into a positive thing, something to be desired and envied, something of power, whereas all Gracie seems to be able to do is hide behind her one good feature, her hair?

Belch of the fog horn, the twisting and turning, rotation of the light in the lighthouse greets her arrival at the end of the breakwater. She jumps a little at the sound, which has been intermittent—as if sometimes it believes that fog will move in and other times it's just your basic cold and starry night. On the level above her Gracie can make out the building itself in the thin light, the peeling of its paint, its raw wood. She leans up against the granite base of the building, feeling the cold rock against the low back of the gown. Roma and her minions had given Gracie someone's jacket to wear, silver threads punched into a crepey, flowery design, machine-spun fabric, your basic chain-store tackiness, as Roma put it, which Gracie guesses they figured went better with a sequined wedding dress than her own sure and comfortable fleece, and this is also too big, stretching down to expose bare, chilled skin. Chicken skin, these goose bumps are called in Hawai'i, another oddity Gracie picked up from one of the scraps in Shark Girl's file box. Some reporter had interviewed a local about Shark Girl: *Get chicken skin,* the local said, thinking about it. *Spirits, akua and 'aumākua in islands, you no question da kine. Local haole girl turn into one shark? Maybe she not all haole. Maybe she not all girl!*

"Gracie?"

This time she really does jump, lurching forward, tripping on the gown straight into Anthony's concave chest. He holds her for a second, steadying her, then lets her go.

"What the hell!" Gracie shrieks, sounding like Roma.

He shrugs, or rather she feels this dismissive movement, close as she is. It's too dark to actually see. "Roma told me to come out here," he says. "I was around the corner. Heard something, wanted to see what the fuck it was. Some believe these lighthouses are haunted, you know."

"You always do what Roma tells you to do? Got no spine of your own?" Gracie's feeling an unfamiliar rage, the unexpected scare, but even more her anger at Roma who clearly manages to get them all doing what she wants because, for chrissake, here they are!

"Well..." he hesitates. Gracie can tell he's looking her over in the ridiculous wedding dress and she feels ashamed.

"It's Liela's," she mutters, the automatic burial response, cheek behind the safety of her hair; then she remembers he can't see this in the dark, her damage.

"Yeah, well Roma told me it had something to do with you. What the fuck?" he whispers.

Gracie stares at Anthony. His face in a darkness that has opened up around them — the stars turn to be out, unraveling of that sliver of moonlight, fog retreating to the outer islands — looks so vulnerable for a moment. *What the fuck?* spoken so gently, almost a sigh. Suddenly she forgets where she is, who she is, the outrageous gown, her own ruined face and without even thinking about it Gracie reaches up, pulling his chin down toward her the way Roma tugged at hers to exhale the pot smoke. He opens his mouth over Gracie's, no coaxing required, those thick berry lips, bristle of chin whiskers and like in her dream of someone else she slides her tongue into his mouth, her hair wheeling out around them in the salty wind. He pushes against her, that chest, familiarity of it the blue-black strangeness of this night, his ambling shape, languid like moving under water, his wet mouth swallowing hers. *Grey shadow.... Something in her notes .... It was like a giant bear trap clamping down..., though what would she know about a bear trap? Compiled by S.G.*

Anthony is prodding Gracie toward the lighthouse steps. "Come on!" — urgent, yet still that halting voice — "something to show you."

Gracie peers up at the lighthouse. "I don't know," she mumbles, still reeling from that kiss, the dark hunch of stairs leading up. The building itself appears three stories, its rocky base built upon the granite, a first floor then a top floor, and another brick wing has the light house tower on it. "I don't know," she repeats.

"Well fuck, Gracie," he says softly, almost tenderly, "nothin' to be scared of, I got a light." Anthony produces a small flashlight from his jacket pocket, as if not being able to *see* the steps leading up to a dark and lonely lighthouse in the middle of the bay, middle of the night is the only problem. "The thing you got to watch out for is the sound," Anthony advises. "Foghorn's so fuckin' loud the Coast Guard has a sign telling you to stay back a hundred feet."

"Are we?" she asks, her eyes needling up to where it might come from, this ear shattering blast.

"Well *duh*, Gracie, can't climb these stairs and be a hundred feet away at the same time now, can you? Don't worry, fog's moved out to North Haven and Vinalhaven. See, you can't even make out the islands' shapes no more."

Gracie peers out into the black, shaking her head and he tugs at her hand. "Come on, you're not chicken, are you?"

Yes! she thinks, but she follows him up, slowly, gripping the metal guard rail tightly on the ocean side. The wind whips up a briny smell. She's close enough to the back of Anthony to inhale the horsey scent of his leather jacket, remembering the feel of it too, against her. "Wouldn't take you for a chicken," he's sputtering, words caught in the wind.

"I'm not much of an adventuress," Gracie says softly, though she doubts he heard her. She wants to touch him again but is suddenly afraid. Maybe she was wrong about what happened, that it didn't mean a thing; he was just responding politely to her moves, like following your partner in the fox-trot or something and here she is out in the middle of nowhere with a guy she barely knows, someone accused of being a rapist! Was he remembering her face when they kissed? Maybe he'd kiss any girl out of politeness, a greeting, like shaking someone's hand, clapping them on the shoulder; tongue on tongue, *hello there, how ya doin*!

"It's OK," Anthony assures her, and she's not sure what is or isn't. After they get to the top Gracie follows him around to the other side, a part of the structure that seems to be brick, cold and scaly in the darkness, moving beside him where he's pointing, the whiteness of his finger a pale twig stretched out in the black, into what appears to be a fist sized broken window pane.

She shivers, "You didn't do that, did you?"

"Gracie, Gracie," he makes a clucking sound through his teeth, "we're just getting to know each other and already you accusin' me? It's that heavy beveled glass they used to make," he tells her authoritatively. "Thick as a man's neck, so how's it going to smash, huh Gracie? Breakwater was finished a hundred years ago, something like 800,000 tons of granite took nine years to build. Don't know for sure on the lighthouse but you can bet it's pretty old. Didn't that sign bottom of the stairs say 1902? That's damn fucking old. Put your face against where it's broken."

Anthony presses his face into the glass and Gracie looks at him like he's crazy.

"Go ahead," he urges. She moves closer, an eerie feeling, heart hammering, the sense of it suddenly being too warm and a sound like a machine, a steady whirring. Jumps back, the strange warmth from inside the glass, a musty, stale smelling wind breezing against her face. Turns toward Anthony, "What the hell?"

"Right!" he nods, clearly satisfied with her reaction.

Score ten points for Gracie McKneely being her usually befuddled self. "What is it?" she asks.

"Don't know," he shrugs. "Haunted, maybe. We're talking *old* here. Lighthouse used to be manned. It's like a whole house, you know. Now everything's automatic, run by some sort of electric impulse or something. Can't change the past though, don't matter how techno things get. What's past is past."

Gracie stares at him. Whatever slowness she thought might have been there has been replaced by something else, almost animated. He feels like someone else, a cartoon of whatever it was she thought of him before sped up, press the fast forward let it rip. "But what could it be?" she whispers. "That warm air."

"What do *you* think?"

He seems to want her to be feeling some kind of reverence here, but living around Berry Waters and her weird group of women, Berry's *spiritualist* ancestry, Gracie is starting to get the impression that Maine is a place maybe a little too caught up in its past, its deaths anyway! Roma said her mother named her after gypsies and that gypsies don't acknowledge death, yet it seems that this *is* Berry's world, life in the what's already happened, trying to bring it back. A chance to play it again, only differently. Not a lot of future-minded conversations happening in that household. "I don't know," she tells him.

Anthony sighs. "Well it doesn't have to mean a fucking thing, Gracie. Just is." Suddenly he grabs her shoulders, she's thinking (hoping?!) maybe to kiss her again but even in the dark she senses the wildness about him. "Let's go in, check it out!"

"What, are you crazy?"

"Nah, look!" Anthony pulls at Gracie's arm, tugging her around the corner, shining his flashlight up on a second story window to the right of where they're standing, the wooden part of the building, and she can see the jagged break in a larger pane of glass.

"I'll just knock that fucker rest of the way out, hoist you up on my shoulders and you reach in, open the window, climb in. Then you can go unlock the door let me in too. We'll check this puppy out. Maybe we can get up where the light is."

"No way, Anthony!" Shakes her head vehemently. "There's no way I'm doing that. This is private property, has to be what, owned by the state? Coast Guard? God, if we get caught!" She's imagining the stricken look on her mother's face, her father's slow ponderance. *We didn't raise you to destroy things, Gracie,* Maizey would say; his frown of disappointment. Life disappoints though, doesn't it? He would know this, would have studied it, the statistics, how many of a group's members will eventually, irrevocably (this would be his word for it) go bad. "It's just wrong," she says.

"Don't you ever do anything *wrong*, Gracie?" He gives her that strained look and even in the darkness she can see this, sense him drifting from her. And he's right. She doesn't do anything *wrong*. But it's not like smoking a joint or something, not this! Chill wind around them now, stale damaged air inside, what is he asking her to do here?

"How do you know, Gracie? How do you know until we get into this sucker how wrong or right or what anything is, just cause people tell you not to do something so you don't do it? They tell you not to deface public property, is that what you're pissing your panties over? The thing's already fucking defaced!" And with that he leans down, unties his boot and in one smooth, almost poetic motion, curve of his arm, his shoulder in the milky darkness lit up by five second rotations of the light in the light house tower, Anthony hurls his shoe through the broken pane of glass taking out the rest. Gracie can hear its shattering somewhere inside, but she ducks just in case.

"Oh God," she moans.

"There," he says smugly, "now we have a reason to go in. I can't walk back on these rocks with just one boot, huh? Don't want me to fall off the breakwater and drown, do you, or trip and break my foot?" He kneels down. "Climb up on my shoulders, Gracie."

Her heart beats hard, its accelerated rush inside her veins. "Can't we just go around this upstairs part from outside, look in the windows? You've got your flashlight, your boot's probably right under the sill." She's remembering that weird warmth and the sound coming from inside. If she goes in first and has to unlock a door for him, then she's in there alone with *whatever*, stumbling around trying to find the damn door!

"Jesus Christ! It's colder than shit and my knees hurt bending down like this; will you just get the fuck on my shoulders? Huh, *Gracie*?" She hears Anthony's aggravation in the way her name is peeled off his tongue, letters sticking, he wants them gone.

Gracie sighs, places her legs around his neck, having to hoist the wedding gown way up her crotch to do so. Sting of freezing wind greets bare thigh flesh. Her face flames and something else, a sort of tingling sensation below her hips, especially when Anthony puts his hands on her thighs, guiding her, holding her up as he rises to a standing position. Suddenly moist and she hopes to God he can't feel this.

"OK," he instructs, "you at the window?"

"Yeah," she chokes, forcing a breath in, feeling again that unfamiliar warmth from where the pane is newly broken. And an even worse smell, rank and damp like urine. "It stinks!"

"That's the smell of nothing used all these years. It's a kind of death," Anthony offers. "Reach in, it's just your basic double hung, not that thick glass from the other window. Unlock it, push the sucker up."

Anthony's starting to pant under her weight, Gracie supposes, though she's not so heavy, at least not that. She does what he says, hating the thought of putting the rest of her on the inside, it's already feeling like a commitment even having her arm in there, unlocks the window, hoists it up slowly.

"Climb in, damnit!" Anthony wheezes. "You waiting for a written invitation?"

"Promise you'll come in right after me? Can't you climb in here too?"

"For chrissake, Gracie, I'll pass up my light, just go unlock the fucking door!" He boosts her through the window, heartbeat roaring in her ears, and she swivels around immediately not wanting to break her connection with the world outside, leaning down. "I'm in," she says. "Hand me the flashlight."

"OK, so now you'll have to find the way back down to where the door is, remember?"

Gracie scans the dark room fearfully, shining the light here, there, chipped and peeling paint on the walls, clutter everywhere, old boxes, wooden crates, metal barrels, scraps of plywood, what looks like an ancient bulletin board lying face down on the floor, old everything. She doesn't want to leave the safety of this window, the way back out. What the hell is she doing here! Squeamish, trying to slip through the world less noticed Gracie McKneely breaking into a haunted lighthouse? The shoes don't fit! Thinking this she bends down and picks up Anthony's boot beside the window, pressing its thick gnarled leather to her chest, some comfort in this. "Anthony?"

Gracie croaks. The sound of her own voice echoes. She peers back out the window but he's already gone, presumably heading toward the door. *What I have to do, all I have to do!* she tells herself, her heart a jack hammer inside her chest, *find the stairs, go down and unlock the door.* Then at least she won't be alone.

A memory, child Gracie, *dog-face*, nine years old and the group of boys, Little League players in another hour but at this moment they are wolves, a pack of them surrounding her, taunting her, howling *dog-face! dog-face!* Herding in closer to the abandoned building where she scrunches down in the shards of glass, stink of pee, wagging their tails threateningly. They have followed Gracie home from school, turning into this lot where she ran trying to lose them, scent of her fixed in their wind thick as sweat, the drool on their tongues, this ancient longing for what she can't know, can they know? Older boys though not by much, and she didn't understand then what they could do but felt the fear of it anyway, and they felt her fear and it excited them. They leave suddenly, crunch of footsteps, screech of a car's brakes. Gracie huddles down, winching her face into the neck of her too-big nylon jacket far as it can get. Feels like she *is* these broken buildings sometimes, sister in stone, not needed, vacated, whatever their business in the world at one time now defunct, trashed, disappeared, slumped into their own decline, reminder of something best left alone. *Will Anthony leave me too? Will he send me away...?*

Gracie shines the flashlight across to where a door is, stepping into the path of its light, one foot, other foot, forward. Another room, appears to have been some sort of bedroom maybe though there's nothing to suggest much comfort, more boxes, some taped shut but most are yawning open, papery looking stuff poking out, stack of metal chairs, a card table with one bent leg and a heavily scratched surface, piles of random clutter on top, nothing official as in lighthouse type equipment. She tries thinking plain old how-was-it-used-before type thoughts to chase away any other thoughts, sounds, the sick and wasted smells, creepy feeling of being where you shouldn't. Tiptoes toward another door. What is she afraid of waking up? Tries to force a deeper breath. The ocean outside, its reassuring rhythmic sweep against the breakwater granite.

Shining her light into a short hallway, an old bathroom, remnants anyway, the filthy tub, stained, nasty looking sink, a place where there might have been some sort of toilet. Gracie thinks of things crawling there, in and out of the rotting drains, spidery, poisoned with age. The light plays havoc on the peeling walls, gritty floor and again that too-warm air; it's either airless in here, shutting out the night's cold or it really is unnaturally warm. Hairs prickle up and down her arms, back of her neck. "Chicken skin!" she announces out loud, squeak of syllables into the deadened air, what they say in Hawai'i when even your skin is spooked.

"Gracie!"

The flashlight careens to the floor, winks out. "Anthony, God!" Her heart does a back flip in her chest. "You scared the hell out of me!"

He bends over, picks up the light. "Worse, Gracie, you broke the fucking light."

"Well how the hell did I know it was you, I was supposed to let you in! How did you get in?"

"What, you think some ghost of an ancient keeper knows your name? Who in Christ's name you think it is? Taking too long. Found an easier way."

"Another broken window?"

"Well," he chuckles, "wasn't a few minutes ago. You deaf or something?"

"Oh Lord," she moans, clutching her head between her arms. "I don't believe this." She considers prayer. It's what Berry would propose. Prayer of the, Dear God please-save-my-butt variety!

"Yeah well," Anthony sighs, heaving the dead flashlight against the wall, "we don't need that sucker. Let your eyes adjust, not so dark in here."

"You better pick up that flashlight," Gracie warns. "Fingerprints."

She can feel him laughing at her. "Oh!" he says. "Duh! Good thinking, Nancy Drew."

"Roma called me that. You two used to read together or something?"

Anthony grabs Gracie's wrist and twists it hard. "Don't mention that cunt in here, here's one place that hasn't been fucked by her."

She pulls away from him, rubbing her arm. "Ouch!" Face burning, that word, cunt cunt *cunt*.

"Sorry," he mutters, "but it's you and me, just us. I know Roma put us up to this and all but, like now it's none of her business, out of her control. She hates that."

Us? Gracie's thinking. Her mind fixates on this, *us*, compelling enough of a thought to block its sister out, that *us* breaking into private property is maybe not the ideal way to start *us* off!

"Come on!" Anthony grabs her arm again, not so tight, just firm. "Let's climb up to where the light is, the metal stairs other side."

She follows him down the short hall into another room, small and cramped, also peeling paint—he's right about their eyes adjusting to the darkness, stuff she just as soon not see!—and that foul, used up air. Gracie can make out what looks like a trap door set of stairs, maybe more for lighthouse keepers or firefighters than real people, skinny silver bars poking straight up. "What about coming down?" she asks doubtfully, heart thumping inside her chest, boom, boom, boom; *doom, doom, doom*!

She can feel his impatience. "Gracie, Jesus. You always got to picture everything you do to its fuckin' finish? Come on, I'll go behind. If you fall you fall on me."

Gracie pulls up the dress reluctantly, swish of its satiny fabric around her knees and she climbs, one step at a time.

At the top they are outside again, only this time high above the breakwater. The fog has retreated completely, massive splattering of stars on the black sky like they were flung there by a giant paint brush. An icy wind whips through and she gasps, "It's like being on top of the world!" She knows this must sound stupid, but it is! Gracie smiles at Anthony, revolutions of the light in the lighthouse tower patterning his face, glowing a pure electric white every five seconds like some weird plugged-in redemption. Would Berry appreciate this? Church of electronic salvation? Anthony gathers Gracie into his arms, kissing her, his cold bare hand pressed against her neck, slipping down on her breast, working its way between the buttons of her "borrowed" jacket, fussing over the satin and sequins of the wedding gown.

"Wish you weren't wearing this thing!" he whispers.

Me too, she thinks, face flaming.

In contrast with most fishes, fertilization in sharks is internal, meaning that the male and female copulate....

"Will you hurt me?" Gracie whispers, or maybe she didn't whisper it; maybe she just thought it. Maybe it wasn't even her, his fingers tugging at whose nipple? *hard as cartilage in his hand.*

Picking their way carefully back over the breakwater Gracie slips, tripping on the dress, slide of the uneven rock and Anthony seizes her arm, his fingers edging around her hand, her fingers lacing awkwardly through his. "So you don't fall," he says. "How come *you* didn't bring a flashlight?"

"Roma didn't exactly warn me I'd be hiking out here in a ten foot long gown!" Gracie mumbles, cheeks burning—she's holding hands with him!

"Uh huh, and I guess you think she came up with the idea like on the spur of the moment?" Anthony laughs, a short unhappy barking sound. "You got something to learn about Roma. She fuckin' cooks everything. She's probably been marinating this in her head for days, just waiting on the right opportunity. She tell you I'd be out there?"

Gracie shakes her head and he's silent and, it occurs to her, maybe disappointed?

"She said there'd be a surprise," Gracie offers.

"Uh huh," Anthony repeats. "You, me, the ghost."

"The ghost?"

"What, you didn't see him? Hovering at the bottom of those metal stairs when you were inching down? I had to bat him away, he was trying his damnedest to see up that Amazon dress of yours. Those keepers got pretty horny, you know. Families lived on shore, just the keeper and his assistant all alone in a little house, middle of the sea, end of a mile of rock. Keepers got needs too, you know." Anthony squeezes her hand and Gracie squeezes back, giggling a little, thinking he'd think she's supposed to. We're like those foghorns, she thinks, one wails the other answers, its timed response.

"Check this out!" He shoves something cold into her palm, metal hard. She peers down but can't make out what is in the dark. "What is it?"

"Don't know. Found it in that tower room, thought we could use a little souvenir of the evening. Some kind of an old something, a compass maybe. Maybe I can sell it to an antiques place, split the booty with you."

She draws back, dropping his hand. "You stole it?"

"What, stole? Nah, Gracie, shit. Stealing is something you plan. Like I said I thought we needed some kind of souvenir. I did it for us. Don't even know what the fuck it is so what's the worth in that? I'm going to steal something I'm going to make damn sure it's worth the effort."

She shakes her head, *us,* that us again. Stares out at the lights of Rockland and Rock Harbor glimmering sharper now, closer they get. "I hope it's nothing they need," she tells him. "What if they miss it?"

"They, who's *they*? What, you think someone still lives out there, uses this thing, whatever it is? Nothing personal about it." Anthony takes her hand in his again, squeezing her fingers. The fog thick around them now and the mournful call of the horns, warning of things hidden, concealed, sudden jagged rocks, sink into the briny mist. Sounds of the sea as it sucks up under the rocks like something breathing; inhale, exhale, if they fell in would it claim them as its own?

They walk off the breakwater hand in hand, back up the sandy bush-lined path, scent of night blooming something in the heavy air, cold as it is, to the parking lot. Roma is there with a couple of the others, sprawled on the hood of a parked car, smoking a joint. Most have gone, the motorcycles have disappeared.

"So!" Roma chortles, she's humming the wedding march of all things. "Here comes the happy couple!"

Anthony drops Gracie's hand like it's weighted and she feels the night's coldness in her fingers, a chill inching up her wrist, arm and neck.

"You love birds want a ride?"

Anthony shakes his head and without another look at any of them takes off down the street, his lanky stride hunched and purposeful. Gracie feels his loss, though it's not like they even had a date. Remembers the press of his hand on her breast and shivers. It's only the night air now, keen and biting.

"Come on!" Roma leaps down off the hood, motions her in. The chunky short girl named Earth, her metal nose hoops glowing like neon boogers in the thin light of the open car door is driving. And Gracie is about to comply as is her way, but suddenly she feels a surge of something in her, hot snap of the blood, some fallout in her bones, organs, something that's surely *not* her—a something that breaks into lighthouses! "No," Gracie tells her, "*No*! I'll walk."

"Oh for chrissake girlie, get a grip, it was just a joke. You can't go walking the streets at 2:00 in the goddamn morning all by yourself in some wedding gown! Christ, that's like pervert perfume. They'll smell you two towns away."

"What would you care? You had me hiking out on a mile of dark slippery rocks in Liela's seven-foot dress, so I guess I can navigate a couple of Rock Harbor town blocks." Then Gracie starts down the same road as Anthony, though well enough behind where if he turns around, he may or may not notice her. And she can rationalize to herself that he *doesn't* see her, doesn't know she's here. And that this is the reason he will not be coming back for her.

The fog reeling in, a dense cloud of it obscuring the boundaries of the houses and street so that it feels like she's walking in a funnel, eyes straight ahead, smell of the sea in her nose down her throat like she's in it somehow. Inhales a deep moist breath, the cinnamon scent of old roses, beach roses destroyed by the cold and frost, planted to look like they grew naturally in the field Roma pointed out to her, where one day a house slid into the ocean. It had been raining hard, Roma said, days of it but no one could have predicted *this*. The people in the house heard a roaring like a train throttling through and they ran outside just in time to witness the earth caving in, swallowing up their lives: children's pictures, diplomas, wedding china, Grandma's antiques, documents, old letters, the chartings of a personal history all a part of the sea, returned to some elemental root. Pale rocks illuminated in the fog mark the boundaries of what used to be, and the rose bushes withered old petals dropping in the cold.

CHAPTER FOURTEEN

It is that blue, that jewel-like turquoise then a sudden darkness, churning, a sea foam green. We are going deeper. I am not afraid; the leg is already gone. Bits of chum floating past, these walls of flesh and cartilage holding me in, bearing me down. I stretch leisurely inside the belly of her, my fingers, hands wrapping around bits of this and that, a tire, a fishing net, femur of an infant something, spine of a medium sized mammal. It is a chronicling of her life as predator, scavenger, top of the food chain in the sea. I peer down at the place where the leg once was and there is just its phantom, that sense of something missing. Suddenly, like a typhoon barreling down her jaw drops open and the ocean rushes in. On the out-take, the updraft, I hear her howl and I am on a wave of her blood now roaring up her cavernous throat, her gaping mouth where the hook flashes fierce in the sudden sun, the gate of razor teeth. Chugging of a fishing boat's engine like the beating of wings in the water, a cormorant, black angel rising to the surface.

When she awoke, heart beat ragged and colder than the coldest flesh, fish flesh, water without breath, it was pulling her, tugging at the nylon sleeve of her nightshirt, *her* nightshirt, *come on! come on!* urging her in. Went right to it like she knew where she had to go, had always known this, tearing through the file box to the journal, tucked inside a manila envelope, a palm-sized brown spiral notebook buried under the last section of the box under the quotes, the reports, more *compilings*, before the sun paled the sky:

I am uncomfortable reading about the lives of the saints, their wanting to suffer, give their lives over to this suffering. Is wanting to suffer what makes us holy? Closer to God? Do I lack faith because I would prefer not to suffer? Should I beg for this pain that comes anyway? Berry Waters says some children are raised to "offer it up"; they fall down, cherry scrapes on their elbows, "offer it up to Jesus!" She says the Bible tells us suffering is a crucible, a passing through fire, a purifying test. If we fail we reject God, increase our unlovableness, dark night of the soul. I do not have it in me to ask for more suffering. I have suffered enough. (S.G.)

P.S. Sharks kill maybe ten humans annually worldwide while fishermen crucify a hundred million sharks each year. A despicable thing known as shark-finning involves capturing the shark, cutting off its fin to sell for the culinary-elitist shark fin soup then throwing the wounded animal back into the sea to die, maybe eaten by its own, crazed by the scent of this blood. How inhuman humans are. One can only improve the gene pool by not contributing to it. (S.G.)

Gracie reads then rereads these words, trying to find the sense, interpret the tone, the feel of her language, her intent, what need behind them. As time allows she slips back into the room in between the vacuuming, the dusting, mopping, sweeping, *the* room, *their* room, pries open the box, *their* box, *her* almost entirely empty notebook: *Journal* it announces in black felt-pen letters on the frayed and faded cover, a scrap here and there, nothing very personal, bits about sharks mostly and this, a note to...who? *One can only improve the gene pool....* Was hoping for, what? Some indication of who she is? Gracie thinks of her own notebook kept *that* summer, cataloging her collections, her lists, done with Dr. Bender's input, her approval, and then the careless, or not so careless—can she even recall what truth in this?— her journal left open on the coffee table: *one cylindrical aqua glass ball, floating in the ocean at dawn; one dead puffer fish washed up on the beach at dawn; two bodies swimming in the ocean at dawn, two heads, long hair short hair; two, no four BREASTS..., now one head, one body... Dr. Bender, Louis, but Louis is a lady!*

Snapping the file box closed again Gracie's feeling less and less guilty, *I do have a right to this, she's left it for me!* Box shoved under their bed for more immediate access. It is dinner time. Gracie will eat no cow, pig, sheep or chicken flesh, nothing that once had a heart, legs, warm blood pumping through.

After dinner is cleared, dishes soaking in the sink for Janie's rotation they gather in the living room. Roma is nowhere anyone knows. "Probably moved out again," Berry grumbles. "All about proving she doesn't need me, that one." Though Gracie won't say it, this time she suspects Roma has left on her account. She's seen little of her since the breakwater night, where after Gracie hoofed it home Roma had arrived before her, chain locking the door so Gracie was forced to ring the bell until a scowling, put-upon Berry dragged herself out of bed, glaring scornfully at the wedding gown and let Gracie in. The thought had crossed her mind to follow Anthony into the carriage house, and with this a wave of fear, of nausea. Who was *she*? Shivering, wind blown cleaning girl in a too-big dress up dress, her caved in face. But once inside Gracie did wonder, Berry stomping back up the stairs, who Roma had tried to humiliate with the wedding thing. Maybe it really was Anthony, shrugging Gracie off as just part of the process.

"Let us join hands and call *Jesus* into our fold," Berry says, grabbing up Gracie's own chilled and reluctant right hand. Gracie is on a straight chair this time, a hard-backed Victorian number with a woven cane seat—someone had shuttled it out of the den and placed it nearest Berry's chair. Janie on the other side of her in an easier chair, worn a slick pale pink like the inside of an ear, Tia and Marie on the couch. Jessie, excusing herself with a migraine retreated to her room.

Earlier this afternoon Gracie showed Berry Shark Girl's note about "suffering," shoving the notebook at her almost angrily. As if it proved something. "But what?" as Berry had voiced, speculating about her supposedly *redemptive* suffering, Berry's words, "Did it prove *that* woman holy? This doesn't even look like Shark Girl's handwriting!" Berry had growled. "What I've seen of her writing, and it don't sound a bit like her."

"But she can't speak!" Gracie pointed out. "How would you know what she sounds like?"

"Ayuh, can't or *won't*! Don't matter nohow, Gracie, for crying out loud, it's not the way she would sound if she *did* speak! Words aren't the whole thing, you know. Everything that woman puts out, I'm telling you this is not its language. She's *uncomfortable* reading about the lives of the saints? Give me a break here, that's yuppie-speak! Only yuppies can afford to be *uncomfortable* about things instead of downright pissed! Besides, I've never known that woman to have a thing to do with saints or the Bible for that matter and here she is yapping about things I said about it. You think that one listened to me? Who knows where she might've picked these things up, scribbled them in her notebook just to throw folks off her trail, plug my name in, make it sound real. Or maybe one of the girls wrote it; at one time they were near as obsessed as you seem to have become. You'd think this woman was the Lord returned the way folks fixate on her. After she took off, you suppose you're the only one been riflin' through her stuff? It's how myths are made, Gracie. Americans love a good shark attack. You best come to our meeting tonight" — Berry shook her head, that fierce needle-straight pony tail — "This time we focus on you."

Unsettled by her dream, Shark Girl in the mouth of the shark only it's *Gracie* in that belly! she reluctantly agreed, or more to the point, didn't object. And here we are.

"Tonight we form the healing circle, a Development Circle," Berry commands. They push their chairs closer around the heavy wooden mouth of the coffee table, shoving the table itself nearer to the couch. "Keep a hold of each other's hands," Berry tells them, "While I ask our newest link an important question. Gracie," she begins, "who or what do you feel haunting you?"

Gracie attempts to slide her hands away from Berry's and Janie's but they grasp hers tighter, Janie squeezing her fingers a bit. "It's OK," Janie whispers.

"What do you mean? I have no idea what you're talking about."

"Ayuh," Berry hums. "You've mentioned those dreams of yours, where you dream you're someone else. If that's not haunting...." she looks around at the others for confirmation and they nod. "You seem fascinated with the pathetic life of that woman, what lived in your room before you. Poor deluded child gets attacked by a shark, grows up believing she's holy. Saint Therese now, her true desire was to suffer with *Jesus*, for the sake of others. Offered herself as a *victim* for the sake of merciful love. Offered herself up to be totally consumed by love! Do you truly believe, Gracie, Shark Girl has this kind of holiness in her, the love of our Lord who took our sins upon Himself, was crucified so we might have the everlasting life? Well?" Berry insists. "'Twas not a rhetorical question."

Gracie tries again to free her hands but Berry's and Janie's are fleshy vices, their fingers clamped around her sweating palms.

"Saint Therese believed to truly love we must give ourselves up entirely for we are loved to the degree that we give ourselves to it. Sound familiar, Gracie? This what's haunting you then?" Berry leans closer, her eyes the eyes of a predator, black and clear as water and Gracie staring into them sees herself. "That's it, isn't it? You believe with your own affliction, the disfigurement done to you by your own father you can rise above it somehow, become *loved*. Isn't that what we all want, to be loved no matter what face we offer up to this world?"

Berry's own face is almost on top of Gracie now, the smell of dinner on her breath, onions from the hamburger helper, the rank and mealy meat, *flesh of my flesh*. Gracie shudders, her cheeks flaming and her head drops forward, willing the wall of her hair down, her hands still grasped by Janie and Berry. Tears are behind her eyes and she prays them uncried. They are the old tears though out of the old wounds and they flow out of habit, their well-carved trails down her cheeks. Suddenly dizzy she slumps over, head between her knees.

"It's OK," Berry's voice, gentle now, cloying, as if in the cutting cruelty of her former words she can now mend, sew back together, make whole again with more forgiving ones. Who is this person, believes in these hurting kinds of powers?

"The path toward healing is to identify the thing what's haunting us, pray for its release, offer it up. This is what we are about, why we have these meetings."

"What?" Gracie asks weakly into her knees, head still down between her legs. *Offer it up*!

"Sometimes it's someone who's passed on to the next level so we bring his presence back to us, help us feel some peace. Jessie's Arnie, for instance. Did you know when we are in Level Two we can create who we want to be? If we were old and bald when we passed we can become young with beautiful hair again. If we were ill we can be whole. If our appearance was not as we wished we can recreate our outward look for the rest of the world. Here too, Gracie, we can choose our reality. Takes a lot of work though and an uncommon faith."

Berry sighs, pauses, the dramatic minute of silence. "In your case, it appears you're haunted by your traumatic childhood, what injured you. It's the situation with Shark Girl too, only, for some reason she developed this other thing, the bleeding bit so folks began believing she's something she's not, some kind of a martyr. Don't know how this happens, maybe she's ill herself for heaven's sake, a hemophiliac or whatever. Yet some even think her a saint! Have to be dead to be a saint, for Lord's sake, and holy! Faultless! Uncorrupted! Evidence of good deeds, not stiffing someone for the rent I'll tell you what. You're not her, Gracie, no matter how many times you put on her shirt. You're not fooling nobody, you know, wearing that. And let me tell you one more thing!" Berry lowers her voice which had been growing more shrill with each point emphasized, gripping Gracie's hand so fiercely now her fingers ache, back of her neck burning under that stony glare: "Chasing around after her boyfriend is not going to make you her, neither!"

At this Gracie's head reels up as if yanked by a string, a puppet, somebody else's design. "Her boyfriend?" she squeaks.

"Hah!" Tia chirps from the couch. "She can have that old yard boy!"

"The yard boy," Janie sighs. "Barely spoken a word since she's left."

"OK, OK!" Berry drops Gracie's hand like it's leadened weight and at its release, a puppet still, her arm pops up and out, mind of its own, wants to hit something. "Just look at what's happened here, will you?" Berry's punishing voice, the voice that announces her pain at having to use it, emphasizing every syllable. "You've gone and done it again, lost the sacred right out of our meeting, your willful chat and interruptions. We've lost the spirit, they'll be no more helping Gracie tonight. Too bad, because I think we were getting somewhere, don't you? Gracie, don't *you* believe we were getting somewhere?"

She's feeling a buzzing again, though not dizziness this time, something hotter, madder, like a cloud of bees doing aerodynamic bee circles in her brain this ferocious buzzing madness. Gracie rises as if propelled, filled with this searing surging air, up and off the uncomfortable chair, staring down at them from this new height.

Berry starts to get up and Gracie's hand punches out, itching to make contact, tugged by that invisible string slapping down against Berry's shoulder, forcing her back. "You are a fraud!" Gracie squeaks, though it's not her own voice squeezing out these words, is it? How could it be? *Gracie McKneely doth not sayeth speaketh meaneth mean kinds of things*! Does she? Gracie McKneely is a wimp!

"Dear *Je*sus forgive her, she knows not what she says," Berry mutters, peering angrily about the group for affirmation. Nobody says a thing.

"Misguided," Berry continues, and the hand that is Gracie's yet is not, lifts off of Berry's shoulder like it's drawn by a magnet, hefty as a block of steel, an uncompromising drag, this time plugging itself against her mouth. Gracie feels the dryness of Berry's lips, the soured rage of her breath. "Silence!" she commands. "You've had your say."

And then what Gracie does is she walks out of that room, so quiet now you can hear the ticking of the grandmother clock pushing the minutes forward, a raw and looming forced peace, out the front door and into the night. Where else is there to go? When you make a scene the dramatic exit is required, and Gracie wasn't used to making scenes.

The night is very cold, a frigid, shocking sense of winter right around the corner now, no more insect sounds, just this frozen silence. Hush of the harbor in the distance, an occasional squeal and sigh of a car, snap of the frost bitten grass under her shoes as she walks. The light is on in the carriage house and she can hear something symphonic floating out from under his door, almost dirge like its despair-filled heaviness. As she walks Gracie unbuttons Shark Girl's shirt. She had not even hovered long enough in that house, that hallway to grab her jacket and the freezing air slams against her chest, her skin, *get chicken skin*! braless, nipples defiantly erect.

She knocks and he is at the door immediately, shunting her inside.

"Jesus, Gracie, what the fuck!"

"You use that word a lot," she tells him. *Fuck.*

He stares at her, wild eyed. "Fuck!" he says it again. "What the fuck are you doing?"

Gracie lets the silk shirt slip down off her shoulders, slithering like a snake to the floor. Reaches into the pocket of her jeans, yanking out the woven elastic band she uses to keep her hair off her face when she washes her face, and she ties her hair back so that her face, her cheek, is fully exposed.

Anthony gazes at Gracie's face, her breasts, back to her face. "They'll probably blame me for this," he says.

"Never mind them. Do you want me?" her voice softer now and quivering, though this still is not her speech, her words, no desperate plea here! Only its weakness, its pitch, is true.

He pulls her toward him, at first burying her in the cave of his chest so that maybe he doesn't have to look at her, Gracie thinks, but then pushing her away from him, just a little, so he *can* look at her: face, neck, breasts, back to her face.

"It was an accident," Gracie tells him. "The palsy could get better. Any day I could wake up and it'll be gone. Not the scar though," she rambles on—he needs to know this, what can and cannot change. "The scar's a scar and it's permanent. Too many skin grafts, and then the palsy. There's a facial nerve there you see, a big one that if it's destroyed would leave my face paralyzed on one side. So no more surgeries. They told me this when I was almost thirteen, then they sent me to Hawai'i like that would make it OK. I was a baby. I grew into who I would be. I'm done."

Anthony is still for a moment, as if considering, then nods. She prays he won't look away and he doesn't.

Gracie is the one who leads him, holding his hand in hers, placing it first against her breast, which is good, she knows this, then lifting it onto her cheek, running his fingers over the tight ridges of damaged skin, tender pull of ancient grafts, then down along the lines of her drooping jaw. "Did you love her?" Gracie whispers.

He doesn't answer, she's not even sure he heard. She ushers him toward the sofa bed, already unfurled, unmade, like some giant wrinkled flag beckoning, unbuttons his shirt, slipping it off his narrow shoulders. He lays down and she unties his boots then her own cross trainers, pulling these off, unzips his jeans then hers, sliding both of them down and off their ankles. Pulls down her underpants. A savage roaring in her ears, her heart beating wildly but with what she's not sure. Fear? Desire? Something... unnamable....? It's as if she's on automatic pilot, doing these things so naturally that she's never done, with a familiarity she couldn't know — except from the movies maybe, or one of her father's books, *Sex and Society*, or better yet *Sex for Dummies, A How To Manual*!

Anthony tugs down his baggy boxer underwear and for a moment, lying naked on the bed in front of her he looks so vulnerable. Of course *she*, Shark Girl would want him, his willingness to please her, be at ease with her maybe just *be* with her. What harm in it? Gracie lies down next to him and spreads her legs as Anthony's long body rolls over then lowers itself down on hers.

"Open your eyes," he whispers, "I need you to see me."

Gracie opens her eyes, her thighs, focusing on this, his face above hers. Something strangely familiar in those words, *I need you to see me*!

In the morning, cold and foggy, dawn sky the color of worn iron, the breakwater fog horn's high pitched cry, Owl's Head's lower moan, Gracie creeps into the big house through the back door not even pausing to wonder why it was unlocked, and as she moves toward the front of the house she hears voices, activity, flashing of ambulance lights outside in the driveway illuminating the room through a wide open front door, cold air clambering in. Berry is talking to an EMT, both of them standing in the doorway. Janie and Marie hovering in the corner. She rushes over to them, "What happened?"

"Jessie," Marie answers, "Poor dear."

Berry whips around, the EMT back outside. "Well, if it isn't Gracie McKneely! Nice of you to join us!" Her frigid stare.

"Is she OK? Is Jessie OK?"

"Considering she went for a late night swim off the breakwater in twenty degree temperatures, I suppose she's just dandy!" Berry's vicious scowl.

"Blue skin!" Janie whistles. "That woman was the color of milk gone bad. I found her, heard her moaning 'bout an hour earlier, after I got up for my shift at the Donut. 'Jessie?' I says, knocking at her door, but she doesn't invite me in. So I come in anyways, there's this little voice telling me to, you know, telling me maybe something's not right. And there she is, lying on her bed soaking wet, her whole body shaking so hard it's like an electric current's passing through, she's the color of a light bulb. That one's usually on the darker side, if you get what I'm saying and I don't mean no prejudice here, she's a sight more attractive than the rest of us no matter *what* color her skin is. There's even a piece of kelp dangling off her hair! Her eyes are open but she's not seeing a thing. Near comatose, I figured. I ran to get Berry who called 911."

"But is she going to be all right!" Gracie repeats.

Berry shrugs. "They'll take care of her at Pen Bay. We'll see. No thanks to you though, Gracie. Your room is closest to hers. Maybe if you were in it you might've heard something, you get what I'm saying? Before she decided to go take that swim. Maybe you're the one could've made the difference!" Cool eyes lingering almost malevolently on Gracie's cheek, Berry Waters flounces out of the room.

She must have looked stricken because Marie, the most-likely-to mother among them (Marie *Osmond's* the mother of seven, after all), grabs Gracie's hand, squeezes it, then slings her fleshy arm around Gracie's trembling shoulders, pulling her taut against a squishy chest smelling of Vicks. "Pay her no mind," Marie whispers, stroking Gracie's hair. "Berry just hates it when this kind of thing happens. She likes to think she can keep us safe. Poor Jessie, don't make no difference that she comes from means — husband's a root canal dentist don't you know, down to Thomaston. Been beaten all her life just the same, just like the rest of us. Gets to a person. Good news is there's something inside her made her come out of that freezing water. Berry will tell you it's Jesus. I'm thinking she just made that choice."

Later, when Anthony comes in for his breakfast Gracie ducks her head inside the refrigerator door, cringing, pretending to be absorbed in an effort to find something to eat.

"I heard," he whispers, moving his body up close behind hers. "Some fucking business, huh?" She feels a surge of panic that someone might come into the kitchen, discover them together. But why should she have to hide this? And anyway, Berry went to the hospital with the ambulance, the others to work. Tia, no doubt, slept through it all;

when she finally does fall asleep nothing can wake that one up. Still Gracie pulls away from him. And still something inside her resists this distance, yearns for his touch.

"Not anyone's fault," Anthony says.

She nods, backing slowly from the refrigerator, shutting the door.

He stares at her, her face which must look haggard, worse even than usual. Gracie cringes again and looks out the window, the day a drenched and misty grey.

Anthony follows her gaze, over an empty kitchen sink; no one could stomach breakfast this morning. "I found two tickets," he starts. "That Rockport concert place. On the street in front of the box office, somebody must've dropped them. Came to ask you...." He doesn't have to finish the sentence. Gracie nods, face flaming, ignoring that busy buzz of a little voice inside her—*should've returned them to the box office*. She's not in the mood for an ethics debate with her own conscience, having just been implicated as someone who might have made a difference in a near-suicide!

He grins, grabbing a bagel from the bread basket on top of the refrigerator, turns and angles back out the kitchen door.

Suddenly she can't bear to see him leave this room, leave her here. Gracie rushes after him, yanking open the door and he whips around like he's been waiting for her, holds out those long branch like arms and just like that she's in them; just like that with Jessie maybe dying or in a coma or who knows what in her cold hospital bed, Gracie is again in the heat of Anthony's body, his bed, the carriage house door slammed shut to the rest of the world. This time it is her, Gracie Kathleen McKneely, who gets to be inside.

Gracie McKneely's Summer List — July 29, 1994 —
Things That Can Hurt In The Ocean:

1. Undulated Moray eel — most vicious Hawaiian eel. Dr. Bender said do not put my hand in coral holes while snorkeling. I asked her if she lost her hand that way and she said no. Louis says it's a story how Dr. Bender lost her hand, but nobody seems to want to tell it.

2. *Yellowhead Moray — prowls in the night, hunts by smell.*

3. *Viper Moray — one of Hawai'i's largest and most dangerous. Its hooked jaw has about the longest sharpest teeth in the moray family. Dr. Bender started to explain about animal families but then she said it didn't seem like I was interested. Well who IS interested in eels?*

4. *Great Barracuda — can grow up to six feet, which is as tall as Louis.*

5. *Tiger shark — very very huge and very dangerous. Most shark attacks in Hawai'i are from tiger sharks. I asked Dr. Bender if it was a shark that took her hand off since she studies sharks on Coconut Island and she said no, but if it did happen that way it would be her own fault she said. People should know better than to put their hands in the wrong place at the wrong time, such as photographing a feeding frenzy, she said. Maybe they would think a person's hand holding the camera is just another hunk of chum. She said sharks are intuitive animals and smarter than most people give them credit.*

6. *Louis North — she's a she who looks like a he being very tall and very strong, bigger muscles than my father's and she has chopped hair. I think Dr. Bender likes Louis better than me.*

7. *Gracie McUgly — no one will ever like her the best.*

8. *Shy Filefish — stays mostly undercover. Can flatten itself against a rock, change color and almost disappear.*

Part V

Many local legends are told of shark-men, always to be known by the mark of a shark's mouth upon the back, who can change form from man to shark and who for a long time go undetected until it is noted that an apparently disinterested warning to swimmers is always followed by a fatal attack by a man-eating shark.... Kawelo is a shark-man living on Kauai.... He has a shark mouth on his back, a tail and appendages on the lower part of his body.... Two rocks shaped like grass houses, one under water in the Wailua river, the other a little below the cave of Mamaaku-a-Lono, represent his houses as a shark and as a man. As a shark-man he lived between Kealia and Wailua and would eat up children who ventured to swim out between those two places. Finally he was discovered and a long line of men formed who stoned him to death.

Beckwith; *Hawaiian Mythology*

CHAPTER FIFTEEN

We were herding ducks just a week before it happened, *the tragedy at the seat of our lives*, Willa Beever attacked by the shark. Nuuanu stream, that cold river green, Father, Willa and me (who knows where Robbie was, was he even then becoming the underexposed negative, part of the photo where not enough light gets in, a shape rimmed in fuzziness, our shadow sibling?). We're bringing these ducks from Honolulu home to our mother, three little yellow baby ducks and their big white mama duck in a wire mesh duck cage, back seat of the Plymouth, quaking their little duck heads off. "Hush up!" Willa orders them, demanding little Willa, pretty fair-haired Willa, gets to sit next to them, did she never question then that the world would always listen? The mother duck, alarmed little pebble duck eyes, squawks and squawks.

Up then over the Old Pali Road, around the Windy Corner, cars shaking like the hand of God's playing jacks with them, shake'm up, splat! To this day if you take pork in your car over the Pali at midnight your car will tremble and rock so hard it won't move forward, and it's not the hand of God, it's ghosts—vengeful Hawaiian soldier spirits, you can hear their yelling in the wind, clashing of their wooden spears and clubs, fierce *manō* shark teeth fastened on the ends of these—warriors Kamehameha the Great pushed off the Pali in 1795, Battle of Nuuanu. They're not keen on pork being schlepped, it's *kapu*! But that's another story. Quite a ride back with a car full of ducks, a *commitment*, and Father decides we can't make it all the way out to Kailua after all, over the Pali these quaking ducks, that they need a bit of a dip first, get their clipped little duck wings wet, clipped so they can't fly away. *But they can swim!* Father said. *A chance to be ducks*, Father said.

Four of them paddling dizzily about that stream, ecstatic and confused in their sudden freedom; not exactly in a line, not little soldiers these ducks—what's that expression, have your ducks in a row? No row, these ducks are all over the place, yellow and white feathers twirling and drifting like clouds, little dartings of yellow, here, there, *everywhere*! And the noises they make, never mind the quack quack, more of a sick and throaty squaaaaawk, like we had been trying to murder the things and at long last they've escaped.

And just what the heck Father was thinking, buying those ducks in the first place, I'll never know. Did he get it in his head that having a family of ducks in the itty bitty pond he built for our mother off the lānai (a wishing well, he told Jaycee) in our Kailua yard might inspire family tendencies among us, Father, Jaycee, Robbie, Willa and me? Did he think the example they set, sated duck mom and her obedient little ducklings might make it such that Jaycee wouldn't want to slip out to the Base, *haole*-hula for the hard shaven marines? Their particular mostly vegetarian duck diets might make her want to eat a healthy breakfast, stop guzzling quite so many gin and tonics, become the sober generous housewife only he could dream her to be? Our mother loved Willa best and that's a thing we all understand now, even better than she loved our father. Do ducks prefer one over the next just because she looks more like the mother duck? Loving the mirror image to love yourself? Gazing at me Jaycee would announce: "Willa favors me, but you..." and she'd ponder this a bit, her slender hand resting under that perfectly pointed chin, staring at the knobby little swells of my own stubby knuckles, my ridiculously long and twiggy *Marfanish* fingers; "You must take after *someone*, Scat, I was there when you were born after all, hah hah hah!" Even the tinkling of their laughs were the same, back when Willa still remembered how to laugh. Mine's more horsey, neigh, neigh, though not Father's either. How could it be? Father rarely laughed.

So we're all flapping around in the cold dark water, ducks, Beevers, the muck, slippery rocks at the bottom covered with moss, algae, grimy, slimy stuff. "These darn ducks are leading us on a wild goose chase!" says Father. Is he making a joke? Willa gets a look in her eyes, little Beever sister's silvery glint she gets in the wake of a joke she would never be the brunt of and she lunges out, grabbing one of the squawking baby ducks by one paddling orange leg, and lifting it upside down out of the black water she whips around, tossing it at me. I see a blur of yellow, the terrified squaaaaawk and before we know it I'm butt down in the cold shallow water, legs splayed, me and the duck, a flutter in my arms.

"You look ridiculous!" Father exclaims. "Get up, Scat, and for heaven's sake hold onto that duckling! We haven't got all day. Why can I not count on you, Scat? I need to be able to depend on *someone*."

I try to do this, try to please my father but the slippery, sloppy, grungy feeling of the moss between my toes on the underwater rocks is so *gross* as I attempt to stand, that down I go again and up goes the duck and my head slides under water for just a second, eyes popping open in the murky green. I see the baby duck feet paddling away from me, fast as they can go. I don't take hold.

Instead I sit there, that slimy rock, and I grab onto the St. Christopher medal hanging by a cheap chain around my neck, close my eyes and think. My mother was outraged when I first started wearing this a couple months ago. "It's a fad," Jaycee insisted to my father, I'm sitting right there in the living room as well. "She's trying to be *with it*. A Catholic thing, and she's not even Catholic. Oh for crying out loud!" Jaycee snapped, when my father said nothing. "What you probably don't realize, Scat, is medals have to be blessed in order to be *holy as holy*, in order to make any difference at all. Yours is unblessed, so what good can it be? Only Catholic girls get to have their medals blessed."

Thinking about this now I wonder what made my mother so uneasy? Probably that others could believe it, believe in something beyond themselves. But what did I know? The necklace was one more thing that irritated her, that was outside her control.

I clutch the unblessed medal in my tingling wet hand. I know a *real* blessing: if you go steady with someone you exchange your medal with his and everyone sees his medal around your neck so this is proof that someone likes you. And I also know the St. Christopher story, because Kathy Connely is Catholic and she told me. He was a giant of a man and he made his living ferrying people across a fierce and mighty stream on his huge shoulders so they'd be safe. So one day he carries such a heavy child he thinks he'll fall down into the raging water. But the child tells him he's Jesus and the heaviness is caused by the weight of the world on his shoulders.

Rising slowly out of the water I climb up on the bank, duckless, hopeless, *unblessed*, my father glaring at me. Then his face softens, that distracted look he gets and I am young enough at this point, innocent enough, *naive* enough to believe everything is going to be all right. I offer him my elbow, bleeding from where I skritched it against a rock. He stares, first at the blood, then at the ducks drifting gracefully away, all in a row now behind the mother duck, down the Nuuanu stream.

"It's OK," my father says wearily, "don't cry." (I wasn't going to, crying got you nowhere in my family; it was merely viewed as someone's last straw, a final indignity, a trip to the bedroom behind a slammed door for the crier.) "Look, Scat!" he says, leaning down closer to my face, pointing. "Those ducks' wings were clipped so they couldn't fly free and will you look at that. There they go anyway, by God!" My father lifts up my elbow, dabbing gently at the blood with his own wet hand.

****

Not all my early memories are bad. Here are two starring the fourth of July, a holiday that for most in Hawai'i meant fire crackers, fire works, barbecue or luau. Good times, summer. What else? Celebrate that which annexed the thrown from Queen Liliokalani? *Ua mau ke ea o ka aina i ka pono*—The life of the land is perpetuated by righteousness. Hawai'i motto. *Thou shalt not steal.* Moses motto. My father said the fourth of July was about being free.

There is one before *it* happened. Though this is more of a conglomeration than an exact and particular fourth of July, maybe a blend of several fourths when my family like most Kailua families went down to the beach for a neighborhood lū'au and to watch the fireworks off of Flat Island. It was a time for feeling together as a family, your family among the other families, you shared the same last name, a place, a position, oldest daughter, middle child, prettiest mother, even if she wasn't like the Other Mothers. It was the fifties. You belonged. Something bigger than just *Scat* of the mossy hair and potato bug buddies. Could I have known to question otherwise?

Jaycee always smelled good, I remember that, before the gin and tonics became so unrelenting no flowery department store cologne could mask the sharpness of gin oozing from her pores, caught up on her breath, sour of the tonic soaked lime. She gathered us up, her good scent, good graces and we ran about the lū'au pit, three little Beevers and Father helping the men with the cooking of the pig, digging the imu two days before, placing the pork on the hot lava rocks, the ti wrapped fish, the laulaus, hefting the whole thing out when it was pau. This was men's work. This was the fifties. And of course Jaycee brought a jello mold of some sort, usually in the shape of a summer star, she called it, which became the star of Bethlehem for our Christmas jello. Miracles seemed almost possible then.

The ocean murmured in the fading light and we would swim, we Kailua kids, barreling down the white expanse of sand grainy as sugar, all of us calling for, demanding our parents watch us perform this or that, a dive off someone's shoulders into the dear and certain blue.

Later the fireworks, smoky ocean air, and once maybe twice it was I who got to curl up into Jaycee's lap, Willa on Father's, Robbie just close enough to be recognized as one of us, all of us on our shared beach blanket, sand slushing and caving in beneath us. Cuddle up under her breasts, her slender arms wrapped around me, fragrance of her skin, know it as my skin too.

Here's a memory from another fourth of July, eight years after *it* happened but still in its wake, its fallout, its renegotiating of the family lines, alliances, who does what, who we could be and with whom now that Willa was...who? Hadn't been dubbed Shark Girl yet, still hidden from the eyes of the world in that bed, breasts poking up under the sheet, that shock of blond hair, the incredible, unsmiling face. She was more beautiful than I, no one ever doubted that she would be. She refused to get up out of that bed and the rest of us—at this point we're talking my father and me, Grandma's moved back to Newwwwengland, and Jaycee? who knows? — we had long since given up coaxing her, urging her, asking Willa if she'd ever get up. Robbie was gone. I was who was there. Just turned eighteen and in my head I too was mostly gone.

I lied, lied, lied about my whereabouts, to my father who did care and Jaycee who became annoyed, anyway, at the things I did, places I went, people I saw. I don't think she was really all that bothered; if anything, she was amused at the ways I could disappoint my father, my lies lies lies. *Her* daughter, of course, didn't lie..., didn't speak, didn't move.

It was 1969 and I was *into it* with relish, gusto, what that year had to offer, *heavy man*, drugs. I hadn't developed my taste, my terrible thirst for alcohol yet but I might've guessed its hovering shadow by how readily I took to dope, a duck to water as they say: grass, hashish, opium, LSD, psilocybin, mescaline, speed, uppers, downers, reds, ludes, bennies, poppers, anything that walked, crawled, flew my way, grew in the ground, grubbed onto my tongue by way of a postage stamp, a blotter, folded into a slip of paper, choked, inhaled, snorted, chewed, stuck in my ear, under my arm, needled under my skin — get ripped, mellow out, *blow your mind* — I did it all. Everything except heroin; I had a few principles, after all. Getting high meant not having to think. Not having to try and make sense of things.

So here's the memory. My last summer in Hawai'i before escaping to the West Coast for college and I had a friend. Foxy *hapa-haole* Meena, one half haole and the other half all kinds of good local stuff, paints your skin that crisp sun-brown, Hawaiian, Chinese, Filipino, etc. etc. All the guys wanted to *ball* her but she was precious and shy and maybe more into chicks anyway. Meena had a much older brother called Rake, for a reason that was never completely clear to me. Rake was a *beautiful cat*, as we said of sexy looking guys then, that olivey-smooth skin, black eyes, shoulder length squiggle of curls, his rakish smile — this the name? He was also a dealer, a *pusher*, we all knew it and this made him the more visible to me. His up front job building surf boards and catamaran sailboats for a shop off Kailua road called Wind and Fin.

Too old for me, my father proclaimed when one day I caught Rake's eye, smoking dope with his sister on their lānai in my bikini, baby oil slathered skin, legs long and pink as two wet tongues. (Marfans was the still uncertain future, whether I had it or not, but by then I had learned to use my height, gangly arms, legs, general gawkiness to its bone-thin, braless, hippie bare advantage. If my heart *was* in trouble, telltale swelling at the root of the aorta, I was dutifully stunting its further engorgement, my near-religious drug intake.) Rake invited me to a concert, the Jefferson Airplane in the Diamond Head Crater, and this time, bad choice, I didn't lie when I asked my father if I could go.

The camping trip to the Moku Lua Islands off the Lanikai coast for the fourth of July was to have been Meena, Rake and me, and so I told my parents I was spending the July 3rd night with Meena. I believed this to be almost true, a half lie, you wouldn't fry quite so hot and if they caught you, you could lie yourself down a different path, plans suddenly changed, a victim in their wake. But when I arrived at their house, my packed hippie-bag, my mother called it, a conglomeration of colorful threads woven from some ancient and well-trod carpet, Meena suddenly couldn't go. And she couldn't look me in the eye telling me this so I knew her brother had got to her in some way, a kind of bribe maybe, baseball cards or a rare shell. Meena had this obsession collecting stuff; back then we never questioned these things, wondered about them, it was just something she *got off on.*

But I saw through it. Rake wanted to get me out on those islands, at night, alone. Loyalties are fickle at just eighteen, easily purchased. I merely nodded at Meena said yes, I could go. I climbed into Rake's flowers and peace sign decaled van (the war in Vietnam escalating but was I thinking of anything larger than my own heart-hammering night ahead, riding in his van?), filled with the food he packed, gear for the boat he borrowed from Wind and Fin, one *he* built, he informed me, that *beautiful cat* grin and off we went. At the least I was anticipating a good high; Rake had some orange sunshine acid. But I knew he had other ideas and this excited me, frightened me, made me ache, jagged breath, unsure. I was more at home with the drugs of the sixties than sex, got stoned way more than I got laid, but I was willing to try anything that would drive me further from my family, release me from the chains of my reassigned future, for however long. Vietnam War. A man on the moon. Equal Rights. Civil Rights. Black Panther Party. Altamonte. The larger, messier world. The Beever that was left. I was nervous and I was ready.

We sailed out to the bigger island, a whale's hump in the near-dark, purpling sky, slap slap of the water against the boat, slap slap of my heart beat. A bird preserve Rake told me, disturbing the terns and boobies, the *iwa* frigate birds as we dragged the catamaran up onto the sand, all rising in a shadowy bird cloud above us. Frigates, *man-of-war birds*, I stared at his sharp brown shoulders in the dying light, sinewy, hard, shuttling the supplies from the catamaran then spreading a lau hala mat on the sand. It was almost night. There were no other humans nor would there be, on this little rock island. I drummed in a breath, slunk down on the mat and Rake passed me a joint then the orange acid tab, psychedelic chaser.

He lit the fire, greasing up our tofu burgers and dumping our canned corn into a rickety handled pan, then suggested I take a swim. I knew what he was getting at. And I wanted to do this for him, I really did, slither out of my clothes like some hippie sea goddess, uninhibited, dive into the ocean a thrillingly sensual, naked arch so he could stare at me, so he would want me. But this was the *ocean*. Swimming just after the sun went down! We knew what was out there, my family and me, if nobody else remembered. (Billy Weaver's leg was bit off somewhere between the Moku Luas and Flat Island, I can see the *Advertiser* even now: *Lad From Prominent Isle Family*, his dark-eyed smile…"The boy died in the water shortly after.") I hesitated, and Rake must've thought it was the naked thing. He shrugged, "Did you bring a bathing suit?" I could hear the letdown in those words.

Well of course I did, this was to have been a camping trip after all, but I shook my head.

He shrugged again, said our meal would be ready soon. *I know what's in that water.*

After dinner I was reeling, acid kicked in, stars burst out, night air steaming, salt and wind, sounds of the birds the roiling waves, things immense. The roof of my mouth tingled and Rake was staring hard at me, giving me the up and down and all over, and what I wanted to do was please him, *belong* to him make him *dig* me, glad he went to whatever trouble, whatever deception to get me out here, away from his sister, away from the world for this night anyway. Tomorrow the fourth, fire works, a celebration. I needed to believe.

"Will you swim right beside me if I go in?" I asked hoarsely. "My sister, you know?"

He nodded, though who knows if he did know, most in Hawai'i had forgotten, had stopped caring. Only when the first article suddenly appeared, late seventies or thereabouts, proclaiming *Shark Girl*! A miracle! did some in Hawai'i remember her, claim her as theirs.

Slowly, fingers shaking, working loose the buttons of my shirt, getting only half way before his fingers were there too, long and quick and certain. And these fingers were unbuttoning my pants, inside my pants, my underpants, me, and I knew I wouldn't have to worry about the swimming part.

He lay me down on the lau hala mat, shifting of the cool sand under us. I could see the shadow of his penis coming down on me, longer than a kiawe branch, *stiffer than stiff* as it poked about between my legs, searching for the *enter*—we were both pretty high and maybe our sonar for this thing was off. For a moment I thought of begging him to stop, sudden panic, choke of fear, what the hell am I doing! And then he's in me and it doesn't hurt and I'm being BALLED, SCREWED, MADE LOVE TO, FUCKED, FUCKING, *FUCK*! Loving the sound of this word in my brain, rattling about in there like something with teeth, something that could tear through those chains binding me to my family, chew up the metal like masticating nails, spit out the shavings and I'd be free of this, *the tragedy at the seat of our lives*.

OK, so here comes the bottom line. Honest to God I actually thought this, high out of my skull on LSD, Rake poking about inside me: I could do what Willa couldn't, stunning Willa, once believed likely to *husband* best, languishing in her bed and I am here GETTING LAID on the beach. When he was done he rolled off of me, sweaty heap, musky sea-smelling air playing down the long cool wet of my body. I shivered, leaned over and stroked the coarse curls on his chest, asked him, holding my breath for his answer, did he come in me? I was thinking even if he did, if I had to have a baby from this it would be OK; I would *experience* it. Acid will do that to you. Makes you damn crazy sometimes.

Rake reached over and scrabbled the top of my head like I was his pet, a child, almost ten years younger than him, after all. "Wow babe," he said, "you couldn't tell? Wasn't hard enough, the orange sunshine, yeah? Felt good though, huh? You one foxy chick, Scat," he said earnestly, positioning my head into the crook of his shoulder, his delightfully funk-smelling arm pit. We lay like that for the rest of the evening, sleeping occasionally, staring at the billions of stars doing their pulsing LSD-induced star dances, birds like dark angels rising off the rocks here and there, a twit a whoop a sigh. Tomorrow was the fourth of July and (foxy chick!) I'd been FUCKED, those hot arms, not another soul in miles, black forever ocean, shush and hush of its waves sweeping then retreating from our shore. Forever was longer in those days, and still with some hope.

I *went with* Rake for the rest of the summer, became with his diligent and regular instruction as nimble in sex as I was with drugs. Lied to my parents for a while about it, then quit lying. What could they do? I was already mostly gone. Wrote him long rambling letters when I went off to the University of Oregon, which he rarely answered, nights up on bennies, revelational soul searching naked before him on a tangle of words. Sometimes I'd get back a *How are you? I am cool. What you doing? This is what I'm doing*, response, nothing personal, nothing heartfelt. But imagining he might have loved me, that he *did* once love me, having to eventually accept that he would love someone else, that he was loving someone else, making love to someone else. Rake, free spirit of the islands, the times, and I craved that in him. How it ached to finally understand something of myself, not being able to *be* that. A few more years I'd be lost to the bottle, staggered days, nights, one drunk to the next, the dizzying blindness, having to wake up occasionally to a dead black sight then collapse into the next needful drunk. Last summer in Hawai'i before college, my eighteenth year, the closest I've come yet to love.

There are other moments, bits and pieces of memory that float suddenly back the way a dream does, unanchored. Willa before *it* happened, my principle playmate, maybe my only friend. Willa assuming every gift I received into her world, assuming *my* world, my things, thoughts, dreams, who I am as her older sister, to be her world. The Betty Crocker bake set given to me by some auntie, some Christmas. Play oven with the shiny black plastic knobs, painted paper wheels for the stove. The message: Robbie with his cowboys and Indians, who would have guessed he'd become the Indian and disappear? Willa, her baby dolls, the children she would never have. And me? Here is where you belong, this gift spoke, Behind a stove is where you can hope to end up.

Willa, mixing up the grainy floaty white contents from the little bake set packaged play foods. *You* can *eat it!* the words announced, not that you should eat it or that it's good for you to eat or even that it tastes good. It tastes like glue, gloppy pasty stuff, the consistency of poi with the flavor of chemically sugared paste and I'm shaking my head, *No way*! And Willa, pouting little pink bud lips, teary eyes, running (still those two perfect legs!) to tell Jaycee. "Play nicely with your sister!" Jaycee demands. "If she fixed you something to eat, you eat it for heaven's sake. Have you no manners? Honestly, Scat, can't you see I've got one of my headaches? Bloody hell. *Do* something, for crying out loud!" So of course I do it, so my mother will love me, so her headache will go away, I eat that soggy, gloppy mess to keep Willa quiet, to keep us at peace. I would have eaten my own hand for her.

My father, pulling me into the bathroom with him after closing tight the living room louvers so the Connelys across the street can't see, can't hear, shutting the door on Jaycee in one of her frantic, shattering moods, who had grabbed up eight year old Willa, maybe a month before the shark? wheeling with her around the living room, singing at the top of her voice—*I'm going to wash that man right out of my hair!* Over and over, higher and shriller, and I could hear Willa's laughter, her delight to be the one included in this frenzy, the one *always* included in our mother's frenzies, our father called them. And Father, who wouldn't speak of them other than this label—*your* mother's frenzies, as if they were something every mother had, just that these in particular happened to be Jaycee's—calmly removing his tie, taking an aloha shirt off the hook inside the bathroom closet where he's carefully hung it, turning delicately away from me to put it on, his bare back, long and tangled web of freckles on such a loose sagging frame. *Where is the Hawaiian in this?* I'm sitting on the closed toilet seat, peering down at my feet, ridiculous toes, the nails that need clipping. Whoever bothered to clip my nails? Tell me to clip my nails? His back still turned, raw neck, the high wobbly sound of my mother's laughter, higher still Willa's squeals. I can see them even now, my mother holding Willa under her arms and she's swinging her, around and around they wheel, that dizzying dance makes nothing else in the world matter, spun moments like your own personal wind blowing you about and everything else disappears, these wholly consumed seconds. He asked me: "Scat, has your mother explained to you about the facts of life?"

I nodded solemnly. After all, wasn't Jaycee always explaining one fact of life or another to me, what I can expect from my future, what I could expect from her?

"Well," he said, hesitating, turning around to gaze at me, that sad, slight smile, the weariness of his too colorful aloha shirt, orange spiky birds of paradise mingling with the lime green finches, wings spread wide like they were flying for the moon maybe, the stars, anywhere just get them out of this shirt! "Well," Father began again, "the reason I ask, it's dangerous out there in the world." Silvery tinkle of splintering glass, she's raging again, throwing things; earlier Father had brought her back from the Base, hauled her out of the Plymouth, kicking and screaming into the house. I imagine Willa face down on the couch now, plugging her ears with her fingers the way she does if I am not there to rescue her, ferret her away into our room behind our closed door. My father sighs, "You just never know, Scat, you never know what you're going to get, what hand you'll be dealt. I've tried, God knows, to give you kids a regular childhood. But I don't even know who I am anymore. You understand me? Caution is in order here. You can't always know."

And this. Why, despite everything, I so desperately yearned for, would die for, still do, still would God help me, my mother, Jaycee Anderson Beever. I'm fifteen, sullen and apart. My grandmother's going back to Newwwwengland and it wasn't a happy day for any of us. It was a giving up, her leaving, giving up on Willa's recovering, giving up on my mother and my grandmother ever being able to share a life again. Recently we had learned that my grandfather, whom I never knew, had finally died. This too a silence in our house. Over the years the most I picked up, Jaycee's slurred and struggled words when she'd been drinking too much: "Got off the bus from third grade," the story would begin, tears drenching her cheeks, "Mother always met me. This time she wasn't there. Ambulance lights in our driveway, I run into our house and everything's broken, turned upside down, such a mess like some furious storm battered through. We stood there like soldiers my mother and me, either side of the door, not touching you see while they wheeled him out, his hands, arms, shoulders bound in white like they've cemented him, or maybe he's a mummy—I remember thinking that, what did I know?—swathed in bandages. The last time I saw him. My father. *In an institution*!" This last part always whispered.

"Keep it to yourselves," our own father would admonish us. "Nothing you've heard goes outside these walls!"

Shame in this, these family secrets, we learned it well. Who knows if our grandmother missed her husband? She never spoke of it. Who knows if she ever visited him after he was institutionalized? Apparently even Jaycee was not allowed to speak it. Her father a silence and now he's gone. Once, years ago, I asked her what he was like and Jaycee got that faraway look, eyes focused somewhere inside, not at me, not at whatever her life had become. "Well," Jaycee said, "my father was very, very...compelling, but difficult, of course, terribly difficult...." She could have been talking about herself. We call our Hawai'i State Hospital (*mental* hospital Robbie said, almost got his mouth washed out with soap), we call it the *pupule house*, crazy people's hospital.

My grandmother wasn't well and was afraid to make the trip back to Newwwwengland. Maybe more afraid not to. She had gained a lot of weight despite the gourmet jello diet she survived these past five years. Her limbs were swollen and immovable with *the arthritis*, she called it. Perhaps she was grieving her husband too, whatever small window of possibility she might've kept cracked open, now shut. Who would know? Gone so many years, might there yet have been hope? "Brain sick!" my mother shrieked once, one of her frenzies, gin bottle pitched against the dining room wall. "Brain sick brain sick brain sick! That's what they said about him and bloody hell! nobody even questioned it."

How much denial can we bear? How drunk must we get to silence the silence?

My father was on the mainland, Robbie already gone and Willa, of course, in bed. So it was I who was forced to accompany them to the airport instead of who knows what I would've rather been doing, just about anything. And of course I let my mother know this. "Bloody hell!" Jaycee snapped. "Your own grandmother and God knows if you'll ever see her again. You can act decent for once, Scat, it's about The Family."

I hung back from them at the airport, dragging Grandma's suitcase behind, embarrassed by them, the old woman in her drab grey Newwwwengland coat and matching hat, despite (to spite?) the grand and sunny tropical afternoon, her swollen, lunging gait; Jaycee, her arm held gallantly out so her mother could clutch onto it, all made up and dressed in a white linen suit like this was some sort of occasion. All the Other Mothers at the airport with their local families, aloha wear, slippers and smiles. My mother in her painted scarlet lips, her *haole* airs.

Where she'd be leaving from was part of the old airport, the new one still in the process of being built, open air decks and steps that led down to the tarmac, more steps leading up into the planes. Grandma was concerned about the steps, kept saying she would fall, she just knew she would fall. We sat on a bench in the yellow sunlight, breezy trade winds, sky the blue of the sea and the heady scent of pikake from the nearby lei stands. Hibiscus in the planters behind us, royal reds and yellow.

My mother dug her spiky painted fingernails into her *lau hala* bag, emerging with two plastic lei bags, an orchid lei for me to give to my grandmother and a red carnation from Jaycee. I rose up off the bench where I was crunched as far from them as I could get, placed the lavender lei around my grandmother's meaty neck, knocking to the side her old lady's pill box hat in the process. I kissed her rouged cheek whispering the requisite *Aloha*, and slunk back down to the other end of the bench, eying the people around us to see who saw, who I would care if they saw.

Then it was Jaycee's turn. She fussed with Grandma's little grey hat first, righting it, clucking gently like Grandma was a child who had somehow managed to mess herself, pinning it into place, then she smoothed out Grandma's crinkly foil colored curls beneath the hat. Such love at times in those fingertips, that patient, tender care. She really was capable of this, you could see it, this caring, the heartbreaking gentleness—how I hungered for its touch! Grandma whimpered a bit, murmured something about the steps, she was scared of those steps. I watched from where I sat, scowling down into myself, and I felt a lump of something so needful, so *wanting* rise up in my throat.

When she put the carnation lei around my grandmother's neck, gently placing it on Grandma's stooped and fleshy shoulders, Jaycee kissed her mother on her mouth then held onto her, not letting go. Her mother, my grandmother, those blue clawed hands, held on back. Jaycee rocking them both, humming a bit; I could hear her whispering to Grandma, her tender voice, the voice that really must believe, after all, in *some* sort of redemption, telling her everything was going to be OK. Everything was going to be just fine.

CHAPTER SIXTEEN

There's a picture I return to in my memory. A rare family photo when Willa had both her legs, Robbie was one of us, and we never doubted, us kids, that our mother and father loved each other, only each other. We were going to be baptized that day, the Beever progeny, in the Congregationalist Church on Kalaheo Avenue, the one with these words chiseled on the altar: *Love Never Faileth*. Was it a concession to a belief in God, our father's most likely, this baptism? A fear of what might happen if we didn't? We hadn't gone to church much before this, and after the shark attack we never went again. Or maybe it was a belief in family, what should be done in a family. Jaycee, who had never been baptized, refused to be baptized along with us. The minister told us before touching our heads with his wet hand, that baptism would cleanse our sins against God.

She is smiling in the picture, our mother, one arm slung around a peevish Willa and the other on my shoulder. Father has his around Robbie, who is standing at attention like a miniature soldier in some boy-suit complete with a tie and jacket that I never saw him wear all together again; sometimes the jacket, sometimes the shirt, never the tie. I was wearing shiny black patent leather shoes with straps across my feet, my thin ankles in their neatly cuffed white socks, and Willa's shoes matched mine. Months later Willa would lose her leg and these shoes, both pairs of them, disappear.

It's the shoes that haunted me. Shoes that seemed to hold some sort of promise, never fulfilled. Shining and important, I remember them sitting in our closet, Willa's and mine when my bedroom was still *ours*, the closet divided by a bulletin board partition that Father put up: Willa's clothes and shoes tossed haphazardly into her part of the closet, mine neatly hung, the black shoes still in their shoe box with the top off, peeking out of a nest of white tissue paper. I had expectations for those shoes, patent leather like our mother's. In a place where footwear was so unremarkable that we weren't even required to wear it to school until sixth grade, these shoes bore a certain weight.

By the time I was in high school my feet had grown beyond the size ten of the standard woman's shoe, and with Hawai'i's mostly Asian population (translate no gargantuan feet!) stores rarely carried shoes that fit me. Shoe shopping became an endurance test, trailing after a tight lipped and irritated Jaycee, through Tom McCann's, Liberty House, JC Penney's, McInerny's: "Wouldn't you know it, Scat, you've inherited your father's big feet!" But back in the time of that photograph, fifth grade, flat chested, skinny legged and hopeful, those shiny numbers in my closet with the Mary Jane straps buckled securely from side to side, looked like dancing shoes, magical shoes, Glenda the good witch, Dorothy shoes, shoes that could carry me swiftly, smoothly, secretly into another life.

The summer after my first year away at college, the only summer I would come home while I was in college, as it turned out, I found the missing shoes, still inside their box in the nest of tissue paper, packed away in our narrow crawl space of an attic in a bigger box, a furniture box, that held various toys, books, knickknacks from our childhood. I didn't remember playing with these things after what happened to Willa; did we ever play again, any of us? The identical shoe box for Willa's patent leather shoes was under mine, but when I opened this only the left shoe was in it.

That night I asked Jaycee where Willa's other shoe was, our baptism shoes, and at first she appeared to not know what I was talking about, but when I persisted she knocked her fist against the mahogany dining room table that she no longer bothered to cover with a tablecloth, white rings like moons marking the many glasses — her gin and tonics no doubt — that had marred its surface. "Well for crying out loud, Scat, what do you think! I gave it to God? He took her leg, her foot, so I figured he may as well have the damn shoe, too? Or maybe he just snatched it away like the shark. They don't tell you this about baptism. You think you're offering up souls, but it was the wrong kind, you see. Apparently what he wanted was her goddamn sole! Get it? It's a joke, Scat, you're supposed to laugh."

That summer was the summer of sex. I couldn't bear being at home. If I slept with someone part of the night then crawled home when everyone was asleep, I could get up just in time to leave for my job as a salesgirl at McInerny's, home again late enough so I wouldn't have to talk to anyone. Who would believe it was about the bed, not the guy? Nameless, almost faceless, they slid through my days, my nights like sperm: always a destination, my job was to let them get just so far between my thighs, my belly, my breasts, stop at the heart, no entry here, *sign seal deliver*—don't slam the door on the way out.

Sometimes after one of these encounters I'd come home, 3:00 AM let's say, quietly open the door to Jaycee and Willa's room and stare at them in their beds. Jaycee snoring, her gravelly gin-induced purrs, but Willa, though I couldn't say for sure, I could swear she was awake, watching me stand there, looking at them. I'd shrug just in case, let her know I didn't care, about anything really, and I'd slip back out, shutting the door. Father was in the garage room at this point, our grandmother back in Newwwwengland. He had abandoned Robbie's room, and it occurs to me now there was a significance here—he never offered an excuse, a reason, to put that much more separation between them, smoothing things, making it seem *normal*. Even this would not last. There will be a time when I come home, how many Christmases later? and Jaycee and Willa will be gone.

Back to the sex. There was Alfonso from Spain. He had a boat moored at the Ilikai where I spent my lunch breaks, a hiatus from McInerny's tedium, sprawled out on one of his little ironing board sized cots, the ocean throbbing beneath us, his hand between my legs. One of the other salesgirls—I was in lingerie, she was in jewelry just around the corner—had a boyfriend who had a friend that was pretty and dumb. Pretty Peter, we called him. Did him too at Charlotte's request, cruising nights in the back of her boyfriend's van, counting how many red lights before he's in me, how many before he's done. It was easier than conversation, which Pretty Peter hadn't figured out how to make, stringing sentences together, responding to another's linguistic cues: Yes? No? Maybe? This other, intrinsic, even a mole could do it.

Jay the astrologist, nude hot tub party nights on his Diamond Head lānai, dark water under us, around us, the reflection of stars like goose bumps pimpling its surface, the ocean just beyond, waiting. Once high on mescaline we swam in it, the path of the moon's light leading us out. I knew what was in there and I didn't care. This is both the beauty and the terror of drugs: they let you forget who you are.

At McInerny's baked tourists would sidle in out of the hot Waikīkī sunshine, and they'd mistake me for a mannequin, tall, thin, bland faced and bored, dug in beside the lingerie counter, rooted as a tree trunk. Let the *real* saleswomen, older, Japanese, Chinese, a work ethic that kept them in motion, dusting shelves, tagging clothes, straightening hangers a hundred times a day, who would *die* in this job, pretend that it mattered. One day it's a photographer, who hires me to model for his own portfolio, he told me. Naked on a hotel room couch, and I knew these pictures would go somewhere, and I knew I should care about this but I didn't. Naked on a couch. Never even hid my face.

A yacht owned by Carlos and "Puki," he called her; who knew what her real name was, a former Miss Hawai'i, gorgeous Filipina with not a thing to say. Met them and their pouch-bellied housemate parading around the Kūhiō Beach Art Fair in full body paint (Puki in her skimpy bikini, her brown skin sprayed with a gold lame), and twenty four hours later the housemate and Mistress Beaver, he called me, are floating on rafts tied behind this yacht, Carlos pumping Puki so hard on the deck the boat shivers and rocks, spouting jerky little waves in its wake. Right before the housemate joins me on my raft, capsizing us both, his hands clutching my breasts like buoys, I imagine the line severed and I'm sailing away, sucked out to sea where *it* waits for me like a starving lover. Me. Me too.

There are the concerts, Diamond Head crater, Waikīkī Shell, and someone's hand down my pants, up my shirt, under my bra when I wore one. The back stage passes, more hands, more mouths, Famous hands! Famous mouths! Later and later I crept home, once even sidesaddle on the back of a motorcycle, sputtering to a stop in our driveway. Tiptoed the biker, head to toe chocolate leather like a giant Hershey's Kiss, into our living room, blowjob under the piano that nobody played. Snake it out; tuck it back neatly inside its candy-coated sheath. Afterwards I threw up in the bath tub—a thin line, sometimes, between desire and despair.

Always the memory of that other leather, patent leather, shiny and black, curled into their shoe box grave like the dead. Willa's, the other shoe, where? Why did she steal mine away too? What did this say? Was I supposed to do this, gather dust, shrivel up and… disappear?

One night, a week before I'm due back for my sophomore year at the University of Oregon, I am tired of it all: the catatonic job, the empty sex, the sneaking around my house in the pre-dawn hours stinking of dope, of some guy's cum, slinking about as if someone would wake up and care. My father maybe, only he's sealed off in his garage room, Jaycee her nightly hiatus from the conscious world, and Willa? Who knew if Willa slept or lay awake, who knew what she thought about dreamt of if she ever did sleep, who even knew *her* anymore? Did she care, at all, that I her sister, two years older snuck back every night after screwing some guy whose name I might not even recall the next day? One time I never even got a name, a beautiful bisexual who was hot for some guy that was hot for me, and the three of us went at it, each with a different objective, like tigers chasing each other's tails. I was sick of it. And beginning to grow a strange thirst, or at least then I thought it strange…. Swigging off Jaycee's gin bottles before I turned down my sheets, slid into my bed, blessedly alone my head spinning, the pungent taste of the gin in my throat washing down whatever was there before it, a drug, a penis, unfamiliar skin, a burning singing fiery wet cleansing ritual, falling asleep with *her* breath becoming, finally, my own.

But on this night I do not do these things. Head home immediately after work, like a normal person I was probably thinking; I'd open the door and dinner would be bubbling on the stove, the smell of it hungering the air, maybe news on TV, my father sitting before it, *Star Bulletin* on his knees, Jaycee cooking us our dinner—even Willa, this is a fantasy after all—stretched out on the couch instead of in their bedroom. A family. We'd have a nice dinner together and the night would end happily ever after, blah blah blah.

Reality check: the house is strangely silent, shuttered, windows without lights darkening in the dusk like empty eye sockets, that lonely, purple time of the evening and no one seems to be about. Then I remembered my father was on the mainland, and Willa would of course be there, in her bed, but why wasn't even the bedroom light on? I slip inside, gently shutting the front door; the house wants me to be quiet, begs it, and I tiptoe through it as I do every night, not high, no sex, not even late. I see there *is* a light, a pale glow from under Robbie's door, but it wouldn't be him, no way would it be him. I approach slowly, hesitantly, already knowing I won't open this door. I hear her laughter then, wobbly and breakable like a glass on a ledge, right before it tumbles, shattering. I don't wait to hear the *other* laugh, low, ugly, an animal growling a warning—unfamiliar yet familiar, all too familiar. I should have catapulted out of the house right then, never looking back, but instead I tug down the recessed folding ladder to the attic, not even caring about the squeaking it makes, stomp up the shuddering steps and grab those boxes out of the bigger box, the patent leather shoes, three of them, Willa's, mine.

It's late when I finally get there, Lanikai Beach. I had driven around for a while debating where to go, a shark heiau where others leave offerings? Something for Ka'ahupāhau and Kahiuka, sister and brother, flesh and bone transformed into cartilage and fin? They live in a cave at Pearl Harbor, protect the people of Ewa from people-eating sharks, *niuhi*. But it wasn't these two, and not just any shark, it was *her* shark. Plus, I didn't feel worthy of any real offering, no ti leaves, no 'awa, no particular food to honor our 'aumakua. How could we have an 'aumakua, who were we kidding? Our father had sold his Hawaiian to the business world, *haole* world, the mainland, to whatever life he managed to eek away from Jaycee, or maybe it was *for* Jaycee. This was before the rumors began about Willa, before Willa became *Shark Girl*, before she was anything but a little girl grown into a bigger girl who had given up.

"There!" I shrieked, standing on a spit of sand at low tide beyond the canal, Lanikai point, its ragged cliff, its concrete marker above me. A stiff, sea-scented breeze kicked up as I hurled Willa's one remaining patent leather shoe into the ocean where the water rippled like stretched skin, pulling back. The Moku Lua Islands were out there, rising like black ghosts in a moonlit darkness. I imagined the birds on them, cooing, crying, guano like spattered paint all over the beach Rake and I had made love on. I have not made love since; sex, only sex. And then I tossed my shoes into the ocean, never even bothering to remove them from their box. "There!" I said it again. Like this satisfied something. Like it could mean something, anything at all.

CHAPTER SEVENTEEN

So what do I look like now? You'll have your own opinion of course, but I'll offer you an image. Let's try the movies, the one defining cultural icon at the start of the new millennium, the great equalizer, democracy at large, Republicans, Democrats, the rich, the poor, price of a Big Mac and fries, the thing almost every American passively participates in: living others lives, their made up stories, celebrities the new gods. Tom Cruise said it then it's got to be true. Combine movies and cable television (miss it on the silver screen you can watch it in your living room *with* a Big Mac and all the fries you can stuff down your throat) and you've got it: the digitally remastered American Dream, coming to a theatre near you.

Rachel Ward, the Australian actress. Rachel Ward at her most angular, her short haired carved out looking self, slim, statuesque. Meld this with *Pooh* from "The World According to Garp" (the movie not the book, of course); she's not a kid anymore, in a nurse's uniform and on a mission, come to the gym to murder Garp. Mousy, fringe of dull colored bangs, sharp, peevish little face, bang! Girl nerd turned adult, all grown up and ready for revenge. The combination of these film fantasies and you get me. I'm long and lean, no Marfans as it finally turned out, just extra tall my father's genes, and that boyish shape, especially from the back, no hips nut-sized little butt. I keep my brown hair geometrically short. People come up to me from the back—*Excuse me, sir!*—and I take real pleasure, no embarrassment anymore in turning around, gracing them with my womanly grin, female face, the sure sharp lines of my androgynous body. I like to see they are the ones who get embarrassed now.

Men go for me, married ones in particular. I see them in public places, grocery stores, restaurants with their wives, gazing furtively, secretly, more than once at me. I am the fantasy they never allowed themselves to have. The boy-woman, child, woman, not feminine, not masculine, like a hermaphrodite who won't allow society to make her the freak, independent and unobtainable. They see me and wonder what it is in their life they lack. Jerk off to the memory of me later, wife asleep, shower running, the empty night.

Perhaps it's because I never really grew up, college to a drunk, they sense the unfinished in me and want to leave their mark. What happened to Willa arrested us all. It's like we were frozen into some other time frame, last possible minutes of the future we were all moving toward. Flash-freeze: my father still watering that lawn, making it green, making that, at least, grow weed-free and pest-free and picture-perfect. Robbie the disappearing brother, gone. Our mother (face it, damnit!), who's only ability to move out of her own self for someone else depended on that someone being Willa. And me. How appropriate I eventually become a photographer, freezing fast those forward marching minutes, holding time, making one moment, one instant, if nothing else, last. And being able to shape this final result, forcing everyone who sees the print to accept the moment I recreate. It's a way of playing God. Perhaps this is why I prefer devastation photography, proof of what God has done.

How many years did I try to recreate the moment we lost Willa in the jaws of that shark? The what ifs? What if it had been me? Or Robbie? What if Fatboy in his visual obsession with Jaycee, his leering and lingering looks, had been watching us instead, little Beevers trailing out after the Lightning in their tubes? Would he have seen the fin, the darkening shadow that now of course, over the years I too can see in my mind, like it was always there to be seen, if only someone was looking? What if our mother wasn't always running so late, didn't have to pack and repack her *lau hala* bag stuffed with the condiments of a life, her just in case she needed it paraphernalia: extra tube of scarlet lipstick in case she dropped one in the ocean; zinc oxide in case her nose started feeling burnt (this, before sunscreens with SPF factors); baby oil to slather on her legs *to* get these burnt; skinny dime-store *novels* in case she tired of talking; *women's* magazines in case she didn't want to start a novel after all; an extra long-sleeved white shirt to put over her suit in case her shoulders get burnt, in case the preferred one she brings gets wet; a floppy cotton hat for her hair which she'd never wear but she likes the idea of a hat; and our packed lunch, those bologna sandwiches on the soggy Wonder bread, which we didn't end up eating until almost supper time. Supper time for sharks too, as it turned out. *Hoover plate*, we were always told we must clean every morsel off our plates because there are starving children in Korea. (Years later I would wonder at the imperialist message in that: telling a privileged American child to eat *her* food because somewhere else another child is starving.) Was that shark circling in for the rest of Willa after it swallowed her leg? Or, *'aumakua*, someone else's ancestral shark god gets a taste of her then spits her out, this mostly *haole* little girl, not even enough Hawaiian in her to be considered *hapa-haole*, not significant enough to eat? *'Aumakua manō*, fierce and venerated, shark black magic in the blood of my sister now? What if... Willa Beever had been completely swallowed up into its mouth, its belly, its own dark and secret history. And disappeared.

****

The how I met alvin-Travis story. I'm traveling in a beat-up Dodge Caravan, the one year they made these with turbo and stick shift, a *cool* ride disguised as a soccer mom's car, relic the moment it was decided to make no more, to some little nowhere town called Rock Harbor, Maine, where rumor has it that my sister and, by default, most likely my mother have surfaced. I'm going to reach them this time before they submerge again, before I'm having to trace them through the *Enquirer* and *Star* and *Globe* articles about my sister, sightings of a miracle. *How to become a saint*, instructs one article: *A saint should have love in her heart; be pure; must practice virtue; evidence of miracles; signs of God's good faith in her....*

I'm going to confront Jaycee with the what-the-hell-do-you-think-you're-doing-capitalizing-on-Willa's-misfortune-to-support-your-own-need-for-attention-and-if-she's-*pure*-I'm-the-Pope! kind of a talk. It could get ugly. Which is why my new husband-of-this-decade (I've had two and we won't get into that, but know that even drunks need to wake up sometimes with something more than just a hangover), the detox counselor who also counsels prisoners, drug abusers, abused women and other disenfranchised, kind of the public defender of the psychologically maimed (alvin-Travis was impressed), thought he should come along to help smooth things out between my mother and me. But it's not just the two of us, because my lover is also along for the ride. My lover is an artist of sorts, a renaissance man, jack of all trades, when a pottery piece isn't thrown right he can whip out his harmonica and blow a tune on that. He's also a yoga instructor, a meditation counselor, a spiritual guide and he claims he can see ghosts, that the dead are all around us, that they never go away. He's comforted by this, but I found myself wondering: what if they watch me when I'm going to the bathroom, taking a shower, committing adultery and fucking him? If they're watching when I'm doing that, then just me and a billion dead people know me for the secret slut I must be. But I digress. It's a talent, one of his many; if there's ever a need for someone who can do these things, Noah is the man.

My husband doesn't know my lover is my lover, of course, which is pretty standard. But my lover also doesn't know my husband is my husband, which is less common, at least among folks traveling in the same car. They know each other, in fact they are friends, friends before either one of them knew me. One of them is the father of my eight weeks in the womb fetus. Neither of them know there's a baby-in-progress inside me. You can see the dilemma. I mean we can't exactly pull up to a Burger King for some road food, hamburgers and fries and I'm saying, *Pass the catsup, and oh by the way, how about a DNA sample from you both?* Luckily they are both your basic every day handsome, evenly featured, sandy haired nothing-stands-out type of *haole* man. A genetic imprint of either of them will be the same sandy-headed, round cheeked generic child.

My husband and I decided to keep our marriage secret until we found Jaycee and Willa, until he could attest, maybe test, to see what affect this might have on two women with such histories of instability. Willa, after all, was the one supposed to marry well and here I'd gone and gotten myself a doctor. The Ph.D. kind of a doctor granted, but doctor nonetheless. We're not talking wood rot or paper

224   Jaimee Wriston Colbert

instead of plastic, those kinds of instability and impermanence. More like balloons. Just when you think you've narrowed in on their whereabouts these two just up and float away. Or jellyfish, drifting on the surface of some mythical sea. At least Willa does. Jaycee makes her presence known when she wants something. Willa never even answers my letters, if indeed I have a right address. Sometimes my mother sticks around long enough to do an interview, draw attention to herself, get them off my sister's trail. I mean, we're not even Catholic and they've got those who believe, enough where she actually has a following of sorts, that Willa can will the pain of others into her own body, take it away from them. Is this a saintly kind of thing? Virtue and purity? My sister was just another gum snapping prepubescent cheer leader wannabe until the shark got her. Some even think that her leg grew back, like she's some kind of lizard, a *mo`o* who can regenerate body parts.

In one of the rare phone discussions I've had with my brother over the years of his own disappearance, his calculated absorption, as he called it, into a culture that does not include our family (using a phone card so I couldn't trace his whereabouts, but I mean really, just how many missing Beevers am I going to waste my life trying to track down?), I asked him how he thought it came about: our little sister the miracle worker. Robbie said it was because of her silence, that in our world mutes are considered either idiots or holy people, wise beyond the rest of us so why bother having something so banal as a conversation? That she survived such a brutal attack as a child elevated her to the holy realm. They think she was saved for a reason, he said. Let the buyer beware....

So my husband and I were keeping our one year marriage a secret, even from my lover, our best friend. We got in the habit of it out at detox where they frown on relations between the counselors and the patients, and we got further into this habit after AA, which I said I couldn't make a commitment to, it was just a little too much like some kind of church I would never go to. But I thought I could make a commitment to Harry and I stopped the drinking to prove it. It was time to stop drinking. He got me Noah as a meditation guide to help take the edge off things, the rest you can imagine. Like I said, men are attracted to me, and after much of my childhood spent as the wallflower, being with two sandy haired *Calvin* model featured men has that sweet taste of revenge. The important thing here is that I'm still dry; I haven't touched a drop of alcohol, though not a day goes by when I don't wonder if just maybe, this is the day I will.

I'm in my mid-forties at this juncture, the time of life when most obstetricians tell you if you haven't conceived by now, it's supposed to be too late! Noah and Harry are both thirty plus. One of them knows how old I am and finds it a turn-on. Will he be the father, schlepping me about in my wheel chair, wiping my drool at our kid's wedding? I managed to survive most of my adult life blacked out, so call me a late bloomer. I inherited a tendency to look young from Jaycee, where instead of my skin wrinkling it just stretches, nice and easy, to fit a little more of me. I look in my thirties but I don't feel it, puking on the roadside weeds, the flatness of Indiana fired up hunters orange and a feverish yellow in the late afternoon sun like something out of an industrial dream.

So there we were, Route 90 east out of Chicago (where I was living before this journey, an unimportant detail, what the story teller deletes to get to the heart, the guts of the matter quicker), through the smoking hell hole of Gary, belches of pink poison licking the sky on a mission to Maine to find my mother and sister. Maybe my sister the victim soul can heal me of this morning sickness, seems to occur any random moment of the day or night, mornings be damned; take it into her own body and let her be the one throwing up, nibbling on soda crackers, tender sips of ginger ale, pretending she just has a touch of the flu.

But it's alvin-Travis I find instead. alvin-Travis, whose agent had seen some of my earlier photographs of rock groups, eighties icons like Duran Duran and Billy Idol after they were no longer big. And my disaster photography, an earthquake in Southern California, Mt. St. Helens exploding, mud slide in West Virginia, sink holes in Florida. Something connected. I posted a Has-anyone-seen-my-sister-the-miracle? ad over the Internet, Last reported sighting in Rock Harbor, Maine, and this agent recognizes my name, contacts me to photograph a New England band called the Head Shrinkers, has-beens who maybe with the right kind of "push," marketing and exposure...? The rest is, as they say, history. I lost the baby just a few weeks later, all those alcoholic years had maybe fermented something inside me, the something that can give birth to, nurture life. Noah and Harry, I realized, had become more about the baby than me. A package deal. The thing can't work without all of its parts.

The ways life damages you. alvin-Travis and me, though we threaten each other with it constantly, spoken or implied, it is possible we will never leave each other. We'll never marry each other either. We don't have to. We're an imperfect fit, two halves that could never be whole. But we have found ways to fit with each other. alvin-Travis needs stories to imagine other lives while he slowly releases any semblance of living his own. It's a sort of passivity addiction, a giving up that is benign, not depressed, just a shrugging off on life. I find it fascinating, addictive personality that I am. I give him his stories. He supports my photography, not because he believes in it, but if I had to do something else to support my own photography I wouldn't have time to tell him stories or play *reality* rolls in some of the stories, his favorite starring me as seductress.

Flash-freeze: He is alvin-Travis's something-or-other and I've been instructed to act like I care. a.T. wants the whole story, nothing left out, all its pieces, its scintillating minutia. This *is* acting; should've been trained in the theatre for it or maybe the porns. Requisite kiss then I reach down into this man's pants and, swear to God, I'm coming up empty. The guy is groaning like there's *something* there so I plunge in again, my fingers creeping ever further between those sticky thighs, all the while I'm holding my breath, praying for contact. I'm not prepared for any other scenario, and somewhere inside myself, a place where in someone else's life there might've been a heart, I'm too kind to turn to this man, blunt panache: "Sorry sir, we've searched and searched, but we simply couldn't find it. We'll have to declare this a Missing Penis." Out of the question. Contact gratefully made, curling into my fingers like a wooly caterpillar, reminds us of winter and all things cold.

We drive to his trailer, a dejected looking camp near Penobscot Bay, most everyone else has gone home for the season (Ex-wife, goddamn whore took his house, his furniture, his daughter, even the goddamn dog! he tells me), that near winter dark, aloof sky and the land looking like it might suck you under, so deep, so lonely, *forlorn*.

He has a Tupperware bread box filled with sex toys in a near empty kitchen (did wifey take the china, the labor saving devices and all the food too leaving hubby only the plastics?). Wants me to put one on, some fuzzy black thing with wings in critical places, a Venus Butterfly he calls it. He takes off his shirt and shows me his scar: "Vietnam," he says, "it's not a grenade or shrapnel or nothing. Appendicitis," he shrugs, "nothing heroic about it at all." I tell him about Willa's leg and how everyone believes she's some sort of god. "What she did is survive," I say.

Later, when I tell it to a.T., the butterfly will be the story's rise, the thing we worked toward, climax, resolution, denouement. I won't tell him how the man cried. Right after I left. Saw him through the partially shut blinds, shadows from the slats on his illuminated baldness like out-of-focus lines on a black and white TV. He was sitting at his gleaming Formica table with not a thing on it, no fruit or flowers, real or otherwise, no newspapers, fliers, catalogs, coupons, cups, cutlery, gloves or maybe a hat tossed down, the chaos of kitchen living; no signs of a life lived whatsoever, his head held between those chubby fingers, saddest hands I've seen.

For this I was the bearer of flesh and grief. But as long as I play some part in our agreement, the unwritten contract of our shared existence, a.T. is tolerant of my obsessive search for my sister, sending her cards, my photographs, moments of secured memory, what's left of my soul without knowing for certain if they ever reach her. These are the ways I try to make sense of my past. He says nothing about it, this need that will always be greater than any need for him.

alvin-Travis lets me live with him away from the world and his own remoteness appeals to me. I know who *I* am, and it's taken years to discover that. What I don't understand is the rest of the world, who I can be, in it. Somehow my sister is the clue, the key, the something that might solve this puzzle, unlock the door, let me back in; the thing that altered our once foreseeable futures, the tragedy at the seat of our lives, as Jaycee named it. And so I keep searching. This is how the dead come back to life.

Part VI

It is related that a girl of thirteen years of age, living at Waikapuna, a long sandy beach directly below Naalehu, Kau, dreamed that a lover appeared to her out of the ocean. Every morning when she told her parents this dream her father thought she had allowed some one liberties and wanted to conceal it, so he kept her carefully guarded. The dreams however continued. After a time the girl gave birth to a shark. Her parents recognized this is the offspring of an akua mano (shark god) called Ke-'lii-kaua-o-Kau, a cousin of Pele, and did not hold the girl responsible.

Beckwith; *Hawaiian Mythology*

CHAPTER EIGHTEEN

Gracie McKneely's Summer List of Harmful Invasive Alien Species Bugs!

Mālaekahana Beach, O'ahu, Hawai'i. Aug. 4, 1994

1. Bigheaded ant. Household pest and major predator. Has exterminated native beetles and ground dwelling crickets!

2. Argentine ant. Kills native moths and bees. Bites people painfully!

3. Big-eyed seed bug. Does bad things to populations of native invertebrates. (Note: ask Dr. Bender to tell me the meaning of that word again, if I can ever get her attention again!)

4. Flies. Gross! Some flies even suck blood. (I saw Louis suck Dr. Bender's fingers on the hand she has, then she pretended to do it on the hook. I think Louis is disgusting!)

5. Black stink bug. Stinks!!!

6. Cockroaches. More gross! Dr. Bender said a cockroach in the ear is a major cause of emergency room visits here. Also they spoil food by going to the bathroom on it. Gross, gross, double gross!

7. Two-spotted leafhopper. Causes many plants to die. (Note: If I died would she be sorry?)

By the time Jessie gets home from the hospital it is winter. Winter in Maine, pale yellow and pink skies, a somber lonesome beauty. They had treated her for hypothermia, for shock, then transferred her to the psychiatric ward where she stayed another few weeks and then another few after that. "Supposing we just pack up her things and help her move in!" Berry had griped. They couldn't be sure she wouldn't do it again, she couldn't *tell* them she wouldn't try it again and maybe this time she succeeds. "Walks out on the water like *Je*sus did," Berry said, "but this one can't never come back, especially now, when the harbor is half froze you could about skate on it."

"Like walking into the eye of God, all that white for miles and miles. If I was to walk into Heaven I'd want it blue," Marie said.

"And curtains!" Janie added. "How about in Heaven there should be curtains so you're not always having to look down on us sinners here."

Thankfully Tia just shook her head. Nobody invited her two cents worth, there were some things they could all agree on.

Gracie's cleaning performance has become mindless, automated sleep-mopping and Berry is beginning to complain. She does the white glove test, she calls it, only she uses some former "housewife's" thrown away (as in she forgot it when she moved out) white sweater. "See the gunk?" Berry prods. "Dust and grime?" She's nodding her head and Gracie is supposed to nod in agreement. Their nodding ritual, two strange and gawky birds, supposed to confirm Gracie's failure. She is to repent and do a dust free dirtless job the next day.

But all Gracie can think about is having sex with Anthony. It's as if something inside her has come undone, unleashed, something so pathetically dormant, hanging on throughout all those years of believing it near impossible that anyone could ever love her. She doesn't know if Anthony loves her. She doesn't know if she loves Anthony. After the years of thinking about it, wondering about it, being sure that love, whatever that was, was not in any future for her, she still doesn't know. And it doesn't matter. Only him inside her every which way now—coming at her from the side, straight down on top of him like she's perched on some dousing rod, shoved up against the door, spread eagled on her stomach on his bed, up on all fours like a beast. She *is* beast. She moans and the sound of it is not her. It doesn't seem to even come from her, or if it does it's been packed away inside her so deep she never even knew it was there, this guttural sounding person, this female who wants nothing but this male, between her legs, in her mouth, everywhere possible for him to be she wants him.

Roma has not moved back in since the breakwater night, as Anthony and Gracie have come to call it. Once she came home to visit Jessie, shaking her head at Gracie hovering in the hallway with her broom. *You're pathetic*, that head shake said, glint of a new metal hoop through her eyebrow.

Berry has also kept some distance, no more invitations to the Jesus Club, barely speaking to Gracie except to criticize her cleaning since she became *connected*, Berry calls it, to Anthony. Like we are attached by some sort of cord, Gracie thinks. Who knows? Maybe they are and one end hangs between those long hairy thighs!

"You do get what he's about," Berry says to Gracie one day, sliding up beside her at the kitchen counter where Gracie is cutting tomatoes for her, to make her gazpacho.

Gracie, wide eyed, "Do you?"

Berry nods, no sarcasm at all. "Ayuh, the woman what lived in your room used him up, threw him away, moved on. Like one of them tomatoes, peel it, cut it, pop it in the broth it's history. You're doing other peoples tomatoes, what can I tell you?"

"Probably nothing," Gracie agrees, amazed yet again at what's been coming out of her mouth. Gracie McKneely, damaged goods and formerly meek as a mole about it, razor tongued as the best of them these days. She could fit in with Liela's girls in a heart beat if she wanted to, even without piercings and tattoos!

"Suit yourself," Berry says, sauntering out of the kitchen. "Rapist!" Gracie hears her hiss, loud enough so she *would* hear.

Today is the last Thursday of the month and Berry has taken the van, along with Tia, Marie and Janie into Portland for their shopping excursion. It is Gracie's responsibility to listen out for Jessie, check on her, see if she needs anything, make sure she is *there*, Berry had emphasized.

She cleans for a while, vacuuming the living room, the parlor, as Berry likes them to call the odd-shaped entry room that has little going for it, with its wood-frame windows painted permanently shut in some other history, and its Salvation Army furniture that nobody sits on; not even a TV in here after all. Then the den. Sweeps up the kitchen half heartedly, not bothering with the corners where petals of ancient linoleum curl up like shriveled leaves, or angling the broom under the cupboards the way Berry has instructed her. Detritus, that which is visible, who cares about the rest? What's unseen goes unwatched. The world is not a polished place. Stares out the kitchen window at the carriage house, mildly considering a midmorning fuck. Anthony is somewhere around these premises. She could put on a skirt, round him up, let him take her from behind, wouldn't even have to pull off her panties, just shove them to one side. Done in fifteen minutes, the length of a coffee break then back to her dust rag. *Cinderella Gets It From Behind*, Gracie giggles, made-up names for porno movies starring her, reeled out in her own sullied mind, delightfully dirtied (having sex changes everything!), its secret grit, flint-grit, catching her blood on fire. *The ability to thermoregulate — which means "warm-blooded" — is another thing that makes certain shark species operate as fierce predators. (Compiled by S.G.)*

Gracie knows it, *her* signature.

She decides to visit Jessie. She hasn't really had a chance to talk to her, no one has; when they poke their heads in she's either asleep or just lying there in bed, staring at the wall, that striking face thin and drawn, squeezed almost into someone else's face seemingly, not all together recognizable. "The medication does her that way," Berry said in disgust. "Antidepressants? Antipsychotics? More like anti-get-with-the-program! Suck them puppies down may as well slit your wrists and be done with it. Only addicts or fools believe happiness comes packed inside some gelatin capsule."

Gracie raps lightly then cracks open the door. "Jessie? You awake?"

She doesn't answer and the room is too dark to see her clearly, shades and curtains drawn. "You want me to open these?" Gracie asks, stepping inside, closing the door behind her then inching over toward the windows. It's a sunny, cold day. Jessie is watching her, those hazel eyes a yellow hunger on her face, studying her movements. Tiger eyes, predator eyes, but not this one, not Jessie! There are the predators, and those that get preyed upon. Gracie hesitates, rocking back on her heels.

"Would *you* like them opened?" Jessie asks finally, her voice small.

Gracie stares self consciously at her feet. "Just thought you might like some sunlight in here."

"Whatever, sure, go ahead."

Gracie does this then gazes at Jessie, slant of morning sun lighting her face which appears older now, all of her years creeping up in just this month or so, sunken, weighted. Jessie sees Gracie looking. "Sorry!" Gracie says, cheeks flushing. "I'm used to people staring at me, well you don't ever get used to it, not really, and here I am staring at you. I'm sorry," she repeats.

Jessie motions, wan flick of her wrist, for Gracie to sit in the cluttered chair by her bed. "Just throw things on the floor," she says. "God knows what's there, nothing I care about. I know I don't look well, Gracie. Fact is I am *not*. So how should I look?"

"Isn't there something they can do for you, something they can give you, something else?" Gracie asks, a little embarrassed though she's not sure why. Maybe because they're talking other peoples ailments here.

"More drugs you mean? The problem is how to fool the brain into thinking everything is A-OK. It's this chemical imbalance I have. Though, I suppose that's all any of us are anyway, right? Chemical combinations, some more successful than others, oxygen or cyanide. Do you know what I used to do, Gracie, anyone tell you? I was a doctor, training to be one anyway, internship at Boston General. Never quite got through. I should've been a vet, maybe that."

"What about Arnie? Is he the reason...?" Gracie starts, then doesn't finish the sentence, lets it hang between them.

Jessie sighs, a slow, shivery outtake of breath. "Arnie is a good example of why I prefer animals to so called humans. They're really more *human*, don't you think? If you define what a human could be in the best sense, top of the evolutionary scale. Animals are all about no grudges, no psychological games, deliberate torments, just their instincts to do what they need to do to survive. No questions, I like that. Keep this our secret, OK? I let Berry use Arnie for our meetings. It's harmless, I know he's gone. I knew what my husband was capable of, after all. Who's the animal there? Berry's a good person. She takes all us walking wounded and tries to help, in her own way. I respect that. She's got a lot of spunk, even if she's a bit off at times. I'm not sure how much Berry herself believes in the spiritualism stuff, she's way too pragmatic to put life in the hands of the unseen. They believe in spirit-guides and Berry's into guiding. Like her mother and grandmother, she comes from women who take things into their own hands. She tries. And she's honest. What more can we ask?"

"Seems like a control freak to me," Gracie says darkly.

"Because you don't need her, Gracie. Shark Girl didn't either. That's why Berry's so bothered by her and you too, I sense. Berry needs to be needed. That's her thing. You can walk out these doors tomorrow and step right into a life. The rest of us? Some of us wouldn't even know where to look. Janie for instance was living out of her car, a true transient. Tia's man beat her, told her she was crazy and she *is*, of course. Mine left me with nothing, though I had already done a pretty good job of that myself. Marie? Well, you can't have someone out and about in the world, harmless as she is, believing she's getting coded messages from Marie Osmond, can you? And Roma, that tough-girl. Talks stink about her mom yet she always comes home. Berry is safe-harbor for her daughter. They're two of a kind, a line of muscle-tongued women only Roma hasn't quite figured out how to use her genetics other than to rankle her mother. You, Gracie, are just fine. I knew that when you didn't run from the mouse or try to kill it; you just let it alone. Live and let live. A cliché but it's the only one worth living by."

"No way," Gracie tells her. "I came here because I didn't know where else to go. I had nowhere, only my home, and it's like I got too big for that or something." Her eyes suddenly tear up.

Jessie touches Gracie's hand. "You could have chosen somewhere else. You *will* choose somewhere else, I predict. Just like Shark Girl."

"Where do you think she went?"

Shrugs, pulling the covers up closer around her thin shoulders. "Shark Girl was beginning to look, I don't know, a little worn, like maybe she wasn't feeling well. So pale. But I gave up trying to diagnose physical failings years ago so I didn't, you know, offer to help her, even ask her if anything was wrong. Not that she would've answered. She had a lot of burdens I suspect, but she was a woman unafraid. She could go anywhere and be just fine. I guess when you live through the worst, losing your leg in the jaws of a shark, well, that's something, isn't it? She was tested in a way most of us will never be. And whether she really is a *victim soul* hardly matters. She isn't a victim, that's what counts."

Gracie leans closer. "I feel..." she hesitates, staring at Jessie's face, unsure if she should go on. The room is warm and smells too sweet, a sickly sweet, too long its contained flesh. Gracie shudders. "Am I making you tired?" she asks.

Jessie fidgets a bit, dragging the covers tighter around her neck. "Finish what you were going to say."

"It's just that..." Gracie leans in closer. She feels like she should be whispering but who else is here to hear it? "Sometimes I feel close to Shark Girl in a really weird way, living in her room and all. I've never even met her and she seems...known somehow. I can't explain it. Maybe because we both have something that happened to us when we were kids, makes us different. Hers is worse of course, I mean I shouldn't be making these comparisons. My accident happened when I was barely a toddler, too young to remember the pain, just what it left. Shark Girl was eight when hers happened. She'll always remember. Her...what she wrote, what she collected from other writings described it as a violence. The violence is what she remembers. I feel a violence too sometimes, something I can't describe, just that it's there. I get these dreams, like I'm not even me anymore, like I'm changing."

"Maybe you are. It's called growing up. I mean that nicely of course, I'm not sure the rest of us here have done much of that."

"What about Shark Girl?"

Jessie smiles, shakes her head. "If you read *Globe* or the *Enquirer* accounts, I suppose she wouldn't have to be a grown up, being a miracle and all. It seems her mother took care of her every need for many years. Berry claimed she was spoiled rotten, but when she came to live here her mother wasn't with her. I don't know how to answer that, Gracie. She wasn't usual, that's all I can say. Maybe the usual doesn't apply to Shark Girl."

Gracie can see Jessie is worn out. Dark curly hair, tangled and matted, head listing a bit to one side on her pillow, eyes flutter then close. She rises slowly off the chair, starts to tiptoe out of the room when Jessie calls out, her voice so small Gracie has to strain to hear her.

"Gracie? Just one more thing. Be careful around Anthony, will you? Just a hunch, a feeling, no real proof."

CHAPTER NINETEEN

What to Do If Confronted By a Shark:
Here are six safety rules from the Department of Fish and Wildlife on how to act when confronted by a shark while swimming or fishing.

Keep quiet!
Keep your spear for protection and retreat slowly.
Do not keep speared fish near your body. Get rid of them or lift them from the water.
Swim in a reefed area as much as possible.
Shout or make a loud noise under water. The concussion may drive the shark away.
Do not panic or thrash. Sharks will attack anything they sense is helpless."
        <u>*The Honolulu Advertiser*</u>; *Dec. 14, 1958*
        (Compiled by S.G. ...day after Billy Weaver....)
        (Noted by G.M. — Why doesn't S.G. finish above sentence?)

That the calendar claims spring, overflowing rivers, leafy trees, liming of the grass, a bluer, milder sky, means squat in Maine. Here the coast is locked under a bruising fog, the damp and constant grey, and though there are those new bird sounds, *a certain melodic urgency* is the way Gracie's father would describe it, cruising birds looking for a ticket to nest, here even love has a less than spring-like meaning. Even *liking* someone doesn't seem to hold a lot of water, her mother's way of putting things. Getting Anthony to do something, *anything*, beyond a bare minimum of responsibilities he has as Berry's yard boy, then sprawling about on his sofa bed wanting to fuck, fuck, fuck. Have you ever done *it* to classical music? Felt those ancient bearded masters in their crescendos like they've crept above you and are glowering down at this unseemly behavior? Try coming to Beethoven's 9th, for instance, that's one description you will not get from Gracie. For the most part in spite of Anthony's barely-hides-his-pissed-offed explanations, she still can't tell the difference between a Mozart opera and a Beethoven symphony, it's just a lot of notes to her. ("Fuck no, Gracie!" Anthony wails. "Not the notes, how many times do I have to tell you! It's about the silences, the silences in between.")

Short of inhaling bud, sucking down a beer, guzzling cheap wine, whatever he's stuffed into his tiny portable refrigerator, then having sex—doing anything beyond these things seems for Anthony an impossible task. Like she's asking him to consider law school, or slip into a Goodwill suit and interview over at MBNA; like he's the sort they'd even offer a credit card to. "It's you that's had the chances, Gracie," he reminds her constantly, that annoyingly slow way he speaks sometimes, "you...who...had...it...all." Translate: too late for them both but she's the one who blew it. Like she really did try getting him to go to medical school or law school or maybe just the community college in Thomaston, night classes to help him get his GED so she wouldn't have to be constantly reminded by him that he's a dropout, not capable of anything more. *Whatever*! Gracie tells him, her Roma-cynic tone. They don't seem to be getting along as well these days.

One thing she doesn't get is why Anthony seems to feel so beholden to Berry, never questioning the grounds for his employment with her, the minimum wage he's paid, the absolutely no chance for any future he has, any advancement whatsoever while living here, *employed* by Berry Waters. Just live he does. And she's beginning to feel restless. One half year as cleaning girl at the America's Haunted Housewives Boarding House seems like maybe it should've been enough. Yet here she is. Diss Anthony for doing nothing, *yet here I am*! Hadn't put much thought into what the next step would be, escaping from home to Maine, and then...? She had hoped it would open itself up to her, writing in the sky, a message, a direction, something extraordinary. Gracie had always thought she wanted a boyfriend, that unobtainable thing, a *relationship*, as if this might validate her, make her *normal* to normal people. So what do normal people want? Some sort of commitment from their boyfriend? A chance to move on, grow, change, *do* something?

A strange thing that's been happening of late is she's waking up next to Anthony in the morning, in Anthony's bed. Maybe you wouldn't think this strange, other than she never actually intends to do it. Her alarm's all set in her own room, she goes out to the carriage house for the usual excitement: hit of weed, slug of beer, fuck Anthony (how easily that word slides off Gracie's tongue now, taut and sexy like it's someone else's language and she's just the vehicle to propel its bidding, some sort of tongue taxi!). Next thing she knows she's waking up to the bleeping of his alarm, luckily set for the same time as her own, her head all fuzzy and strange, a sense of maybe having had too much to drink, yet how is that possible? One beer tops? Gracie feels like she's losing the hours somewhere, offering up the night to some sort of impossibly deep sleep that doesn't even leave her rested. And here she is, next to the sincere, the sincerely concerned Anthony.

"Fuck Gracie, I didn't have the heart to wake you, tired as you must've been. Maybe it's your periods? All that bleeding, you need more iron, some flesh! You're feeling weak, what this is about."

Like Shark Girl, Gracie has become mostly a vegetarian, and clearly Anthony's following Berry's lead in this, convinced the lack of meat, iron, amino acids, says Berry, will be Gracie's undoing. "We are meant to eat meat," Berry says. "Flesh for flesh, law of survival. Strongest takes sustenance from the weakest. It's how our species got to the top. My opinion?" she says, though nobody's asked. "The Lord made us this way and the others to feed us." Berry is of the belief that Shark Girl was a *secret* meat eater. All that bleeding, the iron had to come from somewhere. Her guess? she's as carnivorous as the rest of them.

"Many sharks use a combination of ram, bite, and suction feeding and may change their diet and dominant feeding mode as they grow. Younger makos feed on bony fishes (as most sharks do), with the occasional invertebrate

added to the mix; in general about 85 percent of makos' diet consists of bony fish and squid. The larger a mako becomes, the larger the prey it can and does pursue. This sort of change, in which the diet of an animal alters as the animal grows, is called an ontogenetic, or 'after the beginning,' dietary shift"

<u>The Shark Chronicles</u>; Musick and McMillan. p. 147 (*Compiled by S.G.*)

Gracie is thinking these things while dusting the parlor, the living room and then the den. Dusting is high on her list of the most useless activities Berry has on *her* list for Gracie to do. Moving skin cells and other bits of microscopic debris from place to place, off the shelves, into the air, back it settles upon the shelves, the antique mahogany desk, wooden chair rungs, reinventing itself so Berry can justify the wasted hour doing it all over again tomorrow. It occurs to Gracie her mother would probably have a few things to say about this, or a more successful way of doing it. Maizey hardly ever just *dusted*; dust and polish, *d and p* she called it like some procedural sounding something, *d and c* clean out a woman's plumbing, *d and p* her end tables? And just like that, before Gracie can trod further down this the-excitement-never-ends trail of thought the doorbell rings and damned if it isn't her parents at the door.

She actually does drop the dust rag and her mother frowns at it, all curled up like some dirty little animal on the stoop in front of Maizey's perfect pumps, shoes dyed to match the mustard yellow and screaming peach of her 100 percent chemically constructed fabric no doubt, skirt and jacket. Maizey McKneely believes in supporting human *initiative*, one of the select few who championed polyester as having advanced civilization. Any material that can take a journey through a hot dryer and arrive unwrinkled and unshrunk is a modern miracle, she proclaimed.

"Spring colors," her mother informs her as Gracie studies this outfit, face blazing, shocked. Maizey clears her throat, a curdled sound, her lips tight. "I hope you don't actually clean with that thing, Gracie," she starts, bending over slowly, one hand steadying one ample hip, this too yet another painful effort she is willing to make on her daughter's less than worthy behalf, scoops up the dropped rag with the other launched hand, holding it out in front of her arm's length like maybe it bites.

"Because this needs a good couple of spins through the washer," she adds, barely a breath in between. "Why no doubt you're infecting things with the filth off this rag, never mind whatever it is you're trying to wipe!"

"Mother," Gracie states lamely, offering her arms for the requisite quick hug, "what are you doing here?" Gracie's father stands behind her mother, sheepish, his vague professorial look. Hugs him too and he pats her back, a *there there* sort of pat. "We're on our way up to Bar Harbor and then Acadia," he says. "You know it's a national park?"

Gracie tell him she knows it's a national park. Like this is supposed to explain their sudden reentry into her life?

"It's your father's spring break, and I decided for once we are going to use it like people do, like an actual *break*, and I thought wouldn't it be nice to go to Maine where we can stop for a bit to visit our daughter, who never writes, barely calls, so we can see how she's doing! Will you be inviting us inside anytime soon or are we to just stand out here and catch a chill in the morning air?"

Gracie pulls open the door, though not very much, and her father bearing their two suitcases like some reluctant pack animal has to push it wider so these can come in too. She stares at the suitcases. "You should have called ahead. I'm not sure we have room. It's not a hotel here, in the usual sense."

Gracie's mother sniffs; yes, she can most certainly smell the truth in this, the *usual sense*. "We're not staying *here*, Gracie, it's just that this neighborhood looks a bit worn, you must agree, and I didn't think it a good idea to leave our suitcases in the trunk, you never know." Maizey turns around to Gracie's father, standing stoop-shouldered and bewildered behind her in his best college tweed jacket, the one that looks grey and meshy like all the others, but a better maker, her mother said. "Thomas!" she says, a little sharply, that strained, patient, put-upon voice she used with Gracie when she was a child. "Isn't there something you wanted to ask?"

He scratches his head, tugs at his beard. "Your mother and I thought maybe you'd like to come to Bar Harbor with us, our treat," he emphasizes, shuffling his feet, gazing everywhere but at his daughter's face, eyes rapt on the ceiling tiles above the foyer, Berry's *parlor*. "That is, we would pay for you to have your own room."

"Beside ours!" her mother adds. "And we're promised a water view."

Are you *high*? Gracie wants to say, but that would be just a little too Roma. "Are you nuts?" she asks instead. "I have a job, Mother, I can't just walk out like that."

"You clean," Maizey says.

"Of all people, I thought cleaning was noble in your book. Next to godliness or something."

"Well certainly, Gracie, when it's for you and your father, keeping our home pleasant and welcoming while he's bringing home the bacon, so to speak, and you grow up and pursue your dreams which we did promise to make possible for you within our ability; being a cleaning person for some strange boarding house in the state of Maine hardly qualifies as pursuing a dream, does it?"

"You wouldn't want me to pursue the kinds of dreams I get," Gracie says darkly.

"Yes, well, a dream is a dream I suppose," her father adds — he's sensing where the conversation is going, which circle of hell their words will ride, round and round, no end to the predictable retorts. He was a master at finishing their arguments, some seemingly profound statement that sounds like a thing you'd say at the close of a discussion, but when you think about it later you realize it meant nothing at all.

"Well, so where is the proprietor of this place, Gracie?" her mother asks, *this place* like the words are sticking to the roof of her mouth.

Gracie squirms, staring down at their suitcases. Berry Waters! She's the second to the last person Gracie wants her parents meeting, topped only by Roma who has once again moved back in, this time with a lip ring and a tattoo that spells BAD TASTE IS ITS OWN REWARD, bold black letters on her right shoulder. Now that the calendar says spring, she's in tank tops with scrawny straps to show the tattoo off, her bra fully exposed at its back closure and shoulders, as if this was *meant* to be worn on the outside. Gracie glances nervously about. Berry is at Shaw's getting the week's groceries. Roma could be anywhere.

244   Jaimee Wriston Colbert

She decides to take a chance on Anthony. If she could lead them back outside—luckily it's not rainy today or even foggy, a clear, cool day—if she can round him up from wherever he is, introduce her parents, then maybe she could aim them back toward their car before Roma or Berry appears. Her mother is already angling in toward the living room, her father shuffling dutifully behind her with their oversized hard-backed suitcases. No doubt Gracie's mother feels the hardness makes them stronger, and what would it matter that they are heavier for Thomas? She's got to stop them from actually settling down into the furniture.

"You want to meet my boyfriend?" she asks, her face pink. It's not a word Gracie uses much, in front of Roma and Berry or even Anthony. Just to herself, she speaks it to herself.

They look suitably shocked. "Why Gracie!" her father sputters finally, "How nice!" Like she just told him she scored perfectly on the SATs, something like that. It occurs to Gracie her father doesn't expect much of her in either of these departments, social or intellectual. She's very bright, Gracie's teachers told them, It isn't *potential* that's the problem. Her parents decided it was about ambition, having none.

Gracie's mother is scowling. "Boyfriend. You didn't tell us about any boyfriend, Gracie."

Gracie shrugs.

"Boyfriend," Maizey says it again, trying to find just the right fit for this, some kind of acceptable accommodations, this word, the language center in her brain—define, accept, reject? "Does this boyfriend have a name?" she asks, veering toward Berry's velvet chair like she needs to sit to hear this name.

"He's outside!" Gracie tells her. "Come!" Almost yelling it.

Maizey frowns, sighs, nods to Gracie's father to walk out in front of her. "You needn't shout," she says, "our hearing is the same as when you left us. Name," she repeats. "What is this boyfriend's name?"

"Anthony."

"Anthony? Anthony what? He must have a last name; generally when you tell someone a person's name you give them the whole name, first and last."

Gracie all but pushes her mother out, her hand firm against the small of Maizey's back, the part where surplus flesh overrides the waistband of her mustard and peach flowered skirt, yanking the door shut behind them. "Anthony Gushee," she mumbles.

"Gushee?" her mother asks, Gracie knew she would. "Gushee? What kind of a name is *Gushee*?"

"It's Anthony's name," Gracie says, trying to sound as finite about this as she can. She doesn't want them digging around into any family histories, not Anthony's family whose top intellect, the uncle who *attended* college, as they say when a person doesn't actually make it to the degree, is in prison for masterminding a K-Mart robbery. Stealing must be in their genes. Anthony can't resist *souvenirs* from wherever they go, sodas or a package of string cheese from the QuickMart stuck inside his jacket, even a stack of cheap paper towels from the men's room at the movies so he doesn't have to waste his own hard-earned, he tells Gracie, on such menial things; or—heaven forbid!—buy a real dish towel, all of a couple bucks. Though he'd probably snake this too if they went to the kind of store that sells these. Good thing they hardly go anywhere at all. Suddenly Gracie is dreading finding him. What if her parents start questioning him about his goals? Not like she hasn't of late, but how tolerant will he be of someone doing this that he doesn't even get to sleep with?

She walks hesitantly up to the carriage house door, Maizey and Thomas two steps behind. If I knock, she thinks, most likely he won't be inside since he's got his own little Berry list to work through each day, then they can all go away when he doesn't answer. Her parents to wherever they are going, and Gracie to the bathroom cabinet for a handful of aspirin!

But he does answer, his break, she guesses, and thankfully Gracie doesn't smell any pot, and gratefully she can hear the music of Beethoven or Bach or Mozart, somebody like that in the background. She looks up quickly at her father to register his approval but it's her mother's look she catches instead, stony, hard. You could toss rice at this face and it would bounce right off.

Maizey, whispering loud and shrill, "He lives in *this*? Is it supposed to be some kind of an apartment?" She prays Anthony won't put on his deaf and dumb act no matter how much her mother might have earned not being spoken to!

Anthony peers from one to the other of them, then at Gracie.

Please! her eyes are pleading. He nods, thrusting out his hand for them to shake.

It is decided her parents will take Anthony and Gracie down to the Waterfront restaurant in Camden for lunch, then be on their way. She lied to them, telling them she had no idea where Berry was or when she'd return, praying all the while Berry wouldn't drive up, the van loaded down with Shaws Market bags. The ambiance of the harbor, boats, ducks and geese, blue-green mountains behind, all riveting enough so that when the conversation stutters into silence and no doubt it will, they could all stare out at the shimmering vista. It will be a reason for silence.

She's expecting the million questions game for Anthony from her mother after they are seated, given menus, after Maizey scowls at the prices. "This is not upstate!" she hisses at Gracie's father. Gracie prays Anthony will be up to some kind of answers, something more than stuttered monosyllables or a grunt. But Maizey is strangely quiet and it's Gracie's father who attempts to politely converse, such riveting subjects as America's disappearing middle class in east coast coastal communities; when her father tries to talk socially it sounds like a syllabus rip off, lecture of the hour, Sociology for Sophomores. "With this Republican administration, it's difficult to dispute that the subtext of their mission will be to ensure the invincibility of the wealthier class, everyone else such as the fishing industry and the workers, settlers of these towns, struggling to survive at the bottom."

Anthony, who never had a shot at being part of a middle class to disappear from, who lives so far outside of American politics, Republican or Democrat Gracie doubts he's ever bothered to vote, smiles, that dazed, far away look in his eyes. But he's listening, she'll give him that. She feels a surge of something, good will? Approval? Whatever it is she hasn't felt it in a while toward Anthony. She knows what it's like to be on the outside of things.

It occurs to Gracie that her parents are actually embarrassed, her mother's first loss of words Gracie has seen in a very long time. And it's not Anthony who is doing this to them, however unsuitable they may think he is for their daughter, this hulky, plain speaking young man still in his *gardener clothes*, which Gracie happens to know are the only kind he owns. It's her. Daughter Gracie of the damaged face, her wounded, diminished little life, Gracie Kathleen McKneely with a boyfriend. Not the hypothetical *someday you'll meet a nice man*, but an actual living breathing male, who pulled out Gracie's chair for her, something she could never have guessed he had learned to do. Must've seen it in some movie.

She stares out at the harbor, steely blue, a few boats, fishing mostly, one or two yachts, many more come summer, the knobby Camden hills behind. Listens to her father, watching Anthony politely listening to him, trying to look interested like he knows what the hell Thomas is babbling about. There was a time, she'd been told, when her father was the one who listened; his Ph.D. dissertation, right before he met Gracie's mother, before he got a tenure track job, before his sabbatical and a research grant in Hawai'i then the birth of Gracie. Before all that he was changed forever with his one misfire, a slip of those up until that moment, scrupulously competent arms. (*Maybe it's hot that day? No trade winds blowing, that sucking, airless, humid Kona weather Hawai'i gets, only it's upstate New York now, the unforgiving summers and slippery rubbery too-warm baby girl sliding down, down, down....*) For his dissertation Thomas had studied people's willingness to talk to others, strangers, their need to connect, form a community as audience to their stories. An entire summer he hung out in the New York city subways, Central Park, Port Authority and the train station with a sign: *Talk To Me, I Listen*. And people, after testing him at first, seeing he really would just listen, talked. Told him their dreams, their loneliness, their fears of being not quite *right*.

This was a good choice, Gracie decides, a place where her father can spout his theories about societal ruin on automatic pilot, no tests to give out, no questions to answer. He can rest his eyes on the scenic beauty around them; not ever do they have to actually light down upon the wreck that is his daughter.

A week later Gracie again wakes up in Anthony's bed, again surprised to find herself there, dazed. He'd been distant since her parents brief visit, almost seeming a bit unsure around her. As in, *who am I?* A person who came from somewhere, from *them*, as if it had never occurred to him he might have to deal with Gracie as someone with a family, a personal history, a past; that she didn't just materialize out of Berry Waters' cleaning supplies closet. Anthony is already up, she can hear the shower running, the tiny closet-like bathroom attached to the carriage house, its tight fiberglass shower like climbing into a vertical MRI. Suddenly Gracie doesn't want to be here. She lunges off the sofa bed naked as the morning, grabbing his clothes slung on top of hers on the one folding chair Anthony has for this purpose, and as she does something falls out of his jeans pocket. A piece of balled up paper, and wrapped inside—she unfurls it, thinking it's some sort of note, maybe even one he was writing to her, who knows?—pills, two of them, clear gelatin capsules with a kind of white powder inside. Gracie scowls. Anthony swore he didn't do any drugs other than pot, and he certainly isn't sick, not that this looks like some kind of a prescription medicine!

She slides the paper into a pocket of her own jeans, which she's tugged on, flinging his clothes back down on the chair. Slams the carriage house door even though he won't hear it, the shower still sizzling, clean sound of water gurgling through pipes; she is not particularly comforted by it.

Jogs the path to the big house with the intention of grabbing a quick shower herself, her head foggy and weird. She can't even remember their lovemaking, doesn't recall getting that far last night, just listening to something symphonic on his CD player, Anthony silent beside her.

Jessie is coming out of the bathroom as Gracie's about to enter, her wet hair wrapped in a towel, no makeup, that healthy raisin-brown glow back on her cheeks. She remembers Jessie will be starting a new job today, as a computer lab technician at the University in Augusta and wishes her luck.

Jessie thanks her then frowns, dark brows worming up. "Were you with Anthony?"

Gracie nods, lowering her eyes. Not that Jessie of all people would be judgmental, Gracie coming in all sleep tousled and funky smelling, 6:00 in the AM.

Suddenly Jessie removes her hand from where she had been

clutching her white cotton bath robe and it falls open, revealing her dark and lovely too thin shape, the pokes of her hipbones, still recovering from her illness. She runs her hand, the side of it, down the side of Gracie's face, her scarred cheek and Gracie is shocked but she doesn't jump back. She lets Jessie touch her face.

"She had this look," Jessie whispers. "You hear me, girl?"

"Who?" Gracie asks.

Jessie continues stroking Gracie's cheek, harder now, cool fingers insistent against her sleep-warmed flesh. "That stunned look," she says, grabbing Gracie's chin, forcing her to peer into her eyes. "Be careful around Anthony," she urges. The second time Jessie has said it. Gracie swallows hard inhaling the lavender soap scent of Jessie's hand.

"I never thought much about having kids," she says, releasing Gracie's chin but still standing close. "Game of chance, you can't know what you'll get. It might have been Berry and Roma all over again and I'm not cut out for that, I'm no good in an endurance test. But if I could have had my choice? You, Gracie, would be the daughter I'd have wanted. He can't help who he is I suppose, but damnit girl, be careful around Anthony!"

Third warning, the magical three.

That evening when Gracie goes to Anthony's room she has those pills on the brain but she doesn't say a word. Let him think—hope!— they maybe dropped out of his pocket somewhere and are lost, instead of buried at the bottom of Shark Girl's file box, second section, under a file card marked "Feeding." When he hands Gracie a Corona she pretends she has to go to the bathroom and dumps the liquid down the toilet, masticating a bit on the god-only-knows how old of a lime wedge stuck inside the bottle's neck, to make it look authentic, rinses out her mouth in the sink. She flushes and wanders back out like everything is the way it always is, settling down into his (Roma's!) bloodstained sheets. Anthony kisses her, his hand moving tentatively over her breast. "Can't you take your clothes off?"

"Too tired," she mumbles, closing her eyes, moaning a bit, making it sound real.

"Gracie?" he says, his hand still moldering on her breast, under her shirt now. "Gracie, you asleep?" She doesn't respond.

Immediately he unzips her jeans, yanking them down then off, panties, tugs up her sweater, bunching it around her neck. He reaches underneath her, unhooks her bra, flings this down. *Is he actually going to do me while I'm supposedly asleep?* For some reason this turns Gracie on. Maybe he has a necrophilia fetish and this is as close as it gets. She sighs, stretching languidly like maybe she's having a really good dream. His urgency is exciting.

"Gracie!" Anthony whispers. She says nothing. "You asleep, huh?" He slips her sweater off over her head, pulls the covers over her naked body, tucking her in gently, almost tenderly, then gets up, leaving her there. She hears him rummaging about the room, settling someplace. Slits open her eyes just a little and sees him, his back to her, hunched down in front of the lawnmower box with his stereo switched on, earphones plugging his ears, swaying gently to whichever symphony pumps into his brain, his entire being, apart from her own.

Everything stops. You would hear the wind outside if it was a breath, if it could come alive, enter quietly and witness this, inhale, exhale, the undoing of Gracie McKneely. Because now, of course, it's perfectly clear. She's not a social science professor's kid for nothing. There's a reason behind most every problem, her father would say, clear thinking, this situation calls for clear thinking. Anthony slips her something in her beer and she is supposed to be asleep, *drugged?* out of it, naked in his bed. And he leaves her there. Period. When she wakes up she has no clothes on and believes he was there beside her, believes she still has a boyfriend who cares about her, is attracted to her, at least enough to make love to her. Did she ever even *have* a boyfriend? "What the hell?" she shouts, loud enough so that he jumps a little, swivels around, ripping off the earphones.

"Fuck, Gracie!" Anthony whines. "Jesus, you scared me. I thought you were asleep!"

Hello! she wants to say, but she can't do it, can't be Roma, not now.

Gracie squeezes her head, hands plastered against her eyes as if maybe when she removes them everything will be gone including herself. "What the hell have you been putting in my beer, Anthony, and oh, you missing any pills by the way?" Gracie forces her hands back down at her sides, knees squinched up and the covers tucked firmly around them against her chest, shielding her breasts and she looks hard at him, makes herself do it, staring at him and then she knows it, his red boned, hanging face.

"But why! Why the hell would you? Oh my God, I don't believe this. They're right to treat you the way they do, Berry and Roma, you son of a bitch!" She's sobbing now, her wreck of a face squeezed between her knees, his sheets, the ones he stole Roma's virginity on. "I don't get it! Why would you have to drug me? Am I so awful you don't want to make love to me anymore?" She stares up at his face again, splotched and distressed as meat loaf. He's stood up, inching closer to the bed then stopping in the middle of the room, wringing his hands like something's caught on them, tugging those ham pink fingers one at a time.

"Gracie," he pleads. "Fuck it, Gracie, I didn't mean nothing by it. Sometimes I like to just look. You have a beautiful body, Gracie, really." He says this so earnestly she almost wants to laugh, bit of hysteria thrown into the mix; is he trying to compliment her here, thinks he can get out of this thing by flattering her?

"I don't believe you! You can just *look* on the goddamn Internet! Is this your only interest in me these past couple months? Are you testing drugs on me or something? *Commerce*? My God, you are, aren't you. You're selling those damn things!"

"Gracie!" he wails. "What the fuck am I supposed to do! I didn't get many choices, you know? Think I want to spend the rest of my life working as Berry Waters' boy?"

"Don't you dare turn this around on me, you phony! You can get yourself out and get a real job like anyone else. Just because someone grows up with a mother who's a loser doesn't give him permission to drug his girlfriend! Why the hell can't you just leave this place?" She realizes she said girlfriend out loud and blushes, then thinks — and this is definitely not Gracie here, it can't be because she's always the one in the wrong, isn't she? the one whose life has been wronged? — the hell with that! "And what for? Knocking me out so you can ignore me and listen to your music? How many times do I have to pass out before I pass this drug test? I mean what the hell, Anthony! Why didn't you just tell me you don't want me coming out here anymore?"

"I do want you here, it's just not always about sex." He shakes his head miserably. "She's fuckin' got me. My neck's in her goddamn noose."

"Who? Berry?" Gracie wraps her arms around her stomach, closing her eyes, sickness roiling in like she'll maybe vomit, but goddamnit she could give a damn if she hurled all over his already dirtied sheets! She slides open her eyes, glaring hard at the fidgeting Anthony, her voice low and mean. "Christ, what a fool I've been. I get it now! You really did it, didn't you? You really did rape Roma. That's what they've got on you. The goddamn truth."

He drops his head, shifts from one foot to the other.

"You bastard, you're actually guilty!" Now she's absolutely going to puke, an acidy gurgling at the back of her throat.

Anthony, his voice dark and low, she has to lean closer to hear him: "I didn't hurt her. I don't have it in me to hurt her, much as she deserves it. We were *both* high. I didn't mean to do anything at all. Just to keep her with me…, just a little while."

"You use a drug on her too? What is it, that date rape drug? GHB, or whatever the hell it is?"

He's quiet and Gracie knows this is it, those pills. Jesus, a druggie and she didn't even realize it. *Dear God I promise if you give me a new face I won't ever do drugs.* Gracie wails, "To think I felt sorry for you, all these months I'm pissed at Berry for the way she's been treating you! You owe her and Roma, big time! You should be licking their shoes every day of your miserable life."

"OK, OK Gracie for chrissake, look at it from my point of view for just a fuckin' minute, will you? What do I have in my life? What do *I* get to fucking have? There's no goddamn pleasure in any of it, just the music and I can't even do that myself. Don't you fucking get it? Your parents may be freaks but they're at least nice to you. Your dad hates his life for what he did to your face by *accident*? My mom used to do stuff to me because she hated *me*!"

"Oh wah, wah, wah!" Gracie shrieks. "Let's play pity the *inbred*." She's not sure why she said this, doesn't have any grounds, as her father would put it. *Do you have grounds for your accusation, Gracie?* he would ask, his eyes anywhere but on her. Just that it's supposed to be the worst kind of an insult, around here anyway.

"Fuck you, you don't know, you don't know a fucking thing!" Anthony starts to cry, shoulders heaving and shaking like he's been rigged to the running board of some truck, harsh motorized sobs. She's determined she won't let him do it, try to win back any sympathy, not ever again.

"So what about Shark Girl?" Her voice dropping to almost a whisper, *her* name, a slow new burn of horror flushing her skin. Gracie plasters her hair back off her face, scrunching up closer to Anthony where he hovers now, at the foot of the bed, blubbering, forcing him to look at her. "So? What about Shark Girl?" she hisses again. "You drug her too so you could *look*, one legged miracle, or is it true she grew a new leg? My God, you might be the only one who actually knows. What's a trashed cheek to that? Beautiful body, my ass!" Gracie growls, her blood so hot now she could open a vein, bleed on him, cause second degree burns.

"Ah Christ! You don't get it. You *really* don't get it."

"No," she shakes her head, hard laugh, *hah*! "This time I think I really have got it. What I can't figure out though is why someone like Shark Girl would set foot in this room with someone like you in the first place."

"Gracie," he whimpers.

That's when she starts to cry again, slapping his hand when he tries to reach out to her, letting the covers fall away. It hardly matters anymore. Maybe for *her* it took just a few times before she figured it out and fled, one legged or not. But in the end it's the same reason Gracie has come to this room all these weeks, these months, isn't it? Loneliness, what else could it be? The need for some human contact, flesh on flesh. Truth of it like eating glass. Maybe *she* thought just a night or two, a week, what harm? No doubt she caught on a helluva lot faster than Gracie did! Because the reality is, he didn't want to be with either of them. Just to have them here, in his control, and then perhaps the ultimate power, at some point *he* decides, he doesn't need them at all,

Anthony sniffles, "You got to believe me. I have a good time being with you."

A good time? she thinks. Is that what we were having, a *good time*?

Gracie swipes away any remnants of tears. She staggers off his bed, grabbing her clothes, and gets dressed with him watching, fastening her bra, stepping into her underwear, jeans, readying herself to march out of Anthony Gushee's miserable life.

At the door she turns back and stares at him standing there, sniffling, that loose, jangly frame. "So, how much did you make?" Gracie asks coolly. Something is dawning on her here, something icy and icky, slithering about her gut like a cold little lizard's got in there.

"Gracie!" he pleads.

"I want to know. You used drugs on me, right? GHB, maybe others? So, I want a cut. This wasn't exactly a clinical trial. You made me a test subject. When researchers at my father's university test things on humans the test subjects always get paid. You've got your bank account where? Key Bank? Camden?"

"It's late, we can't fuckin' go to the bank tonight, what the fuck?"

"I want every penny off any drug sales and Shark Girl's too. You were the one who forced her to leave, huh? Not exactly a good rep for the healing business, drugged by a Rock Harbor townie." Gracie hears herself sounding like some cheesy reality show version of a *Who Done It*, but at this point she could give a damn. "You left her no choice! Even that shark didn't defeat her and you choose *this* for her. Who's the shark now? I want that filthy drug money or I go to Berry and I tell her what you've done. She knows you're a rapist. She'll be at the police with this and I'll be right beside her. The date rape drug? Oh boy, you think you have troubles now! Little bit of *souvenir* collecting here and there, a rape and drugs. How low can a life get?"

"Fuck you!" Anthony stamps his big foot, whipping his arms around his sunken in chest, glaring at Gracie that hard, pleading look. "Yeah, OK Miss know-it-all, you figured it out let's say, got my number, *whatever*, but you're gonna hear this first. It's not all like you think. Roma and me, we're the same. It was a matter of who got there first, you know? But that shark woman! Goddamnit Gracie, I know what you're thinking but it didn't happen that way. She's not what you believe she is. She's the one got *me*, I just went along with it, tried to make the best of it. Gracie, Christ, she's...fuck, that woman is some cold. Listen to me, because I'm not even sure she's for real. I'm not talking about that leg. The woman's a mouth, like she could as easily eat me as fuck me, you get what I'm saying?"

Gracie shakes her head, plugs her fingers in her ears; uh uh! she's thinking, she's *not* hearing this. "My God," she snarls, "I may have no ambition, that's probably true, plus all the breaks as you seem to think despite a ruined face, but do you have to be such a living breathing cliché? First thing in the morning we go down to the bank together. In fact, I want to be paid for my time with you! If you try any funny stuff here, rapist! drug dealer!—and I don't know for sure but seems to me drugging people without their knowledge has got to be some sort of abduction—so help me I'm to Berry and the police. Don't even try messing with me, Anthony, I'm a professor's daughter, out of your league," she says meanly. And boy does Gracie know this is mean, her father would shun her and her mother? *Good Democrats never say such things out loud!* Maizey would admonish. *Who are you?*

Gracie walks into the night, trembling, the first time she's managed to leave his bed before morning in quite a while. Clothes on, hair unruffled, her own scent unmingled with his. But it's not as bad as she thought it would be. People survive their broken hearts, fractured lives all the time, don't they? *Who am I?* It hardly matters at this point. She's calling these shots, miserable as they are.

"With their blunt snout, lifeless gray eyes and huge mouth bristling with those wicked, serrated teeth, tiger sharks are exactly what Harold figured Satan would use as his watchdogs."

Shark Bites; Ambrose. p. 71 *(Compiled by S.G.)*

****

"Told you he's a loser!" Roma says triumphantly, though mildly enough. She's being generous with Gracie now. Roma likes it when someone's beaten down before her and will admit as much. She even offers Gracie an evening at Liela's own house, where only the *special* people are allowed. "Cancer victims, AIDS, they'll be smoking pot, getting high, forgetting their pain for a little while," Roma says encouragingly. Gracie shakes her head, smiling sadly as if she's been too emotionally hammered to think about the possibility of a rebound quite yet.

It's several days later and Gracie *has* been hurt of course, though she's had some time to digest this. Figured she'd be feeling devastated and instead is mostly numb. Maybe she had believed somewhere inside herself that it really couldn't last, that as she always suspected she was unworthy of any kind of love, and how she'd usually react is to hide her face. *Who am I if you can't see me?* But this time she's blazing mad and Gracie's more likely to flaunt her face, make people look, see *her*. Of course having the money order from Anthony's bank account (Can you believe it? Meek and mild Gracie McKneely makes him do this and he *did* it, got that money out!), tucked away in Shark Girl's file box didn't hurt this recovery, either. "For you and me," Gracie whispered, slipping it between the articles proclaiming her a healer, a miracle, desperate fan letters, pleas for her to take their pain away, to bleed for them. It's Gracie McKneely who knows her now above anyone else, feels a part of her, bones, muscles, blood, inside her own damaged skin: *knows for a few nights anyway, it was Wilhelmina Beever herself who needed healing.*

Gracie had expected to wake up emotionally shattered, but it was mostly the sex she missed. And missing it, oddly enough, made her feel curiously more alive, having had it, to know its absence. Of course she hadn't realized just how long this *absence* had been absent! Strangely—secretly!—though she's furious at the idea of Anthony's drugging her, secretly Gracie gets off just a bit at the thought of him staring at her body, which is *good*, she knows it, Anthony had told her this over and over his prayerful hands riding her hips. Wondering at what point he lost interest in that was somehow no longer important. It's a feeling of power restored. *She* is calling the shots.

They are camped out in Gracie's room, cleaning day over, both having declined Berry's special stew dinner, her conglomerative history of the month's past meals, Roma's stick shape slung across Gracie's bed and Gracie settled down on the floor where she had once again tossed all of Shark Girl's packed clothes. She needed S.G. around her after the Yard Boy Affair, as Roma is calling it. Gracie lies among *her* things, imagining she can still smell that light sea-foam scent of her this many months later. Gracie made Roma promise she wouldn't tell her mother about Anthony and the drugs, and Roma agreed on the condition she let Anthony know that *Roma* knows—it will make tormenting him all the more satisfying.

"So he really did rape you," Gracie says, confirming what now seems the obvious.

Roma grins. "Girlie, don't you get it? No one, and I mean no *one*, date rape drug or not, GHB, Maine homeboy, cherry meth, liquid ecstasy, whatever the hell name you want to give it, no one messes with Roma Waters if I don't want to be messed with. Call it whatever you want to call it; I'd settle for Big Fucking Mistake. It's Berry who's calling it rape."

Gracie smiles at her. Because Roma, who doesn't know it yet, is a lesser player in Gracie's own design, a support figure, a pawn—her father's chess analogies, the game they used to play together where he could stare at the board and not at his daughter, yet still be with her. *A win for you is not unachievable Gracie*, he would say, bleary eyes studying her moves, the light off his gold framed glasses twinkling, nodding at her queen, her king, the careful and deliberate placement of her figures around them. He approved of the protective way Gracie worked her pawns, taught her this himself.

The bottom line is this: Shark Girl has become more real to Gracie, less out of reach, the person behind the myth as somehow *achievable*, and this time Gracie is the one with the plan.

Gracie McKneely's Summer List of— DANGEROUS ANIMAL SEX
Aug. 9, 1994

> *1. European Praying Mantis — FEMALE! bites off her mate's head! Has to get him either when he's approaching her or after they've done it; if he sneaks up and leaps on her back he can have her and still keep his head. If she gets him first she can have him while he's thrashing around without his head!*

> *2. Some FEMALE spiders do this too. She lures a male over to her pretending she wants him then she pounces on him, wraps him up and stores him for a meal!*

> *3. Dr. Bender told me about a kind of wasp that hunts other bees and wasps, called Beewolves. Males desperate to mate get visits from FEMALES who have already mated and they sting the male until*

he's paralyzed then take them home for their grubs to eat while he's still alive!

4. Pygmy Salamander. Male plunges barbed teeth into female.

5. Female mountain goats can be chased for miles by packs of rams. To escape she jumps narrow ledges on mountain faces. I asked Dr. Bender if she ever falls to her death and she told me an even worse thing, about a flock of sheep on the Arctic circle where the ewes are chased and battered to death by groups of rams. The rams try to mount her, kicking each other off and kicking her, butting her for hours. If she falls they butt her until she's up again and if she's not dead at the end of all that there are giant seabirds called petrels that will disembowel her. (I don't want to write what that means but I know because Louis told me. It's very, very gross!)

6. Crabeater Seals. They bite each other viciously during sex and end up all bloodied and scarred....!!! Even worse are Hawaiian Monk Seals. Dr. Bender said they're an endangered species. She said their greatest threat is each other. The biggest cause of death are mobs of male seals attacking single females to mate them and then the females are either battered to death or they're so weak they get eaten by tiger sharks. She said biologists are giving male monk seals drugs to suppress their sex drive and save their species from going extinct.

7. FEMALE Chickadees. On a nicer note Dr. Bender said, there are the female chickadees who are very fickle (chickadee sluts! Louis called them). She'll find another lover if the one she has doesn't win his daily song competition with his rivals. So now he won't be the only daddy in the nest, says Dr. Bender, and the higher ranked her male is the more likely she will be unfaithful to him. They're accustomed to hearing their high-ranked mate dominate the singing contest and are shocked if he doesn't. Loser, she calls him in chickadee talk and sneaks out before dawn to meet with another male for mating. Then she flies back to her nest to her loser male like nothing ever happened, but DNA studies have shown that not all her chicks are fathered by the same dad. Dr. Bender said they even have something like divorce, that if the highest Alpha female chickadee dies then her Alpha male will sing to the next ranking Beta chickadee who divorces her Beta mate for the high ranking Alpha. It's called trading up, Louis said.

CHAPTER TWENTY

Finally the dream when we are reborn, waking up in the silvery mouth of an ancient river, wiry hair color of the shark, mark of the shark on our backs. By day we walk among others with legs; when the sun sinks we are part of the sea, grey and sleek, dreaming a dream of the deep. Our kind eat crabs. Not the ones that scuttle the beach, digging holes in the yellow sand. Perhaps on a surfboard and we bump up against them. Or in a tube, round black object and those two little crab legs dangling sweet as desire, fresh as a wound that can never heal.

The pathway to alvin-Travis's house is steep and brambly, leading up off a rocky coastal inlet. Low bush blueberry plants poke their ankles, a variety of wild flowers wildly in bloom. Butterflies flit, dragonflies dart, late spring air warm and smells of low tide. Suck in a sticky breath. Roma unnaturally quiet beside her. Gracie asked her to do this, come with her to alvin-Travis's house on foot off the beach (the day before she had noted the locked iron gate at the top of his easier-access driveway), to talk to Shark Girl's sister. Not sure why Roma needed to be included in this, just a hunch that she should. That, and Gracie was a little terrified to go alone! Why the hell was she doing this and who the hell *is* she to be doing this, you dig? as Roma would put it. But Roma is silent.

Gracie peers over at her. "Promise me you won't do anything weird!"

"Oh, what, like reach out for a hug from Daddy-o? Say hi Daddy, meet your long lost daughter! Got any overdue financial support for me compounded by almost eighteen years of interest? That kind of thing?" Roma cuffs Gracie lightly on her shoulder.

Gracie's eyes must have strobbed panic, heels rocking back she stumbles and Roma grabs her arm, laughing. "Jesus, give me a break. *Hello*? If that second rate rocker wanted anything to do with me he would've been in my face long before now. Truth is, if *I* had wanted Scum-Dad in my life I'd have walked this walk years before. You saw how easily my mother got you his address. It's not like he's some big secret. Besides, I may need to blackmail him someday. If he ever does make it big, fat chance, but if nostalgia nerds start buying his CD by the millions or something you can bet I'll be there, claiming my inheritance. What I don't get is why you're so all over Shark Girl that you feel the need to find her through this loser? I mean man, I've known some o.c. disordered girlies but what the hell, Gracie, you're like on some sacred mission. What do you think she's going to do, *heal* you?"

Gracie stares down at her feet. It's as close to any truth as they're likely to get. How *would* she explain such a strange obsession, not even an obsession more like a *possession*! All Gracie knows is something in her has changed since being among *her* things, *her* clothes, *her* letters, her *compiled* information, a place she once was. And there are Gracie's dreams.... Try explain these and they'd certify her a *genuine* haunted housewife, maybe have her committed!

"Far as I'm concerned the so-called Father is about as necessary to me as my toenail clippings," Roma snorts. "Just keep in mind this little pilgrimage is your trip not mine."

Also true. Gracie had been unsure how Roma would take it, asking her if she knew where alvin-Travis lived. The letters in S.G.'s file box didn't include a street address, only Rock Harbor and a rural route number, and he wasn't listed in the phone directory. "Like rock musicians *are*, talented or not!" Roma snapped. She'd once tried to locate Frankie and the Fuck Punch, Roma admitted, and even *they* weren't in the book. "Look in the yellow pages under *rock* and they'll probably send you to a certified geologist or something," she sniffed, and made Gracie ask her mother. "It's your deal," she said. Gracie assured Berry it was his partner she needed to see, his woman friend, whatever she wanted to call her, Susan Catherine, *the sister*.

She had expected a hundred questions, the suspicious, swamp-eyed Berry Waters interrogation. But Berry just nodded, as if all this time she'd been waiting for this request, walked over to her ancient secretary desk in the den and yanked open the top drawer, its tentatively attached antique silver handle. The drawer was stuffed full of scraps of paper, business cards, various contacts, former and maybe future "housewives," lesser used addresses and phone numbers of a life. Snaked her hand through this mess and pulled out from under it her little black address book, dove straight to his name.

Later, the cleaning day over and Gracie making a quick getaway to her room, Berry cornered her in the hall just outside the door. She has been friendlier to Gracie since her breakup with Anthony, though Gracie has yet to be invited to another H.H. meeting.

"You understand that just because I happened to have the man's number in my book don't mean I'm ever going to use it? You keep your bases covered, that's what. After all, he *is* Roma's biological father. But I've done just fine for myself without him, without any man. And Roma, pain in the butt that she is, alive and kicking despite her issues with food. Would having a father in her life have made things so different?"

"Did you enjoy it?" popped out of Gracie's mouth and she had to quickly clarify, seeing the shock and puzzlement on Berry's face. "The rock and roll world, I mean. The seventies."

Berry smiled, eyes watery and distant for a moment. "Ayuh, felt more alive than any other time in my life. Having some wild in you, it frees you in a way. Don't much care what people think of you. Still never got out of Maine though," she laughed, "as here I stand."

That Berry Waters cared at all what people thought of her was news to Gracie. She smiled back.

"Gracie," Berry started, "here's what I come to tell you. I know you're going there to try find Shark Girl and all, and that's just fine, you and a hundred others of her deluded no doubt. First off, if you do find her, try and get me my money, OK? You get her to pay what she owes. I don't ask for much in this life, just what's owed me. Secondly" — and here Berry leaned in close, close enough that Gracie could smell the minty scent of her toothpaste and something else, sweetish yet sharp, hungering under her breath—"Gracie, if you think she's going to change your face for you, think again. She's stumping around on one leg after all. I don't care what they say about her leg growing back, don't buy it for a minute. That woman was humping a prosthesis, had to be. Rumors get started, don't know how but once they're in the world they're hard to put out. Like fire, consumes everything. People want to believe in miracles but I'm here to tell you miracles don't run out on their rent. You think *Jesus* would do that? Saint Therese? Run out and leave the place a pigsty? God decides how He wants you to look out at the world. Maybe His idea putting you in that face was to pay for the sins of your father. Personally I don't buy that about our Lord but some would say it. Maybe it's to make you stronger, so you can bear up under the weight of things. That cheek's like the Lord put a sponge in you, soak up the world's misery and there it sits, a buffer, don't really get into you like it does the rest. But you feel it. You feel Shark Girl's misery and believe it's yours. Think she's the one could heal you? Seems to me should be the other way around!"

Gracie started to protest, always uncomfortable in any conversation about her face having something going for it beyond the burn, the scar (to teach you *compassion*, her mother once said, like she would know!), but Berry stuck up a gnarled hand. "See these bumps on my fingers? Not too attractive, ayuh, and let me tell you they don't feel any better than they look. Our heavenly Father put those there, reminds me I need to work with my head and my heart, not my hands."

At this point Gracie tried to open the bedroom door but Berry looped her hand around Gracie's fingers, tugging them off the glass knob, staring straight into her eyes, still clutching her hand. "I'm going to tell you something I know about her, Gracie, something she wrote for me. I never told this to another soul. Look at me now, this is for real. When Shark Girl first appeared at my place, before I knew a thing about her, even that they called her Shark Girl, she was competing for this room; another woman wanted it also, you see, and I had but the one available. I made them both write me out an application with a statement on the back explaining why they wanted to live here, then I would choose the one that rang true to me, the one maybe *needed* to be at America's Haunted Housewives, cause that's what we're about, right? I know what's been said about the name, that it's a dumb name, doesn't make sense and all. Well let me tell you, folks who say things like this have no clue how it is for some. It's not just about our meetings, contacting the dead like some around here seem to think. A while back I turned on the TV to a show called 'America's Haunted Houses,' only my mind played a trick on me. Housewives! I thought, and I come to understand this was a sign from the Lord; *America's Haunted Housewives* is what I heard. That whole women's liberation thing, back when they said it wasn't OK to be a housewife and then they turn around the next decade, say sure, it *is* OK, women can be anything they want to be! Well none of it applies to poor women, Gracie, women down on their luck, those kinds of considerations are not meant for the ones who fall through the cracks. So here's what Shark Girl wrote, I swear by Jesus this is what she said: *I lay in my bed for eighteen years. One day I decided to get up.*"

It's become clear to Gracie why Roma is here. Trembling at his door, staring at the brass knocker with his a.T. initials engraved on it, without Roma there's no way in hell she'd take that thing in her hand and actually use it. She'd like to turn back down that path, forget the whole thing, heart beat yammering like some ghost is going to open this door. Remembering that night on the breakwater with Anthony, how he made her press her face up against the broken window, those whirring electrical noises, that stale, used-up air. She did it though, did what he asked, even climbing inside! No ghost of some former lighthouse keeper followed them back down that long wet mile of granite, just Gracie's hand hot in Anthony's, daring to think her life really could have some possibilities. Maybe this is why he had her do it, press her face into that unfamiliar air. Then again, she's probably giving him too much credit; probably he was just trying to scare the crap out of her!

Roma glowering, stamps her foot impatiently. "Grow some balls, Gracie, it's a door knocker. Use the damn thing for chrissake. I'm the one should be hesitating, about to witness my own genetic stuff materialize from inside that house. I mean Christ, I don't know why I let you talk me into this idiocy!"

"OK, OK!" Sucking in a breath she knocks before Roma's the one barreling back down that path and Gracie is stuck here alone.

The woman who opens the door is almost as skinny as Roma, hippie garb, float of her long white hair, feathered earrings, patchwork skirt, braless under a purple tube top. Whiff of patchouli oil and pungency of incense burning in the pale oak foyer, dusty slant of sunlight flooding in through the skylight above her frizzled head.

Roma frowns, "Jesus Christ, *this* would be Shark Girl's sister? Wouldn't you know it."

The woman looks flustered, giggles.

"That's not Susan Catherine!" Gracie whispers sharply. "Don't you remember the photograph on the dresser?"

Then alvin-Travis is at the door, appearing about the same as he did in the newspaper article before Roma was Roma but with a receding hairline now, what's left is tied back, bit of a protruding belly, fuller cheeks. He's wearing a tie dyed shirt that looks like it's supposed to be old but isn't, and silky white sailor-type pants. That smug look of prosperity, Gracie's mother had often pointed this out, though what were they, starving?

"Looks like a Buddha-wannabe," Roma whispers harshly to Gracie.

"If you girls are here about that shark business I don't have any information for you!" he blusters. "I'm a little sick of her groupies coming to my home. Let me help you, this is private property!"

Roma immediately chirps, "*One* groupie here maybe and it's not me. I hate the bitch!" She glares at him, intense green eyed stare, stepping closer. He moves back a little, wary.

"Don't fret Pops, I'm not some mental case come here to off you or something, you were never important enough to risk a prison sentence."

Gracie's heart's pounding, "God, Roma!" But alvin-Travis actually smiles.

"Uh huh," he says, "bit of a mouth on you. I give up. Why are you here then? Hustling girl scout cookies?"

"Susan Catherine!" Gracie jumps in before Roma can spit out a retort. Gracie looks quizzically at the hippie woman who has retreated behind alvin-Travis. He follows her gaze as if he too must make sure. "Nah," he says, "she's gone."

"Gone?"

"Not in any permanent sense. A disaster somewhere, Kodak Moment, maybe another Shark Sister sighting."

"You don't know where she went?"

He stares at Gracie, eyes lingering over her cheek but not maliciously, then back to Roma. "What are you two, the teeny bopper swat team?"

"Your kid!" Roma grins, stepping even closer to him, peering up at his in need of a shave chin jutting over her. She blinks almost flirtatiously and Gracie would like to give her a good swift kick, knock her into the next town. "The long lost daughter," she says, batting her eyelashes, silvery glint of her eyebrow piercings. "Happy to see me?"

"Roma!" Gracie croaks. "You promised!"

alvin-Travis frowns down at her a moment, takes another step back, shakes his head. "Too mouthy!" he laughs again, then sighs, rolling his tea colored eyes. "OK, fine, I'll tell you, what difference can it make? You've got more on the ball than the usual geeks who show up here, I'll give you that. Eventually you all catch up with that mutation of a sister anyway, then off she goes somewhere else. She's created herself into a true enigma. If I could've done that with my music I would've been fucking great. You honeys know the meaning of that word?"

"Gee!" Roma chirps, sucking on her finger, "fucking or enigma? Enigma. Isn't that the name of some *other* loser band? For your information, Pops, no enigma would've made *you* great!"

"You know my music?" He appears interested for a moment then shrugs. "Goddamnit, I don't have time for this shit. You look like you've got a story or two, little girl, but I don't want to hear them. OK, I lay it on you and then you disappear, right? Before I get really nasty? I'm a peaceful guy, I just don't happen to appreciate the world at my door, especially in regards to some freak of nature. Susan Catherine split to Hawai'i. Don't have a clue when she'll be back. Not the island with Honolulu, the big one. Something about the volcano. I didn't catch much, because out the door she went. She's like that, a mind of her own. Independent cunt, if you'll permit me that word on my own goddamn property. If I *did* have a kid, that's the kind I'd have."

The hippie woman giggles as he slams the door tight, almost in Roma's face. She pounds her fist against his door, back of her neck blazing. "Christ, *there's* some genetic mess I'd deny if it came to that! Cunt my ass. His taste in women has gone down the toilet since my mother, I'll tell you!"

Gracie bites back a grin. She can see just *whose* daughter Roma is, defending her at that!

Roma whips back around, glaring. "You got your answer Gracie-poo, satisfied? Hawai'i! Not exactly a Greyhound route. And he only told you her sister is there, who knows if Shark Girl is too. Can we go now? This place makes me want to hurl!"

Gracie is quiet as they head back down the brambly path. Volcano? she's thinking, it's what he said, and Shark Girl had to have disappeared *somewhere*, after all. alvin-Travis did mention the possibility of, how did he put it? a *Shark Sister sighting*?

"Well?" Roma continues prodding her. "So Detective Drew, you off to Hawai'i? The *big* Island? Quest for a loser's loser girlfriend and her double-loser sister!"

Gracie stops dead, the Atlantic in front of them a deep cold green, quintessential coastal beauty of Maine, lobster boat steaming out to sea, *this place I am about to leave. Who am I?*

Roma must have seen it too. "You can't be serious, girlie. *Hello?* For starters, what will you do for money? A plane ticket to an island, for chrissake, is it even part of America? This can't be cheap. And where would you stay? Who do you know? *Susan Catherine?* Be real! She must get macked on by Shark Girl's sickos all the time. You don't have that kind of dough, Gracie, not to mention the balls to use it."

Where would I stay? Who do I know? Dr. Bender and Louis driving her to Honolulu International two weeks too soon, that hushed ride, dropping her off at the curb. You burned that bridge, Gracie! her mother tells her a couple days later, dinner time, out on the patio and the hills around them a suffocating, closed in green. Her father staring into the barbecue....

"Maybe I've got it," Gracie says, matter of fact.

"You've got it. What, we're probably talking hundreds of dollars. You've got that?"

Gracie smiles, but not so Roma would see her. *S.G. and me, we've just about got it*, she thinks. The company they kept; hanging out with druggies has *some* rewards, amazing what they'll pay for what comes naturally—silence. "Pretty close," Gracie tells Roma. "I've been saving up," she adds, which is also true. Not much to spend on in Rock Harbor, unless you're into drugs. Turns out she got hers for free.

Roma shakes her head, her color-of-the-month hair, sunflower yellow with a chartreuse tinge. "Well Christ, my mother must be paying you pretty sweetly to clean that goddamn house. Maybe *I'll* take the job if you really go!"

"You could come too," Gracie says, surprising herself about as much as Roma.

Roma laughs. "Yeah right," she says, grabbing Gracie's hand, giving her fingers a hard squeeze. "Listen, Miz McKneely! You made it out of *upstate*, and that's something. I need my girlies around me. I'm not the type that gets out. Like my mother, you dig? We Waters women just huff and puff and wish we did."

Part VII

Na-pua-o-Paula, a pretty girl on Hawai'i, arouses the jealousy of a neighboring family. They give offerings to their shark 'aumakua to destroy her and she is carried away by a wave and devoured by a shark. Her mother goes to a sorcerer. A child is born who resembles the dead girl and is given her name. The other family are afflicted with swellings and die miserably.

Beckwith; *Hawaiian Mythology*

CHAPTER TWENTY-ONE

Flashback: The Worm Scientist. I had been thinking about how I could count my visits home to Hawai'i since leaving for college on one hand, plus a toe. The Worm Scientist was the toe. Jaycee's 50th birthday and my 27th summer. I'm an alcoholic but not admitting it, believing I can control it, that it's perfectly normal to start every day with a Bloody Mary—it has tomato juice after all—and that every day can start at one or two in the afternoon, whenever I finally wake up, crusted eyes, hammering head, skin a shade of ground up taro, hungover from the night before, the night before that, a darkness that begins in the afternoon, beginning again the next afternoon. Time loses its definition when the hours are determined by which drink and how many.

I don't think I even came close to loving The Worm Scientist, but it was not without a concentrated effort on my part. I believed I would never find anyone nicer or more "appropriate" as Jaycee might label it, "husband material." I wasn't exactly a catch myself, staggering from one boozy bout to the next—and so I brought him to Jaycee's birthday party, a gift of sorts, my hat off to *normalcy*. Jaycee took me aside after he had gone to fetch us, my mother and me, yet another drink, and rasped into my ear: "You'll have short children if you marry that one."

Short or not he gave me back the gift of the sea, made me love it again, that which I had feared, for the time we spent together diving into its cool blue below the surface world. A summer night he takes me to see the Fireworms, or *Ahahuluhulu* as Hawaiians call them, which translated means hairy cord. Floating orange bristles they are heart-achingly brilliant, abundant, their spawning triggered by the full moon, clouds of eggs and sperm like blown bubbles.

He teaches me about other sea worms, some that are filter feeders, some that stalk their prey, some who even eat their kin, a riotous bunch of whiskered and segmented animals slithering over coral heads, inching out from tubes, having evolved, these sexual beasts, into eighteen ways to reproduce themselves, including breaking into pieces. I think about that, breaking into pieces, eliminating any need for another person—like my photographs, I realize now, pieces of me. When the Worm Scientist is asleep I slide away from him and curl into my own nutibranch form—"to move in a sinuous manner suggestive of a worm" the American Heritage Dictionary defined this—my lonely, separate thirst.

On our last dive together, what will turn in to our last day together, we drive out to Kawela where the shallow bay water is a clear, pale aqua and the deeper ocean, just beyond the reef, dark as dusk. It's there we are headed, the long swim out, our masks, fins, tanks, regulators, weight belts, tools that will let us become a part of this world for as long as our oxygen holds forth. We both take a long pull off our water bottles before submerging. Mine is mostly vodka—thank heavens for the clear ones, I learned this from my mother—gin, vodka, you can funnel it into bottles where it's disguised as the 'other' you poured out. We used to watch Jaycee before heading uptown, dumping 7up into the sink, her gin into the 7up bottle. If the Worm Scientist suspects he doesn't say it. *Don't ask; don't tell....*

Bobbing on the surface of this inky water, he tells me what we'll be looking for: carnivorous worms, ones who use their jaws to nab other worms, fish, creatures much larger than themselves, and acorn worms. Acorn worms, he tells me, have toxic skin that discourages predators and their head can regenerate if severed. Plus they have gill slits, like an embryonic human—or a shark. Then he dives down, our usual game plan, him first with me following closely behind…, only this time I didn't.

Because at first when I hear it, it sounds like a song. I am entranced, all grin; in love with the sea again and it's singing to me! Imagine sirens, low and mournful, though not so mournful, sort of unearthly, like the ocean has brought forth whatever is in its deepest, strangest depths, a world unknown, uncharted, untouched, *unfouled* by humans and put this to music; the kind of music waves make, wind over the waves, the slapping, pulling, slithery sounds of the water itself, undulating, alive. Then, I see it. It is not the sea, after all. Not close but not far either, sort of taking its time, humming, gliding, humming, swimming, sidestroke, breaststroke, leisurely in control of its world this ocean, its curving commands, meandering through it the way we might part long grass in a field, stalks of corn, something rooted to the ground that we walk upon, thrusting it aside, certain of our destination, our place, So she approaches me. For I know she's a she, must be a she, must have always been *she*, her fin in the low sunlight kaleidoscopic, like it too is made of this translucent water, this world that is hers and not mine.

A singing, humming, beating, and I'm aware that it is my own heart too, contributing to this song, this keening, erratically and painfully alive, pushing up toward my throat, a rogue wave, a fierce and ancient blood. I do not move, not even a panicky kick of my fins. What's the use? Her fins are cartilage, something that belongs, not the rubber of mine. Mine were made in imitation of hers, after all. I should have been afraid, is what I will imagine afterwards, terrified in fact but instead am mostly numb. It seems fitting somehow, my sister, me. I think about the worms we were supposed to collect today, the ones who can regenerate their heads. In another year Willa and Jaycee will begin the first of their disappearing acts, and the rumors will start—the regenerated leg—but of course I can't know this yet. What I know is she's directly in front of me now, and I imagine us staring into each other's eyes, eye to eye, hers like mirrors, deep and sure, my own reflected in their glassy surface. Though naturally hers would be under water, but I can picture it unfolding, slow motion, frozen time, like in one of my photographs, the moment before whatever it is we think we know ceases. My final thought at the end of this story will be one of regret: that I wouldn't have a child, that I wouldn't get to prove I could be a better mother than Jaycee.

Of course the Worm Scientist saves the day, flash of his long handled knife for cutting worm colonies off coral heads (or the occasional shark?), and he'll be so disgusted at my inability to be grateful, my lack of *caring*, for chrissake, that I was about to be *chum*! that he won't call me the next day or the day after that or any of the long sultry days for the rest of the summer. And this in turn will become yet another excuse, a reason to drink, so much that even Jaycee notices, suggesting that maybe it's time for me to leave.

Of course it didn't happen that way. The Worm Scientist surfaces with his *specimens* he calls them in his collector's bag—a word that in most cases means that which was alive and will be no more—and no doubt he asked me (he'd rightfully be annoyed) why I didn't follow him down, floating *willfully* (he did use that word!) on the ocean like I am my own raft, drifting away so that he had to swim out even further to fetch me, tired as he was. I'm fairly certain this was the moment when we both stopped pretending to care.

Photographer's Log - Susan Catherine Beever
<u>Breasts</u>

After the miscarriage my breasts seemed to still believe there would be a baby to nourish, nurture into this world. How could this be? losing the baby before even my belly popped out and yet my breasts grew heavy, tender, swollen I could've sworn, with milk. They ached for a release, for the chance to do what they were intended to do, succor this child that the genetic mapping of my body, anyway, seemed more certain of its place than I. Life craves to live. Breasts, I title these; Breasts.

****

The last story I would tell alvin-Travis before leaving for Hawai'i was about Pele, the Hawaiian volcano goddess, how in 1960 she destroyed the town of Kapoho, all but one light tower where the keeper, an old man, had befriended an old Hawaiian woman the night before. Pele, in her old woman guise. She saved his tower by carving the path of her molten lava around it. "You can see it to this day," I told a.T. "Perky white structure staunch in a field of nothing but black lava and ohia lehua, its red blossoms breaking through. Lava that buried the entire town. Furthermore," I told him, ratcheting up the drama as any good story teller knows to do, "you can go to Kalapana, the site of the Waha'ula Heiau, 'Red Mouth Temple' they call it, and see how Pele buried the land in an ocean of rock all except this temple, carving her lava around it to preserve it. The day before it happened a beautiful Hawaiian woman, tall and stately, flowing hair in a long white dress with a little white dog was seen roaming the area. The goddess Pele, in her young woman shape."

"Why did she?" he asked. Meaning why did she save the one light tower or the temple, not why she got angry enough to destroy Kapoho and Kalapana in the first place. When Pele is displeased, her raging, unsettled moods, watch out! Or maybe it's simply a warning, a reminder of who *is* in charge.

"Because they were nice to her," I told him. "It was the old Hawaiian man and his wife who took her in, fed her, served her gin her favorite drink, put lehua blossoms, her flowers on the table to honor her. When she left she spread ti leaves around the border of the place so her lava would know not to destroy it.

"Here's something else," I told a.T. "You can look this up in Hawaiian history books. Princess Ke'elikōlani became a hero to the Hawaiian people in 1881 when she asked Pele to stop a lava flow before it reached Hilo. She made Pele an offering, then she and her party spent the night in the path of the lava to show her faith. And what do you think?" I asked a.T., who had no answer. "When they awoke the flow had stopped right before them!"

"Does Pele have a lover?" alvin-Travis wanted to know. So I told him how as legend has it, this red-eyed goddess (Ka wahine'ai honua, the earth-eating woman!), led by her brother Kamohoali'i the shark god, brought her brothers and sisters to the island of Hawai'i. Pele's favorite sister was the youngest, Hi'iaka, a healer, goddess of the dance, earth-mother type who created bloom out of Pele's destruction. In a dream Pele traveled to the island of Kaua'i and fell in love with a handsome young chief named Lohi'au. When she awoke Hi'iaka volunteered to travel to Kaua'i and fetch this mortal for Pele, but she's gone too long and Pele became angry and in her jealous rage burnt Hi'iaka's beautiful groves and ohia forests. Hi'iaka brought Lohi'au back to the big island (it took a while because he had committed suicide over his brief encounter with a beautiful, mysterious woman who disappeared and Hi'iaka, the healer, had to bring him back to life!). When she saw the destruction her big sister had caused she embraced Lohi'au to make Pele jealous. Pele exploded and turned Lohi'au to stone.

"But wait!" I told alvin-Travis who was staring at me, his grey, incredulous look, shaking his newly blonded head (I know he's been dying his hair and I know the tide of it still willfully recedes, not much he can do about that). "There's a happy ending, a.T.," I assured him; story tellers must be mindful of their audience's limitations. "Hi'iaka and Pele later made up and the ghost of Lohi'au was resurrected for Hi'iaka's pleasure."

alvin-Travis didn't like the story because there was no explicit sex. "A beautiful woman appears with long flowing hair and nobody wants to nail her?" He shook his head. "And little sister gets the ghost? That's twisted, Susan Catherine, you've got to do better than that."

Photographer's Log - Susan Catherine Beever
<u>Volcano</u>

In Hong Kong they have what is known as Face Mapping. They believe if you read the face you can read a person's life. It is my belief that land destroyed in some irrevocable way has this mapping as well. In this ravaged Earth we read the face of God. Kapoho, buried by molten lava and more recently Kalapana, the Queen's own bath in Kalapana, swimming hole of royalty and the gods. This wounded land, the fingerprints of divinity? In the abyss, sublime? Catharsis in a landscape gone amok? To be a photographer is to be a chronicler of immortality. Land under its own molten burial emerges reborn in the image. Not the photo, the photo is a stop in time, a hiccup, one moment frozen from the rest. But what another might see in it! Truth as perception of its own self. My camera bears witness to the burying of Kapoho and Kalapana by Kīlauea volcano:

1. Set camera on tripod, snap on the wide angle lens; big image needed when photographing the breadth of ruin. Not much scale reference on a town long spread of lava. Tree branches poking out white as bone, a chimney, four stripped metal poles, highway signs, warnings jutting haphazardly out of the black: **No Parking; Reduced Speed, 25 Miles.** *Life buried under itself. Who's in charge now?*

2. Study light for the perfect exposure. Ropiness of the pahoehoe lava, sharply defined shadows, what little contrast there is on this flattened land. Another bent sign: **Extreme... Beyond This Point** – *Danger burnt mostly away –* **Collapse Of Lava Bench Occurs Without Warning, Causing Violent Steam Explosions And Ocean Surge**. *Extreme. I title these, Extreme.*

3. Angle tripod, back lighting highlights of fractured rock, twisted tree, scope of ruination. How important are we, how necessary, when a land can turn on us this way and in hours whatever it is we believed we built, its significance, presumed permanence, burnt down under its own new beginnings? Check lens, field of view: violence of a cobalt sky over devastation of black; crippled ohia struggling out of the broken down rock with its one fiery red lehua – Pele's flower. Like trying to cage God.

****

I had a dream she was calling me and she needed my help. On a cell phone no less, and the Rock Harbor area of Maine is a black hole for cell phones. Not enough signals out maybe, or too many hills, mountains, or the way the coast crunches in on itself off Penobscot Bay, its reclusive bowled-in shape. Maybe the people of midcoast Maine just want to be left alone. At any rate there she was on the other end of my dream receiver, her lilting child voice back when she still had a voice and the ragged stretches, the gulps of air in between her words like she had been crying, everything hopeless, beyond repair.

And that's when I awoke thinking, Fatboy! When it came back to me, just like that. I'm not sure you can call what happens from a dream recovered memory, or whatever the psycho-babble for this they are trumpeting these days. And yet can't a dream itself be memory, images buried under an avalanche of lava, let's say, because we are told to be good, or quiet, or private, *those family secrets* – and eventually these molten hot and gaseous moments come bubbling forth as disturbances below the surface inevitably must, exploding back into consciousness, reshaping themselves again as memory?

It was maybe a year after the shark attack, Willa home and in her hospital bed in Jaycee's room (soon this room will become Jaycee and Willa's room, but at this time there is still hope for Willa moving back into the room we shared together, Willa moving back into some semblance of a life). Father's moved out of their bedroom, onto the couch in the TV room. It's late, a milky moon-striped night, shadows from the spider lily outside eking across the louvered windows, cricket sounds, too quiet. I awake in the middle of this night feeling afraid and alone. My sister is no longer in my room. Tiptoe out to Father on the couch, the likeliest source of comfort, forgetting he's on the mainland, one of his trips. My heart is a raw and aching little mallet, battering my chest. The hallway's tile cold under my feet.

Slip silently into Jaycee's room, the door cracked slightly open. My plan is to slide down on the floor, wiggle across the carpet near my mother's side of the bed and sleep there. I won't let her know I'm here though, because she might send me back. "You're my big beaver," she'd insist. "Too big for this fraidy-cat nonsense."

But as I contemplate this, still hanging back in the corner near the door, I notice the hump, the moving lump on her bed and then the moaning and groaning, the puffing and pumping of this lump, the sighs of my mother under it all and then, horror of horrors! a beam of dust coated moonlight ricochets off the wide open window louvers lighting up the half moon of Fatboy's bulging bottom. Jaycee cries out and I cower back against the door, slapping my hand over my mouth to hold in my own shriek, that shriek of Jaycee's when *it* happened, how it flew into my own mouth, hunkered down deep in my throat and comes back and back, you never know when, its hot little sword of a yelp on my tongue, threatening to slice open my lips, hack its way out my jaw and howl.

Eyes wrench away from my mother's bed, focusing on Willa in her bed near by. Her eyes are open, at least I think they are, looking at me. Drop soundlessly as a gecko down onto the carpet, slithering my body up beside Willa's bed, away from our mother's. Peering up through the darkness I see her hand hanging over me, dangling down, her fingers knitting and crossing and weaving and if ever I know terror in the years to come, it will be accompanied by this image: Willa's small fingers worrying themselves in the fouled darkness of our mother's room.

When they are done Fatboy rises up out of the bed. I see his blubbery huge shape, a monster in the shadows, grotesque semblance of the Pillsbury dough boy come to life *hee hee*! towering over us from where I lie on the floor between the two beds, pressing myself into the gold shag carpet like maybe I really can just disappear, get swallowed up be gone from this. One of my hands now laced through my sister's, the other still against my mouth, forcing my scream back back back! down my throat, choking down its heat, violence of *this* silence. For haven't I always known it? The time I saw him jiggle her on his lap, their *routine*, the laughter in the middle of the night that was not our Father's, surely we have *all* known it.

He will slip through the sliding door that leads onto the lānai, into the dark, I know this too, vanish like cloud into the thin air of *what*? This too, that mustn't be remembered? But as he prepares to do this, yanking his clothes on, rip of his zipper in the darkness, a shuddering movement against my sister's bed on the way toward the door, I know something else. I feel it in my sister's hand, how she grabs onto my fingers, the silent plea. What is it I could have done to save her, to save any of us? Do I dream this? Fatboy's leaving, his slow shuffle past Willa's bed, meaty hand drifting down upon the bed, over her body, its lingering, achingly slow journey on. And how do I explain now what I couldn't then, the horror of this — that it wasn't her *body* he was feeling for, but the *absence* of it. The place where her leg should have been.

The next shape over Willa is Jaycee herself, Jaycee bending down so close to me if I moved my foot an inch I could touch her ankle and she'd know I too am here, the one who is not supposed to be here, I'm here here here; do you know it, can you remember it, did I exist at all for you my mother beyond the space I took up, the *other* one? The chemical stink of gin on her breath in her pores mingling with some deeper funk.

"Sweetie? You awake? Nothing happened, do you understand me?" she whispers harshly. *Not a word! This does not go outside these walls.* "You have no idea how hard all of this has been for me, how lonely I get, dear little Willa."

Willa's hand falls out of mine and I let it, do not try to catch it.

Let it fall. Who am I, this bigger beaver, protector of the Beever girls? I have failed.

Photographer's Log - Susan Catherine Beever
<u>Hand</u>

Seems significant enough in its whole, four fingers and a thumb's worth, able to accomplish most anything the brain orders it to do: pick up pencil, put foot in mouth, grab onto another, hold tight. Cold feet warm heart, or should it be warm hands cold heart? Splays of light playing over the fingers like these are something. Fingers touching fingers. How could they hold on to what no longer is? The sound of one hand clapping is… nothing.

CHAPTER TWENTY-TWO

You're probably wondering how it all came together; how I went from telling Pele tales to a.T. and having nightmares about my sister, to packing up and doing it, 6,000 miles closer to my vision of the little lau hala hut at the base of Kīlauea, my version of retirement— or giving up. This, then, was the moment inspiration hit: I had been tending alvin-Travis's garden—a couple days after the cell phone dream, Willa's child-thin voice still faintly buzzing in my ears like a worrisome gnat—cutting back the spring growth, taming it, making it manageable. Life is just a little harder in Maine for most people. Maine's famous beauty, its green and uncluttered spaces mean less business, less industry, less jobs, less income, less families that get to enjoy life above the poverty line, less of whatever else so many others in this country seem to feel their due. But not for alvin-Travis. And I helped see to this, played my little part in securing his personal comfort so I in turn could be left alone. The revelation was so simple I could've slapped myself. Maybe I did. Felt bruised from the inside out. It was not my sister I should have been seeking all these years. It's him. Fatboy must be connected somehow, I sensed this burning in every fevered cell of my flesh.

I rented the cabin outside Volcanoes National Park off the Internet. I had been wanting to photograph Kīlauea volcano's encroachment on the land over Kalapana for a while, its fiery advance over the Chain of Craters road into the sea as convenient a reason as any for my leaving. Fatboy could be anywhere, but our history, his with my family's is in the islands. This is where to begin. Call my father at the Kailua house, see if he knows how to contact Jaycee. She'd know where Fatboy is. Jaycee moved out of our home years ago, though she still claims a closet full of clothes, still her room, just in case. She is mostly gone, either with my sister or who knows where.

My mother is the second most lost woman I've known. Only Willa is more irrevocable, lost to that shark and returned to us as something else, something more fierce in her silence than our mother could muster, even in her frenzies. Jaycee is a woman born out of her time: twenty years later she would've found her niche, an executive of some company, making millions on paper, shuffling paper, nothing solid nothing built but her own needful empire. Perhaps my sister finally kicked her out, and wherever Willa is now she is there without Jaycee. I'd wish it so, for Willa's sake. Must be hard to work miracles with your mom hovering in the background critiquing. Fatboy left our Kailua neighborhood before I finished high school. Surely Jaycee would know where he went; she would have made it her business to know this. And maybe I need to see them both, for wasn't it Jaycee, really, who stole my sister's voice? Gathering her up like one might a wounded bird, feeding her, petting her, caging her, letting her forget what it meant to fly? Perhaps it's Jaycee who was the real *tragedy at the seat of our lives*, her insatiable demands. My sister's catastrophe was just that, a terrible accident.

I call from my rented Volcano cabin, one of those stripped boxy numbers, corrugated iron roof, surrounded by cindery soil with numerous giant hapu'u ferns, wild orchids, sweet yellow and white ginger and its own catchment tank to supply water. Outside a *pueo* hoots, a sign of death the Hawaiians believed, or perhaps somebody's *'aumakua*, protecting them, whistling its warning. Right now I'm feeling too torn from this land to fully accept any of it. My mother's needling at my father — *Your Hawaiian blood could fill a big toe!* I am on a mission and until I talk to Jaycee, ferret out Fatboy, Dark Prince of the Beever childhood I won't be able to concentrate on anything else. Perhaps I'll ensnare him in one of his own Trapper sets. How much would the market bear for a corpulent pelt of corrupt flesh?

My father's voice on the phone sounds the same, always that

lingering in his words, the vague reassurance. I've come to believe he wanted to be there for us, this partly absent father, he just wasn't sure how to *be* a father to both a wife and his kids. What he had wanted to be was a husband.

"Of course I know where she is," he says, as if all these years of Jaycee's leavings he's always known exactly where to find her. "Shouldn't you, Scat?"

"Susan Catherine," I remind him, "I prefer Susan Catherine now."

"A daughter by any name is a daughter," my father says, sounding a little hurt. "Couldn't you have just tried a bit harder to keep in touch with her?"

"Willa?" I ask, confused by the strangely worn tone of my father's words.

"No Scat, Susan Catherine, your mother. She feels rejected by her own children and she's not getting any younger, neither of us are. So she wasn't perfect, who is? But she did give birth to you, isn't that worth something? And she cares about you, all of you. Robbie who never writes or calls, I'm not sure where he is or who he is anymore; how did it come to this? And you only seek her out when you're trying to find your sister, just like everyone else."

"What about Willa?" I ask quietly, trying to sound at least a little contrite, but I'm having a hard time with it, seeing Jaycee as some sort of aging martyr-mom.

"She's the one who told your mother she doesn't want to see her anymore, about broke Jaycee's heart."

This I have to smile at. She really did it then, after all these years, the miracle cuts free of the mom!

"Willa has a fan club; your mother has nobody. Willa makes it so nobody can find her and your mother just wanted to be found, doggonit Scat, *Susan Catherine*, that's what she wanted."

"So where is she then?" I ask, suddenly annoyed at his drama. Of all the people Jaycee stepped on my father provided the easiest target. It's like he had one of those kick me signs engraved on his rear end. Why is it he's chosen never to see what Jaycee's been up to? To love her despite?

"Kāne'ohe!" my father snaps.

Kāne'ohe? At first I think he means the Base, but that couldn't be. Jaycee's hula dancing days have long since ended. Then it dawns on me. "You mean the state hospital? The *pupule house*! Jesus Christ, Dad, you had her committed?"

He snorts, a sad sort of laugh. "Good lord Scat, surely you don't believe for a moment your mother would let anyone commit her? She checked in herself. After Willa told her to disappear, well, she just about did. She became...so lost." His voice choking up.

I roll my eyes, frown. Something is not clicking here. Jaycee checking herself into a mental hospital? *Brain sick*? Maybe she had her talons out for some rich shrink there!

"You know she's manic-depressive, don't you?" He says this so casually, like you know your mother doesn't really have dark brown hair! "I guess they're calling it something else now, and of course back when I first met her I don't believe they had a label for it at all. We just thought she was exuberant at times. I loved that about her. Even her frenzies, you could excuse them because sometimes, once in a while, she appeared so happy. Good grief, we don't want to question *happy*, do we? And her low periods always seemed to have a cause, you know, like when you kids were born. You could make sense of it anyway, a lot of the times."

"They've got medication for that," I snarl, most of me not wanting to see any truth in this, yet another excuse for my mother's failures at being a mother! And the other part of me, a sour choke of a voice going, yes...this could makes sense. Her own father, my grandfather I never got to know locked away. It's hereditary, isn't it? Then I think about my sister. Could this be what happened to her, in part maybe? Shut away into some prolonged mental illness-induced silence?

"Your mother refused to take it. Said it would make her fat. I suppose maybe I should've mentioned something to you kids, you know, when they gave it its name. Just seemed a bit much, all that sickness, Willa and then.... Well anyhow, they have her on something there. I've talked to her on the phone. She sounds... lucid I guess you'd call it. But I wouldn't know for sure. She won't let me visit her, Scat, Susan Catherine. She won't let me come see her there at all. I tried, and they told me there's a note in her chart, says patient requested that I not be allowed to see her. Her husband, all these years. I'll never abandon her, you know that about me, and they won't let me in. I have no say, you see, she's the one who committed herself. I'm not even on her "Call" list, some list that says who she'll accept phone calls from. She'll call *me*, if she's so inclined. *Voluntary client*, that's how they've labeled her, like she's in there to have some legal matter resolved."

I hear a catch in his voice and my own eyes are wet. I swipe at them angrily. Why am I getting upset on his behalf? It is his excusing her behavior all those years, his ultimate forgiveness, choosing to ignore whenever and whatever he could, that allowed Jaycee to be Jaycee. No doubt it's even his medical insurance paying for her "visit." Our father chose to love our mother no matter what, and over us.

I fly to Honolulu the next morning after paying for another two weeks at the Volcano cabin, making sure I have something to come back to. Leave most of my clothes, extra film, my Log and several camera lenses I would not want to be without for too long as escrow. I refuse to get sucked into the Jaycee orbit.

Engage an Aloha cab at the airport to take me out to the State Hospital via the H-3 highway, goes all the way to the Marine Corps Air Station, the *Base*. It's my first time on this newest freeway, over the green mountains and through the brown hills, Kāneʻohe Bay a silver gleaming in the distance. About the time I graduated from high school they finished Hawaiʻi's first freeway, H-1, the downward spiral into a mainland chaos of traffic since. During the time H-3 was being built, blasting through Halawa valley workers came across a heiau, an old Hawaiian burial ground complete with bones. And then more *iwi* other places. What to do with the bones! Always a problem when tearing up these islands. The protests that resulted slowed the building of H-3 down for so long it became the most expensive federal highway ever built. Of course I was on the mainland drunk during most of this, but I remember my father's phone calls, dutiful accountings of the news from Hawaiʻi. What else would we talk about? His absent wife? My sister the miracle? The runaway brother? My inability to hold onto a steady job? A dry drunk is, after all, only dry until her next bottle, and no one appreciates the sunset-eyed employee stumbling in hung over no matter what time her shift. *Iwi kupuna.* Building the thing right over the ancestors. Whose side was my father on? After the Reagan eighties when the divide between the rich and the poor became more obvious and the middle class began to shrink he even started voting Democrat. *Democrat,* like *Catholic,* like *divorce,* whispered words usually relegated to the silences in our house, when they were used it was as some derisive explanation: That's a *Catholic* thing; she's *divorced* and a *Democrat,* what can you expect?

When I was a kid the big deal was the new Pali Highway, its double lanes climbing up the side of the sheer peak, making it so commuters from Kailua to Honolulu, instead of sometimes a two hour trip over the Old Pali Road, trembling assault inching around the Windy Corner, or the Waimanālu route, halfway around the island past the iron pink bad boys and girls homes, the pummeled coast, could now have a smoother under an hour commute. This was finished, maybe 1961? Then they built the Wilson Tunnel and about half the commuters, the ones closer to Kāne'ohe, used that. Funny thing about the Wilson tunnel: when they blasted the two sides of the mountain to form the tunnel, the two *pukas* didn't connect properly. In the eighties when they constructed onramps from the airport to join H-1, they built these too high to meet. It's as if the very land here trembles under this weight of *progress,* trying by any means, sacred bones to incompetent engineering, to stop it.

We pull up to the security booth at the Hawai'i State Hospital. I give the guard my name and the name of the person who gave me the OK, heads-up she called it, permission to be on these grounds. He frowns, checks his records, asks to see my ID then hands me a photocopied map pointing me toward the buildings, long and cream colored with red tile roofs. Concrete? Something that won't burn? Most of them just one story, can't jump either, I'm thinking. Study my choices: Skills Development, Neuropsychology, Prep A, Prep B, Adult Closed Ward, Adult Open Ward, *Ma`ele`eli.* My mother is there.

I still have alvin-Travis's credit card and the cab driver swipes this easily through his portable register. I plug in a good sized tip. Figure I'll e-mail a.T. a story as payment, make up some breasty brainless weather goddess since he all but dismissed Pele. This made up goddess, who always wanted to learn to blow a horn, has no talent other than making rain, drought, etc. So she settles on blowing old tie-dyed and dyed headed musicians—he'll appreciate that.

"Thanks, eh?" the driver grins, winks. He's a local boy, very cute, bit of a flirt. "You going tell me you holo hele Windward College down street instead of pupule house, yeah? You one professor?"

"Nope," I don't smile back. "The pupule house." No professor, just the daughter of an insane mother! I think. I'm not in a flirting mood, and I don't need any more empty encounters of the male persuasion for alvin-Travis, stories like invoices, earning my keep. Here my keep is my own. Gaze up at the claws and trenches of the emerald peaks behind, the Ko'olaus. Wild Hawaiian chickens run across the road in front of the guard house. *How did the chicken get to the other side of the street?* A day like any other, I tell myself. Inhale a ragged breath.

Entering the heavy doors I clutch nervously at my stomach, figuring I'll immediately hear screaming, my images of mental institutions coming mostly from fiction, *I Never Promised You a Rose Garden, One Flew Over the Cuckoo's Nest*, etc. I expect saucer-eyed souls pushing brooms, nodding off to television, chatting with invisible companions. My worst moments as a teenager I used to wish a lobotomy on Jaycee, slice everything out of her that enraged me. *You're a crazy lady!* I shrieked at her once, some indignity she wanted me to do or wouldn't let me do, who knows. Maybe she embarrassed me, eating jello with her fingers. Whatever the things my mother did and was became, during those pre-adult years, their own raw humiliation. "So then what's *normal*, Scat?" she'd ask me. "What your father says?" Suddenly I'm scared and trembling all over; it's my mother who is inside these walls somewhere.

But these walls are silent, early afternoon, perhaps the inhabitants had retreated to their rooms for a nap after lunch.

"It's quiet in here," I say uncertainly to the flat-faced receptionist, *Aloha I'm Denise*! her name tag announces, who had looked up Jaycee A. Beever on her computer and is now rifling through my mother's chart. Denise has a pink acrylic sweater draped over her shoulders held on by a fake pearls sweater guard, a piece of costume jewelry I thought went to whatever fashion trends graveyard hoop skirts and girdles are buried in. Her blue-black hair is squinched tight into a French twist, a fake orchid bobby pinned at the top. "Is that a silk flower?" I ask her, not that I care, fake is fake, but I feel a need for some conversation, some sense of *normalcy*. She plunges a plump fingered hand to the back of her head, touches the orchid for a second, shrugs, asks me for my ID. I show her my license, repeating the person's name who had given me permission to be here. "Like I *want* to be here," I joke. Or try to.

She shrugs again; what difference can it make in her day if I come here or I don't? "Down the hall turn right, last door on left," she says, tart voice. "Allowed only one hour visit, yeah?" Denise glances up at the clock significantly. I follow her eyes. I hadn't figured on *that* much time with Jaycee.

"Are there particulars I should know?"

Denise knits her pencil brows, frowns. Clearly she hasn't been exposed to the same reading list I have. I start down the hall.

"Has one roommate!" she shrills after me.

The door is wide open and it's the roommate I see first, sitting on her bed, knees drawn up to her chest, head of bright red curls face down and pressed against the tops of her knee caps, rocking back and forth. Sharp pigeon-wing shoulder blades, skinny calves the bluish-white of skim milk and huge bony feet; this woman is all angles and hair. She doesn't look up when I enter the room and I move slowly, almost on tiptoe, toward Jaycee in her bed near the window. My mother appears to be asleep, lying flat on her back eyes closed. I blink, swallow hard, shocked at how bloated she looks. Those fine facial features that elevated her to *pretty* among the other mothers, the one thing she had that they did not—Jaycee never *looked* like a mother—are sunken into two pounds of cheek flesh. Even her arms, poking out above the sheet that's pulled up taut over the rest of her, are thick as bowling pins, barely a hint of an arm's implied shape. Her fingernails are painted though, thank God for purple polish! I could almost weep out of gratitude for this, her one familiar feature.

She slides open her eyes as I approach the bed, peers up at me, closes them again and without any surprise, no hello, arms hoisted out for a hug, nothing to indicate we haven't seen each other in two years, my mother, her voice husky, rusty sounding like she hasn't been using it much lately says: "Fat, aren't I? It's the meds. Signing yourself into this place means letting them pump you full, it's what they do. Either that or electric shock. Lobotomies are passé, of course, the ruin of that unfortunate Kennedy girl."

My cheeks burn, as if she could know what I had been thinking before. "Well hi yourself, Jaycee," I say crisply. Take an upbeat tone, I instruct myself, like nothing at all here is unexpected, unusual, not *normal*! I lean down, give her a quick peck on the cheek. Her skin smells strangely dusty. Force back a need to sneeze.

"Your father told you I was here, I assume. He doesn't come himself, gets someone else to. Typical."

"*Someone* else? He said you won't let him come see you!"

She shrugs, those thickly entrenched shoulders like she's got some kind of padded jacket on instead of the thin straps of a nightgown, flicks her wrist, a dismissive gesture, she is bored with this conversation. "You meet my roommate? Her name's Cairn, like those rock piles they mark journeys with. Your father and I had an argument about that once, I remember it like it was yesterday. *Ahu* is what they are called here, he said. He lets the Hawaiian out when it's convenient, you see, when he thinks he knows a word or two. *Cairn* is what they are to the rest of the world! I informed him. Some journey. Sits there all day long, just like that. At night the nurse comes and lays her down flat, so that's how she knows it's time to sleep. Journeys like this, who needs frequent flier miles? Quiet though, I'll give her that. It's like sharing the room with a bug."

"What's wrong with you, Jaycee!" I blurt, prickly edge to my voice. I didn't come here to talk about cairns or ahus, *or* her roommate. I glance over at the head of rocking red curls. How does life turn on one this way?

"Remember long time ago, Scat, the cow that came into our yard?" My mother has opened her eyes wide now and is staring eagerly up at me. I reluctantly drag the straight wooden chair nearest the bed closer to her, sit down. The chair is padded at its seat, back rounded, nothing sharp in this place. Feels like a commitment, sitting here.

"You should do something with your hair, Scat, it's absolutely devoid of any wave whatsoever. And so short. Are you trying to look like a man? You're middle aged now," she nods, as if digesting this herself. "You tend to lose your femininity. Every curl counts."

I peer again over at the red curls, shake my head. "What about that cow, Jaycee, never mind my hair. And it's Susan Catherine. Haven't been calling myself Scat for years."

"You don't need to call *yourself* Scat. What's a name but what others call you? I wasn't really scared of the escaped cow, that's what I was going to tell you. You all thought I was."

I frown. "What do you mean?"

"You thought I was scared of it. Help! Wild cow! Not true."

I shake my head again. "I asked what's wrong with you, Jaycee! I mean, you put yourself in *Kāne'ohe* for chrissake, and you're going on about the damn cow, happened years ago."

"Do you remember the Italian donkeys?"

"The *what*? What is this, some sort of twisted Dr. Doolittle game? Farm Animals Jeopardy? I get a box of animal crackers for the right answer?"

Jaycee's green eyes, little gleaming slits in the folds of her face cloud over, look confused. "Oh dear, wait a minute, just where were those donkeys anyway? That wasn't Kailua, was it? And how, my God, how was it I knew they were Italian?"

"Jaycee, I don't know what you're talking about!" My stomach lurches, acid taste at the back of my throat. All of a sudden, excess flesh be damned, the part of her that seemed like my mother before, even her bitchiness, the arrogance, seems like it's sliding away, something vague and uncertain, scared! taking its place. Her eyes look damp and she's swiveling her head from side to side.

"I just can't think where they were now, where were those poor little donkeys, anyway?"

"Jaycee?" I plead, but then I'm unsure what to follow this with. I reach out and touch what I guess would be her upper thigh, under the covers, just to hold my hand somewhere in the vicinity of her and she jerks back, wincing. "Ouch!" she says. "Not there. Don't touch me there."

"Why not? Why shouldn't I touch you there, is something wrong?"

Jaycee ignores this, batting at the air where my hand was. "Well, so maybe they were right here after all, right next door. Yes, that's probably it, when they let us out on the grounds to smoke, I'll bet those Italian donkeys were right next door."

I peer doubtfully out of a high small window, its reinforced Plexiglas, seeing nothing from this angle but white empty space. I feel like I'm in prison, figure that's how I'm supposed to feel though most of these poor folk were in prisons of their own making before ever coming here. Decidedly, there are no farms beside the State Hospital, no donkeys. *Funny Farm*! Kāne'ohe courthouse, Windward Community College, tract houses packed into subdivisions off the roads leading up to it, tropical scents in the rain and grey mingling with too many newcomers, too much traffic, the spreading sprawl of Kāne'ohe. In the middle of all this was Tiki Tops, where we ate Sunday nights when we were *good*; where we begged our father for a Peppermint Patty after dinner if we were *good*; the restaurant owned by Spencecliff Corporation, Billy Weaver's uncle and dad. What did our mother get if she was good? Remember her pitching a fit there one night because Tiki Tops didn't have a liquor license.

Jaycee continues, "There were two of them, Jimmy Beam and Juniper Berry, if you can believe those names. Italian donkeys, small and grey and very old I remember I was told, old as old. Never could get it straight which was the girl and which the boy, but I do recall there was one of each. Anyhow one of them died."

My mother stops here, inching herself up to a sitting position, shaky, a monumental effort. She has breasts, this new heft of her, large ones that droop down, pear shaped shadows inside her thin nylon gown.

"Don't they at least have you get dressed?"

My mother grins that fake sort of grin, all in the teeth. "I'm not naked!" she sings. "One of them died," Jaycee repeats, and I see her eyes suddenly tear up, fumbling about the night table, I assume for the tissue box and I hand this to her.

"But that's not really the sad part," she sighs, blowing her nose fiercely. "We all have to die. If you're alive it's just a matter of how much time before you're dead. Isn't that what life is? The time you have between your entry and your death? The sad part is the one that's left. Jimmy Beam or Juniper Berry, I don't know which. But one of them has been left."

I stare at my mother. Her dark uncombed shag of hair has the distinct skunk stripe of grey roots; not so long ago she would've shaved her head before letting her hair go this far without coloring it. All that flesh, I get the sense of a person sinking down inside her own self and I feel like I should *do* something for her but haven't a clue what. Then I remember my mission here. Trembling, I stamp my foot on the vinyl floor, shake my head, shoulders, like shrugging water off of myself. This will be done, I remind myself.

"Wait a minute, just a damn minute here!" my voice wavering. "Jaycee," I say sharply, her head has slipped to one side of her neck like she's about to fall asleep, eyes winking shut. "Do you remember Fatboy?"

Eyes pop open again, green cat-eyes. "Who?" she says, *meeowwww*.

"You know, I know you know, from the neighborhood. He was driving the boat!" I say meanly. That will jog any memory lapse.

"Hmmm," she hums, "oh, yes. Haven't thought about that one for a while."

"Do you know where he is?"

Her eyes gleam up at me, newly alert. "That was a long time ago Scat, what are you getting at here?"

I nod. "Yeah, though if you can remember the escaped cow I guess you might remember him! He moved somewhere, didn't he? Figured you would know where."

Jaycee shakes her head, that vague look again, then suddenly smiles, almost a flirty glance up at me. "Now why oh why does my dear older beaver want to find the likes of Fatboy, hmmm?"

My stomach curdles, a sour taste in my mouth. I glare at her, the old anger rising. "Maybe to kill him," I hiss. "For starters, maybe that!"

My mother considers this a moment, bowing her head as if in prayer. I study those roots the metallic color of paper clips. "Hmmm," she sighs, nods. "You're probably too late. Most likely somebody already has. He was the type just begging to be shut up, you know?"

"So why didn't you?"

"Kill him?"

"No, shut him up at least! I mean, how could you stand him, Christ, how could you?"

"How do we stand most of the people that snake their way into our lives, Scat, even family. Especially family. Just because we share genes or a marriage doesn't mean our hearts are the same, you know."

"Oh, gee, do tell!" I clutch at my head as if this is suddenly hurting, but the ache is undefined though familiar and it's all over. "I repeat, Jaycee, where is he?"

She sighs, smiles almost sadly but I refuse to buy into that. My mother is not sad about any part of our shared past that has hurt anyone other than herself. Her usual line, We press on!

"Oh Scat, poor Scat, you didn't have a clue, did you? I was better at hiding things than I thought. Why on earth would I know or care where that one went!" Jaycee sits up straighter, leaning toward me and I smell a chemical tartness on her breath; the medication I'm assuming, no gin and tonics here. "He was only one of them, Scat, do you get me? Why would I have cared where Fatboy moved to? He wasn't that special. He, most of them over the years were as interchangeable, as replaceable in my life as..., let me think now, yes! as light bulbs." Smiling proudly at her analogy.

I shudder, close my eyes. My head's reeling, so dizzy I have to hold it down between my knees. "God!" I moan.

"For heaven's sake, Scat, get a grip, will you? Are you still judging me? You're still judging me, aren't you! Is that it? The reason you are here? Would've thought as a grown woman yourself, a *middle-aged* woman you'd have gotten over that by now. By now you should know life doesn't always feed you what you thought you were cooking up, now does it! Look at it this way, I was filet mignon in a meat loaf life. You figure tying on a frilly apron and playing Betty Crocker was enough? I had an *adventuresome* spirit, goddamnit! And now I ask you Miss Betterthanme, how you think a *lady* in 1950's Hawai'i was going to find adventure? Bloody hell, I would've been stifled completely if not for the others. They were my Wild West, my gold rush, an *audition* of sorts. At least I always knew I was appreciated, treasured even. I know your father loves me and I'm not saying he didn't then, but he didn't treasure me. I was something he owned, like a good couch, a coveted car, the name on his tax deduction. Willa's tragedy, horrible as it was, I had some purpose there, a function, can you understand that? What was I supposed to do, curl up and die?"

"Couldn't you have just gone to secretary school?" I hiss. Lift my head slowly, stabs of grey behind my eyes threatening to engulf me, grey grey grey. She's got it right though, I'm thinking, pretty astute for a goddamn mental case. Curl up and die. Times when I too wondered if that wouldn't be the easier thing, for my mother, certainly for my sister, and for me, me too. "Do you, can you, have any idea of the ruin, the absolute devastation you and that *Fat*man caused? And you're telling me there were others, that *he* was not enough?" My voice is harsh, strained, choking. Feel my words cutting out, can hardly hear some of the syllables myself. It's like the cell phone from my dream, my sister's voice, or what I imagined I remembered of her voice back when she had one, calling for help and I can barely hear her, barely believe it. No signal out. I shudder, "You were a worse predator than the goddamn shark!"

Jaycee reaches over and touches my hand. For a moment I almost let myself think it's to comfort me, then she grabs my fingers, her own fingers cool and clammy, tugging to get my attention. I look away from her then slowly swivel my head back, force myself to stare into her eyes, dragged back into those gleaming green blades.

"She made me leave!" my mother whines. "All I did for her and she forces me to leave, tells me from now on wherever she is, I'm not to be there. Can you imagine? All I did for her!"

I stare at my mother. I'm comprehending this sudden subject change but I don't want to; want to yank my hand from hers, slide my chair back into the corner of this room, far as I can get to hear these words. But she has me, her hand now wrapped like some creeping flesh vine around my wrist.

"I tried to see her after she left Maine. She hadn't wanted me there either but it wasn't an *imperative*, and I had other business at that point anyway so it was mutually agreeable, I thought, and just for the time being. She came back here, you know, the islands. I was living in San Francisco at the time, a real estate mogul, very successful. And I flew out to be with her, gave things up do you hear me? I gave things up! and she tells me no. You think that man would take me back now, looking like this? All I've got is what you see, Scat, at least you can take pictures of something *else*."

I think about my recent photographs; with the exception of the volcano they are mostly of me, parts of me. Log titles: neck and shoulders, breasts, hands, hips and thighs, toes. I feel suddenly ashamed. There are tears in Jaycee's eyes and I'm hoping she'll grab a tissue and release my hand, but she doesn't. Just lets them slide down her cheek.

"Willa called a sort of press conference, if you can imagine, on Kailua Beach. Where the tragedy happened. Not the respectable papers, mind you, the gossipy ones. A few of her fans were there, the afflicted, hollering out, begging her to notice but she ignored them. I came too. In fact the letter she wrote told me she wanted me to be there. I was hopeful because she invited me, but nervous, you know. Couldn't imagine what she was up to. She had an interpreter there, some nice looking young man who read aloud the note she handed him. I wondered if maybe they were together, you know. She's always been so lovely, despite all that's happened. She could *get* someone that age."

I roll my eyes. "Right, Jaycee, so what did the note say?"

"She's just a regular person, nothing special, the first page said. Just a girl whose leg was bit off by a shark. Just a *haole*, Willa told us, via this young man. Not even the popular Billy Weaver. Would've been better if he was the one who survived his attack not her, the second page said, because she's nobody at all. She was wearing this long white mu'umu'u, her hair tied back and a pikake lei around her head. She looked so beautiful, almost like she was going to get married, like something wonderful should be happening in that outfit, like she was some sort of angel. But suddenly she's lifting the mu'umu'u and I'm shrieking out to her, 'No! Don't do it!'"

"And then?" I ask, curious in spite of myself. My mother has gone silent. She looks confused again, almost scared. Slowly the pressure of her fingers releases and she's about to drop my hand. I hold onto her. *This* time, I hold on. "What happened next?" I demand.

"I need some water," Jaycee whines. I grab the plastic pitcher off the night stand, pour her half a plastic cup full, slide the cup up to her lips. She sips, that blank stare. "Tell me!" I order her. "You're the one who started this."

My mother sighs. "I want a cigarette. Pass me one, they're on the bureau."

Annoyed I glance up at the plain wooden bureau, other side of the window. A mess of her clothes, some knickknacks, plastic bottle of half gone lotion, blooms of used tissues, but no cigarettes that I can see. "Jaycee, you're not even allowed to smoke in here, the building is no smoking for chrissake."

"I want one!" she says petulantly. "Nobody tells me what I can or can't do. I want to smoke, I bloody well smoke!" I stare at my mother, the purse of her lips, set of her jaw, and I don't know whether to laugh or cry. The old toughness, her stubbornness, so pathetically out of place here where they've clearly drugged her, where she languishes about in their bed, unable to get by in her own life without their intervention.

"Tell me what happened, Jaycee," I say quietly, my words as controlled, as measured as I can make them, "then I'll walk outside with you. I'll get permission, a pass, whatever we need. You can light up out there, suck down that poison to your heart's content."

She nods; this, for the moment, seems satisfactory. "There was a woman on the beach," Jaycee continues, "watching her children swim. You could see she wasn't well. It was a warm afternoon but she's all wrapped up in a blanket, hunched over on the sand. She had one of those scarves tied up around her head, the kind that's supposed to hide the fact you've got no hair. I figured from chemotherapy, most likely." Jaycee shakes her head, clamps shut her mouth, tears glittering greenly in her eyes.

"Mother!" I howl in frustration. And we both startle at that, because I called her mother, not Jaycee. "Just finish telling me, will you please!" I sputter.

"OK, OK, so all of a sudden your sister falls face down on the sand and I rush over to her, we all do. And..."

"*And*!" I shriek. The rocking on the other bed wavers for a split second, just a measure off beat, then picks up again. "Jaycee, for chrissake!"

"She's bleeding! I'm telling the truth, goddamnit, bloody hell, she was bleeding! A red stain creeping under her white mu'umu'u all over the white sand. The sand again, do you see? Jesus, the blood stained sand!"

"What are you saying? Those ridiculous rumors about her? Are you telling me Willa's got a stigmata or something? Give me a break!"

Jaycee shakes her head, looks annoyed. "No, no, that's a Catholic thing. Bleed from the palms, supposed to be Jesus' nail wounds. I'm saying your sister was bleeding in her chest area. She fell down flat on the sand. And that woman on the beach, she stood up then, called to her kids. Let the blanket drop and I could see!"

"See what? For chrissake, Jaycee, will you just tell it!"

"That woman had no left breast. They had removed it, breast cancer no doubt."

"Yeah, so!" My heart pounding, pulse roaring, a waterfall in my ears.

"Don't you get it, Scat?" She grabs my hand again and this time her fingers are icy cold. "It's real, goddamnit! Your sister was bleeding for that woman! Bleeding on the left side of her chest! It's real, and all this time I thought it was more of...a thing we created. An image. Well we had to do *something*, she was too pretty a girl, too special to just let fall through the cracks, you hear me? I thought we were a team, Willa and me, and all along... bloody hell! All along she's really doing it."

I yank my hand back from my mother, lunge up and off the chair, claw at my forehead, my neck, then collapse back down again. I can't take it standing after all. I'm not even sure what of all this I *can* take, or what, even, *this* really is! "I don't know what the hell we're talking about here, Jaycee!"

She shrugs. "I have no use that's what," she says quietly. "Useless as useless. No use at all."

"You do realize this was all a fucking coincidence, a goddamn fucking coincidence? What if Willa herself is sick, have you considered that? Maybe she fell down and she's bleeding because she's the one who's ill, and here you are, hanging out in the *pupule* house feeling sorry for yourself! You you you, it was always about you!"

My mother's head droops down on her neck like some awful wilting flower. Hoarse sobs, her ragged breath. I realize this was a pretty terrible thing to say to someone in a mental institution (especially someone whose own father died in one!), but there's this rage I feel and I can't help this, and I know now I have always felt it, even when I was a child—the bigger sister having to assume the role of caretaker because my mother couldn't or wouldn't. Now my little sister maybe *is* sick and who is going to help her? Not her own mother, that's for certain!

"You said *fucking* to me," Jaycee wails, her head still down and rolling now, side to side. "Who gave you permission to use that kind of language with me, I didn't raise you that way."

"*You* didn't raise me period! *Manic depressive*," I snarl, my voice softer but I know she can hear me. "That's just a label for how you made the rest of us feel, crazy that's what, you made us all hopelessly crazy. No wonder she bleeds, first the shark and then you. Who else would package illness into a goddamn miracle?"

"How's your father?" Jaycee asks suddenly, lifting her head, eyes fish colored and vacant, no real interest, as if now we are to have a polite conversation.

"Broken!" I growl. "Like the rest of us." *Humpty Dumpty sat on a wall....* I know that one and most any other nursery rhyme by heart. I was the one who read to Willa, when our father wasn't around; who knows for sure if Robbie even learned to read?

"We were a team," she moans, "like those two Italian donkeys."

"You know, you don't seem any different than usual," I say nastily. "Maybe that means you should've always been in here. Maybe you should've been here and we should never have been born. Whose loss would that be? The shark's, no doubt, got to dine on the miracle leg!"

Jaycee peers suddenly over at the other bed, the rocking red head. "Cairn?" she calls out. "Did you meet my daughter? Not the one I told you about, this one here is the other one!" My mother swivels her head slowly back at me, her eyes glittering up.

I nod. Heart wants to crumble but I won't let it. This much, after all, I have known.

"You want to see my bandage?" Jaycee asks. She doesn't wait for an answer, pushing the sheet down over her swollen belly, hips, two bulbously dimpled legs, sliding her nightgown up. Her right upper thigh is swaddled in heavy gauze, all the way around at the top. She doesn't have any underwear on and the dark nest of pubic hair next to the white bandage makes me queasy. I look away.

My mother sighs, exasperated, as if I'm being criticized for having a weak stomach, that this is what it's about. "You can look or not,

Scat, it's not going to change things. There's an artery here, a big one, pumps blood from your feet back up to your heart, floor to ceiling, down again. Keeps us going."

I say nothing, will that bile taste back down my throat.

Jaycee continues, a monotone voice: "My ticket into these hallowed walls, moment the blade first pierced my flesh. These days to call a bed your own in an institution you've either got to take someone else out, but then I'd have to be in the Closed Ward—I shudder to think what goes on in there—or make a damn earnest attempt on yourself. Trick is knowing when to stop. How deep to slice versus RPM of flow versus how quickly you can be found. My father's times now, back then it was easier. Someone complains, a neighbor maybe, maybe a wife. You lock them up, you never see them again. Before managed care of course. Insurance company would consider the cost factor, three squares a day and all the meds versus the possibility of a successful suicide. I keep chipping away at it, no matter how close they cut my fingernails. You like my polish?" She shoots me an anxious look, as if she cares whether I do or not. "I have to get permission from my doctor for them to bring the bottle in, even for five minutes."

"You want to be here?" I ask dully, there's a ringing in my ears and my own voice sounds so far away, like it's coming from someone else, somewhere else, not even of this room.

She lowers her eyes, strokes the bandage almost tenderly. Those lost hands, the world on my shoulders when she put them there. "I'm tired," she sighs. " Try to understand this, Scat. I'm so bloody tired."

This time I stand up and I stay up, sliding the chair firmly back against the wall. I take her hand loosely in mine again, to shake it goodbye, but my mother grabs onto me. "Will you try to find her?" she pleads, green eyes begging up at mine. "My guess is she's still in Hawai'i, probably the big island, she always loved that one best."

I shake my head, and suddenly I feel almost unbearably sad. "No, Mother," I say, fighting back tears, deliberately calling her that, Mother. "It's about time for me to be done with looking. I lost Willa Beever a long time ago. We all did, even you, goddamnit. Even you."

I wriggle away from my mother's grasp and start toward the door, turn around and she hisses at me: "He's in here, you know! I hear him, see him!" Grins wildly. "Wants me to go and be with him!"

"Who?" I ask, dreading her answer.

But she just smiles. "Family, Scat, can't break away no matter what you do. The chains are in the blood."

At the door I turn around again and she's slipped down flat on her back, sheet pulled tight over her ruin, eyes squeezed shut. She's mumbling and I strain to hear, against my better instinct I still need to hear her. Something about donkeys, the one that was left, bless its little heart, but that's what it is, she's whispering. "Maybe it doesn't know it was left, senses something's missing but it's a beast after all, doesn't know, doesn't get it, no hope, you see, hopeless as hopeless."

Stare hard at her, letting my eyes linger over the still pretty if fleshy face I so desperately grieved, more so than for my sister, I understand this. My mother, Jaycee Anderson Beever, all caught up in her abundant new skin, her inexorable despair. And then I look over at the woman rocking on the other bed, rhythmically, back and forth, never breaking her stride if you could call it that, neither slow nor fast, like she's tuned into some secret pulse, some heart beat deep inside the world the rest of us mostly ignore. Rocking to it, those blood colored curls the only true color in this room.

CHAPTER TWENTY-THREE

A group of Hawaiian caterpillars have evolved from gentle plant eaters into ferocious carnivorous caterpillars, catching flies and other insects for their dinner. They ambush then strike, holding their prey with their evolved legs and sharp new claws. This is called an adaptive shift. (!!!) The nene goose has done this too, evolved from geese with webbed feet who need water to living on lava wastes, the lava flows of Hawai'i.

(S.G. Noted by G.M. – Those exclamation marks!!!)

Something I Did, by Gracie McKneely. 2:00 P.M. August 13, 1994.

1.   *Looked at Dr. Bender's notes on DOLPHIN SEX while she and Louis were at a lunch party that I wasn't invited to. She's writing an article, she told me, for a journal. So I'm writing this in MY JOURNAL. I only wanted to surprise her by knowing something important she knows.*

2.   *What I found out about bottle-nosed dolphins: males are seen copulating (I looked the word up, it means SEX) with turtles by inserting their PENISES into soft tissue at the back of their shells. (Gross! I don't think the turtles would like this.) They also copulate with sharks and eels her note said. (This comes from her stuff with sharks on Coconut Island maybe.) But Eels? Said the male has a hook on the end of his penis and the dolphin uses it to hook a struggling eel. Said the males also do it with each other and that the Amazon River Dolphin penetrates another male dolphin's*

blowhole with his penis. I asked Louis (because after they came back from the party Dr. Bender had to go someplace and give a lecture) if it would be rape when a dolphin makes an eel do it. Rape is what we learned about in seventh grade health class. Louis told me that there is an Asian monkey, a macaque, where the females mount each other to achieve orgasm. Louis asked me if I knew what that meant and I said I think I do and she said I should stay the ... (she used a bad word here) out of Robyn's business. I didn't mean anything by it, just to know something she knows already before she has to tell me about it.

3.   *I saw them. Dr. Bender said in some species of gulls females pair with each other, build a nest together and help each other incubate eggs that a male from a different nest has fertilized. They will mount each other, Dr. Bender said, and display. I SAW THEM I SAW THEM I SAW THEM.*

****

On the plane to Hawai'i the chipmunk cheeked little boy in the row in front of Gracie keeps squeezing his fat face into the crack between the seats, staring at her, rolling back his eyes like he's maybe retarded then grinning evilly. Each time Gracie meets his eyes he snaps his head back in like a lizard, next moment popping over the top of his seat. This might be considered cute in someone else's life. She tries a vague and distant smile, rewarding him for his existence in such a way he might feel fulfilled but not encouraged and move on. It's in the knowing when to quit that separates most kids from most adults, the *adult* adults anyway. Gracie is beginning to learn this, when to quit. Though there are some things she can't seem to give up—because here she is. He grapples urgently at his mother's shoulder: "Mommy, that lady's ugly!" Slinks down behind her hair, habitual response, the cruelty of boys.

"Shush!" the mother hushes him. "You're the one behaving ugly!" She turns around to apologize, sees Gracie's face, blushes. "Sorry!" she mumbles.

"It's OK," Gracie assures her, smoothing away the embarrassment of others. But she's thinking, you are right woman, it *is* your son who's the ugly one!

So when he pokes his mug between the seats again she is ready for him, classic passive aggressive, sticks out her tongue, tugs down on her scar, the flap of her cheek into an exaggerated droop, crossing her eyes. He shrieks and the mother slaps mildly at his arm. "Sit right!" she commands him. "Turn around again you're gonna get it." Gracie grins smugly. She can feel the disapproval of her seat mate, a sour jawed older woman who's entire face sags as much as the right side of Gracie's and for no reason beyond her years of being a squinched up, humorless hag. Gracie offers her full frontal, scarred half, pretty half, grins again.

"Sharks don't kill each other just because they hate each others guts!! In fact they love each others guts. And talk about self-appreciation! Shark hunter Vic Hislop of Australia has reported sharks caught twice – using the shark's own intestines for bait!"

Hawai'i's Shark Stories; Barnett. p. 110 *(As compiled by S.G. Noted by G. M.*

Question: Whose exclamation marks?)

Leaving Maine seemed a more sure step than getting there. Once Gracie purchased her ticket there was no turning back. The Housewives came out to the Portland Jetport to see her off along with Roma and Berry; timing was right, fourth Thursday of the month in the city. Gracie chose to feel honored. Apologized to Berry for deserting the job and Berry shook her head. "Won't hear of any of that, you weren't so good at it nohow, Gracie. Didn't your mother teach you a thing or two about cleaning?" Her quick efficient hug and a brief prayer for Jesus' blessings on Gracie's journey. Gracie glanced over at Roma who was smirking.

She had invited Roma and Jessie, the two Gracie would actually miss to visit her if she ended up staying there, if she found a job. Jessie looked doubtfully at Roma. "Pretend I'm a mouse," Roma offered, "too big to flush down the toilet."

"Keep denying your stomach its right to a decent meal and you won't be!" Berry muttered. Tia cautioned Gracie about space travelers from another dimension known to pluck people right out of their airplane seats. "You're the one who gets to get away!" Janie howled as Gracie drifted out from security down the long white aisle toward her gate. Maine, blur of green islands, jewels in an ice blue sea, disappearing out the left side of the 737 window.

Last night Gracie had called her parents to tell them she was going, making sure to first confirm the one way nonrefundable ticket, Portland to Chicago, Chicago to Honolulu, Honolulu to Hilo. "Can't turn back now," she said. Her mother predictably hysterical, her father strangely, insistently neutral. "Let her go, Maizey," Gracie heard him say in the background, Beethoven or something symphonic on the stereo — for a moment her stomach churned and a bad taste snuck into her throat. Tried to picture *their* stereo, not *his* CD player perched upon its lawnmower box table, the gleaming wood top covered with her mother's obsessively dusted figurines, a vase of flowers perhaps, white daises, yellow roses, whatever they were they'd be all the same; her mother's ordered life that in the end, in spite of her undisputed love for them barely tolerated the messier presences of Gracie's father and Gracie, however different they too are from each other. "She's already gone anyway," her father said. Gracie imagined him clutching his glass of wine, prayerful hands, the ways we get by.

Wiki Wiki Motel, back streets of Hilo, no place the guide book mentioned or that she would have had a chance of stumbling upon on her own without the help of grinning Alika. Figured she'd pick a place out of the book when she arrived but when she called these were already full. Gracie could hear her mother: *You should have reserved your accommodations before you set one foot on that plane!* Gracie's mother, queen of the shoulds, the should nots, life according to Maizey McKneely. *You should never have been holding that baby while you were barbecuing, what were you thinking!* Enough to put someone off meat for a good long time.

She's hovering about the information booth with its Where To Stay pamphlets when he zeros in on her, the flower scented airport, raw ceilings open to the muggy, tingly air, looking helpless, her shrinking self again. "I'm Alika! Need one ride or what?" He's wearing a Wiki Wiki Motel tee shirt, salmon pink with neon orange lettering.

"Hi," she says unenthusiastically. (*Aloha spirit!* the guide book chortled in that personable, hyperactive guide book voice. *Watch for it, famed friendliness of the islanders.*) "So, what does it mean?" Gracie asks him, trying to sound interested. She's not really. Exhausted from the long journey and feeling a little sad, defeated before setting one foot out of this airport. What's the point? In search of some elusive healer? Why not just become a Jesus freak, a *haunted housewife* and be done with it!

"What, Alika? Hawaiian for Alex. You rather call me Alex or what?"

She lowers her eyes, cheek tucked neatly behind her hair. "No."

"OK then! You need one place to stay? I got one, you know," pointing to his tee shirt. *Off Historic Hilo Harbor*! it announces in smaller neon.

He's handsome, dark skinned, a sort of blubbery soft look, comfortable in his bigness. Gracie is reassured by his too-much smile. This really is business. "Whatever," she tells him, voice like a shrug, voice not hers. "Suppose I can check it out at least." *Sharks are sleek, mean and intelligent compared to the big dull fish, say a grouper. Searing eyes, a purposeful look.* Looks at him purposefully: "But if it doesn't work you'll take me somewhere else, right?"

He grins, that seemingly tireless, slathered on smile.

Leaving the airport, cinder gardens and hibiscus, crotan and hala trees alongside the lava wall. She had studied the guide book's photos of plant life, social scientist's daughter already categorizing, though her father at one time found botanical life less *compelling* than society, studying it that is. She suspects these days he'd prefer a habitat with plants over one with people. Ferns, for instance, which this island has an abundance of, are seldom cruel, will never do something someone would regret.

Alika's driving an ancient VW Beetle painted pink, of all the unlikely colors for a German car, scripted black lettering *Wiki Wiki* on its battered doors. He lets Gracie know how lucky she is to have found him, that all the hotels, bed and breakfasts, *whateva*! are booked because Pele—"She blow, yeah?" he winks. "Everyone like come see her tantrum. Her name mean meander. Ho'ohele down Kīlauea, set fire to kīpuka one time, take forest right into sea, eh?"

Gracie wonders if he really talks this way or whether he's putting it on for her. *Pidgin English*! the guide book chortled, *Also referred to as Hawaiian Creole. A saucy linguistical stew of different cultures and their languages, Hawai'i's melting pot.* Tries to picture Alika as an accountant-in-training by night maybe, something sober like that, with a Midwestern twang. "The volcano," she whispers. (What she's thinking is *her,* the photographer. alvin-Travis had said it—gone to the volcano, a *Kodak Moment.*)

Gracie in the passenger seat, her right cheek pressed to the glass as if to hide it, but then she thinks what the hell! and rolls open the window. The island of Hawai'i is like nothing she's ever smelled, rich with rain, air so thick and moist it's like breathing under water. The scarred red earth and all manner of flowers and fruits; even in downtown Hilo, just minutes from the airport, its colorful mix of two story buildings, some single level store fronts, wooden, concrete, most with green or red corrugated iron roofs, a chunky bright little city that manages to appear so even under a dark shrug of clouds. Palms, *hala, hau, kukui,* she can still identify these from *that summer,* and gracefully spreading trees dropping strange wiggly things off of them; Monkeypod, Alika informs her. Gracie breathes deeply, feeling newly alive, almost as if at some point in between the interminable plane ride, shedding her mainland jacket and being here she's actually begun to grow a new skin. Born in these islands then shuttled so soon to the mainland, as they call it, she wonders if maybe, possibly she might feel at home? Make it hers though she was gone before she could even speak its name? *Maybe the voice for home is not in words.*

Alika tells her the weather is volcano weather. "The kind rain and mist when Pele blow, goddess-style depression, yeah? Wants even the sky to announce her pissed off mood, spit rain, you know. Been erupting two decades. Tourists come watch her *hele* her lava into the sea, get big steam this one. That why you here?"

Gracie peers doubtfully over at him, crinkly black curls, skin the color of some beautifully polished stone. Turns back toward the window. But of course, she imagines herself telling him, this is where *the sister* would be. Of course she would, she's the photographer, isn't she? Haven't I flown 6,000 miles just to see her? *Christ*! she groans like Roma would and Alika glances at her. "Huh?" he asks, "Said what?"

"Nothing," she says. "So, is Pele clinically depressed or is it more of a situational thing?" Gracie tries to imagine a situation that might upset a goddess but can't do it. Surely life is just a little easier for someone who has fire at her fingertips! *Dog-face, dog-face, whoosh*! Burn baby burn.

Alika smirks. "One *wahine*, no?"

He tells her in his mother's lifetime Hilo was destroyed by a series of five giant tidal waves. The year she was born, 1946, Laupahoehoe was hit, a school, students and teachers swept out to sea. "One *pilikia* land," Alika proclaims, "but we rebuild, what else you going do? Downtown Hilo buildings? Way back from harbor now cause others destroyed, yeah?"

Gracie is grateful for his easy conversation. He's got the good side of her face, her left profile. Wonders if he noticed all of her isn't the same.

Alika turns into a street, Kinoole, heading immediately uphill. He maneuvers the VW deftly against the curb in front of the Wiki Wiki Motel, a hunched pink building with a mossy corrugated tin roof, and of all things one of those pink flamingo yard ornaments perched up on the roof like it's chowing down on the moss. "Wow!" Gracie grunts, "Somebody's vision of paradise?" Chickens scatter about the entrance. From a nearby yard a rooster crows; that burdened smell of rotting fruit (guava? papaya? her guide book didn't do odors!) and clumpy wet soil.

"She like her pink!" Alika laughs, jumping out of the car, hurrying around to Gracie's side, yanking open the door. "We call it Quonset hut style, reflect Hilo's plantation past, eh? Nah nah," he winks, "just *is* one Quonset hut!" He grabs Gracie's suitcase from the back at the same time she's reaching for her carryon. Their fingers brush and she's startled by how warm his feel, another's hand. Their eyes meet and his free hand suddenly shoots out toward her face. She immediately draws back, a turtle tucking in its offending head, as he gently lifts her hair.

"Whoa!" he whistles, "Birth mark or tattoo?"

Gracie sighs. Here we go again, she thinks. Maybe if she barely acknowledges that he spoke he'll back off; it's either this or they pretend not to notice at all while mapping their exit.

"Good luck you know, kissed by one angel."

"I doubt that," she mutters.

"Oh, so a tattoo? Could be tattoo," he nods, brows knit together thoughtfully. "I'm part Maori. Maori get cheek tattoos to show they are warriors, women too, for identity."

"You're not Hawaiian?" she asks, though at this point she really couldn't care less, mostly to change the subject.

"Oh, for sure! Little bit Maori, Hawaiian, Fijian, Chinese, Portuguese, even your basic *haole*. One poi dog style! Anyhow Hawaiians get tattoos, Fijians, ancient Polynesian art. Watch the hula dancers sometime, real ones, not the ones dance for the *haoles*."

Alika is looking at Gracie's face with interest, no embarrassment, no pulling back, just conversation seemingly. She forces herself to meet his eyes, keeping a steady gaze. "My name is Gracie Kathleen McKneely," she tells him, offering her hand. "About as basic a *haole* as it gets."

"Gracie Kathleen McKneely," he says solemnly. "One basic *haole wahine*!" helping her out of the car. "*Pohaku wa'uwa'uili*," he winks, his hand still holding hers.

"Huh?" Gracie mumbles, heartbeat accelerating, a roar in her veins, the warmth of him! Clutching her carryon, her purse with her free hand, shutting the VW door with her hip, leaning back against it her other hand burning up in his. God, she thinks, not this again!

"Means stones that claw the skin. At Waikapuna in Ka'u, not too far." Alika leans so close she can smell a sort of fruitiness on his breath, his teeth white as shells. "One powerful love potion, you know."

Gracie's cheeks blaze. "Whatever," she whispers.

He releases her hand, ushering her inside. The first thing she sees hanging over the golden wood desk (he tells her it's *koa*, what canoes were made of) is a framed poster of the goddess Pele, *the red-eyed goddess*, her ropey lava hair, holding an egg with the naked curves of another woman nestled inside. A double-hulled canoe is in front of her and in the foreground, a large sleek shark! *A gurgling in my throat, pectoral fins stick out like wings of a jet, provide lift as I swim, mouth open lets the oxygen rich water wash over my gills, if I stop swimming I could drown. Skin tight as a drum, hula drum pounding out the rhythms of the dance.*

"You like?" Alika asks, gazing at Gracie intently. "Pele's brother, Kamohoali'i, Shark God, king of sharks, keeper of the water of life. In human form he appear without a loincloth, privilege reserved only for gods, yeah? Pele's favorite little sister in egg, Hi'iaka, spirit of hula. Shark's my uncle's family 'aumakua. One time he went night fishing by concrete tower at Moku Ola, shark cave underneath. Rogue wave come along and knock him in, current dragging him out, ocean all black and rough and what you think?" Alika looks at her expectantly. "A shark leads him safely to shore! He now one 'aumakua kahu, a keeper. Goes Moku Ola to feed his shark now, yeah? instead of his own opu. Offer food and 'awa, show respect."

"We grow up believing they are dangerous." Quietly, her words barely there, did she even speak?

Alika nods, "'Jaws' generation. Some are some aren't, like people, eh? Trick is to know who's who. Shark kill you he one people-eater. You kill 'aumakua is like murdering your relative. Some folks born human turn into a shark. Ka'ahupahau and Kahiuka, sister and brother. They live in one cave now, near Pearl Harbor. That area of O'ahu have plenty man-eating sharks too, *niuhi*. Who you going kill? This not Hollywood."

"*In the fish-eat-fish world beneath the waves, few fish regularly feed upon the shark—except the shark. There are creatures that may challenge the shark—killer whales and an occasional swordfish. Like human beings, however, sharks are normally prey only to their own kind.*" Shadows in the Sea; Allen, p. 191 *(Compiled by S.G. and G.M. Note: A P.S. in her own words about how in the womb the strongest fetuses eat the weakest. I was surprised to find out sharks bear their young live! Why didn't Dr. B. mention this? Makes them seem more human than fish! S.G. wrote something about siblings, her own I guess but she scribbled over it. Seems like she mostly doesn't acknowledge having a family, just the articles referring to them as a personal history, interviews with her mother—but these are all about S.G.— and the mostly unopened letters from her sister. It's like she's not even part of them anymore.)*

After checking in with the help of the generously pink mu'umu'ued local woman she assumes is Alika's mother, a giant pink hibiscus pinned over her right ear, Alika offers Gracie his Wiki Wiki VW to drive out to where the volcano is erupting. "You won't find one bus, taxi, car rental, nothing," he says. "Tourists take them all. They flocking to Pele, not one clue what she capable of. Got to help out here or I'd *holoholo* with you. Means go someplace, for pleasure!"

Face flaming, she starts to pull her hair down over her cheek then lets it go. *Let it go.* "You trust me with your car?" Gracie asks doubtfully. It's been a while since she's driven, though she appreciates that he's chosen to separate her and her mission, whatever *that* is, from the throngs of *other* tourists. Alika is looking Gracie over again, head to toe and in between. Smiles, that dazzling white grin. *Shark teeth anchored in gums replaced by a never-ending supply.... Apparently he's not finding me so bad.*

The afternoon is cool and the air feels gritty, clouds the color of pencil lead the closer Gracie gets to where the volcano is spewing into the ocean. Vog, Alika called it, the gaseous fog the volcano makes. He outlined the route in yellow marker on her map, climbing Kīlauea, past groves of ginger, fern, papaya and banana, heading up Volcano Highway into the koa and ohia, the *kīpuka*, musk scent of the rain forest in Volcanoes National Park, then following the Chain of Craters road down toward the sapphire sea until suddenly it stops.

"*Stops*, not ends," he emphasized. "Flow come over the road, *pau*, just like that! They try charge tourists to see eruption. Pele no like they make money off her so she seal the buggah up!"

As Gracie approaches the area not only does the air seem coarser but the two lane road, for miles a stark lava waste land has become suddenly crowded with parked vehicles on either side. Up ahead two park rangers are stopping cars. She rolls down her window.

"You'll have to turn around," one of them informs her, an extra tall khaki shirted ranger bending stiffly down from a black belted waist to peer into her car. "Lava flow crossed this, no more road in about half a mile."

"Follow the cars? Park at the side?"

He nods. "Got any breathing problems? We're warning people who have asthma or any other breathing ailment to stay away. Smoke from burning asphalt is dangerous. Plus the lava creates acidic steam plumes and the fumes can be overwhelming where it enters the sea. Could also undermine the lava crust and there can be sudden collapse. We're telling folks not to go near the edge, the lava ledge is unstable. You'll see the new black sand beach. Very dangerous, may not have even cooled."

"Right," she says. "Anything at all good about doing this?" *Who talks this way?*

Shifts his weight from one black booted foot to the other, nods, doesn't smile. "It's about the most powerful thing you can witness. Just be careful. Carry enough water when you hike in, it's almost a two mile walk to where she's acting up today. We recommend good shoes, it can be tough going. We know only as much as she lets us. She'll blow where she wants to."

He hands Gracie a pair of disposable gloves. "Protect against burns," he says, eying her cheek then looking away. "There's a barrel to put them in when you're done. Keep as much of your body covered as possible."

Tugs a shank of hair over her cheek, lets it go. "No problem."

After parking the Wiki Wiki mobile, Gracie ties her cross trainers extra tight, grabs the bottle of *Menehune* island water Alika gave her then follows a group of tourists inching their way over the rough, dried (she's hoping!) lava flow. "This is a'a lava," they are told by another ranger whose dark red-streaked hair is swept up in a loose bun, herding them away from what must be the less stable lava, intensely black and shimmering, marked with yellow police tape. The ocean roars in the distance, an immense, luminous blue.

"Follow the white flag markers while you can, yeah?" the ranger tells them. "When they stop you folks are on your own."

"Head toward the steam?" A heavyset man in a floppy Hawaiian print hat asks. She gives him a duh! sort of look. "Watch for skylights," she warns, "where the lava drops away, forms a lava tube. Folks break bones, or worse."

Gracie steps gingerly over the rough, gritty surface, heart beat drumming, da-*dum*, da-*dum*. She doesn't do much in her life by a long shot considered dangerous and in less than twenty-four hours she has flown through four time zones to a tropical island, standing near the edge of an erupting volcano. *"Pau Pele, pau manō – May I be devoured by Pele, May I be devoured by a shark...if I fail."* Old Hawaiian Chant. *(Compiled by S.G. G.M.) Who are you?*

Gracie follows the flow of tourists picking their way toward the eruption, a mile or so in, past scatterings of steel highway markers, warning signs: Watch your speed! Fumes May be Hazardous! Bent over, curled by the advance of boiling lava like they're made of paper, origami highway signs. The going is slow, the afternoon stifling now, muggy, the trail a crumbly and uneven glimmer of violet, green and gold minerals in the cooled stone. She slows, sucking down a swig of water. Her mouth feels parched. The once cool and overcast day has become a steam pit, she thinks, this lava waste land a humid hell. Stares out at the ocean, so richly blue the sight of it after all this black makes her ache, throbbing in her throat, a longing for something but what it is she couldn't name. Gracie's eyes are wet. She swipes her hand against them then presses it to her chest. As if she could hold it, this yearning, then release it to flow through her veins to her heart, back into the blood and away. Wipes her eyes again and gazes toward the billowing steam, Pele pouring hers into the sea.

And that's when she spots me. Knows immediately it has to be me. My cropped hair, mannish elongated shape, that commanding sense of me (Gracie would see it this way), as of course I'm completely ignoring the yellow tape, other side of it humping a camera pack, a tripod, holding up my hand to shield my eyes from the harsh glare, the grit and glitter of volcanic air, straight over the shiny new lava ledge toward the sea. I am who she imagined I'd be.

Gracie stops dead in her tracks and an urgent chalk-white woman in shorts behind her is forced to also stop. The woman stumbles, grumbling, glaring at Gracie as she turns around to apologize, notices Gracie's cheek, looks away. Some things are worse than tripping on a'a, she's determined. But take a look at our Gracie! She's deciding on the spot, watching the snarly, jelloy, overripe shape try to navigate its way over the lava away from her, maybe she wouldn't trade. Not for that one anyway.

She steps to the side, closer to the yellow marker, out of the stream of foot traffic. Stares at me, the photographer, still a ways ahead of her. How simple things can be sometimes. She's come here to find me and, what do you know, she has. I'm not moving in a direction anyone else is. If she follows me, not only will it be obvious she's following me, but doing so means disobeying the yellow tape, the rangers' request, maybe putting herself in mortal danger, she'd be thinking; there's a reason the area is roped off. To Gracie I would not appear in any hurry to get to where the plumes of steam are rising. But if she lets me go?

She walks slowly, mimicking my movements only keeping to the inland side of the marker. And what the hell do I say to her, she would wonder? *Are you Shark Girl's sister?* It would sound inane! And then what? What does she really want to know anyway? Suddenly this mission of hers, if we could call it that, seems totally ridiculous to Gracie. She feels like a fool, face blazing, stumbling across this massive stretch of rock that looks like the moon (would she guess they actually trained astronauts on the Ka'u lava desert, close as we get to a lunar landscape?); no signs of biological life but for the clusters of gaudy, yammering tourists creeping across the dark field like so many brightly clad bugs—may as well wear double-knit and plaid, heft a bag of golf clubs and be done with it. (Gracie, I should note here, is accustomed to looking for signs of biological life, her formative summer spent studying wildlife and not so wild life, courtesy of Dr. Robyn Bender. But I jump ahead of myself, as of course I couldn't know this yet. Stories are like that: you don't always get to have all the parts when you need them. Time is flexible in a narrator's world, and timing, needless to say, is everything.)

Gracie stops dead between where I am and where the rest have moved away, head scrunched down to examine her ankle scraped up against a rocky outcrop, bubbles of boulder-sized lava spewn here and there, its grainy porous surface. Ouch! When she peers over at me again I too will have stopped, turned fully around so Gracie can see me better, see that I am staring at her. She'll blush of course, and most likely contemplate an about-face to the Wiki Wiki mobile, but instead stands there like an idiot (she would think) as I stroll back in her direction. She inches forward as if she didn't really stop, like she doesn't see me approaching her.

I call out when we are within easy voice range: "If you're stalking me I'm afraid I'll have to shoot you."

She pretends to look around like maybe I'm not even talking to her, though there's no one foolish enough to be near us, this close to marked danger. *Do not speak! There are no words for this....*

I'm practically on top of her now, smirking, pointing at my camera. "Shoot, get it?"

She nods, her hot face, dry throat, steam from the cracks between the rocks curling up, destination sinuses. Sniffles.

My voice is low, she'd think, a little gruff. "Do I know you?"

Stands there dully, shaking her head and feeling like an idiot she'll tell me later.

"You speak English? Something familiar about you." I examine her cheek. This, my first close-up of Gracie; she'd expect me to look away but I don't. Damage doesn't bother me, on the contrary I am drawn to it. This pummeled land and my sister for starters. I am much more compelled by the wounds one can see than psychic wreckage, rampant in my own family—but that's the old story. My eyes linger over Gracie's face then down the rest of her, appraising.

She looks at me skeptically. "Sorry," I laugh. "I was composing you in a shot actually, you'd be a nice contrast to this."

Gracie wanted to laugh too, she'll tell me, but it doesn't come out. *No words for this! No words no words no words.*

"It's in the eyes, good portraits are set through the eyes. I'm not just a lava junkie. In fact I was looking around for a different sort of shot when I noticed you behind me. If you call Park Headquarters they'll tell you there's a new lobe of lava to the east of this flow, moving more than 300 feet a day. That's Pele's playground right now. We're too far west. If the vog lifted you'd see the sun sinking. No good volcano shots today, close as I can usually get."

She manages a weak smile. I'm guessing she has a need to keep me talking because I can see now she just can't speak, no voice coming out, no language lingering behind her tongue, her brain willing it out. I'm an expert on silences, after all; how many years did I live with a sister who became a mute? Or perhaps muted is the better word, as mute to me indicates something you can't help, like being born deaf or blind. My sister could talk, then she couldn't. No reason for it. The shark didn't chomp off her tongue. Likely Gracie's thinking it's as though she's lost her language, somewhere between where jello-thighs glared at her and she gracefully bloodied her own ankle. Could she follow the path back and find her voice, white flags and yellow tape?

I flash what I know appears to be an orange badge, clipped to the nylon jacket tied over my shoulders. My arms are bare, thin and tan. Gracie stares at them, then the badge. "Looks like press," I say, "but it's not. I'm my own press. They see the photography equipment and they don't bother me. Clearly beyond a home video, know what I mean? Where are you from? You do strike me as familiar. I don't usually have much to do with strangers, particularly tourists and here we are. You walking my way?" (These were honest enough questions. Please bear in mind at this point I do not know her.)

Gracie is studying my face, clean lines, handsome more than pretty, the face in the silver framed photo on the bureau (we discover!), Shark Girl's sister. She peers down at her feet, then a worried glance toward the ocean. *Lava ledge, breaks off into the sea*.... Heart pumping, blood shooting down to her fingertips, tingling. Merely to swallow her own spit would be like sipping stones through a straw. Stares at her hands. *Can jump in any moment now, brain to language to tongue and out, just ask, that's all, what harm could it be? Are you Shark Girl's sister? But I know this, so what's the point!*

When Gracie looks up again I will have started back out.

"Come if you want," I call to her, "I won't shoot you." I move ahead, closer to the edge, the intense heat. Gracie is hot, sweat glistening on her forehead. Is it the sun now too, she'd be wondering, finally out and reflecting the black lava like a furnace, daggers of light flashing off an indigo sea that hurting blue? *Where the water's dark the sharks*....

I've hoisted the camera bag firmly against my shoulder. Gracie stares at my path over the newly cooled flow, doubt churning, remembering again that night at the Rockland breakwater (this too I learn later, but let me tell it here for the integrity of the story), the wintry cold of it, pressing her face to the broken lighthouse window, stagnant warmth in the dead of night. And then going in! My God, crawling into that ancient lighthouse! *And here I am.*

"Christ!" Gracie mutters, very *Romaesque*, inching her way over the yellow tape, ropes of luminous rock, boiled egg stink of sulfur, following Susan Catherine Beever, devastation photographer of some distinction. Somewhere in cyberspace it says this, statistics on Shark Girl's family, her sister, *devastation photographer of some distinction*. Gracie would have read this in my sister's files. Willa kept us, her family, as *I* will discover, locked away in that box with everything else about her former life in scrupulous, documented detail. Perhaps it was easier that way than letting us move on, grow old with her, the ones who knew her as she was, and loved her anyway.

A sour taste curdling in Gracie's throat. What's the worst that can happen? she's thinking. Bit of a burn? Lava not quite cooled enough and her shoe, maybe some of the skin on the bottom of her foot shriveled away? Well it's not like she hasn't been burned before! Ledge caves in, the fall into the sea.... *We swim our sleek streamlined shape, top of the ocean food-chain, our well-developed eyes have light amplifying layers, nostrils sense odors in minute concentrations, sensory pits detect electronic fields emitted by prey; we swim we swim, if we do not we suffocate.*

Twenty minutes later we are on a lava cliff stretching over a foaming shore, less than an eighth of a mile from where the volcano is dumping into the ocean. Pele sluicing her fires, fierce heat of the spray searing our faces. Waves sizzle in against grainy sand, pulling back like burnt skin. Gracie pushes her chin down under the neck of her tee shirt, grateful, she'll tell me, she had followed Alika's advice and worn one with long sleeves. Slides on the disposable gloves. "Nothing like it!" the ranger stated. What she's feeling is a little sick.

"Here," I say, offering her an extra long sleeved cotton work shirt I've yanked out of my camera bag. "Wrap this around your head covering as much of your face as you can, just let your eyes peep through. I'm used to this shit, don't need it. You can't see it as well in the daylight, but look over to where the funnel of steam is most intense, that creeping dark red lava toe? Looks like a moving mound of congealed blood!"

Gracie nods numbly. Believes I've taken pity on her, taken her in, little mute *haole* retard of the lava waste, she'd think. Or maybe she senses the outcast in me too, one inner-outcast to another. I put my arm around her neck, guiding her face to where I am pointing. She'll feel my warmth, my tallness bearing her, covering her in a shroud of my own skin, the scent of me. I'm feeling familiar to her, like her own sister might if she had one. Gracie's parents, who chose not to have more children after what happened to her. Tears pool in her eyes.

I pull away, staring at her. "Steam getting to you? We should turn back. Couple of tourists died last October somewhere around here inhaling this junk." I push my hand gently over her nose and mouth, pressing the sleeve of my shirt against the hot skin of her cheeks. My other hand is on her shoulder, leading her away from the coast. I will discover in time that this was the moment when Gracie had an impulse to lick my fingers, to see if even this felt known, the taste of my skin. But she restrained herself.

"I love it here," I tell her, matter of fact. "Where else in this country is land building itself instead of gobbled up by yuppies and the like for their Mc-Nests, their own greedy interests? That's the thing about being rich. You can afford to have interests. In a lava field, nothing but sky, sound of the wind over earth laid bare, no bullshit. At times I believe I could live here, I've felt this before. Weave myself a little lau hala hut, make another if that one burns, lie down and be part of this. When I'm here I feel somehow enlarged, yet wallowing in my insignificance at the same time. We humans take ourselves too seriously, don't you agree? Other species, crabs for instance, it's all about food, scavenging for it, eating it, reproducing, dying. We make our food, our sex, have to mean something. What can it mean? In the end we too are dust, rich, poor, the genius and the moron, all just a Pledge can away. There!" I say, "You OK? This is a good place. The light is perfect."

We are back a ways from the ocean now, the roar of the waves subsiding into a dull rhythmic throbbing. I untie the shirt wrapped around Gracie's head and it falls away lightly like old skin. "I don't like things posed," I tell her—she runs her hand through those wavy locks. "So be natural." Knits her brows and I laugh. "Yeah, I lied. I would like to shoot you, if it's OK. What's your name anyway? I never even asked and here I am about to freeze a moment or two of your life for posterity. Oh!" I smile (*slyly?*), "I forgot. We're not on speaking terms. Never mind, you have the look going for you, who needs talk? Like this land, it's what's below the surface. When you explode I'll bet watch out!"

I start to set the meter on my camera then pull back, frowning, staring at her hard. Something has occurred to me that I'm embarrassed took this long for me to sort the wrinkles out, but I say it to her in such a way she'll think it's just dawned on me. "You're not here because of my sister, are you? Tracking me to find out where she is? It's happened before and let me tell you, I hate that! Am I my sister's keeper?"

No words for this! She plasters on a vague, puzzled look, gazing out over the parched landscape. We stand there in silence for a minute or two inhaling the sulfur, the vog, the strangeness. Then I smile so she can see this is OK, really it is, the crinkling of lines around my sharp brown eyes. Hers too are brown, she'd be thinking, but less certain, more like a dog's, *dog face*? I look straight into those eyes. "Never mind," I tell her.

Gracie lets me take her picture, gazing out at this stunned land. She becomes for a moment its rawness, though we learn this is not her; no Gracie McKneely waiting silently to explode, rage bubbling under the patina of a not so smooth face. That is not her way, is it? (Or it never used to be….) Gracie goes forth, goes on, hurt held carefully inside, secured and precious and offered to no one. *I will not ask where her sister is.*

Back at our cars, the Wiki Wiki mobile and my rented Jeep which, as it turns out, oddly enough is parked near the VW, I wave at her as she's climbing into her car. "Just a second," I call out, signaling Gracie to wait like I've had some sort of afterthought, laying my camera bag down on the passenger seat of the Jeep, collapsed tripod on the floor beneath. Gracie has already fastened her seat belt but has left the door open. I stride over, my long legged blue-jeaned gait, bending down so that I'm leaning on the door, peering in through the open window as if the door really is shut.

"OK," I tell her, "Here's the deal. I'm not even sure she's still alive. You get me? I don't mean physically, I don't think, I mean alive in the sense of being a part of it all. She's been so fragile, just never fully recovered from the shock is the medical establishment's educated guess. But shock, I'm here to tell you, is not salvation."

She squirms a bit, shaking her head like she hasn't a clue what I'm talking about, staring up at the sides of Kīlauea, or is it Pu'u O'o, she might wonder? Or are they one, the same cindery yellow, arch of lustrous black rock cascading like Pele's own hair across older, greyer rock, youth to age its own life cycle and here and there the ashy waste, fern and ohia lehua, her fiery flowers breaking through. Note the intensity of these blossoms, life triumphant! Gracie's inner guidebook.

I lift my eyebrows, gaze straight into her eyes. "You know," I say, "I know you know. It's just a tip I'm offering here because you let me photograph you and there's something about you... can't explain but my sense is she would want you to know. I honestly don't know what to tell you. Our mother is in the state hospital. You get what I mean? In Kāne'ohe. They used to always be together. Then they weren't. I'm not making some sort of talk-show confessional here to a stranger; you can get a lot of this stuff from the tabloids or the Net. What I'm offering you is a way to see it."

My eyes are suddenly damp. Damn! I think, the plan had been to stay completely rational. If my father were here he'd tell me that this is what's important, keeping rational in an irrational situation. And so he's spent his life doing just that. My eyes leave her face, staring in the direction of Mauna Loa, the long blue mountain, Mauna Kea stretching its higher, craggier peaks behind. Highest mountains in the world, Gracie will have read in her guide book, if you measure from below sea level. She inches her neck around and stares too. Because now neither one of us can look at the other. It's like we've been set on some path to another's heart, but we're not sure we're up to the hike.

"Don't you get it?" I sigh. "We've got some kind of need here in common and it's futile, damnit. I've wasted a lot of years trying to figure it all out, the disintegration of my family, piece it back together like it's a puzzle. What happened to Willa happened, we can't alter it, but that everything else could somehow fit back in, just without the missing piece, you see? The goddamn leg! Well, turns out there are a whole lot of missing pieces and some that shouldn't even be inside the frame. It's just too messy. I don't know what your interest is in her but if it's because you think she can give you some kind of redemption forget it. There's fracturing beyond even my own comprehension and you're staring at someone who threw away twenty years of her life over it. Look at this land, will you? Absolute ravagement then it rebuilds itself over time into something new. My God, don't you wish people were like that? Be like a damn *mo'o*, a lizard, leg chomped off a new one grows back in its place." I rub my forehead, sweat breaking out, dampening my armpits. "But then, that's the myth, isn't it?"

My gaze again locks into hers. "Do you want to know what I think is really bizarre? That nobody seems to ask the question you'd think they'd ask, the only one that matters, in my opinion, as in Just how did Willa Beever, *your sister*, get from scabby-kneed eight year old brat to a miracle? It's like they want it to be true, so by golly it is. I mean hell, if that's the outcome you'd think everyone would be trying to get them, shark bites!

"You want to know how I think it might have happened?" Gracie shifts uncomfortably but I won't let her not hear this. "It's a scenario I came up with when I was still drinking, stalking her, trying to figure out how to make contact with her, how to redeem my past through her, my elusive little sister. Sound familiar? Some days I believe this, other days I don't, but it's something, you know? Hear me out for just a few more minutes."

Gracie starts to look away then doesn't. We look at each other.

"Listen. In 1979 Willa Beever gets out of her bed at the age of 26; this much we know. I'm 28, a college graduate and an alcoholic. My life was going nowhere but at least it was nowhere near home. Home was San Francisco, my favorite bar out at Point Lobos. I could stare into the Pacific, listen to the sea lions roar and medicate myself into oblivion. Our brother was long gone; who's around to pay attention to little sister? Do you hear me? I'm telling you she just one day got up.

"In 1979 the newspapers were filled with the latest shark attack, on the heels of three in 1976, one in 1977, one in 1978 and then an elderly man fishing off South Kohala on this very island. Fire department divers found only his hand and a flashlight. One of the 1976 attacks was pretty gruesome: Danson Nakaima passed out while scuba diving for black coral off Lahaina, Maui at a depth of 180 feet. Thirty sharks were seen near the partially devoured remains of his body. Stephen C. Powell was also scuba diving in 1976; only the lower parts of his body were recovered. This is all documented. You can look this stuff up.

"Let's say some of Willa's behavior, her silence, lolling about in her bed for years was for attention. OK, she's my little sister and she did get a lot of our mother's love so sure there's some jealousy there. But let's say it's so, in part. The other part was as the medical establishment called it when they closed the book on her—unremitting shock. Stole her voice and her will to get better, that's what most believed and I'm not saying this isn't partly, maybe even mostly true. I can't imagine what she must have gone through, the pain, reliving the attack again and again, forever in her mind and her voice just closes up in there too. But Willa also craved attention, and boy did she get it. Until the 1970s anyway when the rest of us grew up, moved out, moved on.

"Maybe she heard about those attacks and the excitement they stirred up in the community, and maybe she felt even more neglected. She gets up. No grace; there was no reason why physically Willa couldn't get out of that bed. But no doubt our mother, a full on lush herself at that point went frenzying about the neighborhood: It's a miracle! It's a miracle! Innocent enough, as I'm sure when your daughter goes to bed for 18 years you've got to see it as something pretty significant when finally she gets up.

"Let's say one of the neighbors was paying particular attention, Birdie McPherson, mother of the brats I used to babysit, wah wah wahed all the time. Turned out one of them actually had something to cry about, Teddy McPherson diagnosed with leukemia. He'd have been around twenty at that point, not expected to live to adulthood at twenty-one. Imagine if she and Teddy came over for a visit, not expecting anything other than to be in the presence of some other mother's good fortune, maybe something would rub off. Meanwhile our father sets little sister up with a prosthesis—he'd have been real quick on that particular task, I'll tell you. But the McPhersons didn't know this and when they knocked it was none other than Willa Beever walking!!! to open the door.

"Bingo. Within a short period of time Teddy's leukemia goes into a dramatic remission. These things happen. Willa still didn't talk, she's the color of paper and about as flaccid, since she just spent eighteen years in her bed! But anyone looking at her might assume the worst—Willa was ill. Gossip diagnosis: Teddy got better, Willa got it. Given leukemia is not exactly like catching a cold from someone's sneeze, you can imagine how the victim soul thing might have started.

"That's one borderline rational scenario, and believe me when you're a drunk whose irksome little sister is suddenly humping that cross with Jesus you need to hold onto anything remotely reasonable. People want miracles. She got up. Teddy McPherson's leukemia went into remission. That's what we know. Who dug out those shark stories, I haven't a clue. Half shark half person, the *mo'o* regeneration trick—Willa on her feet thus her leg's grown back—this on top of the bleeding, healing thing? I mean come on, it's like fusing Slavic fairy tales with Buddhist ancestor worship and Barbie!"

Gracie slides her gaze away from my face, peering down at her fingers, short and pale, drumming lightly, nervously on the Wiki Wiki steering wheel. Stares back up at me. She can't keep her eyes off me.

I grin, reach in through the window and tousle her bangs like she's some little kid. "Hope it didn't sound like I was lecturing you there, my dear, I'm the last one fit for that. Folks who've tried to find my sister through me I say to them, boy, are you ever barking up the wrong tree! Used to be kind of fun, back when I was a drunk. I'd mess with their heads, they'd walk away smiling, believing they found the light. What light? I was darkness incarnate, dying inside and they're coming to me to find some sort of answer to life. My baby sister. Unbelievable. Don't you guys get it? She was a little girl who had something terrible happen to her and she survived it. End of story."

There are tears in Gracie's eyes. I shrug dismissively. "I don't know, just some stuff I've thought about. Are you OK? Suppose you couldn't tell me if you weren't, huh?" Gracie nods uncertainly, up and down, as though whatever's real in this is just now dawning on her—a little slow I'm thinking, but what else can she do?

NO VOICE, NO WORDS, STRANGLED IN MY THROAT, LIKE AFTER I SAW THEM AND I WANTED SO BADLY FOR HER TO LOVE ME TOO, AND THAT'S ALL I WAS THINKING, ALL I EVER NEEDED BUT I JUST COULDN'T SPEAK IT WHEN I CRAWLED INTO THE BED BESIDE HER, AND THEY MADE ME GO HOME....

Smile my biggest smile, angle my face in through the open Wiki Wiki window near hers, her breath lemony, that imprisoned breath of a voice unused (I remember this breath!) and I say: "I must confess, sometimes I feel very close to the people trying to find my sister, you folks have a way of getting under my skin. We're all missing something and wouldn't you know it, we're looking for salvation from someone who's maybe missing her very soul. Victim soul? Who's the victim? Try this out, my dear. Maybe a miracle is something we want others to do for us because we're too goddamn lazy, we're worn to the bone and we've given up trying to do it ourselves. Huh? What do you think? Am I ready to audition for the next Saint Beaver, or what!"

She's tearing up again, those moist brown eyes, so what I do is I take that chin into my warm fingers, lean in even closer and I whisper: "Anyway, guess what? I'm not the one who gets to grow a new skin in this story. What I get is to be sober." Then I kiss her cheek, reaching all the way around to the right side to do it.

CHAPTER TWENTY-FOUR

There's a Hawaiian tale called *The Little Yellow Shark*. I discovered it in my sister's file box when Gracie gave this to me along with her own notes, a few days after our Volcano meeting. Gracie (who had recovered her voice!), said she didn't need them anymore. It's about a good shark who trapped an evil shark in a hole on the coral reef off Waīkikī, where it was killed. When this *niuhi* was sliced open they found human bones and hair in its stomach. The people were so grateful to *The Little Yellow Shark* that they had a great feast around their *imu* in a ceremonial spot known to this day in downtown Honolulu. "I guess even heroes have their victims," Gracie wrote in her notes. Maybe Fatboy the Trapper was on to something. It seems one is inevitably either the hunter or the hunted.

As for me, I take pictures. What I like about photography is its visual language. Life is always in the process of becoming, never arriving; if you're alive this is true. A photograph stops time. Consider Gracie. If I could choose to photograph Gracie at a telling moment in her life, here is what I would take:

A golden hot afternoon, summer of 1994, some colleague of Robyn Bender's, her Koko Head home. Louis and Robyn and Gracie too this time, cocktails, the clinking of ice, *pūpūs*, droll buzz of conversation, the occasionally emphatic musings of adults. The talk was about morning sickness, only as Gracie told it, she thought it was *mourning* sickness. Feeling awkward, foolish, ever the child (sick with love, though how could she understand this?), just *wrong*, she slipped out into the back yard where there was a carp pond. Stared down at the fish swishing about, gurgling of the decorative faucet, this too the iron image of a fish, offering them a never-ending gush of fresh water. They were well cared for these carp. Imagine their mouths as they open and shut, open and shut, no worries that one day there might not be anything to fill them, gills flapping — they extrude fat from their gills, did you know? I learned this too, an efficient eating machine. Gracie had a sudden impulse to stick her own face in, where that lucid water poured into the dark scent of the pond, feeling it there, her face, the slick sure shape of a fish; to *be* one of them, orange, red, yellow flashings, life as simple as the next doomed fly, snapping shut. I would freeze that, when what's there for this moment is no longer her.

I have a memory, not so long ago but it comes back to me like a recurring dream only this was real. I'm walking on the breakwater, where Gracie used to walk, late spring early summer, who can tell the difference in Maine? — right before I returned to Hawai'i. And the fog was so heavy, so all encompassing that I had a sense of what it might be to live life blind, or mostly blind where the world is all greys, no specific edges only silhouettes. This fog was alive in the way things are that are beyond our control, existing in a realm that is maybe part dream, maybe part God, something that will thrive long after our own brief appearance in time.

In this fog Gracie too would be a silhouette to anyone else, her defacement meaningless because how does it exist if no one can see it? Only the boundaries of us all that inhabit a particular space, all diminished in the breath of this fog, the smoky sea smelling breath like what might come from a great whale off the coast, inhaling, exhaling. To be blind like in this fog relying only, so sharply! on your other senses, sounds of the various horns — breakwater foghorn's high wail, Owls Head's answering moan, boats creeping timidly into the harbor, chugging churning engine sounds. The lick of the sea where I walked, a sucking noise, rocks solid under my feet and the waves roiling on either side in that timeless rhythm. It was at this moment that I felt my sister, in a way I hadn't felt her before, as though she had become a part of it: the wind, the rocks, the fog, the sea. So much is bigger than us, after all.

The lighthouse finally rose out of the fog its staunch and withered face, its light barely glimmering those five second revolutions. It occurred to me how little anything at that moment mattered. In the fog we can be anybody, anywhere, in a field perhaps, bending and rustling of wheat tassels in the wind, crickets, locusts, grasshoppers, birdsong, all awash of sound — who are *you* in all this sound?

Remembering this now I think about another ocean, the one in Gracie's dreams as she described them to me, blue as breath, luminous, bluster of the surf the sun beating down, all vibration and sensation. Is this the moment when she understands, not our Gracie of the perceivable world but the other underneath, those three layers of skin? And how do I capture *this* in a photograph, save it as proof, label it, classify it, paste it into my Log: some knowledge of the world that isn't what most of us know; a door we dare not open, a place that may not take us in.

Photographer's Log — Susan Catherine Beever
Endings

Snapshot: two little girls floating on that tube in my dream, but it's real enough and I sent it to her. One's future as a saint and the other a drunk; one is here the other is...? Was it determined even then, our lives could go this wrong? Two little girls in the finite sea, drifting.

Willa had her ways of pushing us all over the edge.

Snapshot: Gracie gave it to me, had been schlepping it about in her wallet, bent and dog-eared and cut in half, scissors snipped straight as a blade, and Louis has disappeared. Robyn Bender's slender arm, the one with its original hand, slung around the leggy, cowering young Gracie who angles her face into a sun blazing white as salvation. The camera has captured her left side, same as anyone's.

Snapshot: the one from the tabloids, stunning Jaycee holding baby Willa, Robbie and Scat behind in the shadows, not in her light. Not in her light.

I became the photographer yet never once did I take her picture.

Correction, I title these: **Absence of Proof**

Know the world as a lesser place if you, my beautiful and beloved sister, are no longer in it.

EPILOGUE

Volcanic remains of Kalapana Beach, what Pele has left. Someday soon maybe I'll be in that little lau hala hut, trade winds whistling over my head, Pele's roar in the distance, staring out toward the purple horizon, dot of blackened fins like a pattern of geese, maybe you see them maybe you don't, rising and falling with the swell of the sea. "Maybe we'll find her maybe we won't," is what the detective with the Hilo Police said, my concession to Jaycee, handing over the search to those who do this professionally; "can you folks understand how few of the missing person cases are satisfactorily resolved?" But I had told my mother the truth: I am done looking for my sister.

Pack up my camera bag. I'm heading home, but not to Maine after all, salacious stories like a gathering of airport souvenirs for alvin-Travis: plastic leis, bleached shells, macadamia nut candies, pineapple jellies and passion fruit teas and who needs them? As easily forgotten as consumed. Aloha Airlines to Honolulu and then the old Kailua Taxi if it still exists (if it doesn't I'll improvise; I've learned at least this, how to finesse the details to suit a story) to Kailua. I'm hoping it won't be completely dark, that good rosy dusk, evenings of my childhood before *the tragedy*, and three little Beevers chasing joyfully down the lane after the mosquito truck, spraying its scented fog of DDT, becoming lost in this cloud of poison not knowing then that it *was* poison (except for mosquitoes!), boundaries obscured, the land around us reinventing itself so that when finally the fog cleared there you were.

Our father still watering our lawn, shooting water he called it.

How many years did it take me to understand that for him, choosing to do this rather than drop a sprinkler down, standing there willing each blade's growth, arching that mist from the power nozzle over the tender green, this was our father's way to God. He'll nod serenely at my return, as if he never doubted I'd be back. Perhaps he'll drape a lei around my neck, made it himself from the red plumerias off our back yard tree, stroking my cheek, sleek as the petals. Aloha, he'll say, *Aloha kāua* Scat. This much that is Hawaiian in him.

And Jaycee? She'll come back to us or she won't, but what I know is this: I am the one who is like her after all, not Willa. Sex for shelter, summer of sex, sex as currency, the flesh standard, whether to quell our lonely thirst or for a roof over our scheming heads, walls of our creation around us, the power dynamic: Who is using whom and how? Sex is what we ended up with. Love, or its possibility anyway, is what we live for.

Maybe deep down where dreams are dreamt, where the seeds of our stories are discovered, laid bare and we piece these together like stringing a lei, what happened, what did not, hope, regret, what cannot be changed and what has forever changed, spinning these out a tenuous yet continuous thread, lei needle silvery thin and fine as *pinao*, a dragon fly's wing, futures created and recreated over and over again. Maybe it is here where the myth begins.

Is it a dream? You will ask yourself this, must ask it as it seems like your eyes are open and you're seeing yourself sitting upright and forward on a sun-warmed rock the way the hala tree bends over the cliff, leaning into the wind, the sea, oldest of stories, watchful and thorny, trusting its roots because what else is there? At the place where a strip of sand meets a surging sea, watch what suddenly appears; watch her walk to the end of the point, such grace, possession of this land, this ocean her fluid and sinewy movements. Though she isn't really walking, couldn't be walking as it appears she has just one appendage, maybe a leg, but more like a fin, shivery play of the light, a fish's fin, long and metallic, body and tail. Hair hanging golden to her waist, eyes the color of the sea, shimmering gunmetal scales, long graceful curving of a fish. Her voice (is it a voice? resonate as wind, as breath): Would you like to swim with my friends? Ten of them, their fins dark and precise, cutting the water like so many knives. And with that the fish-woman arches her splendid shape and leaps. As she pivots, her projectile straight into the ocean, see the long curve of thigh, her muscled lower calf, the arched foot. Now there are eleven and the new one rising up through the luminescent sea so light and fine it appears almost translucent in the setting sun.

From The Files Of Wilhelmina Malia Beever (S.G.)
As Compiled by Grace Kathleen McKneely (G.M.)

"...It is said that these are "sharks who have exchanged souls with living men." It is a process of adoption, and what injures one injures the other."

Beckwith; <u>Hawaiian Mythology</u>

From the <u>Honolulu Advertiser</u>, December 14, 1958
Lad From Prominent Isle Family
"A shark at least 15 feet long slipped inside the reef off Lanikai yesterday afternoon, moved unnoticed past a group of happy boys out surfing, and bit off the right leg of 15 year old William (Billy) Weaver. The boy died in the water shortly after."

..."30 Feet from the boys in the water he saw the shark surface. "Shark" he screamed. The shark lay still for a moment, its tail swishing lazily. Then it rolled over with a splash."

Same page as Lad From Prominent Family: Boy Butchers 5 in Family In California "The Murder rampage one of the most vicious in Southern California History.... A suitcase and hunting knives found at the murder scene matched descriptions of articles taken when young Eder left home..." (Noted by G.M. — This, pre Charlie Manson and "Helter Skelter.")

What to Do If Confronted By a Shark (G.M. — Same paper/same article)

Keep Quiet!

Keep your spear for protection and retreat slowly.

Do not keep speared fish near your body. Get rid of them or lift them from water.

Shout or make a loud noise under water. The concussion may drive shark away.

Do not panic or thrash. Sharks will attack anything they sense helpless.

Same page: "Billy Weaver, a ninth grader at Punahou School, was one of the stars of the school's baseball team. He was good at all sports, but he loved most of all swimming, diving and surfing."

Honolulu Star-Bulletin, August 7, 1959

Breeding Ground

"...Reppun said that Kaneohe Bay is a breeding ground for tiger sharks and hammerhead sharks. An interesting sidelight Reppun gave about the boneless beasts, which date back 10 million years: a shark with cancer has never been found, and it is thought that something in the shark's liver may account for this...."

Honolulu Star-Bulletin; October 7, 1959

New Substance Is Tested, Believed Successful as Shark Repellent

..." Dr. Albert L. Tester, Senior Professor of Zoology at the University of Hawai'i..., {Developed} substance as per a contract agreement with the U.S. Office of Naval Research, which is sponsoring his shark behavior studies.... Dr. Tester reports the substance is an organic compound. Specifically what element in the compound is the actual repellent has not been pinpointed yet. The scientist's ...studies also yielded many significant findings on shark behavior. Briefly, that sharks are:

1. Highly intelligent. They train rapidly in conditioned response experiments....

2. Do not have particularly sharp vision....when sharks bite a body they just snap at whatever's available..., do not aim for the thigh, arm or anything specific like that.

3. Don't appear to differentiate between colors. This is a controversial question and still problematical, Dr. Tester noted....

4. Have a terrific sense of smell....

5. Have a well-developed sense of taste.

For taste-smell tests, a few sharks were blinded and a few others had their nostrils plugged. The latter could see. When natural squid was tossed in the test pools the blind sharks went right to {it}. The ones with plugged nostrils got to the bait, but took a long while to find it. When another batch of squid {was offered} (this time the taste was washed out in alcohol...,) the blind sharks did not go for it. Sharks with their sense of smell hampered did not take to it at all. Normal sharks (with taste and smell) started munching and then spat it out, proving that normal feeding must have some taste."

6. Are not repelled by decayed shark flesh or tobacco, which some persons believe make good repellents. Dr. Tester said whole human blood, on the other hand, startled and excited them. He could not tell whether they were attracted or repelled by it..... Sharks showed no particular response to human urine.

7. Are not effected by sound, however loud.... Also, he said no amount of shouting, even the use of rough language, shook them at all.

8. Do not feed on bait if a flashlight is on it....

9. Are very individual and localized. The men got so they recognized the sharks ... that swam around their work area. They were all six footers and appeared to have personalities of their own. Their feeding personalities went something like this: Black-tip, always cautious; white-tip fearless—rushed in where others feared to tread; grey, always circled and then struck; nurse shark, least dangerous, sat at the bottom most of the time....

Star-Bulletin; December 13, 1959

566 Sharks Killed in O'ahu Waters During Past Year

"Five hundred and sixty-six sharks have been killed in O'ahu waters to avenge the death of Billy Weaver one year ago today. In addition, 375 pups carried by mother sharks in the catch were destroyed....

"The Shark Control Program is being financed by $16,476 contributed by public subscription plus $11,000 provided by Governor Quinn from his contingency fund....

Contributions may be made to the Billy Weaver Shark Control Program in its care at Box 2390, Honolulu 4."

Star-Bulletin; July 10, 1960
Along the Miracle Mile; with Dale Richesen
"Make-I-Ka-Mano in Hawai'i means: Death by Sharks! ...Even though the experts tell us that our chances of being attacked are about equal to those of being struck by lightning, most of us retain the knowledge that it has happened and could happen again—perhaps this very hour!

Only a little more than a year ago a boy named Billy Weaver was killed while swimming off Lanikai.... But does this mean we stay away from the water? Not at all!

... In the last few years, according to the Shark Research Panel of the American Institute of the Biological Sciences, sharks have been increasing and so have the number of attacks. ...Shark repellents are being developed and used, but not with any universal success...

One of the most reliable repellents was developed and used— and held as a top secret—during World War II. It consists basically of copper acetate.... the same chemical given off by rotten shark meat and apparently the smell sounds some sort of danger warning inside the brain of a shark.

One of the leading scientists in shark research lives in Hawai'i and has carried on extensive psychological studies of sharks, trying to figure out just how a shark thinks. He is Dr. Albert L. Tester of the University of Hawai'i. In specifically constructed tanks, he carries on Pavlov-like stimulus-response experiments to determine how the critters will behave when such and such happens.

Someone is forever coming up with a new set of rules on how to behave when you suddenly discover you've inadvertently gotten chummy with a hammerhead....

1. Always dive with a companion. Do not provoke small or seemingly harmless sharks. Place speared fish in a boat or dinghy so they won't attract sharks.

2. As a rule, a shark will circle several times before attacking. Get into a boat quickly; swim with a regular beat, and do not make undue disturbance in the water as you move toward the boat.

3. If there's not time to reach a boat, you can sometimes discourage a shark by releasing bubbles or hitting it on the snout with a club. Do not hit with your bare hand. Shouting under water may help."

Star-Bulletin; November 20, 1960
Shark Worship and the Kapu of the Sea; by Inez Ashdown
"Through experience primitive people learned to avoid dangers. For the welfare of their children, the experienced ones made rules, or kapus, for the less experienced....

The Kapu of the Sea, for instance, urged cleanliness of waters and beaches. In order to make it meaningful, the kahunas, or teachers, wove fantasies around the kapu.

The kahuna set up a genealogy called Mo'o, who were the spirits of deified parents noted for their perfection, who could assume the form of lizards, owls, and sharks when protecting their descendants on earth. The ancestral spirits were 'aumakua, or guardian spirits.

... it followed that such spirits would assume shark form, or inhabit the bodies of certain sharks....

Anyone who broke the Kapu of the Sea by throwing refuse on beaches or into the waters of streams or the sea was punished. The offender was killed, the corpse was left on an altar to decompose for two to three days, and then was lashed to the outrigger of a chief's canoe and used as shark bait to destroy man-eating sharks....

April 20, 1961
Excerpts from: Billy Weaver Shark Research and Control Program
Final Report; Isaac I. Ikehara, Aquatic Biologist

Division of Fish and Game/Department of Agriculture and Conservation.
State of Hawai'i

"...This (tiger) shark appears to be an indiscriminate and opportunistic feeder to a greater degree than other sharks examined, for some of the ingested materials found in the (79 stomachs) examined were birds, turtles, garbage {such as} mammal bones, grapefruit rind and discarded vegetables and trash such as pie plates, pieces of corrugated fiber board cartons, shoes, slippers, etc. Judging from the frequency of shark flesh found in tiger shark stomachs, cannibalism appears to be more pronounced in this species than among the others. In most instances of cannibalism, it appears to have occurred on sharks which were caught on a hook. As with the sand sharks, the majority of live organisms fed upon by tiger sharks were of the slow moving or bottom dwelling forms."

"...One female caught was observed giving birth to pups after she was hooked and tied to the bow of the vessel. Ten pups were still in the uterus when the shark was cut open and 6 pups were observed following the vessel...."

"...The results obtained {in the final report} strongly indicate that species of sharks such as the sand, tiger and small black-tipped are highly vulnerable to continued fishing pressure and that their population can be controlled through the application of judicious fishing pressure."

"Stories are many of sharks' struggles against death and their apparent insensitivity to what in other creatures would be intense pain. But a headless, disemboweled shark writhing on the beach is not really struggling against death. Rather, its biologically simple body is throbbing with reflex actions. It is death that is doing the struggling; snuffing out such a vibrant, basic form of life takes a long time."

Allen; <u>Shadows in the Sea</u>. 195

Kamehameha at Laupahoehoe: *Let the old men, the old women, and the children lie down by the wayside and harm them not.*

Bibliography of Works Consulted and Cited

Allen, Thomas B. Shadows In The Sea: The Sharks, Skates, And Rays. New York: Lyon and Burford, Publishers, 1996.

Allen, Thomas B. Shark Attacks, Their Causes and Avoidance. New York: The Lyons Press, 2001.

Ambrose, Greg. Shark Bites, True Tales Of Survival. Honolulu: The Bess Press, 1996.

Ashdown, Inez. "Shark Worship and The Kapu of the Sea." Star Bulletin [Honolulu] 20 November, 1960.

Barnett, Fred. Hawaii's Shark Stories. Kailua: Fred Barnett-Ottis Media, 1996.

Beckwith, Martha. Hawaiian Mythology. Honolulu: University of Hawaii Press, 1970.

Borg, Jim. Tigers Of The Sea, Hawaii's Deadly Sharks. Honolulu: Mutual Publishing, 1993.

Crites, Jennifer. "Shark Gods of Ancient Hawaii." Leisure Around Town; Oceanic Time Warner Cable of Hawaii, (1998-2002 Oceanic Cable), August 27, 2002. {http://www.hawaii.rr.com/leisure/reviews/jennifer_crites/2002-06_sgoahawaii.htm}

Crow, Gerald L. and Jennifer Crites. Sharks And Rays Of Hawai'i. Honolulu: Mutual Publishing, 2002. pp. 143-153.

Ikehara, Isaac I. "Billy Weaver Shark Research And Control Program, Final Report." Honolulu: Division Of Fish And Game, Department Of Agriculture And Conservation, State Of Hawaii, 1960.

Kane, Herb Kawainui. Ancient Hawai'i. Captain Cook: The Kawainui Press, 1997.

Kane, Herb Kawainui. Pele, Goddess of Hawai'i's Volcanoes. Captain Cook: The Kawainui Press, 1987.

Krystek, Lee. www.unmuseum.org/bigsnake.htm, 1996-1999.

McMurray, Terry. "Boy 5th Killed By Sharks in 72 Yrs." The Advertiser [Honolulu], 14 December, 1958.

Morse, Gordon. "Lad From Prominent Isle Family." (Shark Kills Boy Off Lanikai). The Sunday Advertiser [Honolulu], 14 December, 1958: continued p. A-14.

Musick, John A. and Beverly McMillan. The Shark Chronicles, A Scientist Tracks The Consummate Predator. New York: Henry Holt and Company, 2002.